THE
LONDON
SÉANCE
SOCIETY

Also by Sarah Penner

The Lost Apothecary

SARAH PENNER

THE
LONDON
SÉANCE
SOCIETY

PARK
ROW
BOOKS

PARK ™
ROW
BOOKS™

ISBN-13: 978-0-7783-8711-4

The London Séance Society

Copyright © 2023 by Sarah Penner

Park Row Books
22 Adelaide St. West, 41st Floor
Toronto, Ontario M5H 4E3, Canada
ParkRowBooks.com
BookClubbish.com

Printed in U.S.A.

For my big sister, Kellie.

(And for you, Mom.
After all, you were the first to say,
"Let's go to a séance…")

THE
LONDON
SÉANCE
SOCIETY

GRAVES, YAWN AND YIELD YOUR DEAD...
—WILLIAM SHAKESPEARE

THE SEVEN STAGES OF A SÉANCE

I
ANCIENT DEVIL'S INCANTATION

*The medium recites an incantation to protect
séance participants from rogues and fiends.*

II
INVOCATION

*The medium issues a summons to all
nearby spirits to enter the séance room.*

III
ISOLATION

*The medium rids the room of all spirits except
the target spirit, i.e., the deceased person whom
the séance participants intend to contact.*

IV
INVITATION

*The medium compels entrancement
by the deceased's spirit.*

V
ENTRANCEMENT

The medium is entranced by the deceased's spirit.

VI
DÉNOUEMENT

The medium ascertains the information desired.

VII
TERMINATION

*The medium expels the deceased's spirit from the room,
ending the entrancement and concluding the séance.*

1

 LENNA

Paris, Thursday, 13 February 1873

At an abandoned château on the wooded outskirts of Paris, a dark séance was about to take place.

The clock read thirty-two minutes after midnight. Lenna Wickes, spiritualist understudy, sat at an oval table draped in black linen. A gentleman and his wife, the other séance participants, sat at the table with her. Their faces were somber and their breathing uneasy. They were in what was once the parlor of the dilapidated château, which had not been inhabited for a hundred years. Behind Lenna, blood-colored paper peeled from the walls, clusters of mildew hiding underneath.

If all went well tonight, the ghost they sought—that of a young woman, murdered here in this very place—would soon appear.

Above them, something skittered. Mice, surely. Lenna had seen the droppings when they walked in, the tiny black kernels scattered about the baseboards. But then the skitter turned to a scratching noise and—was that a thud she'd just heard? She fought off a chill, thinking that if ghosts did indeed exist, this derelict château would be the place to find them.

She glanced quickly out the window into the darkness. Fat, wet snowflakes, rare for Paris, drifted down around the château. They'd set a few lanterns outside, and Lenna's eyes fell on the metal gate at the front of the estate, wrapped in dead ivy vines and quivering in its brace. Beyond it stood dark, thick forest, the needly evergreens dusted with white.

The séance participants, called *sitters*, had gathered at midnight. The parents of the victim—whom Lenna had met several days prior to this event—arrived first. They were followed soon after by Lenna and her teacher, the renowned medium who would lead tonight's affair: Vaudeline D'Allaire.

All of them were dressed in black, and the energy in the room was neither warm nor welcoming. As the parents waited in their seats, their movements were nervous and abrupt: the father knocked over a brass candlestick and apologized profusely. Lenna, opening her notebook from across the table, couldn't blame him. They were all anxious, and Lenna had wiped her damp palms on her gown a dozen times already.

No one wanted to spend this agonizing hour under Vaudeline's guidance. The price of admission was terribly high, and that wasn't accounting for the francs she required up front.

The spirit they meant to conjure tonight was not of the everyday sort, but nor were any of the ghosts Vaudeline invited to come forth. These were not old grandmothers in white nightgowns, lives lived long, stalking through corridors. These were not the casualties of war, valiant men who'd known what they were getting themselves into. No, these ghosts were victims of violence, and gone too soon. They'd been murdered, every one of them. And worse, their killers had gotten away.

This was where Vaudeline came in, and it was why people sought her out. People like the couple trembling across the table now. People like Lenna.

Vaudeline, aged thirty, was known throughout the world for her skill in conjuring the spirits of murder victims in order to ascertain the identities of their killers. An esteemed spiritualist, she had solved several of Europe's most baffling murder mysteries. Her name had made headlines dozens of times, especially after her departure from London early last year, the circumstances of which yet remained unclear. Even still, this hadn't dampened her loyal, worldwide following. She lived now in Paris, her city of birth.

The forgotten château was an unusual place for a séance, but then, much was strange about Vaudeline's methods, and she claimed spirits could only be conjured at the location where they'd died.

Two weeks earlier, on the first of February, Lenna had crossed the English Channel to begin studying under Vaudeline. Lenna knew she wasn't her teacher's most devoted student. She wavered in her beliefs often, struggling with the necessity of the *Ancient Devil's Incantation* or the *palo santo* or the bowl of warbler shells. It wasn't that she didn't believe; she simply couldn't be *sure*. None of this could be proved. None of this could be weighed or analyzed or turned over in her hands like the stones and specimens she kept back home. Where other students might have readily accepted even the most far-fetched theories about the occult, Lenna found herself constantly asking *How? How do you know for sure?* And though she'd attended one séance a few years ago, nothing convincing had come of it. Certainly, no ghosts had appeared.

It was maddening, this truth-versus-illusion business.

In her twenty-three years of life, Lenna had never seen an apparition. Some claimed to feel a cool presence when walking among old estates and cemeteries or said they'd seen a flicker in the candlelight or a humanlike shadow on the wall. Lenna would nod along, wanting badly to believe. But couldn't these be explained by something more…reasonable? Tricks of the light existed everywhere, prisms and reflections easily explained by science.

If Lenna had been asked a few months ago to travel to Paris to participate in a séance, she might have laughed. And studying the art of séance itself? Quite the waste of time, what with so many rock specimens waiting to be collected along the River Thames. But then came All Hallows' Eve—the night Lenna found her precious younger sister, Evie, stabbed to death in the garden of their parents' modest travelers' hotel, the Hickway House, on Euston Road. It was clear there had been a struggle: Evie's hair was in disarray, and there was trauma—blanching and bruising—to various parts of her body. Her satchel, emptied of its contents, had been flung next to her body.

In the days that followed, the police had given Evie's death as much attention as they gave the murder of any middle-class woman, which was to say not much at all. Three months gone, and not a single answer. Lenna was desperate—and desperation prevailed over disbelief; she knew that now. She adored Evie, more than anything else in this world. Magic, witchcraft, poltergeists. She'd commit to any of it, if it meant finding a way to reconnect with her beloved younger sister.

Besides, even though Lenna hadn't made up her mind about ghosts, she considered that her treasured fossils might be proof that remnants of life could still exist after death. Evie had first posed the idea, and now more than ever Lenna yearned to see the truth in it.

Evie had been a budding medium, an unyielding believer in spirits, and a former student and devotee of Vaudeline. If anyone could find a way to breach the barrier between life and death, it would be her. Lenna needed to communicate with her, to learn the truth about what had happened. The police might not have been willing to pursue justice, but Lenna was. So she had chosen to set aside her doubts and learn—if not master—this strange art of séance.

She could not even properly grieve, so consumed was she with untangling the crime against her sister. Lenna didn't want to mourn, not yet. Before she mourned, she wanted vengeance.

Knowing Vaudeline wouldn't travel to London—she hadn't been back, not since her abrupt departure the year before—Lenna had decided to make the trip to Paris. She was determined to solve Evie's death, one way or another. Even if it meant spending a month under the tutelage of a stranger—albeit a stranger she'd decided she quite liked—and even if it meant learning the sinister subtleties of an art in which she was not sure she believed.

Besides, perhaps tonight that would change.

Perhaps tonight she would see her first ghost.

Lenna pushed her hands between her thighs: she was trembling and did not want anyone to see it. She wanted to appear a brave understudy, an adept student. And she needed to demonstrate her levelheadedness for the sake of the parents across the table, who were visibly terrified about what might unfold tonight.

She was glad she'd met them a few days ago in a place far less ominous. They'd visited Vaudeline's sizable flat in central Paris, and the four of them had gathered in the parlor to talk through their questions about the upcoming séance.

And the risks.

Lenna knew the risks of séance already—she and Vaudeline had discussed them when she first presented herself as a prospective student—but during the meeting in the parlor, the hazards seemed of greater consequence.

"You will not find any Ouija boards or planchettes in my possession," Vaudeline had explained to the parents. "Those are the playthings of children in attics. My séances are apt to take a different, more dangerous, direction."

The parlor door opened, and a guesthouse maid brought in tea for the four of them. She set it on the table in front of the

group, next to a diagram Lenna and Vaudeline had been studying earlier noting the proper setting of a séance table with its
many *outils*. The black beeswax candles, the opals and amethysts,
the snakeskins and salt bowls.

"A trance state," the mother offered, once the maid had gone.
"Precisely."

Having been under Vaudeline's tutelage for some weeks,
Lenna didn't need to ask for clarification. She knew that in
mediumship, a trance state, or entrancement, occurred when a
spirit quite literally took over the medium's flesh, once again
subsisting within a living, breathing body. Vaudeline described
it as a sort of dual existence that allowed mediums to cognize
the memories and thoughts of the deceased while also maintaining their own, in parallel.

The mother took a sip of her tea, then leaned forward to withdraw something from her bag: a newspaper clipping. Her hands
trembled just as they had upon her arrival, when she'd stared at
Vaudeline a long while before being able to speak.

Lenna had reacted the same upon first meeting Vaudeline,
though it wasn't because she'd been dazzled by the medium's reputation. It had more to do with her cloud-colored eyes and the
way she'd held Lenna's gaze a few seconds longer than convention permitted. The brief moment had revealed plenty: Vaudeline
was self-assured. And like Evie, she didn't care much for rules.

Both of which were traits that Lenna found quite transfixing.

The mother handed over the article. Lenna couldn't understand the French headline, but the date of the article indicated it
was a few years old. "It says a man died at one of your séances,"
the mother explained. "Is it true?"

Vaudeline nodded. "Spirits are unpredictable," she said. "Especially the ones we seek—the victims. The risk is greatest early
in the séance, after I've recited the *Invocation*, which invites all
nearby spirits into the room. It is like turning on a water spigot.
To manifest the spirit of a murder victim and solve a crime, I

must also deal with the dead at the periphery. I try to get through this stage quickly, but I cannot keep them at bay entirely." She nodded to the article.

"Did the police ever determine how the man died?" the mother asked.

"Heart failure, officially. But those of us in the room saw it happen, the shadow of a hand over his mouth." Vaudeline handed the article back over. "In a decade of doing séances, only three people have died on my watch. It is very rare. More common is the sudden appearance of wounds, which are connected to the traumas suffered by the victim before their death. Lacerations, twisted ligaments, bruises."

The father dropped his head forward, and Lenna fought a sudden urge to leave the room, maybe even vomit. Their daughter had been strangled. What if a rope burn spontaneously appeared on someone's neck during the séance? The mere thought of it was intolerable.

"There are lesser dangers, as well," Vaudeline continued. Perhaps she sensed it would be wise to move on. "The things someone might...*engage* in, for instance. At a séance a few months ago, two of the participants—under the influence of spirits— began to fornicate on the table."

Lenna gave a small gasp. For all the stories Vaudeline had shared with her in the last two weeks, she hadn't heard this one. "Were they lovers beforehand?" she asked, thinking surely the parents were as curious as her.

Vaudeline shook her head. "They'd never met in their lives." She turned, and Lenna's gaze fell on the tiny freckle at the tip of Vaudeline's nose. So small it might be mistaken for a shadow.

"Despite the risks," Vaudeline said, looking back to the parents, "trances are the quickest and most effective way to get the information needed to solve a case. This is not about entertainment or peace-seeking. If that's what you're after, I'd direct you to any number of reputable ghost hunters throughout the city."

The father cleared his throat. "I am concerned..." he said, gently taking his wife's hand "...well, I am concerned about my wife's well-being if we hold the séance at the château, where our daughter died."

Where our daughter died, he'd said. Easier words to say aloud than *where our daughter was killed*. That was too much to admit, too sharp on the tongue. Lenna knew this better than anyone.

Vaudeline looked at the wife. "You will need to find a way to remain composed, or I suggest you do not attend at all." She sat back and folded her hands together, inviting no further discussion about it. This was, after all, one of Vaudeline's key beliefs: a spirit could only be conjured within proximity to the site of their death. If she could perform a séance from afar, Lenna wouldn't be here in Paris at all. She'd have written Vaudeline and asked her to perform Evie's séance in France and then report back to Lenna with the results.

But as Vaudeline had publicly stated, she wouldn't be returning to London anytime soon. Lenna would have to learn the art of séance herself in Paris, then return to the site of Evie's death with the hope of conjuring her sister's spirit on her own.

"Plenty of mediums carry out séances in their own homes," the mother said now. "Nowhere near the place where their loved ones have died."

"And plenty of mediums are frauds." Vaudeline swirled her cup of tea and went on, undeterred. "I understand it is difficult to be at the site of your daughter's death, but we are not there to be delicate with our emotions. We are there to solve a crime."

This might have come across as cold, but Vaudeline had said it countless times. She could not intertwine herself with the grief of the family. Grief was weakness, and there was nothing so dangerous in the séance room as weakness of any kind. Spirits— the dangerous, free-roaming ones, apt to haunt and tease sitters whether summoned or not—liked weakness.

"It will be just the two of you, is that right?" Vaudeline asked.

The father gave a single nod.

"Was your daughter married, or did she have a beau? If so, it would be helpful to extend an invitation to him or her. The more of your daughter's latent energy we can gather in the room, the better."

"No," the father said. "Not married, and no beau."

"That we're aware of, at least," the mother added, giving a small smile. "Our daughter was quite...independent."

Lenna smiled, musing on the woman's delicate word choice. Perhaps her daughter had been a bit like Evie. Free-spirited. Unbridled.

The mother coughed lightly. "Might I ask," she said, looking at Lenna, "what role you will play in the séance?"

Lenna nodded. "I'm Vaudeline's understudy," she said. "I'm still memorizing the incantations, but I'll be taking notes on the seven-stage séance sequence."

"She is not part of my traditional cohort," Vaudeline added, "which typically has three to five students. Lenna's circumstances were such that, after she arrived between cohorts a couple of weeks ago, I opted to take her on for an individualized training program."

This was all factual, if not grossly short on detail. When Lenna arrived in Paris and told Vaudeline that Evie—her former student—had been murdered in London, Vaudeline found the news staggering. She quickly ushered Lenna in, set her up in the empty bunkroom typically set aside for students, and began an accelerated training program. Typically, cohorts studied under Vaudeline for eight weeks, but she aimed to have Lenna's training done in half that time.

"I didn't realize you taught mediumship," the mother said to Vaudeline, "in addition to conducting séances yourself."

"Yes. I've been a medium for ten years, a teacher for five." She leaned forward, her tone more serious now. "Regarding the séance, there are things you can do to diminish the risks I've just laid out. Foremost, no wine or liquor beforehand. Not even a drop. And do your best to keep any tears at bay. Don't dwell on memories. Memories are weakness. And in the séance room, weakness is your downfall."

The peril posed by weakness was one of the first lessons Vaudeline had taught Lenna when their studies began. The world teemed with ghosts. Every bedchamber, every meadow, every seaport. Over millennia, so long as people had lived, so too had they died—and they did not go far. Because of this, Vaudeline explained, many séances resulted in the appearance of spirits who weren't invited. Most of these were benign and merely curious. They longed to feel the sensation of embodiment once again, or they meant to playfully tease the sitters. Vaudeline had no problem steering these affable spooks away.

It was the malicious spirits and destructive poltergeists who posed the danger, and much could go wrong during a séance on their account. They might entrance Vaudeline before the target spirit had a chance to do so, or they might entrance the sitters, a phenomenon known as *absorptus*. These entities were intelligent and knew exactly who to prey on: The crying. The young. The inebriated. The lustful. These were all forms of fragility, a sort of porousness allowing the diabolical being inside.

To prevent such fiends from interrupting a séance, Vaudeline carefully assessed the sitters before the affair began. She did not permit anyone under the age of sixteen to attend, nor anyone with liquor on their breath. Crying family members were sometimes tossed out.

This diligence, together with the ancient, protective incantation that Vaudeline read at the start of each affair, and the two expulsive injunctions that could be used as a last resort, kept her séances safe.

Most of the time.

Nothing was guaranteed. This was an *art*, Vaudeline said time and time again. And spirits were terribly unpredictable.

At the château, Lenna glanced up from her notebook and looked again at the parents, studying their expressions. The father's face was hard, both hands set firmly on the table. He looked ready for battle. The mother, meanwhile, had a gray, dazed look in her eyes, and a streak of dried tears had carved a rivulet through the rouge on her cheeks.

Lenna was proud of her. Proud of both of them. But their strength might put her in a vulnerable position. She shuddered, wondering whether a spirit might find *her* the weakest person in the room, or if something else might go awry. She recalled a few of Vaudeline's stories, tales of people pulling weapons on one another while in a trance state, or candelabras thrust across the room as if by their own accord. Lenna glanced around now, thankful there were no candelabras to be seen.

Vaudeline unlocked a leather suitcase and pulled a few items out. Everyone else had taken their places, and a nervous silence descended upon the room. What, Lenna wondered, would transpire in the minutes to come? She chewed mindlessly at her fingernails, a lifelong vice, and watched Vaudeline closely for any signs of trickery. She could find none.

Vaudeline retrieved two lengths of black linen from her case. She delicately hung them over the brick hearth and the lead-latticed window at the front of the room, which overlooked the entrance to the dilapidated château. The bottom portion of the window glass was broken, so the fabric would keep out the drafts. But Lenna knew the other reason Vaudeline covered it now, for they had reviewed it in their studies. Windows were portals of light and encouraged the entrance and movement of uninvited spirits who had died close by. Hearths, too. A rogue spirit could swoop down a chimney as easily as it could come through a window. Thus, it was best to encapsulate the room if possible. *Close and dark.*

Well, things certainly felt close now. Vaudeline finally took a seat, pulling her chair closer to Lenna and angling her legs toward her. Lenna wondered if the movement was inadvertent. She hoped not.

As Vaudeline opened her book of incantations, her long lashes cast shadows on her cheeks. A wisp of hair slipped loose and dangled in front of her face, but she paid it no mind as she turned the pages of her book, the fabric of her silk gown sliding easily over her pale arms.

Lenna caught the father gazing at Vaudeline. His pupils had gone wide and black, and his lips were parted. Lenna recognized this look—lust—and she didn't blame him a bit. One might call the man deviant, even debased, for having the capacity to feel desire while still so overwhelmed by grief and loss. But not Lenna. She knew this twist and tangle well.

Indeed, they might have made an ugly pair, grief and desire. But Lenna couldn't blame the man across the table, for she suffered both agonies herself these days.

The room grew very still. The candle did not flicker, nor did the window covering rustle. The séance had not yet begun, but it was undeniable: Vaudeline had established full and complete control of the room. Anything she asked, the participants would do.

Lenna was glad for it, comforted by Vaudeline's steady expertise, so in contrast with the eerie feeling about the room. She recalled her teacher's promise en route to the château. *No harm will befall you,* Vaudeline had said softly. *You would be the first I would protect, if needed. Ma promesse à toi.*

Now Lenna repeated these words, this promise, in her mind. Her own incantation.

Vaudeline withdrew a small watch from inside her cloak. She studied its face, then returned it to an inner pocket. "We will begin in forty seconds," she said. Across the table, the mother of the victim sniffled, and the father cleared his throat, straightened his back. Lenna could not fathom the emotion plaguing them, the nuanced temptation and terror of what they were about to experience. What must it feel like to approach an encounter with one's dead daughter?

The same, probably, as it felt to approach an encounter with one's dead sister.

The thought jarred Lenna. Tonight, and indeed her entire course of study, was not just about learning the art of séance. This endeavor, ultimately, was about communicating with Evie and learning the truth about her murder.

Lenna offered a warm smile to the mother across the table. Candlelight glinted in the woman's eyes; she was fighting back tears. Lenna wished she could whisper a few words of comfort to her, but the time for that had long passed.

The sitters kept their eyes low as the forty seconds ticked slowly by. Lenna could hear the timepiece inside Vaudeline's cloak, the movement of the tiny mechanism within its metal encasement. She knew Vaudeline was counting the ticks, and then she would begin her first incantation, the protective *exordium*, the prelude, extracted from a thousand-year-old Latin text on demons. Lenna had already memorized the first four stanzas, but there were twelve in total.

She waited for Vaudeline's long intake of air: the incantation needed to be recited in a single, unbroken breath. Breath control was another thing Lenna needed to practice. While reading the incantation from her notebook in recent days, she could only get through half of it before feeling faint and gasping for air.

The candle closest to the hearth flickered, and somewhere nearby—was it outside the room, or above it?—a *thump* sounded.

Lenna froze, looked up from her notebook. It had not been mice in the floorboards—that much was clear. The pencil fell from her fingers. Instinctively, she leaned closer to Vaudeline, ready to clasp her hand if it came to that. Decorum be damned.

"Something is coming," Vaudeline said suddenly. Her voice remained even and low. She kept her gaze down, eyes closed.

The *thump* sounded again. Lenna tensed, jerking her head toward the family. Across the table, the mother's eyes were wide, and the father leaned forward, looking hopeful. Surely, they thought this thumping meant the spirit of their daughter was nearly upon them. But Vaudeline hadn't covered the detailed seven-stage sequence with them, so they couldn't know that it was too soon for a manifestation, that the séance had not even begun.

Lenna might have been the only one of them to know it, but something was not right. The sequence was off: Vaudeline would never begin a séance without the *Ancient Devil's Incantation*, meant to protect them all. For a moment, terror seized her. Was there some demon making its way into the room at this very moment? Something sinister enough to have disrupted Vaudeline's sequence? A chill ran down her arms as she waited for the medium to act.

Still, Vaudeline had not moved. Bravely, as a sort of second-in-command, Lenna turned to her. "Something is…coming? A spirit?" she whispered.

Vaudeline exhaled, frustration writ on her face. She shook her head and held up a finger as though to say, *Just wait.*

At once, the door to the room flew open.

**SEVERAL DAYS EARLIER,
ACROSS THE ENGLISH CHANNEL,
IN LONDON**

2

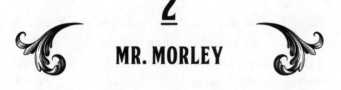

MR. MORLEY

London, Monday, 10 February 1873

On the second story of the London Séance Society, a West End gentlemen's-only establishment, I sat hunched over a mahogany desk in my private study. In front of me a lantern flickered, its blue-orange glow illuminating the items scattered about my desk: a few blank sheets of Society stationery, a monocle on a silver chain, an inkwell in the shape of a bell.

I spent a few moments massaging the swollen half-moons beneath my eyes, evidence of strain and worry. I'd not slept well for several months, and my jaw was in a constant state of clench.

We were facing a few problems here at the Society.

Not in the Department of Clairvoyance—no, that unit was clean as a whistle. Rather, the problems lay within the Department of Spiritualism, where I'd served as vice president since joining the Society a decade ago.

Like any good gentleman of authority, I knew all there was to know about my department. I knew which séances we'd done last week—indeed, I was the one who made member assignments—and I knew the location of every reference guide in our library, every volume on the occult. I knew the department's revenue numbers, the names of members' wives, and what we would serve for breakfast at the department assembly three days hence.

No matter how personal or trivial the information might be, I knew it all.

So when it came to the mess we were facing at the Department of Spiritualism, the responsibility to clean things up fell on me, and me alone.

An empty brandy glass sat at my right; my lips still stung with the last unsatisfying sip of it. I poured myself another, gazing straight ahead at a small frame affixed to the wall. Inside the frame was the Society's mission. *Established in 1860, the mission of the London Séance Society is to provide clairvoyance and mediumship services throughout the city of London, with the intent of providing peace to mourners and satisfying the populace's growing curiosity about the afterlife.*

I crossed my arms, dwelling on this. Providing peace and satisfying curiosity were indeed what we excelled at.

More than two hundred members belonged to the Society. Roughly two-thirds of them were members of the Department of Clairvoyance, led by their vice president, my counterpart, Mr. T. Shaw. Shaw's department performed hundreds of readings across London every month. Its reputation was impeccable and its revenue consistent.

Shaw's vetting process had something to do with it. Before admission to the Society, prospective members of his department were required to demonstrate their skills in clairaudience, numerology, divination, or whatever other talent they possessed.

Things were done somewhat differently in my area, the Department of Spiritualism. For one, we did less business. We performed only a dozen or so séances each month. (But even still, the per-booking revenue was higher—much higher—than anything Shaw's department brought in with a street-side palm reading.) Further, members in our department were invite-only, and my vetting process was less…precise. Unlike Shaw's clairvoyants who could identify the date on a coin in my pocket, I could not rightfully expect my prospective members to conjure a ghost on command in a boardroom.

This meant that membership in my department was determined based on trusted references, the old who-knows-who. But have no doubt about it: my vetting process might have been less rigorous, but I was no less picky. My standards were high.

Both Shaw and I reported up to the president, Mr. Volckman. Volckman had founded the Society twelve years ago, just as the notion of ghosts began to take hold of the city. Séances, spirits, spooks: they were all *en vogue*, and London could not get enough. Seeing a financial opportunity, Volckman got to work, bringing Shaw and me in early.

He'd been an admirable leader.

Before his death, that was.

On the corner of my desk was yet another article about that unfortunate night, published in this morning's paper. I glanced at the headline: *Still No Answers for London Gentleman Murdered during Evening Soirée*—and read the brief report in its entirety again.

The Metropolitan Police Service continues to investigate the circumstances surrounding the murder of Mr. M. Volckman, Mayfair resident, which occurred more than three months ago. Volckman was an esteemed gentleman: father, husband, and president of the renowned West End gentleman's club, the London Séance Society.

Volckman's body, badly mauled, was discovered on the thirty-first of October in a private cellar near Grosvenor Square, managed by a Mr. M. Morley of London, vice president of the Society's Department of Spiritualism.

An All Hallows' Eve soirée had taken place at the cellar that evening. Volckman's body was found in the cellar's subbasement by Mr. Morley himself. At least a hundred partygoers attended the event held on the premises that

evening, a fact which the Met reports is a significant complication in their investigation.

Mr. Volckman was an upstanding family man. His
friends insist he'd accrued no gambling debts and had
never antagonized anyone. An exemplary gentleman, his
loved ones report, leaving us still to speculate: Who might
have wanted him dead?

I set the article down, agitated, and stood from my well-worn
leather chair. I began to pace the small room and approached a
mirror, affixed to the wall next to the Society mission docu-
ment. I took a long look and frowned, as I always did, at the
reflection that met my eyes. Thirty-six years old with a handsome head of hair—no thinning, no receding—and a sharp jaw,
a straight nose.

But my complexion—I despised it. A birthmark, deep red
in color and mottled, stretched its way from below my left eye
and across my face to my ear. This wasn't a small blemish, easily
covered with a spot of rouge: it was the width of my palm, and
while once it had been smooth, over time this area of skin had
thickened. It now took on a raised, rough appearance.

During childhood, the feature had endeared me to adults. It
would disappear someday, everyone assured me. But it hadn't,
and how shamed it left me now. None of my friends were
plagued with such a flaw. Among London's finest gentlemen, I
stood out, and not in a good way.

If only the blemish could be scrubbed away or bleached. As
an adolescent, I'd rubbed it raw with sand and lime. When that
gave me nothing but splotchy lesions on the entire left side of
my face, I made a homemade concoction—vinegar, mixed with
a brightening cream I found among my mother's things—and
applied that to my skin overnight. Week after week, I tried such

absurd tactics. Not a single one of them worked. If anything, I
think the birthmark grew darker, maybe even larger.

The worst part of it? The way women now looked upon me
for a second too long, as though I were a strange, foreign specimen. Having such a blemish didn't bode well for my marriage
prospects, either. Not only did it prove a hindrance in attracting women, but no one could explain what exactly had caused
the imperfection. My parents hadn't had enormous birthmarks
on their faces. What woman would risk such a thing afflicting
her children, too?

Now I ran my hand along my cheek. My facial hair hid a
small portion of the birthmark, but I considered the rest a pathetic visage upon which to gaze. I turned away. Shame at my
appearance was something with which I had eventually made
peace, but still I hated mirrors.

Mr. Volckman had always looked past my appearance. In all
the years I knew him, he had not so much as remarked on it.

I missed him dearly. Despite being a decade my senior and a
man of extraordinary demands, he had been a mentor, a confidant. A partner.

He'd been a generous man, too—the very reason my mother
and I hadn't floundered financially a decade ago after my father,
a successful textile merchant, had died from pneumonia. The
two of us tried mightily to keep my father's fabric shop afloat,
but neither of us had the talent or the showmanship for sales.
In a matter of months, a veneer of dust settled over our inven-
tory: the silk panels precut for drapery, the lengths of wool for
winter gowns, the bright pink cottons meant for livery attire.
All of it went out of style, as we hadn't the funds to purchase
the latest patterns or refresh our product. Our upper-class clientele wasted no time closing their credit accounts and taking
their business elsewhere.

Mr. Volckman, a longtime patron of the shop, took pity on
us. I wondered if he felt sorry for me, a twenty-six-year-old

gentleman with class and manners, yet unmarried, burdened by a failing business and an aging mother. Mr. Volckman had just founded the London Séance Society and was in search of someone reliable—someone *loyal*—to establish and lead the Department of Spiritualism. He took me under his wing and paid me a handsome salary, enough to provide for my mother. She closed the textile shop, selling off what little she could, while I buried my face in countless texts about spiritualism: the nature of souls, the ways in which spirits relay information, the tools to facilitate these communications. Volckman gave me plenty of rein to run the department as I liked. As revenues began to accrue, I could tell he was pleased. Pleased, and maybe even somewhat surprised.

I would be forever indebted to Mr. Volckman. His generosity had not only saved my family from financial ruin, but it had renewed my social standing and provided me with a circle of posh friends.

I wanted to do right by him.

Volckman had been a man of high expectations and low tolerance for error, and of particular concern was the Society's reputation for credibility, authenticity. He gave no grace when these were threatened. He was none too happy, then, when a groundswell of rumors began in early 1872, mostly parlorroom whispers that the Society laced their séances with ruses and magic tricks. The information was brought to him by one of his close associates, someone who knew the occult circles in London quite well.

These rumors, specific to my department, reflected badly on the entire organization. It implied that the whole of the Society's work consisted of hoaxes and ploys and that we were nothing but illusionists. Men of theater magic.

Never mind the good will between us, Mr. Volckman was irate, especially with me. It was my department causing problems, after all. And I couldn't disagree with him. The thought of the Society's impeccable reputation marred by rumors of such misconduct made me sick.

Beneath the mirror was yet another frame, this one containing newspaper clippings, all of them written by satisfied customers. *I am utterly delighted with the outcome of the séance held a fortnight ago,* one of them read. *The gentlemen of the London Séance Society manifested my dead husband, and when they asked his ghost if I should be set free to love again, a wild hammering came from inside the chimney...*

I remembered that séance well—the look of delight on the widow's face, the look of relief. It was better than the money.

Not that the money wasn't also quite good.

The Society's honorable reputation over the last decade meant plenty of commissioned work for the organization, and at the end of each quarter, profits were aggregated and distributed via a dividend to Society members. For many, these dividends were the most attractive benefit of membership. It encouraged them to hone their skills in clairsentience or spirit-channeling, so better to keep business flowing.

For others, it wasn't about the money so much as the gentlemen's camaraderie. The Society headquarters was a place to escape the monotony of home life and partake in stimulating conversation, exclusive parties, extravagant meals.

And for a remaining few, the most appealing benefit to membership was neither the income nor the exclusivity. It was the women with whom we tended to work.

The nature of our services meant unhindered access to many homes throughout the city. The Society was quite discerning, and especially in my department it was no coincidence that nearly all of our clients were wealthy widows and left-behind heiresses. I monitored the obituaries, and I knew well the aristocratic bloodlines, the surnames associated with landholdings or politics—in other words, the sort of women not apt to balk at expensive séances.

Though we worked with them often, women were not allowed at the Society headquarters, and they never had been—not since the Society's founding. During the last leadership meeting Volckman attended, in late October, one member had made a motion to strike the rule. Shouldn't women be permitted as special dinner guests, at least?

Despite being a family man himself, Volckman had laughed at the notion. "Gentlemen retreat to the Society to escape their wives," he'd said, "not to consort further with them. We wouldn't invite our wives to Morley's cellar parties in Grosvenor Square, would we?"

We'd all laughed at this. For several years, I'd thrown large parties in the underground space, which was large enough to host a hundred guests. I'd been managing the cellar for years as a way to earn extra income. It held nearly two hundred casks— gin, vermouth, blended whiskey—and an ample amount of wine. My responsibility was to turn the barrels, transport them in and out, shoo the rats away. The barrels and bottles themselves were owned by a distributor in North London.

None of our members told their wives about my cellar parties. We were good secret-keepers, all of us, and especially Volckman. He was immensely loyal to the things he valued.

For a decade, we'd done just fine at the Society, going about things the way we did.

Until those rumors began.

On the heels of the gossip, business started to decline. In my department, commissions sank 14 percent quarter-over-quarter. Shaw's weren't far behind. The declining revenue was alarming enough, but the reduced dividends were most problematic. A few of the members—dissatisfied with their distributions—threatened to leave. The citywide chatter was dangerous, but members abandoning ship? These defectors would do us no favors. People would start asking questions, more than they already had.

No, I could not let it happen. I could not let the Society implode. The merrymaking, the money, all of it was too good.

Volckman demanded I get to the bottom of things: we needed to identify the problem and resolve it as quickly as possible. He, too, promised to do some digging.

Only, his efforts had eventually gotten him killed.

Somewhere outside, beyond the windowless walls of the room, a warbler began to sing its cheerful tune. The bird had taken up this evening song in recent days. Strange behavior for an animal that normally sang a morning chorus, but so it went with wild things.

I glanced once more at the article about Volckman's death, tapping my finger on the final sentence: *Who might have wanted him dead?*

The warbler sang louder. I spared a few moments listening to the tiny vocalist, envying its glee. Then I hung my head and pinched the bridge of my nose.

It would be perilous, this task ahead of me.

3

LENNA

Paris, Thursday, 13 February 1873

At the château, the door of the old parlor swung open.

The mother of the murdered woman let out a horrified scream. Lenna turned to look, and she could make out the dark shadows of something humanlike in the doorway. *If this is a ghost,* she thought, *then I have been so terribly wrong about everything.*

The shadow stepped forward into the parlor. More clearly in view now, Lenna noticed the dark uniform, the stubble on his chin. It was the very corporeal form of a young man, lantern swinging in his hand. Four brass buttons on his coat caught the glimmer of candlelight, and slung across his chest was a leather messenger bag. He stood there panting, his cheeks flushed with cold. A few snowflakes stuck to his coat, melting as he stepped into the room.

"Who is this?" the father muttered, his voice low and heavy with confusion. He glanced at his wife, an incredulous look on his face. She remained silent.

The father's ferocity, paired with the mother's meekness, reminded Lenna very much of her own parents. After Evie's death several months ago, their mother had left for the countryside with a cousin. She'd tried to endure the city for a couple of weeks, taking callers in the parlor of the Hickway House, a crepe veil draped over her glassy eyes. But with her daughter's death unsolved, everyone took on an air of suspicion. Whether strangers or old friends, Lenna's mother trusted no one.

This left Lenna's father to oversee the hotel. It was manageable—only twenty-four beds, mostly travelers stopping over from King's Cross and St. Pancras—but even still, Lenna knew the strain on her father was great, and she looked forward to the day when her mother felt well enough to return to the city.

Now the grieving father across the table shifted in his seat. "Is this man real?" he asked aloud.

Lenna wondered the same. For all she and Vaudeline had covered in the last two weeks, she had not asked the most fundamental of questions: What, exactly, did a ghost look like? She wondered if ghosts were supposed to resemble the floating, ethereal forms depicted in children's books, or if they were as tangible and lifelike as the man standing now in the doorway.

Quickly, she looked down at her notebook, where she'd made diligent notes in recent days. She flitted her eyes over the page, looking for some clue that she might have missed.

The way he pants, Lenna thought, *and the flush on his face. He seems entirely real, but how can I know for sure?*

Evie wouldn't have worried herself with such questions. Her beliefs had always come effortlessly, not plagued by misgivings, by science, by reason.

Lenna, in contrast, liked to think of herself as a girl of logic and practicality. She'd always been interested in the natural world, but never more so than when she met Stephen Heslop.

Stephen was the twin brother of Eloise, who had been a close friend of Evie and Lenna's. Stephen was only a few months older than Lenna, and the two of them became acquainted when he returned from his studies at Oxford to work in the Museum of Practical Geology on Jermyn Street, studying minerals and fossils.

Stephen regularly came to the Hickway House to call on Lenna, and he often brought work with him, like chisels and brushes needing repair. Lenna would sit with him while he tended to his tools in the garden, and her interest in naturalism grew as Stephen explained to her the science of fossils. She even accompanied him to the museum a few times, familiarizing herself with the wide range of stone collections.

One day, Stephen brought her a small round stone, but it was not like any Lenna had seen before. It was translucent, the color of whiskey, and called amber. By giving her the gift, Lenna knew that Stephen was trying to spark a courtship. But although she liked spending time with him, she was unmoved by his romantic interest. What most excited her was the resin stone itself and that which lay within: the skeleton of a tiny arachnid, no larger than a fingernail, and the nearly invisible strands of her web, still spun in perfect formation. It was a young stone, Stephen told her, less than one hundred thousand years old.

"It's yours," he said, a glimmer of sweat on his upper lip. He reached his hand forward to touch Lenna's arm, but she gently leaned out of his reach, studying more closely the tiny hairs on the spider's crooked arms.

So began her collection of ancient amber specimens and a desire to know more of things like this: relics made of minerals, or fossilized spiders discovered in far-off places by explorers who braved to leave this city of fog and damp.

A few weeks later, Stephen returned from the museum with waste materials from the laboratory, including a bag of half-dried clay and a few broken tools. He let Lenna experiment with making some fossil casts herself, and she went out to gather a dead perch from the Thames. With its spiny dorsal fin, it left a nice imprint for Lenna. It was something she could touch with the pad of her finger, which appealed to her. She was fascinated by anything physical, viewable, *provable*. Just like the little spider in her amber-soaked web. It did not change, did not vanish.

Unlike the subjects with which Evie occupied herself.

Evie had always preferred subjects ethereal in nature: apparitions, premonitions, dreams. She dutifully did her work at their parents' hotel each day, and then she delved into her vague, strange studies at night. She believed ghosts existed everywhere, beneath some layer of life as yet invisible to her. With the right formula—the right spell, or the right amulet—she believed this realm might be unveiled.

She believed she might make a good profit from it, too. In London, ghosts had come into fashion only a few years earlier. Evie spotted the opportunity: her personal obsession could make her good money. She believed she could get rich off this—very rich—if only she could obtain the necessary training. Thus, a couple of years ago in London, she'd been thrilled to secure a place in one of Vaudeline D'Allaire's cohorts. Vaudeline was a worthy name to drop in smoky, shrouded parlors, and Evie knew the experience would give her a leg up.

It wasn't greedy, Lenna had to admit. It was brilliant.

More than the sisters' interests differed. They lacked any physical resemblance, as well. Evie had short black hair and watery blue eyes, just like their mother, but Lenna had inherited their father's butter-colored waves and hazel eyes. Further, while Lenna was quite feminine, Evie had always been a bit rugged and boyish. Unadorned, if not downright plain. In looks, anyway; certainly not in demeanor. She was as smart and spunky as anyone Lenna had ever met. Too smart, if Lenna was honest with herself. Cunning, even.

Like all sisters, the girls quarreled often. The week before Evie's death, they'd been sitting alone in their shared room at the hotel. While Evie read a book, Lenna studied her fossil casts.

She'd just held the perch cast up to the oil lamp, observing the intricate dips and hollows made by the flesh of the fish.

"You have just proved that I am right," Evie said. She looked up from her papers, light glinting off her pink cheeks.

"Sorry?"

"Your little perch cast that you cannot stop staring at. The fish is dead and gone. Yet the form of him is right in front of you, just as it will be in that clay for all of time. It's the same of ghosts. We may die, but we are never really gone."

Lenna traced her thumbnail along the round belly of the imprint. She hadn't thought of it this way, but still, she wouldn't cede so easily to her younger sister. "Isn't that full of ideals."

Evie huffed. "Something cannot be an illusion if it still exists after we think it has gone. Including the fossils and stones you obsess over. Last week, you went on about a leaf fossil your beau had brought from the museum. It was, what, a thousand years old?"

"Four thousand. And he's not my beau."

"Right." Evie crossed her hands in her lap. "Well, the leaf itself is long gone. Decayed. But it left its mark, did it not? There is still something of it left behind. Or are you to say the leaf itself was an illusion because it exists no more?"

Evie had a point. Even Lenna's amber stone with the spider inside was evidence supporting the argument. The spider was perfectly preserved. Dead, and yet not disappeared. Still, Lenna would not surrender to Evie. She'd rather stay silent than admit she might be wrong.

"You have spent too much time with Stephen, worrying about things that can be *touched*," Evie continued. "You ought to join me on a ghost hunt someday. You might be surprised."

"You haven't spotted a single ghost."

"They are there, I assure you." She curled a leg up beneath her and lifted her book again. "As much as your perch was once in that clay."

Evie absentmindedly toyed with a lace on her shoe, returning her gaze to the reading material spread out around her: a manual on table rapping—whatever that was—and another on identifying the nature of orbs in photographs. There were ads for what appeared to be vials of phosphorous oil, a diagram on séance-cabinet construction, and a booklet titled "Catalog of Apportations."

"What are *apportations*?" Lenna asked. She'd never heard the word.

Evie's eyes lit up. "Oh, they're so fascinating. Apportations are little tokens that appear during séances. Or any place where ghosts might be present. Coins, seashells, flowers, and the like."

"They just...appear? From the sky?"

Evie shrugged. "Sometimes. Or you might look away and turn back and find the token right in front of you." She reached for the catalog and turned it to a dog-eared page near the center. "These apportations are for sale at a fortune-telling shop on Jermyn Street. I visit often. I want this one." She held up the page to show an illustration of a feather. "It's from a blackcap warbler. They're terribly noisy."

"You and your birds," Lenna said, smiling. Evie had loved birds since she was little. It suited her well, given her wild, independent streak.

"It's the only feather apportation at the shop," Evie said. She turned to another page. "Dozens of seashells, though."

Lenna went back to her fossil cast, musing on the likelihood that a token might actually fall from the sky. She couldn't get behind the idea; shells and feathers didn't spontaneously appear. These were the sort of fantastical topics that marred spiritualism for Lenna, making it hard to believe in any of it.

"Huh," Evie said suddenly, shaking her head. She'd returned to her newspaper.

"What is it?"

Evie nodded to the paper in her hands. "A mechanism for

applying false images of spirits onto photographs." She read on, brow furrowed in concentration. "They've charged a man named Mr. Hudson at a photography studio in Holloway for double-exposing negative plates." She turned the page. "Studio was closed down, just last month."

"Serves him right."

Evie chewed her bottom lip. She looked as though she might reply—might even defend the man—but then she lifted the pen and the black notebook next to her, fervently making notes that Lenna could not see.

This minor squabble about fossils and ghosts was not the last quarrel between the girls. They'd argued the morning of Evie's death, in fact. It had been the worst row the two of them had ever had.

Three months might have passed since Evie's murder, but their argument that morning was too painful to think about, even now.

Inside the château parlor, the newcomer in the uniform reached into his messenger bag. He withdrew an envelope, his hands trembling. Lenna did not know what to make of him— did not know whether he was of this world or of Evie's.

"Une lettre urgente de Londres," the messenger said, his eyes wide. He thrust forward a small envelope. Faintly, in the low light, Lenna could make out a hasty scrawl on the front and a bloodred stamp at the corner.

It isn't a ghost, she decided—not unless a ghost could intercept the postal service and lay hands on an envelope as real as this one. Still, the post didn't show up at abandoned châteaus at midnight. Clearly, this was not just any messenger. He must have gone to the guesthouse in Paris, asked of Vaudeline's whereabouts, and then—given the sweat on his brow—pushed his horse hard to get here. Now Lenna was less concerned with who the messenger was and more curious about who had sent him. The letter, whatever it contained, must have been of utmost importance.

Slowly, Vaudeline outstretched her hand, but she startled at a sudden commotion on the other side of the table.

"What is this?" the father cried out, looking at Vaudeline. He stood with such force that his chair tipped over, its clatter echoing about the room. "Is this a prank?" he asked her. His words seeped with hostility, but beneath them, Lenna saw the statement for what it really was. This was *grief*. Ugly, unresolved, complicated grief, like the kind Lenna suffered herself. This was a man who feared he would never see his daughter again, and he'd lost her in the worst possible way. He pointed a plump finger at the messenger. "How much did she pay you to interrupt? Tell me now, boy."

Lenna threw the father a glance, her eyes wide. It was a brave accusation, but then again, the timing was uncanny. The young man had arrived just seconds before the protective incantation...

Coincidence, or no such thing?

She turned to look at Vaudeline, who had recovered herself and now waved the messenger over. She took the envelope from him, muttered a word of thanks, and slipped the letter out. No sooner had she unfolded the paper than Lenna spotted it: the thick black border around the edge.

The letter, then, was an announcement. Someone had died. But who?

"My God," Vaudeline whispered as she read. A look of horror crossed her face.

"What is it?" Lenna asked, pretending she had not seen the ribbon of black framing the words. On the other side of the table, the father remained standing, the knocked-over chair at his side.

Vaudeline folded the letter up, placed it back in the envelope, and tucked the envelope into her cloak. Her face was grim. Was it grief or fright? She locked her gaze on Lenna. "Let's finish this quickly," she said. She turned to the father. "Please, take your seat."

As the parents settled back in, Vaudeline fussed with a few of the *outils* on the table. She reached first for a jar of crushed warbler eggshells—the shells were apt to make spirits more communicative during a séance, or so Vaudeline claimed—but she knocked the jar over, spilling the shells onto the table. Lenna bent forward to help her pick up the mottled pieces.

Meanwhile, the messenger left quickly with a look of relief on his face. A few moments later, Lenna spotted him outside, through the window, mounting his black pony. The snow outside had stopped, and the atmosphere in the parlor felt more sober even than a few minutes ago.

At last, Vaudeline began the first stage of the séance, the *Ancient Devil's Incantation*. It went smoothly, without complication, but just as she was to recite the second incantation—the *Invocation*—she paused, stifling a quiet sob.

"I'm very sorry," she said to the room. "I just need a moment."

Lenna reached over, gave her hand a quick squeeze. Vaudeline had warned the parents to keep their tears at bay, yet here she was, fighting them herself. Vaudeline knew well the risks of séance and the importance of remaining stoic, so Lenna could only imagine how intrusive Vaudeline's emotions must be now. The black-bordered letter must have brought very bad news, indeed.

Suddenly, Lenna wished this séance over and done with. She reminded herself that this night was about justice and peace for the parents sitting across the table. But if she were honest with herself, she longed to know who'd sent the letter and what news it had divulged.

"Can I help?" Lenna whispered to Vaudeline. She hadn't memorized the incantations, but she had them written in her notebook and could easily read them aloud if need be.

Vaudeline gave her an appreciative look. "Yes, actually." She dabbed her eyes again. "Go ahead with the *Invocation*."

Lenna hadn't actually thought Vaudeline would agree, and she now flipped through the pages of her notebook with a trembling hand. They'd only practiced this a few times. Vaudeline had always been complimentary of the way Lenna articulated the challenging Latin words and the rhythm with which she recited the verses. Still, Lenna had never performed a real incantation. In such an ominous setting, no less.

Her fingers began to tingle, a pins-and-needles feeling underneath her nails, and a burst of sapphire light flashed several times in her peripheral vision.

Nerves, surely. But she forged on. The sooner this was over, the sooner she could ask about the letter.

She located the *Invocation* and began to read.

4

MR. MORLEY

London, Tuesday, 11 February 1873

The next morning, alone in my study, I half-heartedly perused an article on ectoplasm. It was a topic I knew well. I'd given a closed-door, invitation-only lecture on it last summer, about eight months ago.

That day—the sixth of June—the discussion had centered around the substances sometimes remaining after supernatural occurrences. Ectoplasm—a viscous white paste, or gel, occasionally excreted by mediums during séance—was the most well-known of these.

After the lecture ended, I displayed a few samples I'd preserved from our own recent séances. As I arranged the bowls in an even row, I noticed a youthful man I'd never before seen. His unexpected presence in the room alarmed me. He was spending quite too much time amid the samples, and he even had the gall to reach his fingers inside one bowl and play with the material.

I swiftly approached him. "Good day, sir," I said to him, aiming to keep my voice steady. "Who is your sponsor for this lecture?" I looked around for an escort.

The young man turned his face, cap askew. I nearly fell backward at the first sight of those blue eyes, a lock of black hair falling into them.

Suddenly, a knock on my study door. It jolted me out of the memory, and I gave a quick glance at the papers on my desk, flipping over a few confidential indentures. Christ, it wasn't even nine o'clock in the morning. Who needed me already?

"Come in," I called out.

It was Constable Beck, a member of the Department of Spiritualism who also sat on the Metropolitan Police. He dropped yesterday's paper onto my desk with a *smack*, pointing at the same article I'd read last night. The one posing the all-important question about who might have wanted Volckman dead.

"Three interminable months of this mockery," he said, crossing his arms over his burly frame. He was twice my size, mostly muscle. "I'm bloody tired of it. By God, they drop the Met's name every time. We'll be crucified for incompetence if we don't get to the bottom of it."

Beck had always been a touch melodramatic. Misbehaved, too. I didn't know the specifics, but I'd heard the Met had threatened to oust him several times. Subversion, mostly, and there were rumors of petty bribes.

He went on. "I'm considering asking the commissioner about hiring a fresh team of private investigators, or perhaps—"

"No," I said suddenly. "I...I have a better idea."

He frowned. "What is it, then?"

Nervously, I doodled for a moment in my notebook, thinking of how I might frame this up for him. I would tell him only the most necessary of details. "Vaudeline D'Allaire," I began.

He cleared his throat, dislodging something wet. "Didn't she leave the city abruptly last year? If I recall, she refuses to return."

I had intimate knowledge of the circumstances surrounding this. "Her concerns were—are—related to security," I replied, "and—"

"'Security'?" he repeated. "What do you mean by that?"

"I'm not authorized to expand on details."

He hesitated for a moment, then: "Fair enough."

I ran the heel of my shoe along the plush Persian carpet. "Would you agree to help me if I invite her back to the city to perform a séance for Mr. Volckman? To provide her personal protection while she's here for a brief time?" Beck's Met uniform, his weapon, they'd be advantageous, and Vaudeline would be more likely to agree to a summons knowing someone was looking out for her.

He raised his eyebrows. "You think she'd return?"

"She and Mr. Volckman were associates, fond of one another. I suspect she'll want to help if she can, but only if her safety is guaranteed. A member of the Met acting as escort would be of great comfort to her, surely."

"Well, of course," he said, more eagerly than I might have expected. "I'd be happy to."

Melodramatic or not, he was serving some purpose now. "You understand the confidentiality, Beck. She'll be in disguise. No one but us can know she's here. I absolutely must keep her safe. I will need you to sign an oath, promising to keep classified any details you might learn while she's here."

"It would help to know who, exactly, she's trying to hide from."

I kept silent, under no obligation to expand on particulars. Leaders have that luxury.

"Very well, then." He paused, moved on. "It shouldn't be terribly difficult to lie low with her. Doesn't she only perform her séances in the place where the victim has died? Lucky for us, that's your private cellar. It isn't as though we'll have a crowd of onlookers."

"Precisely. The most difficult piece, I think, will be managing the risks. You've seen the newspaper reports about her work over the years?"

"Outbursts among those in the room," Beck said, nodding. "Violence. Fornication. Seizures. Spontaneous fires. Ceilings caving in. A few have died." He gave a shrug as though amused. "Nothing we don't see at the Met on a regular basis."

I nodded, more optimistic than I'd been just a minute ago. I feigned a tight yawn and tried to appear casual about this conversation, despite the very real implications of it. This would be dangerous, this entire affair. "Right, then. Assuming she accepts the invitation, I'll let you know her planned arrival date."

He gave a nod and left my study. I sat motionless for a few minutes, ruminating on the way I wanted things to go.

I glanced at the sofa. Underneath, out of view, was my small revolver.

I'd be keeping it close in the days to come.

I returned my attention to the article about ectoplasm, thinking again of the lecture on the sixth of June. In fact, the chap I'd approached at the end of the lecture was not a young man at all.

It was a woman, eighteen, maybe twenty, and she was well disguised in men's clothing: a woolen Guernsey jumper like the fishermen wear, charcoal-hued trousers, and a plain wool cap, under which her hair was neatly tucked up. Now that I had a better look, I noticed how very slender her face was, with lovely shadows beneath her cheeks and in the dimple of her chin. I thought, briefly, there might be a look of familiarity about her. Perhaps I had seen her around town, but I could not be sure.

"I'll ask you again," I said. "Who invited you here today? I'm sure you know our rules—laypersons and prospective applicants may only attend our lectures if escorted by a member of the Society."

"Who invited me?" the girl repeated. She seemed suddenly nervous. Next to us, a bowl of ectoplasm congealed, foul-smelling. "Why, a..." She hesitated. "A Mr. Morley." She looked toward the door, alarm fresh in her eyes. "He is just out there, waiting for me, I'm sure."

I couldn't help but laugh then. The little liar, pretty as she was. She must have sneaked into the building and spotted my name on one of the placards. Unfortunately for her, she picked the wrong name. "In fact, *I* am Mr. Morley, vice president of the department, and as I said, these lectures are invitation only."

I watched in delight as her oval eyes grew wide and round. That blue, like mazarine. I had a sudden desire to dive into them headfirst, to drink them in or drown.

Instinctively, I looked down, though I'd have been a fool to think she hadn't already noticed the birthmark spread across the left side of my face.

Then I did something very unusual. I have always been so awkward about women, but perhaps it was her appearance as a boy that gave me courage, made it seem briefly that she was one of us. "Have you any interest in going for a stroll?" I asked her.

"A stroll?" She stammered a moment, glancing at the door again. I thought she might flee. "Y-you are the vice president, you said?"

I nodded, taking a step closer. "That's right."

I was sure then that she was about to decline. I thought quickly of my rebuttal. I would remind her of the repercussions of trespassing, and I would inform her that, in fact, several members of the Met were in the building at this very moment. Not that I would have reported her. I only wanted to continue the conversation. Yet, as it turned out, no rebuttal was necessary.

"A stroll sounds lovely," she finally said, and there was a glimmer of delight in her eyes that I had not yet seen. Perhaps she had sized me up in that brief interim and decided I was not as unsightly as I believed myself to be.

We walked a nearby park for two hours, with hardly a pause in the conversation. She was extraordinarily interested in the spirit world; luckily for her, I could speak quite intelligently about it. Eventually my voice grew hoarse, so I invited her out again the next day.

She quickly accepted, and we agreed to meet at the Hickway House on Euston Road, where she lived and worked. "When you arrive, ask the front desk for Miss Wickes," she said, just before we parted. Then she held up a hand, gave a small smile. "But there are two of us. My sister is Lenna. Be sure to ask for me—Miss Evie Wickes."

5

LENNA

Paris, Friday, 14 February 1873

After the château séance, the women returned to Vaudeline's guesthouse in Paris. It was very late, but both women expressed their restlessness, and Vaudeline decided to make tea. As she did so, Lenna kept silent, ruminating on the way things had gone following the messenger's interruption.

After Lenna's assistance with several of the incantations, Vaudeline had composed herself enough to recite the *Entrancement* incantation and ultimately reach her *Dénouement*. She identified the woman's killer as a jilted lover, providing his full name and where in Paris he lived. But at this revelation, the parents had acted underwhelmed. They'd never heard the man's name, they said. The father openly questioned Vaudeline's declaration about the man who murdered his daughter, saying that she might have fabricated any name at all. He promised to follow up with police, and if the lead went nowhere, he assured Vaudeline he'd be knocking on her door.

Naturally, Lenna felt defensive of the séance outcome—after all, she'd been the one to perform a couple of the incantations—

but even so, she couldn't blame the parents for their skepticism. Was it possible Vaudeline had provided a fictional name? Her *Dénouement* had come quite easily, especially given the emotion with which she'd struggled earlier in the evening...

Lenna couldn't deny it, the sense of letdown now that the séance had concluded without a whit of evidence about ghosts. She'd hoped something more tangible would occur, but nothing in the room had so much as moved an inch. For all the warnings about sitters being entranced or tables flipping over, tonight's affair had been remarkably...tidy. Just a medium closing her eyes, then announcing a name no one had ever heard.

Sitting at Vaudeline's table, Lenna could not wait a moment longer. "The letter," she said. "I saw the black border."

Vaudeline stepped toward her, a teacup in each hand. A candle flickered in front of them, plus a few on the mantel in the adjoining parlor. "Yes," she said, setting the cups down. "I was informed that someone I knew quite well during my time in London was—" Her voice quivered. "Well, he was murdered the same night as Evie. All Hallows' Eve."

"Oh," Lenna said, clasping her hand over her mouth. "Was he a friend?"

"A very dear one, yes. He and I met years ago, before London's web of occult practitioners had grown so large. He is—was— the president at an organization known as the London Séance Society, a West End gentleman's club. They make quite a lot of money running ghost hunts, séances, and the like."

"Yes," Lenna said. "I know of them."

Vaudeline looked up in surprise. "Oh?"

She nodded. "A few years ago, they performed two séances for a family with whom I'm close. The Heslops. I attended the first of these, which was a séance held to contact the spirit of my close friend Eloise. She and her father both died in a tragic drowning accident. Those of us who cared for them were desperate for a chance to say goodbye. Evie and I were permitted to attend her séance."

"I'm very sorry for your loss," Vaudeline said. "What about the second séance?"

Lenna gave a small shake of her head. "The second one was for Eloise's father, Mr. Heslop. He'd been a wealthy railway magnate, well-liked among town. But the gentlemen who performed his séance didn't permit anyone who knew Mr. Heslop to attend, other than his widow." Here, Lenna hesitated. "It was all quite strange, actually. Mrs. Heslop had been delirious with grief, but after her late husband's séance, she seemed almost... recovered. Quite a lot better, at least, and she fell deeply in love with one of the Society members, a Mr. Cleland, who'd apparently participated in the séance for Mr. Heslop." She paused. "Mrs. Heslop and Mr. Cleland were married not long afterward. It caused quite the scandal for a while."

Vaudeline raised her eyebrows. "Scandalous, indeed. Did anything come of Eloise's séance?"

Nothing but a slew of tender memories and a page of nonsensical images the men drew on a sheet of paper during the séance—symbols they insisted Eloise had communicated from the dead. Evie believed the images would make sense someday, once properly interpreted. But Lenna? She thought it a farce, all of it. If ghosts existed, Eloise would have communicated something logical. God knew there were plenty of memories and secrets on which Eloise could draw.

"No," Lenna answered softly.

"Sometimes that happens, unfortunately." Vaudeline took a sip, wrapping her hands around her tea. "I hope it doesn't cause you to question the skill of the medium who led the séance. Certainly, Mr. Volckman was a discerning judge of talent. Perhaps you know that he was the original founder of the Society? He was a keen businessman, to be sure, but also a man of principle. Truth mattered to him, and he often complained that there were too many spiritualist impostors practicing in London and endangering all of us. He hoped the work of the Society would give credibility to the art of mediumship, rather than tarnish it." She shook her head, rubbed her eyes. "I will miss Mr. Volckman terribly. He was such an admirable colleague, but also a wonderful husband and father. His poor wife. I hope she is provided for..."

Vaudeline reached into her cloak and withdrew the letter, tapping it against the table. "I have not told you much about my departure from London, have I?"

Before her death, Evie had followed Vaudeline's work closely. She'd mused aloud on Vaudeline's swift exit from London, noting that for all the outspoken statements Vaudeline had made about the art of spiritualism, she'd been conspicuously silent on the reason for her departure.

Now Lenna shook her head.

"Before I left," Vaudeline explained, "I'd begun to suspect that there were a few rogue men within the Society who were running fraudulent-mediumship schemes. Parlor-room tricks, mostly, but fraud nevertheless. I only knew this because, given my position among spiritualists in the city, rumors had managed to make their way to me. I intended to investigate—discreetly— so I could provide Mr. Volckman with as much information as possible. But once I brought my initial concerns to him, he took the rumors very seriously. He promised to get to the bottom of things. I believe he meant to interview every widow and mourner in London who'd enlisted the Society's help in recent months. To his credit, the Society has always done a magnificent job of maintaining its reputation for authenticity. Volckman was not one to tolerate mischief."

Vaudeline leaned back in her chair, a morose look on her face. "Soon after talking with him about what I'd heard, Volckman told me he had indeed discovered evidence of something crooked within the organization—schemes meant to swindle money out of mourners—and he even knew the identities of the few men to blame. He needed to gather more evidence before bringing it against them, but what he'd learned was alarming. Not only did the scheme go deeper than he first realized, but these Society members seemed to know I was privy to the rumors, given my role in London's occult circles. They knew I'd begun asking questions, knew I was friends with Volckman. According to him, these men had plans to interfere with my meddling. And given what he'd gleaned from his own investigation, he felt confident my personal safety was at risk.

"Mr. Volckman suggested I return to Paris, quickly and without ceremony, until he resolved matters at the Society," Vaudeline said. "I took his warnings very seriously. It would be temporary, after all. And this was not the first time he'd looked out for my professional interests. In prior years, he'd defended several of my more controversial essays, even offered to connect me with his lawyers a time or two. Over the years, his wife, Ada, and I also became friends. I'd joined them both for meals, met their children. So I was inclined to follow his guidance." She fluttered her fingernails against the table, then shook her head. "Seeing as how Mr. Volckman is now dead, it is clear he gave me sage advice."

At last, she handed the letter over to Lenna. "You're welcome to have a look, if you'd like."

Lenna took the letter and angled it toward the low light.

Miss D'Allaire,

I regret to share with you that dreadful circumstances have fallen on the London Séance Society. A friend to both of us, Mr. M. Volckman, was found murdered on All Hallows' Eve, the thirty-first of October. The Met have yet to identify a perpetrator.

As the vice president of the Department of Spiritualism, and

Volckman's closest friend and confidant, I believe that the man—or men—who killed him is connected to your departure from London early last year. After you left, Mr. Volckman shared with me the reason behind your escape from the city and the threat posed to you by the rogue members sitting within the Society, the same members he believed were rigging our séances across town. For my own protection, he refused to identify the members by name until he had finished his investigation. It is my personal belief that these members learned of Volckman's investigation and sought retribution on him before he could obtain irrefutable proof of their wrongdoing. They would have known, as much as you and me, that Volckman was a man of integrity. He would not tolerate any members misaligned with his aims for the Society.

I am determined to sniff out the culprits within my department and bring them to justice. However, knowing the depth of Volckman's inquiries and the danger it caused him, I am inclined to go about things in a different way.

With that said, I should like to invite you to London to discreetly perform a séance for Mr. Volckman, with the intent of identifying the man (or men) who murdered him. I am sorry to say it, but I suspect his killer is connected to the Society. It could be someone who was hired to silence Mr. Volckman, or, worse than this, one of the Society members who has been performing crooked séances and causing the rumors you heard last year.

I endeavor to put your mind at ease regarding any (well-warranted) security concerns. Metropolitan Police constable and Society member Mr. Borden Beck has promised to accompany you for the duration of your time in London. Further, I am able to provide suitable lodging and disguise for your brief time in the city.

I do hope you will consider accepting this appeal, especially given your friendship and professional relationship with Mr. Volckman in years past. He was a good man; you know this as well as I do. You are a vengeance-seeker, Miss D'Allaire, and I implore you now to help me identify the men who took our beloved friend too soon.

If you are interested, enclosed I have provided travel instructions. Your every expense will be reimbursed. Please do inform me of your decision in the overnight post, including your planned arrival time.

With warmest regards,
Mr. Morley
Vice President, Department of Spiritualism
The London Séance Society

After reading the letter, Lenna gave it back to Vaudeline and walked over to the parlor window. She placed her palms against it, letting the coolness of the glass seep into her sweaty palms. On the outside of the window, a thin layer of frost melted in the shape of her hand. She glanced back at Vaudeline. "Have you ever met this Mr. Morley?"

"In passing, yes, at various mediumship events across the city. We've exchanged a few pleasantries, nothing more."

"His request seems very dangerous," Lenna said.

"It does, but I do not see how I can refuse it. Not when considering all that Mr. Volckman did for me over the years." Vaudeline exhaled slowly. Then she walked over to Lenna, joining her in front of the window. "You can understand why this letter has left me so upset," she said. "Not only have I learned about the death of a friend, but it seems the rumors I brought to him might have sent him to his grave. Mr. Morley was kind enough not to say it outright, but I am humble enough to admit it. I'm a spiritualist trying to solve crimes, and yet I feel very much to blame in this one." She paused. "I agree—the request is a precarious one. But a guilty conscience is not much better."

Lenna bit her bottom lip, suddenly pitying Vaudeline. It was a heart-wrenching story, and Lenna understood now why Vaudeline had been so devastated by the news. Devastated enough to ask for assistance with the incantations, even.

"I wonder if the Society has tried their own séance for Mr. Volckman," Lenna said now.

Vaudeline gave a small shrug. "Even if they have, their séances are not meant to solve crimes. Not like mine. Their aim instead is to uphold belief in the afterlife. They do this mostly by fostering tangible signs of spirits, otherworldly sounds, sights, and so on."

Tangible signs of spirits. This made sense, given the strange images the Society had written down on paper during Eloise's séance a few years ago. Ambiguous as they were, the scribbles were indeed something visible.

Lenna caught her hazy reflection in the window. Suddenly, a realization occurred to her—so obvious, so logical, she hadn't considered it until now. "If you're in London," she said, "then perhaps you can perform Evie's séance."

"Yes," Vaudeline said. "Assuming the Volckman séance goes well. If it does not, I will need to find my way back out of the city. Quickly. Which is why we cannot abandon your training merely on account of this letter." She patted her cloak. "Especially given the very natural skill you continue to exhibit." Vaudeline drew her lips together in an O shape and blew out one of the candles on the hearth; it had melted down and was dripping wax on the mantel. "I assure you, the incantations you read tonight would not have been so effective if another student had recited them." She gave a small smile, the first Lenna had seen all night. "Including our beloved Evie."

Lenna raised her eyebrows, surprised by this. "Evie always told me she was one of your best students."

"In terms of enthusiasm, yes. But she could, on occasion, be a bit overconfident about her skill."

"Impossible," Lenna quipped. "Overconfident? That doesn't sound like Evie at all."

Vaudeline smiled. "Once, we worked together on a very simple clairvoyance exercise. I set out ten wooden tiles, each with a number engraved on the underside. I picked one up at random and held it tight in my palm. She thought for a while on it, methodically working through the intuition exercises I'd taught her. She declared the tile a 9. I flipped it over; it was a 6." Vaudeline gave a wistful smile. "I was encouraging about the error. Evie could hardly be blamed for flipping the numeral in her mind. But she refused to believe it was a 6. She refused to admit her mistake, which was such a minor one at that. I showed her the engraving, how the tiny loops of the numbers were, in fact, subtly different. Her cheeks went red, her voice got higher. She questioned me, her teacher, saying that perhaps I was wrong. Well, I've had the tiles for years. I assure you, I know quite well which is the 9 and which is the 6. But she could not be convinced, and eventually, I gave it up and we moved on."

Lenna could hardly say she was surprised by this story. Such obstinacy was Evie's way.

Vaudeline waved away a wisp of smoke hovering near the women. "I haven't wasted any of your time on clairvoyance, as your recitation of the séance incantations is most important. Still, I sense you would know the 9 from the 6 perfectly well. You've been a marvelous student, quick to master everything we've covered. A natural, as evidenced tonight." She reached for Lenna's hand and gave it a squeeze, then let go. In the darkness, the sweet odor of her breath hovered between them.

At her touch, Lenna felt like she'd been flipped upside down, then righted again. "Interesting," she said, "that Evie believed so strongly in these matters, yet she struggled with the mastery of skills. I am just the opposite. I struggle with belief, but according to you, my skill in séance comes naturally."

"Yes. I see it all the time. I am convinced the spirit world quite enjoys chipping away at reluctance. When given the chance, ghosts are more cooperative with disbelievers." She cocked her head to one side. "Did you feel anything strange tonight when performing the incantations?"

Lenna thought a moment. She'd had the odd tingling sensation in her fingertips and the vibrant flash of blue light in the corner of her eye, but she'd experienced these in the past and had always attributed them to nerves, anxiety. "No," she said. "No, nothing strange."

"Well," Vaudeline said, giving a shrug. "We cannot forget your training. In fact—" Vaudeline paused "—I think you ought to join me on Volckman's séance."

"J-join you?" Lenna sputtered, sure she'd misheard.

Vaudeline gave a quick nod. "It seems quite the wasted opportunity," she said, "for an understudy to stay at home twiddling her thumbs while her teacher is out solving crimes. There will undoubtedly be much to learn at this gentleman's séance."

Lenna shook her head. "I won't be twiddling my thumbs. I'll be practicing the incantations again, until your work is done."

Vaudeline's face softened. "Admirable, but self-practice still will not compare to seeing another séance in practice."

Another séance with nothing provable? Lenna thought. *Just claims that can't be substantiated? Names that no one has heard of?*

The reward didn't seem worth the risk.

Suddenly she shivered—bone-cold, fatigued, and exasperated not only with Vaudeline but with the idea of spirits as a whole. She wanted to see a ghost, not just hear that Vaudeline had been entranced by one.

But this would not happen tonight, and for the first time since their initial meeting, Lenna wondered if her fondness for Vaudeline might have swayed her ability to discern truth from illusion. She looked now at her with more than a hint of skepticism. Vaudeline was, after all, a thirty-year-old ghost-hunting woman with few friends. She'd built her international renown on rumor—even hearsay.

And as if this were not enough, tonight's séance had proved an utter disappointment.

Lenna crossed her arms, feeling her temper rise and the heat in her chest, too. "After more than two weeks with you," she said, "still I have no proof that any of this is real. Even—" she swiped away an unexpected tear, knowing she couldn't take back what she was about to say "—even this séance, tonight. I can't help but agree with the father on a few points." She knew she was being bellicose—she was implying that her own lack of belief was Vaudeline's fault, when in fact it had always been this way—but she was tired of being strung forward with talk of spirits and never any proof of them.

Vaudeline stepped away from the window, and where her warm body had been a moment ago, now a chill hung in the air. It was plainly written on her face, the sting of Lenna's comment. "You sought me out," she said, "not the other way around." Her voice had risen above its normal volume, and now she stammered for a moment. Lenna wondered if she was fighting back tears of her own. Again. "I never asked you to believe in any of this, and it isn't my fault that your closed-mindedness keeps you from believing in anything that is not made of *rock*."

Closed-mindedness. It was the sort of accusation Evie had made more than once, and Lenna remembered too well the frustration of those never-resolved quarrels about illusion and tricks of light. Evie and Vaudeline were terribly similar in this way.

Lenna knew her sudden shift in mood was disproportionate to the situation. Vaudeline had merely invited her to join the Volckman séance, and now Lenna's harsh reply had left them both in tears. But her temper and grief felt so raw tonight. The way Vaudeline spoke about death, it was not a finale so much as an entr'acte, or interlude. Behind this curtain, she believed, spirits were as real—as alive—as they'd been in life. It was infuriating to think that Evie could be so close, yet so out of reach. All of these veils, whether in life or death—Lenna hated them.

She knew the rhythms of her moods. She needed to get out of this stifling, low-lit room. A pair of double doors led from the parlor to a small garden outside. Without another word to Vaudeline, she let herself out.

Into the moonlit night she went, taking a seat on a frigid metal bench outside. She wished the snow had not stopped falling earlier that night. What she wouldn't give now to disappear into the swirl and silence of it.

She sat for some time, arms crossed, watching a cream-colored cat stalk along the stone wall. The brisk air and the smell of woodsmoke were a welcome reprieve and eventually subdued her.

Even still, the tears kept falling. She'd never felt so alone.

After a while, she became aware of footsteps behind her. Vaudeline. What had happened between them tonight? This felt greater than a disappointing séance: it felt like a moment of reckoning between them. Their beliefs were so very different, but tonight might have fixed that. It might have been the night Lenna's beliefs changed. But now her convictions were even stronger. And she found that she suddenly did not trust a single thing about Vaudeline.

The summons from London loomed ahead of them, a juncture. Where would they go from here?

Lenna had not expected to end this night sitting alone amid snowmelt, as unenlightened about ghosts as she'd always been. In the frigid air, the warm tears running down her cheeks felt as though they might freeze into tiny crystals. *I just miss Evie*, she told herself. *I am crying because I have held it all in. I have not grieved her properly.* But as she sat in silence, arms still crossed, she knew this was not the full truth. There was more to this weeping, and it had everything to do with the woman whose footsteps now approached close behind her.

Vaudeline took a seat next to Lenna, though Lenna kept her gaze straight ahead. Somewhere in the tree arching above them, a horned owl swooped past, diving into the shrubs in pursuit of some unseen prey.

A moment later, Lenna felt the brush of fingertips against her own. It could easily have been an accident, a mere graze of hands. Or maybe it was not an accident at all. Either way, it didn't matter; Lenna moved her arm away, not at all in the mood for reconciliation.

The two women remained in silence this way a long while, their bodies just inches apart. But to Lenna, it felt like miles all the same.

6

 LENNA

Paris, Friday, 14 February 1873

Eventually, Vaudeline stood from the bench and went back inside.

A few heavy clouds rolled in, obscuring the moon. The garden was so very dark, and Lenna began to shiver, impossibly cold. How long did she intend to sit out here, anyway, sulking and sour?

She willed herself to snap out of her mood. Vaudeline might not have proved anything tonight, but it wasn't as though she'd done anything wrong. She'd merely been the nearest person for Lenna to release her frustrations upon. *If only I could run myself through a sieve,* Lenna thought, *and separate the feelings inside of me so to better deal with them one by one.*

The feeling of despair tonight reminded her of the quarrel she and Evie had had on the morning of Evie's death. It had been their worst and their last.

They'd been alone together in the breakfast room at the hotel. Soon, they would assist the kitchen maids in serving the table d'hôte breakfast. The hotel was full that day with an unusually high number of business travelers.

Neither of the sisters knew that Evie's death was but hours away. Not on this lovely autumn morning with a plate of glazed pear tarts in front of them. But Lenna didn't have much of an appetite that day. Yet again, she'd awoken dizzy, with flashes of colorful light—orange, violet—at the periphery of her vision. The tips of her fingers tingled, and her tummy churned, despite having not eaten anything since the night prior. This had gone on for several days now.

She stared down at the tart on her plate, eyes glazed over, feeling exceptionally unwell.

"Have one," Evie said. "Or I'll have it for you."

"I'm not hungry."

Evie raised her eyebrows. "But these are your favorite." She sliced her own tart in two and took a bite, smacking her lips.

"Whose hat is that?" Lenna asked, pointing to the rim of a grayish-brown felt cap protruding from Evie's satchel. There was a tiny notch on one side. She'd seen the cap a few times before but always assumed it belonged to yet another of Evie's beaus. Now curiosity got the best of her.

Evie's mouth fell open, crumbs sticking to the corner of her lips. She glanced at her bag. "Pardon?"

"It's not the first I've seen it." She eyed Evie warily. "It's a man's cap, clearly. Last time, you left it on the dresser. It smelled like tobacco."

Evie shoved the hat deep into her satchel and resumed chewing. "I hate that you do this."

"Do what?"

"Stick your nose into my business."

Lenna exhaled, rolling her eyes. She lifted a tiny flake of sugar glaze from her plate and put it on her tongue.

"Do you know what day tomorrow is?" Evie asked. How very like her to divert the conversation like this.

"The first of November," Lenna said, though she knew this wasn't what Evie was referring to.

"Stephen's birthday," Evie said.

Lenna nodded. "And Eloise's."

If she were honest with herself, Lenna wondered if this might explain why she'd been feeling so unwell as of late. She hated the first of November—hated that it marked another year her dear friend would never get to see.

The circumstances surrounding the death of Eloise and her father, Mr. Heslop, still haunted Lenna. A few years ago, midwinter, they'd been on an evening walk around the boating lake at the Regent's Park. Mr. Heslop walked the path nightly, but on this particular night, Eloise had accompanied him. Part of the lake had frozen over, and while no one had seen the accident occur, police believed Eloise slipped into the icy water, and her father went in after her. Both bodies were discovered the next morning.

Almost as painful as the accident was Mrs. Heslop's swift remarriage to another man, Mr. Cleland, who was a member of several West End gentlemen's clubs, including the London Séance Society. He was a brand-new member of the Society and had met Mrs. Heslop at her late husband's séance.

To this day, Lenna could hardly stomach the knowledge that Stephen and Eloise's mother had so easily moved on to another man—particularly Mr. Cleland, whose gambling habits had been ridiculed in the gossip columns more than once.

"I wonder what Eloise would be like today," Lenna mused aloud.

Evie crossed her hands on the table in front of her. "I've been trying to contact her."

Lenna pushed her plate away, suddenly thinking she might be

sick. The sugary smell of the tart repulsed her. She reached for a pitcher of water at the center of the table and poured herself a glass.

"I wish you wouldn't make her part of your games," Lenna said irritably. It was one thing when Evie played with a needle on string, waiting for movement, or when she talked about the latest photographic evidence of apparitions. It was an altogether different matter when she brought Eloise into it. Even now, existing just as a memory, Eloise remained terribly precious to Lenna.

"It isn't a *game* to me," Evie said. "It's real. And I think I've pushed my way through to her. I've been…seeing things. Drawing them out."

"Like the men of the London Séance Society claimed to do?" Lenna retorted, her voice like ice.

Toward the end of Eloise's séance, the Society member who'd led the affair—a man named Mr. Dankworth—retrieved a sheet of paper and drew wildly on it: rudimentary illustrations of furniture and insects, plus a variety of strange symbols, none of them relating in any way to Eloise or what her interests in life had been.

"Automatic writing," Mr. Dankworth said when he had finished. "A common skill among mediums, in which we act as a conduit for the spirit to communicate. Without knowing what, exactly, we're writing down, we reflexively transfer the spirit's desired message onto paper." He handed the drawings over. "Eloise established a connection with us today and bade me to produce these drawings."

Eloise's mother, grief-stricken as she was, believed that the images and words on the page had indeed been communicated from her daughter. Evie, too. They were intent on translating the meaning of the images in the days to come.

Lenna, meanwhile, thought the entire séance a sham. No one ever did make sense of the images, which gave Lenna a strange sort of satisfaction.

Now Evie glared at Lenna. "Don't let that one experience ruin it all for you. Those mediums the Society assigned were novices. Besides, we still don't know that the drawings were a hoax. We can't prove it either way."

"Exactly my point about all of this. I agree it can't be proved wrong, but it also can't be proved right."

"Then maybe you can help clear something up for me. One of the drawings I did while communicating with Eloise was, I think, about you."

Lenna set down her glass hard, so hard that water sloshed over the side of it. "Pardon?"

Evie gave a nod, took another bite of her pear tart. "When I felt like I'd reached her spirit, I closed my eyes and began to draw, aware that I was making lines on the paper, but not really knowing what the lines formed—what shape or image. Then I felt myself making little scratches on the paper, as though writing down letters. A few minutes later, I opened my eyes to see what it was that I'd put on the page."

"And?"

Evie reached into the small pocket sewn into her gown, withdrawing a sheet of paper. She passed it across the table to Lenna, who quickly unfolded it.

On the page was a single, simple shape: a hexagon. And inside of the hexagon, the letter *L* with a pair of interlocking hearts.

Lenna gasped. "Impossible," she whispered.

Before her death, Eloise had written Lenna a short, intimate note. She'd folded the paper into a tiny hexagon, then given it to Lenna. On the front of the hexagon was Lenna's first initial, and inside, next to Eloise's name, were two miniature hearts. Almost exactly like Evie's illustration.

"Do you know what it means?" Evie said, leaning forward excitedly. "The hexagon?"

The folded hexagon with its tender edges, having been opened and closed countless times, was now tucked discreetly into a trinket box under Lenna's bed. "Yes," Lenna said. "I do." But then she frowned. She'd found Evie rooting through her things a few days ago, claiming she'd lost her favorite pair of gloves. "Wait. Did you—" Her chest began to burn, and she sat forward, looking her sister hard in the eye. "Did you find the note she gave me?"

"What?" Evie went still. "What note?"

Lenna eyed her warily, not sure what was worse: the possibility that Evie was trying to fool her own sister into believing in ghosts by way of using something she'd found among Lenna's private things, or Evie having opened the note and reading the contents of it.

Yet Evie must have read it, if she knew the note was from Eloise.

Not only was this a violation of Lenna's privacy, but the note contained a very dear—and very private—sentiment. A message meant to be shared only between Lenna and Eloise.

Lenna flushed, feeling embarrassed now, too. "Eloise gave me a note before she died," she said. "She folded it into the shape of a hexagon and wrote my initial on it."

"You cannot be serious." Evie's eyes widened in delight. "This means—oh my—it means...I was successful." She looked down at her drawing, delighted, touching it like it was made of gold. "You see, Lenna? It's real, so much of this—"

"No," she snapped. To Lenna, nothing about this was delightful or enlightening. She didn't believe her sister, not for a second. "I cannot believe you invaded my privacy. And I cannot believe you're using it now to try and convince me of something I don't believe in."

Evie suddenly stood, her hip knocking the table, and Lenna's fork clattered off the table and onto the floor. "You think I'm lying about this?" Evie cried, her eyes welling with tears.

"You were looking through my things just a few days ago," Lenna said, now standing eye to eye with her. "The timing of this so-called automatic-writing exercise feels quite convenient. Especially so near Eloise's birthday."

Outside the room, down the corridor, their mother's voice rang out, something about a guest needing a tour itinerary. Evie glanced toward the door, took a step toward it. "I'm going," she said, wiping away a tear.

Her dismissal provoked Lenna; something in her burst open, a blister of exasperation with her insolent, dishonest little sister. She grabbed Evie's paper with the illustration, clutched either side of it, and ripped it down the center. She tossed the two halves onto the table.

Evie went white, staring at the pages as though not believing what she'd just seen.

After a long moment of silence, finally Evie spoke. "I—I—" she stammered. "I cannot believe you did this." Then, very delicately, she picked up the two halves, folded them together, and tucked them back into her pocket. No longer did Evie have tears in her eyes. Instead, she looked furious. "Goodbye," she said, sweeping out of the room.

Instantly a flash of color struck Lenna's vision, vivid and disorienting. She didn't reply but instead stood there trembling, her stomach churning worse than it had all morning.

After Evie had gone, Lenna went up to her bedroom. She pulled the trinket box out from under her bed and sifted through its contents. There, at the very bottom of the box, tucked between a dried fern leaf and a childhood drawing, was the hexagon. Eloise's note.

It appeared untouched, with the complex folds perfectly intact. The note was exactly as Lenna had left it. And Evie, well, she was heavy-handed. Often careless. Lenna felt confident she wouldn't have known how to refold the hexagon, nor would she have thought to replace the note back in the box in exactly the manner she'd found it.

Lenna was now certain of it: Evie hadn't been in this box.

Unfolding the paper, Lenna read the note for what must have been the thousandth time.

> *It will always be this way, won't it? Endless things we'll feel for each other, and yet we cannot breathe a word of it aloud. I find solace in knowing that a friendship between two women faces no threats, and we can go on this way forever. So long as you and I know what it really is between us, that will be enough for me.*

At the bottom, Eloise had signed off with two hearts, their sides looped together.

Lenna pressed the page against her chest, inhaling deep. A year ago, the paper had still carried the subtle scent of Eloise; it was long gone now, but Lenna still touched the parchment to her nose every time, hoping to catch a remnant of it.

We can go on this way forever, Eloise had said. How very wrong she'd been. Nothing had gone on forever—neither their guise of friendship, nor the true affections hidden beneath it. Not their long walks arm in arm, nor the furtive glances they'd shared after their first kiss. Or their second.

It had always been that way with Eloise. A hesitation had existed between them, a resistance born of timidity and fear of rule-breaking. As badly as Lenna wanted to explore this territory with her, she feared growing too close, knowing they could not be together, not really. Their families would not permit it. Certainly, proper London society would not permit it. Why, then, would Lenna let such feelings grow and intensify? Better to quell them while early and young.

Eloise had clearly felt the same. Hence, the message inside her note. *So long as you and I know what it really is between us, that will be enough for me.*

Lenna folded the paper again into its perfect hexagon. There was no way Evie could have seen the note, no way she could have redone the folds correctly. With a sigh of regret, Lenna closed the lid, put the box back under the bed, and went in search of Evie. She'd apologize for her frustration, her false accusations. Those two halves of Evie's paper, the jagged edge on either side—she wished badly she could fuse them back together. The healing of a cut.

And this was to say nothing of what it actually meant about Evie's exercise in communicating with the dead. Lenna would need to think more on this. She might have wavered between belief and skepticism, but Evie's drawing was strikingly accurate. The initials, the interlocking hearts on the inside. If Evie hadn't read the note, how could she have possibly known such details?

Lenna rushed downstairs, searching for her sister. But Evie had gone out for the morning; one of the maids explained that she'd begged off early and left the building to assist a lodger with directions.

Lenna wasn't able to say *I'm sorry.*

And she never got the chance because she never saw her sister alive again.

Lenna left the garden bench, making her way back into the parlor. Vaudeline, bleary-eyed and yawning, sat awake in the dining room, writing a letter. It was nearly three o'clock in the morning.

"I'm writing my reply to Mr. Morley," Vaudeline said. "I'll send it via overnight post in the morning. I didn't mention a traveling companion. I'll leave Saturday morning." She folded the letter up, secured the envelope. "You're welcome to arrange whatever return travel you'd like, and we—or *I*—can do Evie's séance as soon as Volckman's is over."

"Thank you," Lenna said. She sat down and reached for her

mug of tea. She took a sip and cringed—it had gone cold—then set it back down. "And I'm s—" She interlaced her fingers, an apology on the tip of her tongue, held back by pride. But she knew too well the repercussions of waiting to make apologies. "I'm sorry for what I said earlier. About the séance, and my lack of belief. You've had a terrible night, and I did nothing to make it easier on you." She held very still, waiting to see how Vaudeline would reply.

Vaudeline tossed her letter onto the center of the table, pushed back her chair, and stood. She gave Lenna a long, inscrutable look. "I have, indeed, had a terrible night," she said, giving a nod. She stepped around the table, toward Lenna, and knelt just in front of her. "But the worst part of it was not the letter about my friend Mr. Volckman, nor the father's claims about my séance, nor even *your* claims about my séance. The worst part of my night was out in the garden, when I reached for your hand and you moved it away." She looked down. "I can withstand the rigors of my job—the macabre nature of séance, the accusations of fraud. But I do not have many companions, and I have never grown accustomed to conflict with the people I consider friends."

Something in Vaudeline's tone seemed…different. Consequential. At once, Lenna regretted her pouting. How childish it had been of her.

"Good night," Vaudeline finally whispered, her voice laced with sadness. She bent forward and gave Lenna a slow, tender kiss on the cheek.

Lenna's breath caught. No other woman, other than Eloise, had let their lips linger so long against Lenna's skin. "Good night," she replied, taken aback by the exchange. She and Vaudeline had always shown each other minor displays of affection, but never had it been like this, so brimming with intimacy and frustration.

She watched Vaudeline walk away, toward her bedroom. Then

she touched her fingertips to her cheek. Already, the sensation of Vaudeline's lips against her skin had disappeared.

Lenna lay awake in bed a long while after that, eyes affixed on the pale ceiling.

If Evie were here now, she'd be pleased with Lenna for feeling something. She'd always teased Lenna about her apparent lack of interest in romance, reminding her that Stephen Heslop was not only terribly handsome but clearly in love with her.

What Evie didn't know was that, several years ago, Lenna did have a romantic interest. Only, it hadn't been Stephen.

Still, she'd kissed him once, on the street behind a lamppost. It was an experiment of sorts. She'd hoped it would stir something within her, possibly make her forget about Eloise altogether, but it decidedly had not.

Afterward, she'd run home and closed the door of the girls' shared bedroom. She proceeded to share every detail with Evie. After all, this kiss was nothing to hide.

"His teeth kept knocking against mine," she said.

Evie cringed. "It gets better in time."

Of all people, she would know. She'd been kissing boys for years.

"And it was wet," Lenna went on. "His lips were just…" She touched a scratch on her chin where his facial hair had scraped against her. He'd been more insistent than Lenna wanted, his breath damp and smelling of coffee. "Scratchy and forceful. I didn't like it. Not at all."

"Nor would I, the way you've described it."

Lenna lowered her voice. "His hands, he kept running them along my waist," she whispered. "And the back of my neck." She toyed with the lock of hair behind her ears that he'd inadvertently pulled loose.

"Well, that doesn't sound all bad. I quite like it when gentlemen put their hands on my waist." Evie's eyes glinted. "Perhaps you would like it if it were someone else."

"I can't think of any man I want to do that with again. Any at all."

"Who said it has to be a man?"

Lenna's stomach had lurched at this. Might Evie have suspected her secret fondness for Eloise? She'd changed the topic quickly, and they'd never circled the subject again. But now, lying alone in her bunk at Vaudeline's guesthouse, Evie's words came back to her. *Who said it has to be a man?*

Lenna thought of the kiss with Stephen, the amber stone he'd gifted her, the occasional brush of their arms and hands. None of it had done anything for her—and had, in some instances, left her feeling sick to her stomach, even ashamed. Not true to herself, certainly.

Yet how very different it had always been around Eloise, and the last two weeks with Vaudeline, too. Inconsequential chatter with Vaudeline often left her breathless. And the way Vaudeline had gazed so intensely at Lenna upon her arrival in Paris… Gooseflesh had run down her entire body. Though it left her skin chilled, still she'd tugged at her bodice, feeling marvelously warm inside.

In recent days, Lenna had felt all the things she hadn't felt since spending time around Eloise, like heat in her face, dampness under her arms, and an inexplicable urge to forgo responsibilities in favor of daydreams. This, plus a constant curiosity about Vaudeline: what she was thinking, what she was reading, to whom she was writing her letters.

And that kiss on the cheek, earlier tonight… Lenna couldn't recall anything so tender or soft in all her life.

Lying in her bunk, Lenna finally admitted it to herself. A mere whisper in the dark, she said it aloud. *I want her. I want Vaudeline, just as I wanted Eloise.* And she did not mean as a teacher or even a friend. She wanted more of Vaudeline than a teacher or friend would dare to give.

The admission gave her a thrill. She might not have shared the secret with anyone else, but at least she'd said it aloud to herself. It was a brave start.

And maybe this time, she'd be bolder—more so than she'd been with Eloise. They'd only put their friendship on display, and still the time had been stolen from them. Their *forever* hadn't existed at all.

Well, Lenna had learned the lesson twice over now. Nothing was promised. Not sisterhood, not friendship. Not the next love note, not the next argument. All that was promised was now—this lone, ever-fleeting moment—and Lenna was tired of missing her chance to do or say the truest thing while she still had the opportunity.

Slowly, brazenly, Lenna reached out and placed her hand against the wall next to her bunk. She knew that mere inches away—through the plaster and wood, in the adjoining room— Vaudeline was lying in her bed. Asleep, or maybe not.

With one hand still resting against the wall, Lenna slowly pushed her other hand underneath the lace coverlet, finding the bottom edge of her chemise. She toyed with the fringe of it, noticing how the tips of her fingers felt especially sensitive, almost ticklish.

She pulled her chemise upward, trailing the tip of her index finger along her hip bone and then along the crease at the top of her leg. She paused for a moment, feeling some resistance in her mind as she thought of London, of the stuffiness of the city, of lace gloves hiding hands. She thought of all the things women couldn't admit to doing, wanting. Such rules had kept her from revealing her romantic feelings several years ago—not just to Eloise, but to Evie, even to herself.

But now she knew too well the curse of such rules. The stifled, never-explored possibilities. She continued to move her fingers downward, inching them along, imagining that perhaps

Vaudeline was not asleep on the other side of the wall at all but doing something similar.

Suddenly Lenna's knee jerked involuntarily. She'd only done this a few times—always burdened by shame and, later, remorse. Now she pressed harder than she ever had, not giving a whit for decency, reveling in the sensation of it, breathing with the rhythm of it. With her other hand, she pushed her palm flat against the wall, wishing there was some incantation to make it crumble and fall away, to get her closer to the woman on the other side.

In her imagination, at least, she could make the wall disappear. She felt reckless now, not bothered by decency, and trembled with every whirl of her fingertip. One hand on the wall, one hand between her legs, she pictured Vaudeline's bed next to her own with no barrier between them. She imagined Vaudeline doing precisely this same thing, thinking of her, wanting not to be a teacher or a friend at all but a lover. She remembered the soft warmth of Vaudeline's lips against her cheek a short while ago, the sensation of her breath as she said good-night—

Suddenly, Lenna pushed her head back into the pillow and lifted her hips in a reflex she couldn't have thwarted if she so desired. Her hand slipped away from the wall. She clasped it over her mouth as she shuddered violently, four times, five times.

Beneath her fingers, a shameless smile.

7

 MR. MORLEY

London, Saturday, 15 February 1873

I was delighted to receive Vaudeline's swift letter of acceptance. She informed me that she'd depart Paris very early on Saturday morning, the fifteenth of February, with a planned arrival of eight o'clock in the evening.

I began preparations immediately, foremost with the small storage room on the ground floor of the Society, apart from the common areas where the members spent their time. The storage room was full of boxes and discarded furniture pieces: podiums, broken chairs, a heavy bookcase. I set some of it just outside the room, in the unused corridor, and threw away the rest.

Once I'd tidied the room, I brought in a cot and placed clean sheets and a few pieces of clothing on a chair. Vaudeline wouldn't be residing in the room for very long, so I didn't worry much over comforts or convenience.

Finished with the arrangements, I closed the door and made my way back to the front of the building.

As I went, I passed the rarely used servants' door, leading outside to the alley at the back of the Society headquarters. This door was the one through which I would admit Vaudeline, and I gave a small smile, remembering the other woman who used to furtively sneak her way in via this entrance.

Evie Rebecca Wickes.

By our fourth walk, her obsession with the spirit world was painfully obvious. It was all she wanted to talk about: what ghosts we'd seen during our séances, what reference volumes we kept in our library, what spiritualist contacts we had made around the city.

On one particularly memorable morning, she made a passing remark about a woman she idolized, the famed medium named Vaudeline D'Allaire.

"I simply adore her," Evie said, all smiles. "I've read everything she's ever written, and I was fortunate enough to partake in one of her training cohorts here in London." She turned her blue gaze on me. "Have you heard of Miss D'Allaire? Surely you have, given your aligned interests. She left for Paris, without explanation, about six months ago."

I tripped slightly on the pavement, cursing at my scuffed shoe. "Yes, I know of her," I said. "We ran in similar circles."

Evie gave a nod and, to my great relief, did not press the matter. Miss D'Allaire's departure was a confidential subject, linked to things I couldn't possibly get into with this young woman: rumors, rogues, reputational damage.

"I do enjoy breaking a few rules, Mr. Morley," Evie said suddenly, looking up at me through her eyelashes. She stopped short, there in the middle of the park, and turned to face me head-on. "I'd like to meet you somewhere private next time."

It was an improper proposal on her part, but nothing about Miss Wickes was what I would term *proper*. It nearly dripped from her, that wayward youthfulness. She was unusually high-spirited for a woman and totally unconcerned with convention. I had tried, on a prior walk, to steer us into a more traditional courtship, but when I asked for permission to call on her father, she laughed.

Oh, but I relish in the excitement of this, she'd said that day. *We have a special connection, don't we? I quite like that no one knows about us—and I've never been one for etiquette, anyhow.*

It was impossible to be angry with her about it, despite the underlying snub. I was under Evie's spell, and I believe she knew it.

Now her request for a private assignation caught me off guard, and I fumbled a moment over my reply. I remained burdened by a lifetime of embarrassment over the birthmark on my face, and I had never been so overtly propositioned by a woman. An attractive one at that, all bergamot and sweet-smelling skin.

"I am quite surprised," I finally said, glancing down at my feet. Try as I might, I could not muster a jot of self-confidence just then. I touched my cheek, wishing more than anything that the blemish on my face would evaporate or otherwise disappear.

She stepped closer, her gaze very serious now. She pulled my hand away from my cheek. "Why do you always hide your face from me?" she asked. Above us, a few tree branches swayed in the breeze, and rays of sunshine glinted erratically around us. "I find it exquisite," she added, before I could respond, "the ways in which you are different than every other gentleman."

No one had ever said such a thing to me. *"Exquisite,"* I repeated, drawing out the syllables. For the briefest of moments, I thought I might cry.

"Yes." She gave a little shuffle of her feet like she might begin to dance, there in the broken sunlight. "Have you any engagements tonight?" she asked, more playful now.

In fact, I did. A few of us Society members had reserved a box for a showing of *The Miser* at the Theatre Royal in Drury Lane.

"No engagements at all," I said anyway.

She gave a little grin. "Excellent."

We agreed to meet at ten o'clock, after the members had gone.

I told her to go to the servants' door at the back of the Society building. No one meddled near it, other than the ratcatchers and sewer nightmen who were too drunk to remember what they saw anyhow.

I advised her to dress in men's clothes, like she'd done for the ectoplasm lecture. We would have plenty of privacy.

Never mind the rules. I greatly looked forward to welcoming a woman up the back stairs of the Society that evening.

8

LENNA

Paris, Saturday, 15 February 1873

L enna opted to return to London alongside Vaudeline. On Saturday, two days after the séance at the château, the women situated themselves in a small, second-class compartment toward the back of a steamer car, departing Paris and en route for Boulogne. There, they would board a steamship taking them across the Channel, up the River Thames, and directly to the London Bridge Wharf. It was a quicker route by several hours than Lenna's journey into Paris.

As the train pulled out of Paris, Lenna laid her head back against the headrest, letting the motion of the train lull her into a deep sleep.

Sometime later, the rattle of porcelain woke her. Lenna blinked her eyes open, disoriented. Through the haze of her sleepy eyes, she could make out the form of Vaudeline across from her in the train carriage, flipping the pages of a book with a contented look on her face. A porcelain pot of tea rested on top of a small tray affixed to Vaudeline's seat.

"You slept for more than two hours," Vaudeline said quietly, not looking up from her book.

Lenna checked her watch and nodded, then briefly closed her eyes again. She'd had the strangest dream about Evie dancing gleefully in the rain, wearing that strange felt cap. She'd been surrounded by upside-down candles that did not melt nor extinguish in the rain, and at some point, the rain had turned to coins and seashells and feathers. *Apportations.*

Then the rain had turned luminescent and bright green—like phosphorous oil. It reminded her of her conversation with Vaudeline a few days ago. They'd gone on a walk in Vaudeline's neighborhood and discussed Evie's strange behavior leading up to her death. Including what clues, if any, Lenna had found after the event.

"Evie went to a party the night she died," Lenna had explained to Vaudeline. "I don't know where—the city was full of parties that night—or with who. She had lots of friends, and they all believed in ghosts. She did this disappearing game often, sneaking out of the hotel, day or night, without telling our parents. She wouldn't even tell me what she was up to. I assumed she had a beau, maybe more than one." Lenna stepped carefully along the sidewalk, wrapping her arms tight around her chest. "And as for the gathering she attended that night? Well, I can't even be sure it was a party, in the traditional sense. It could have been a ghost chase or a séance or anything like that."

"And you didn't find anything in the days to follow that might have shed some light on the gathering or who she'd gone with?" Vaudeline asked.

Lenna shook her head. The morning after Evie's death, she'd blazed through their shared room. The instability of grief had made her wild—violent, even. She tore open Evie's mattress with a knife, looking for love notes or money or hand-scrawled admissions. She ripped a drawer from its casing, searching inside and underneath for pasted-on secrets. Anything she could break into pieces, she did, locked or not. It was cathartic for a brief moment, the transfer of her fury into a piece of splintered wood, but Lenna found no answers. She couldn't even find the notebook, the one Evie had written in so many times. Before leaving the room, she kicked the rubbish bin for good measure. It clattered across the room, but it was empty, of course. No clues there, either.

"I went through her things the morning after her death, looking for any clues or information. I found nothing about the party. I could only find quite a few...clippings. Articles."

This piqued Vaudeline's interest. "Of what nature?"

"Quite a lot about you." Lenna chewed at her bottom lip. "But I also found articles on pyromancy, a vial of phosphorous oil, a book on automatic—"

"You found a vial of phosphorous oil?" Vaudeline asked, pulling up short on the sidewalk.

"Yes," Lenna said slowly. "What's wrong with phosphorous oil?"

Vaudeline began walking again, and then she cleared her throat. "I make no claims about your sister's amusements or intentions for her mediumship business, but I must tell you that phosphorous oil is a favorite tool of swindling spiritualists, one of the most blatant forms of imposture in this field."

Lenna balked. "How so?"

Vaudeline went on. "Phosphorous oil is luminous—it glows—and fraudulent mediums will often douse objects in the oil to give them the impression of being otherworldly. Sometimes, mediums will use the oil to paint humanlike forms on the wall or even bedsheets. There is no reason a spiritualist would ever keep it among her things, unless it was with the intent to deceive."

Lenna suddenly felt defensive of Evie. If Vaudeline meant to call Evie a fraud, why, two could play at that game. "Well, among her things, there were plenty of articles about your séances, too."

"I did not mean to give the impression your sister was involved in imposture," Vaudeline said quickly. Then she'd pressed her lips together and changed the topic.

Now Lenna frowned, chasing the tendrils of her strange dream before they escaped her memory, but suddenly the train veered left on a hard turn, jarring her attention. The dream dissipated, fragile as it was.

She reached down into her bag, looking for her tin of peppermints. As she searched, her hand brushed up against a paper bag. Within it, she knew, was the downy, tender feather of a blackcap warbler.

After her terrible, last argument with Evie on the morning of All Hallows' Eve, Lenna had gone immediately to the fortune-telling shop on Jermyn Street in search of the feather apportation Evie had shown her in the catalog. It felt inadequate as an olive branch—anything would be inadequate after tearing Evie's paper in half and accusing her of reading Eloise's note—but it was something.

To her great relief, the feather was still available for sale. The shop owner carefully wrapped it in paper, and Lenna handed over a few coins. She'd put the package in her room for safekeeping, hoping to have the chance to talk with Evie that night and apologize. It didn't matter that she considered apportations fantastical, imaginary, or downright fake. All that mattered was Evie. She'd wanted a feather—*this* one—and after their argument, Lenna would have given her the world.

Now, it seemed, the warbler feather belonged to Lenna forever. A reminder of what she'd done and the apology she never got to make.

"Would you like tea?" Vaudeline asked, motioning to a second teacup sitting on a saucer.

Lenna nodded; her tongue felt dry, cottony. She watched as Vaudeline carefully poured, struck—as she'd been upon their first meeting—by Vaudeline's impossibly long lashes. "Thank you," Lenna said, taking the cup from her, before adding, "I had a dream about my sister."

Vaudeline smiled warmly. "I dream every so often of my sister, too." Her smile fell. "But the dreams are not happy ones, as I suspect yours are."

Lenna knew Vaudeline had a sister, but they had not talked at length about her. "Why are they not happy dreams?"

Vaudeline set her book down. "She lives in Paris," she said, "as do my parents. I have not seen any of them since I was nineteen, more than ten years ago. That was when I became a medium and began traveling across the world. My parents and sister shunned me soon after. They've been interviewed several times over the years. Once, my mother told a reporter I was better suited to an insane asylum. She much prefers to boast about my younger sister, who is a mother with a brood of beautiful children." She toyed with a black bangle on her wrist. "Quite the irony that families are willing to pay me to reach through the realm of the dead for their loved ones, yet mine will not so much as make the trip across Paris."

Lenna remembered, two nights ago, what Vaudeline had said: *I have never grown accustomed to conflict with the people I consider friends.* Perhaps the pain of her family's rejection had also been buried in that statement. Lenna couldn't fathom it, this public and private exile. It was a wonder Vaudeline had any kindness left in her at all.

"Maybe this is why I care so much for solving cold crimes," Vaudeline said. "Who wants to be neglected or disregarded, whether in life or in death? None of us. And though I won't seek vengeance against my family for shunning me, I have directed those frustrations into my work. I suppose, in some ways, my family's rejection prepared me for what was to come. Communing with the dead is a lonely thing. As I've said, I do not have many companions in this business." She pursed her lips. "You've seen how stoic I must be when sitting across the table from a grieving family. Such a demeanor does not exactly invite...friendship. I've been called *cold, apathetic. Uncaring.*"

"Your stoicism isn't because you don't feel for the séance participants," Lenna said. "You're trying to protect them." She frowned, thinking how Vaudeline's chilly demeanor was mere illusion, a facade. "Just because you keep your empathy locked away doesn't make you insensitive. The empathy is there. You're simply very skilled at setting it aside."

A thin door separated their compartment from the train's central corridor; outside, a boy pushed a cart down the aisle, offering newspapers and cigarettes and fresh croissants. Lenna hailed him down, suddenly very hungry.

Vaudeline looked down at her hands in her lap. "No one has ever put it quite that way before. Thank you for saying it."

Lenna might have been a mere understudy, but she felt a singular sense of pride, knowing she'd just exposed something about Vaudeline—something she'd observed on her own and ventured to say out loud. She wanted to dig deeper, to keep exploring and revealing what she thought lay underneath the exterior of this famed woman. Based on Vaudeline's comment a moment ago, it seemed others had not taken the time to do this. Her profession meant that people considered her nothing more than a conduit, a means to reach their deceased loved ones. How must it feel for Vaudeline to exist as a means of connecting people but never being truly seen? Never relishing such connection herself?

"Why did you become a medium?" Lenna asked. "If it is so rife with loneliness and skepticism..."

"For exactly the same reason you came to Paris. I lost someone, too. A man I loved very much. His name was Léon. We'd known each other only a year, but I'm sure someday we would have gotten married."

Lenna took a small bite of her croissant, chewing thoughtfully. "Where did you meet him?"

"In Paris, at a street fair. Léon was an artist. Watercolor. I walked by his stand one morning, awestruck by his work and his way with colors and movement. Everything from his depictions of children running along a lake to tears rolling down a cheek. Sailboats, daffodils, dogs. There was nothing he couldn't paint. His work was terribly lifelike, as though you might reach through the canvas and pluck a flower petal straight from it. I went to his stand every weekend until, eventually, he understood that I was not only interested in his art." She gave a mischievous smile, her eyes glimmering. "It did not take long for us to fall deeply in love."

"Was he—" Lenna cleared her throat. "Well, you said you lost him. How did he die?"

Vaudeline nodded as though expecting the question. "He suffered a head injury, a bad fall from the stairs tucked behind his town house. One moment he had been so alive, his hand creating landscapes and emotion from nothing but pigment on a brush, and then he was merely…gone. A cold body, soon to be laid in a grave. And the paintings. I could hardly believe that they would cease to exist from that point forward." She gazed out the window. The train passed through a field of winter snowdrops with their humble, downward-facing blooms. "It sickened me, the thought of what the world had lost. What *I* had lost. Desperate to get something of him back, I studied everything I could about spirits and séances and entrancement. I became very good at it, and I found quite a lot of peace—for a while."

Now Vaudeline gave a slow shrug as the train forged on. A beam of sunlight came through the window and fell across her lap, and she traced it slowly with her fingers. "Anyhow, I am glad you dreamed of your sister. Dreams are healing." She lifted the book from her lap: it was evident that she was not interested in discussing Léon any further today. "My dreams tend to be abstract and strange," she went on, "but I suppose my unusual taste in books does not help." She turned the spine of the book toward Lenna. *The Island Clairsensories*, it read. "It's a novel about six Arctic islands, each inhabited by a princess with some kind of clairsensory power. Soon, I will probably dream of beautiful women surrounded by ice or little seals..."

The passage of time might have soothed Lenna's temper, but not her skepticism. As she chewed a piece of croissant, she was glad to keep her mouth busy—anything to keep her from asking for more information about these invisible, unprovable ideas like clairsensory abilities. She wanted to keep the peace, so even after she was done eating, she remained silent and gazed out the window at a frozen, dismal field. This vista, she could believe: the formation of ice, the measure of cold. Somewhere beneath the packed surface were layers of sediment, like sandstone, limestone, and chalk. She could dig for these things—albeit very deep—and lift the pieces out, let the sediment crumble between her fingers. She might even be able to spot a fossil or two.

She exhaled, her breath fogging a spot on the window and obscuring the view outside. She wanted badly to meet Vaudeline halfway on something, anything. It seemed imperative now, if the two were to keep their friendship intact. Lenna had been stubborn and argumentative two nights ago, but still it was maddening, the lack of proof about any of this. She wanted to believe, but she was beginning to feel that evidence of the spirit world was evading her. Teasing her.

Life and death are not as black-and-white as I want them to be, she admitted to herself. *Maybe my resistance is part of the problem. How can anything of the spirit world show itself to me if I simply write it off as illusion?* She resolved to be less stubborn, to see if she could permit science and spirits to coexist, even in a small way. Without this, she considered that her faltering beliefs might stand in the way of someday reaching Evie, wherever she was.

She became aware of eyes on her. She glanced away from the window to find Vaudeline looking curiously at her. "Did you know that your lips move when you're deep in thought?"

Lenna flushed. "No," she said, embarrassed. No one had ever told her this, not even Evie.

"What are you thinking about?"

She chose her words carefully, wary of causing friction between them. "How easy it is to believe in the things we can see and touch. We cannot do either with spirits."

Vaudeline shook her head. "You mustn't speak for us all. What you mean is that *you* cannot see or touch them. Not yet." She paused. "Clergymen and scientists believe we spiritualists imagine these things or that we are talented actors seeking attention and fame." She gave a little laugh. "Believe me, if I sought fame, I would not have embarked on a career abounding with so much sorrow. And cynicism."

The train moved easily across the tracks, rocking their carriage slightly. Vaudeline gave her a warm smile. "I did not give you a proper apology two nights ago, as I should have. *Moi aussi, je suis désolée.* I've encountered skeptics my entire life, but I took greater offense to your doubts than I might normally have."

Lenna wondered why this might be. Was it because Vaudeline had been shaken by the letter from London? Or because Vaudeline held Lenna's opinion above other skeptics she'd encountered? She hoped it was the latter, that Vaudeline was more sensitive to the things Lenna believed—or did not believe—when compared to the average person. Lenna did not want to be an average person in Vaudeline's eyes, not at all.

"I shouldn't have invited you to the gentleman's case in London," Vaudeline said now. "It is not safe or practical. I cannot teach you properly, not while remaining focused on something that has such high stakes for them and for me." She crossed one leg over the other, placing her hands neatly in her lap. "As for Evie, I will keep my promise. After I finish with the London Séance Society, I will perform your sister's séance."

"Thank you. I hope—" Lenna could not hide the quiver in her voice. "Well, I hope it all goes safely."

Vaudeline's eyes flashed darkly. "Yes." She nodded. "Me, too." The train slowed as they approached the station at Boulogne. "Until then—" she pointed to the rugged ground along the tracks "—we will part, and you can return to your fossils and rocks. It is the safest option for you, anyhow."

Her words were laced with a gentle resignation. Whereas over the last two weeks, Lenna had felt pulled forward by Vaudeline— like her new friend would continue to chisel away at her disbelief— she now realized Vaudeline had given up the fight. What terribly unfortunate timing, given that Lenna had just decided to release a mote of her stubbornness and was determined now to find illusion in everyday life.

Both women had softened their stances. And yet, while Lenna meant to move toward Vaudeline's beliefs, Vaudeline seemed ready to set Lenna free of them.

Lenna gazed out at the Liane River and, beyond, the English Channel they would soon cross. The tide was low, and she knew that among the rocky riverbed were countless objects that would make for good exhibits at a museum: ammonites that could be measured, silica that could be weighed, even the remnants of bone that could be traced down a chart of taxonomy.

But this? This forlorn feeling stirring inside of her, knowing she would depart from Vaudeline at the London docks tonight— it could not be identified, could not be touched, yet it was entirely real.

Just when I realize that my stubbornness might be the problem, Lenna thought, *she and I must go our separate ways.* It seemed terribly unfair. Lenna glanced down, swiping away a stray tear before Vaudeline could take notice of it.

That evening, the steamship arrived nearly an hour early in London. The women disembarked and made their way down the gangway plank onto the dock at the London Bridge Wharf. It was after seven o'clock, the sun long down. Vaudeline pulled out a handkerchief, covering her nose and dabbing at her eyes. As if the reek of the Thames weren't distasteful enough, the shroud of fog hanging over the city this time of year could make a person's eyes sting and water. Vaudeline wasn't used to this, not like Lenna was.

Stepping onto the dock, Lenna did not remember the last time she was so run-down, so weary. Still, they'd disembarked early. Mr. Morley wouldn't have arrived yet, and Lenna couldn't fathom letting Vaudeline sit here alone among the crowd.

"I'll wait over here," Vaudeline said, motioning to a bench across the dock. Ahead was a sign, lit by a gas lamp, bearing the words *General Steam Navigation Co.* She turned, as though about to wish Lenna goodbye.

"You don't really believe I'm leaving you here to wait alone, do you?"

"It's getting late."

Lenna raised her eyebrows. They'd stayed up later than this many times in Paris, talking well into the early hours of the morning. Vaudeline had always enjoyed Lenna's long discourses about the fossil collections and preservation techniques she'd learned about in London. Similarly, Lenna enjoyed hearing of the many places Vaudeline had traveled as she gladly recounted stories of her séances in Cape Breton, Tunis, Serbia. Lenna didn't know what to make of the more outlandish claims—levitating bowls and spontaneous scars—but the travel bits, at least, were fascinating. The spice markets and sunny climates. Lenna hoped to someday see it all for herself.

"We've stayed up much later than this before," she said.

Vaudeline smiled. "Very true." She took a seat, reached into her bag. "While we wait, we can play a game." She withdrew her novel, the one about Arctic islands and clairsensory women, and angled it toward the gas lamp.

Lenna sat down, too, inching close to her. "A game of…reading to one another?"

"No. I will choose a random word on the page. Then you try to guess what word I've chosen."

"So, it isn't a game at all. It's a way for you to coerce me into practicing my clairvoyance." Lenna grinned. "Always a teacher."

"I'll give you a hint or two. No clairvoyance needed." Vaudeline glanced at her. "I'd like to think we are not *only* a teacher and student." She angled the book toward herself, frowned, then looked up. "I have the word. Your clue is *float*."

Lenna smiled. *"Iceberg."*

"Agh," Vaudeline said, smiling. "Far too easy." She turned to another page and skimmed her finger down the page. "Ooh, I very much like this next one. Your clue is...*les seins*."

Lenna poked her playfully on the leg. "This is just a lesson in French, then. I haven't the slightest idea what that means."

"Very well, then. A clue in English: *bosom*."

Lenna flushed. *"Chest?"*

"No."

"Breasts."

"Oui."

They began to laugh then, so loud that several porters turned to look. Amid the giggling, Lenna looked down. Her hand had found Vaudeline's, and their fingers were now intertwined.

She remembered Vaudeline's comment in Paris, after the château séance: *The worst part of my night was out in the garden, when I reached for your hand and you moved it away.*

Yet just now, without thinking, Lenna's hand had reached for hers. Almost of its own volition.

Vaudeline closed the book and set it aside, and the two women leaned back against the bench, their hips pressed close. Neither of them moved to release their intertwined hands. For a long while they remained like this, in silence, looking out at the River Thames, dark and shadowy as it was. Lenna couldn't help but wonder what was beneath the surface of the water, how much life must exist there, awake and alive even at this gloomy hour.

Time went by too quickly. Just before eight o'clock, Vaudeline lifted Lenna's hand to her lips and laid a tender kiss on the top of it. "The nature of my work is that it cannot be seen," she said, her voice low. "And that goes for my affection, too. I quite like you, Lenna, but affection is not always tangible. I hope you will still believe it exists."

Very slowly, she disentangled her hand from Lenna's and looked toward the awning.

"Mr. Morley indicated in his travel instructions that he'd be waiting over there," Vaudeline said. She stretched her neck to look around the crowd. Then she stood, turning to Lenna. "You'll give me your address? I'll make my way over as soon as I can."

Lenna gripped the leather handle of her wicker luggage case. *I quite like you*, Vaudeline had just said. But what could she say in return, particularly at this moment, teeming as it was with danger and uncertainty? All she could dwell on was the worst possible outcome: the rogue men within the Society learning about Vaudeline's arrival in London, or her and Mr. Morley's clandestine plan.

"Please, be safe," was all Lenna could manage.

"Yes," Vaudeline whispered. "Of course. Your address?" She gave a quick wink in the darkness. "If things do not go well, I may need to seek asylum. If you'll take me in, that is."

Lenna's throat tightened. "I don't know how you are able to talk so airily about it. You do not seem half as worried as I am." Still, her concerns served no purpose, not now. They were already in London, and underneath the awning several yards away, a group of official-looking men had just arrived. Mr. Morley was likely somewhere among them. Relenting, she took a step closer to Vaudeline. "I'm at the Hickway House. On Euston Road."

Vaudeline nodded, then motioned to a man who had left the lineup under the awning and now walked toward them. "This looks like him," she said.

Lenna fumbled around in her bag and withdrew a small piece of paper, quickly writing down *Hickway House*, lest Vaudeline forget. Her fingers shook as she wrote. "Here you are," she said, handing the slip to Vaudeline. Then, fighting the urge to cry, Lenna leaned in to embrace her friend, letting her hand linger between her shoulder blades. Vaudeline pressed in closer.

With her head resting on Vaudeline's shoulder, Lenna could clearly see the man approaching them, the man who must be Mr. Morley. He wasn't in gentlemen's attire but in standard workmen's clothes—a brown wool coat and breeches—like he meant to remain inconspicuous. The left side of his face bore a dark birthmark, and perched on his head was a tawny-colored felt cap. It was flattened and quite worn, with a frayed notch above the left ear.

Suddenly, Lenna gasped.

She had seen this cap before.

It was the same one she'd seen among Evie's things, several times in the months before her death.

9

 LENNA

London, Saturday, 15 February 1873

L enna pulled out of her embrace with Vaudeline, no longer bothered with the hard task of saying goodbye. A moment ago, she'd intended to split off from Vaudeline and go call her own coach.

Now Lenna's skin prickled. She would not be calling her own coach to go home. Not yet.

Mr. Morley was still a few strides away, just long enough for Lenna to pull away a strand of Vaudeline's hair and whisper into her ear. "The man approaching is wearing a cap that Evie brought home more than once. I'm sure of it."

By the time the words were out, Mr. Morley was next to them, giving the women a small bow. "Miss D'Allaire," he said under his breath, glancing around him to ensure no one was listening. A pipe dangled from his lips. "Welcome, and thank you for accepting my invitation." From a bag slung over his shoulder, he removed a dark brown overcoat and a wool cap. "You must put this on at once."

Vaudeline did as instructed, all the while keeping her eyes

locked on Lenna, as though trying to discern what she was thinking.

Evie had been in touch with countless spiritualist societies in the city, and even those abroad. Further, she'd known of the London Séance Society, given the séance they'd performed for Eloise. This wasn't what Lenna found shocking.

What she found shocking was the *hat*.

Women didn't wear articles of clothing belonging to strange men, and it made the connection between Evie and this man... personal. She eyed the cap again, resting innocently on Mr. Morley's head. If she looked closely, might she find a remnant black hair belonging to her beloved sister? The possibility left her feeling ill.

"Hello, Mr. Morley," Vaudeline said, her voice equally low. "Quite some time since we've seen each other. More than a year."

"Indeed." He gave Lenna a curious look. "And this is?"

"My understudy," Vaudeline said. "She traveled with me from Paris."

His eyes widened. "Quite dangerous of you to keep a companion on the journey over. I do hope you did not draw more attention than necessary or share any confidential details." He looked away, toward the awning. "I had a lively discussion with a driver, earlier. I'm happy to enlist him if your understudy needs a coach."

Vaudeline raised her eyebrows. A moment ago, she might have simply told him *Of course, thank you*. But now she turned to Lenna. "You were waiting until our arrival to make a decision about your training here in London and whether to participate in my next séance."

It was a trick, a lie—both women knew that the decision for Lenna to forgo the séance had already been made. Vaudeline had all but retracted her invitation on the train this morning, citing the danger involved and the high stakes.

Yet everything had changed in the last few minutes.

Lenna looked again at the cap on Mr. Morley's head. She could so easily remember it sitting upon Evie's dresser—could even remember Evie shoving it back into her satchel on the morning of her death as though she hadn't wanted anyone to see it. *I hate that you do this*, Evie had said, referring to Lenna's tendency to pry into her personal affairs.

But Evie was dead. And Lenna would pry for as long as it took to get to the truth of things. "I'll participate, yes," she said.

Mr. Morley gave a laugh, then looked at Vaudeline. "She's English? Why, I assumed she was French. Either way, Miss D'Allaire, this was not our agreement." He took a step closer, placed a hand lightly on her arm. "This case is highly confidential, and it has been enough work for me to coordinate the discreet arrival of one woman at the Society, much less two. I cannot approve of this."

A boy walked by selling half-penny cups of hot elder wine, and Vaudeline purchased two. "Mr. Morley, I do not want us to make adversaries of one another. We were both dear friends of Mr. Volckman, and your letter did not state that I must arrive in London alone." She handed one of the cups to Lenna. "I fully trust my understudy, and her skill in the séance room is exceptional." She threw her wine back quickly.

Mr. Morley glanced warily at the gangplank as though weighing his options. "Really, Miss D'Allaire, I think it would be best if she did not join. There is so much risk, you cannot possibly—"

"She will join me, or I will need to respectfully decline the séance altogether."

He let out a long, resigned exhalation. "Very well, then," he said, his face pained. "A few terms." He motioned to Lenna. "Term number one," he said. "She cannot come and go from the Society as she pleases. The séance is late tomorrow night. We thought you might like to spend the day resting after your journey in."

Vaudeline looked to Lenna for a response. Lenna hadn't no-
tified her father that she was returning to London, so for all he
knew, she was still out of the country. No one was expecting
her, and she nodded her approval.

"Perfectly acceptable," Vaudeline said to Mr. Morley.

"Very good. I have prepared a small room at the Society headquarters. It's quite small, but inconspicuous. Hardly more than a
broom closet." He motioned to the two of them. "There is only
one cot, but I can track down a second one, I'm sure.

"Term number two," he continued. "Recall, this is a gentlemen's society, and women are not permitted inside the headquarters, nor are they permitted to partake in any of our affairs,
on- or off-site. It is one of our strictest rules, though I'm willing
to make an exception for you, given the circumstances. Still, the
other members cannot know about it, so I ask that you both remain in disguise at all times. I presume this will come as a relief
to you anyhow, Miss D'Allaire, given the reason you're here. I
do not know who within the Society to suspect of Mr. Volckman's death—who I can trust, and who I cannot. Keeping you
in disguise is paramount for your safety."

At her nod, he went on. "Term number three. We must be
very cautious about your movements. If there is any reason to
leave—a short walk, for instance—I will escort you in and out
via the servants' entrance at the back of the building, which
is very close to the room where you'll be staying. Constable
Beck—who I mentioned in my letter—is on hand, as well." He
motioned to Lenna. "But I cannot guarantee her safety while
she is here in London. Constable Beck was prepared only for
your arrival, Miss D'Allaire. He's waiting now, in the omnibus."

At this, Vaudeline raised her eyebrows. "Fair enough. She has
not made enemies of anyone at the Society, as I seem to have
done. I cannot see why she would need protection, anyhow."

Mr. Morley, having apparently finished with his terms, waved the women forward. But suddenly he stopped, turning on Lenna. "Might I ask your name?"

Lenna tensed. She knew he had a yet-to-be-determined connection to Evie, but he'd have no way of knowing that she was Evie's older sister. Unless Evie had shared Lenna's name at some point...

No matter. Mr. Morley stood very still, awaiting her answer.

"Lenna," she said.

He frowned, pausing for what seemed a beat too long. "And you live here in London?"

"Yes. My family owns the Hickway House."

There came a low whistle from behind them. A porter was maneuvering a large case through the crowd. Vaudeline and Lenna stepped aside to let him through, but Mr. Morley remained in place, suddenly looking...what?

Not obstinate, but stunned.

Finally, the porter tapped him on the shoulder, and Mr. Morley stepped aside. He cleared his throat as though forcing aside whatever it was he wanted to say next. Then he ushered the women through the throng of passengers, out a side gate, and into the low-lit city.

10

MR. MORLEY

London, Saturday, 15 February 1873

As I walked the women away from the docks and toward the omnibus, I tried my best to remain relaxed, nonchalant.

In truth, I was greatly alarmed by what I'd just learned: Vaudeline's unexpected companion was none other than Evie's older sister. I suspected it the moment she said her name was Lenna—there could not be that many of them in London—and she confirmed it a moment later, stating that she lived at the Hickway House.

Evie had mentioned her a few times, said the two were very close. Beyond that, I'd never given the older girl much thought.

What a fool I believed myself now. It was something I should have foreseen, Lenna's studying under the same famed medium Evie had trained under.

After all, Lenna had a crime to solve. Her sister was newly dead. She hadn't revealed this to me when we met on the docks, but there was no need.

I already knew.

★ ★ ★

Evie and I continued to grow close that summer. It was a classic *quid pro quo* arrangement, from her point of view. I had access to what she wanted, an array of mediumship knowledge: the hard-to-find books, the instruments, our confidential written records of séances and ghost hunts.

As for what I desired? Well, it would take a fool not to sort it out. Evie Rebecca Wickes was as vivacious and lovely as a twenty-year-old woman could be. And she not only looked past my mottled birthmark, but she had called it *exquisite*. There was something between us—a connection. She'd said it aloud herself.

How could I not yearn for her?

As the summer went on, it would go like this. She would arrive at the servants' door at our preordained hour, generally quite late. (Upon opening it and seeing the person on the other side, I was always fooled for the briefest of moments, thinking a porter had shown up at the wrong place.) I then whisked her up the back stairs to the library and into my study.

Those first few evenings, she would grant me only a long kiss, maybe a caress or two. After these brief encounters, she was quick to state what she wanted to see in the library stacks, typically some method or technique she had heard about from one of her friends.

In those early days, our meetings were more about intellectual exchange than romance, but I sensed a yielding in her as the weeks went on and she let my hands wander lower, longer.

Once, Evie asked if we had any library volumes on the construction of spirit horns, or even the horns themselves.

"Yes," I said. "But I'll admit, it has all begun to feel a tad unfair."

She cocked her head to one side. "Unfair?"

I nodded. She knew exactly what I meant. Still, I'd lay it out for her. "I've let you explore quite a lot around here. More than you've let me explore of you, surely."

She gave a little laugh, puckered her bottom lip. Slowly, she unfastened the top button of her boys' breeches, then the second and third. The fabric loosened around her hips, and she tugged it downward, revealing the flesh of her lower belly and the curve of her waist, features of her I'd never seen.

Down her breeches went, an inch and then another, until she revealed that beneath her clothes were the stockings and garters she'd worn under her gown that day. I went bloody senseless for a moment, thinking I might have died, thinking this would be it, at long last.

She let me look for a while, even let me snap a garter against her thigh. Eventually, I skirted my hands across her belly, wanting more of her.

"The spirit horns," she said, pushing my hands away. "Let me see them. The construction diagrams, too."

I dropped my hands at my sides. "Evie."

She tugged her breeches back up. "I'm sorry you think our arrangement is unfair. I do not." She refastened the buttons. "If anything, I believe I've hardly scratched the surface of all there is to explore out there." She nodded at the door, behind which was the library.

With a sigh of resignation, I directed her to the shelf where we kept several books on the construction of spirit horns.

The mahogany bookshelves were twice her height. The stacks stood nearly twelve feet tall, with footstools placed every few yards for anyone needing a volume on an upper shelf. Each row of shelves held hundreds of titles. There were books on the history of the paranormal, ancient séance lore, sketches of ghosts observed over hundreds of years, and plenty of guides on technique.

While she perused the section on spirit noises, I left to retrieve the half-dozen horns we kept in storage. As I showed them off, I explained the sounds the horns would make in the presence of spirits or energy, and then together we looked through the charts in the books, indicating what each noise meant, like the presence of an animal spirit or a demon or a child.

She got what she needed, taking copious notes and making a few illustrations in her black notebook.

This was how our arrangement went for weeks and weeks, all stifling summer long. Evie gradually let me see and touch more of her, and in return, I was generous with the Society documents I allowed her to peruse. I let her read our meeting minutes, and I showed her our ghost-hunting tools and implements, and I provided her nearly unlimited access to our library stacks.

She was hungry for it, I'd begun to realize. And greedy. She devoured it all like a dog with a bone.

One morning in mid-July, I went to my study, startled to find a small white envelope on the carpet. Someone must have slid it underneath the door.

I opened it, immediately recognizing Mr. Volckman's handwriting. *We've something serious to discuss. Let's talk at your soonest convenience.*

My stomach plunged to the floor. I looked over my shoulder, suddenly feeling caught or watched. Was this about Evie? Had he spotted us together, despite her disguise?

I immediately went downstairs and into the Society common room, where I asked of Volckman's whereabouts. Someone had seen him in the smoking tower not long ago, so I quickly made my way there, glad to find him sitting in his usual chair, a pipe dangling from his lips. No one else was in the room. The afternoon sun came in through a round window, and a smoky haze hung in the air, lending the space a bright, dreamy feel.

"I got your note," I said, taking a slow inhalation. "Something serious, you say?"

Volckman looked up from his papers, crossed one leg over the other. He pointed to a sheet of parchment in front of him, scribbled over with numbers. "Revenues are down again."

Relief washed over me. This was just about money, then. I wiped away a bead of sweat from behind my ear. "So, we'll do more prospecting or—"

"No." Volckman shook his head. "We need to address the root of the problem, not tighten a tourniquet around it." He paused. "We need to figure out what's driving the rumors—the talk—about fraudulent séances."

I closed my eyes, briefly. This bloody topic again. He'd first brought it up early in the year. "I'm dealing with it. I'm... figuring it out."

"This is important, Morley. I asked Miss D'Allaire to leave the city, for God's sake."

"I know."

He set his pipe down. "It's a mess, all of this." He tapped his finger on the sheet of parchment, a disgusted look on his face. Then he looked me hard in the eye. "Get it sorted, Morley. The numbers, the talk, all of it. I've more than a few men willing and able to take over your position with the department."

I blinked at him, hardly able to believe what he'd just said. Half of this organization we'd built together. Now he was threatening to dismiss me?

I bit my lower lip, wanting to snap back at Volckman's threat, but I knew it would do me no good. Might even exacerbate things. I was his subordinate, after all. Everything I valued, I'd acquired on account of his generosity to me a decade ago.

I wished him a good day, assuring him a final time that I'd get this all resolved. One way or another.

As I made my way out of the room, something tickled against

my neck. Instinctively, I reached for it. On the collar of my coat was a straight, dark hair, several inches long. Evie's, of course. I brushed it away, quickly, as I might if one end of it were on fire.

It floated to the floor, slowly, like a feather.

But as it went, at last it struck me: a rather very good solution to all of this.

11

LENNA

London, Saturday, 15 February 1873

After leaving the docks, Mr. Morley helped the women lift their luggage onto the top of a black-lacquered omnibus, large enough for eight or ten people. A pair of onyx-colored horses were harnessed at the front, plumes of black feathers secured to their heads as might be seen in a funerary procession. *The London Séance Society* was embellished on the side of the omnibus in plain gray script. All of this lent the carriage a rather grim appearance, but if these men led séances, their clientele were mourners. They wouldn't dare arrive at a grieving household with white horses and colorful plumage.

As Lenna stepped into the carriage, she was startled to see someone already inside, toward the back, hidden in the shadows. Then she remembered—the constable. As the group made brief introductions, Constable Beck—broad-shouldered with thick eyebrows and a scar, several inches long, across the bottom of his chin—avoided eye contact and spoke as few words as possible. He kept his arms crossed, and he made no effort to hide his slow, up-and-down appraisal of the women. He was meant to serve as protection for Vaudeline—a means of reassurance—but to Lenna, his manner gave the opposite impression. In truth, she found him quite unsettling.

Further, she wondered how much Constable Beck knew about the Volckman case. Had Mr. Morley told him about the wrong-doers within the Society?

Lenna took her seat on one of the benches running along the length of the carriage, frowning at a pair of wooden barrels at the back of the omnibus.

"I keep a spirits distillery," Mr. Morley explained, "and occasionally use the Society bus to make deliveries." He pointed at the barrels. "Those will go out later this week."

Mr. Morley tapped the driver on the shoulder. He was an attractive young man in dark livery with a high, crisp collar. Lenna expected them to begin conversing, but she was surprised when the driver handed Mr. Morley a small slate and a piece of chalk. Mr. Morley quickly jotted a few words on the slate. Then he passed it over to the driver.

"Our driver, Bennett, neither hears nor speaks," he explained, seeing Lenna's confused expression. "The slate is how we communicate. I informed him we'll go straight to the London Séance Society. I imagine you both are quite exhausted."

Lenna was glad for it: not only was she tired, but she had developed a horrid headache in the last few minutes. The stench in the air, perhaps. She untied the kerchief around her neck—she felt strangely hot, despite the season—and set it next to her on the seat, quietly strategizing how she might glean any insight about Evie's involvement with Mr. Morley.

"I gather from your letter that you and Mr. Volckman were as close as always," Vaudeline said, leaning forward on the bench so Mr. Morley could hear her over the clatter of the horses' hooves.

"Yes." He cleared his throat, ran a hand over the back of his neck. "Very close."

"And have the men of the London Séance Society taken any measures to contact his spirit?" Vaudeline asked.

"Indeed. The outcome was…concerning."

She frowned. "How so?"

Mr. Morley and Constable Beck shared a wary glance. "We attempted a séance," Mr. Morley said. "Twice, actually. Both times, we weren't able to gather any energy. The room was as still and quiet as could be."

"No quivering in the air or warmth?" Vaudeline asked.

"Not a whit."

"And you performed these incantations in the place he died?" Vaudeline asked.

Mr. Morley nodded. "Yes. We held the séances in my private cellar. I know it was the place he died, because I was the one who found his body." He frowned, rubbing his chin. "I've wondered, Miss D'Allaire, if there is such a thing as a counter-incantation. The miscreants within the Society—"

"Before we discuss further," Vaudeline interjected, "how much does Constable Beck know?"

Morley gave an approving nod. "How conscientious of you. I've told Beck enough, and he has signed an oath of confidentiality, as well." He cleared his throat and went on. "Is it possible these rogue men might have done something to hinder our séances, even if they were not in the room with us?"

"One can dispel encumbrance incantations in a room, certainly. They're difficult to do effectively, however."

Mr. Morley shrugged. "Well, our members are quite skilled, as you know. Perhaps an *encumbrance incantation*, as you say, explains why our séances have been ineffective. Anyhow, we've tried a few other things. Even a—" he gazed down, fiddling with his fingers "—a planchette."

Vaudeline blinked as though she'd misheard. "A planchette?"

"Yes. It's a board on wheels, with a pen that—"

"I know what it is, Mr. Morley." She gave a little laugh. "But a planchette is a children's toy. Not a reliable tool for mediumship."

"I am desperate," he said softly. "I will try anything. Even a children's toy."

Chastised, Vaudeline tenderly squeezed his arm and leaned back in her seat.

Eventually they turned onto York Street at the north end of St. James's Square. The driver pulled the reins to the right, directing the horses toward a narrow passage behind a row of buildings.

They quickened their pace, and Mr. Morley let out a chuckle. "The closer they get to home, the faster they tend to go." He pointed down the passageway, littered in places with straw. Ahead, the mews were clearly visible, the entrance flanked on either side by mounted gas lamps. Above this, on the second story, Lenna could just make out a pair of light-colored curtains through a mullioned window. She presumed this was where the driver lived and slept.

She gazed back at the Society building, several stories almost entirely in shadow. The facade was of Portland limestone. She could spot it easily because Stephen had taught her what it looked like: he'd shown her samples and explained how the stone was used all over the metropolis. The limestone was easy to identify with its pale gleam, though in London it was often stained from the fog and soot. Lenna knew that if she looked closely at the facade in daylight, she'd find tiny spiral and screw fossils— gastropods—embedded in the stone, as well as the imprints of coral from an ancient reef.

They approached a door at the back, where a gas lamp flickered. Here, Lenna noticed an inconspicuous inscription at eye level: *The London Séance Society, Est. 1860.* How ironic, she thought, the mention of *séance* etched into this fossil-studded stone. Two sides of the dead, the illusory and the tangible.

Once inside, Mr. Morley and Constable Beck led the women down a short corridor. Pushed to one end of the hallway were a few old pieces of furniture, including a heavy mahogany book-case. They reached a closed door, and Mr. Morley stepped into the room and raised the lantern in his hand, better illuminating the space around them. It was indeed sparse, with a cot and a pile of clothing. Underneath a window was a chair, the sturdy wooden sort that might be found in a lecture hall with a hun-dred others. There was a waist-high table in one corner with a ceramic bowl and pitcher for water, plus a few flannel wash-cloths. A makeshift toilet table, pitiful as it was.

"I'll bring another cot," he said. "Members occasionally stay overnight, so we have a few spares." He pointed at a paper bag next to the clothing pile. "In there you'll find a few things left over from the Society luncheon earlier today. Breads and jams and chicken cutlets. All quite good." He turned to Constable Beck. "I believe we're all finished for tonight. Thank you for your assistance."

Constable Beck gave a stiff nod. "I'll be in tomorrow, prob-ably around seven, should you need me." Without so much as acknowledging the women, he turned on his heel and left.

Vaudeline set her bag down, taking in the small room. "You mentioned that tomorrow is a day of rest for me and Miss Wickes," she said. "In fact, there is a better use of our time, if the séance is to be a success."

Mr. Morley widened his eyes, and even Lenna grew still, wondering where Vaudeline intended to take this. "Yes?" Mr. Morley said hesitantly.

"The day of Mr. Volckman's death... Do you know his movements, his whereabouts? We'll need to pay a visit to those locations, if feasible." She reached into her traveling bag and withdrew a notebook and pencil.

"His *whereabouts*? You sound like a member of the Met." Mr. Morley smiled and turned the knob on the lantern, lowering its flare as their eyes adjusted to the low light. "The Met has al-ready exhausted every forensic opportunity, I assure you. There are no clues, or evidence, to be found in the places Mr. Volckman went on All Hallows' Eve."

Vaudeline shook her head. "Oh, to be sure, this is not about forensics, Mr. Morley. Have you read any of my publications about clairtangency? It was a favorite topic of discussion between Mr. Volckman and me."

"I have not, but I'm sufficiently intrigued." He reached for the bag of luncheon leftovers, offering it to Vaudeline, but she waved it away.

"Clairtangency relates to the energy transferred by a person into the things they touch," she said. "This phenomenon is particularly strong when we're feeling powerful emotions like anger, lust, envy—emotions people often battle in the minutes or hours before their death, depending on the circumstances." She carefully slid her fingers down the red velvet curtains on either side of the window. "I am able to absorb this energy, which in turn allows me to more easily manifest the deceased during a séance. For this reason, I'd like to access any places Mr. Volckman went on the day of his death, to see if I can pull any latent energy from the items he might have touched."

Mr. Morley blinked, not bothering to hide the look of disbelief on his face. Clearly, clairtangency was not one of the techniques used by the London Séance Society. Still, Lenna could sympathize with the position he was in. He'd coordinated Vaudeline's arrival in London and situated her here in the Society headquarters. No matter what he thought of this clairtangency technique, Lenna could only imagine the pressure he felt to get this right—to get this case solved.

"All right, then," Mr. Morley said. "A few hours before Mr. Volckman's death, the Society performed a séance for a widow who lives nearby, Mrs. Gray. I did not attend, but Mr. Volckman did."

"Do you know where she lives?"

He nodded. "Yes. I oversee the commissioning and contract

process for all department séances. I assign participating members, as well. She lives over on Albemarle Street."

Vaudeline made a few notes in her book. "We'll call on Mrs. Gray, then, in the morning. I should like to call on Ada Volckman, too, on Bruton Street. It's not but a few minutes from Albemarle."

"I did not anticipate us going about errands all over town tomorrow," he said gently. "Perhaps the visit with Mrs. Volckman can wait until after the séance, once this is all resolved."

"She and I were friends, Mr. Morley. I dined at her table more than a few times. Why, I've even read bedtime stories to her children." She paused, her eyes sorrowful. "I should like to call on her tomorrow, if only for a few minutes." Suddenly, Vaudeline frowned. "Does she know you've enlisted me for her late husband's séance?"

Mr. Morley paused, cleared his throat. "No. I didn't want to trouble her with the details of your visit. She has enough to concern herself with. Which is why I'd ask you to consider, once again, whether there is really any advantage in calling on her so unexpectedly." He drew out the word *advantage*, like a merchant or salesman might.

Vaudeline studied him carefully. "Have you ever lost a loved one, Mr. Morley?"

"Yes. My father."

"Recently? Were you close?"

"More than a decade ago. And yes, very close."

Vaudeline nodded. "After his death, were you fortunate enough to have friends checking in on you? Or did you feel lonelier as the weeks went on?"

Mr. Morley blinked a few times. "The latter, certainly."

"Precisely. After some time has passed, only the immediate family and friends seem to…ache. It feels as though everyone else has moved on. The visits dwindle. People gather again, laughing as loudly as they ever did. The empty seat fills with someone new. Thus, I agree with you," Vaudeline went on, "that as it relates to the investigation, there is little *advantage* in calling on Mrs. Volckman tomorrow. But consoling a friend who lost her husband three months since? Why, I can think of no better reason to pay her a visit."

The three of them were silent a moment. Then Mr. Morley intertwined his fingers. "Very well, then. We shall call on her in the morning." Was it Lenna's imagination, or had a trace of defeat—frustration, even—seeped into his voice?

"Excellent." Vaudeline looked down at her notebook. "Now, any other ideas about where Mr. Volckman went on the day he died?"

"I cannot say. I did not keep his diary for him." As he spoke, Lenna looked down, uncomfortable. Mr. Morley was their source of information and protection over the next couple of days. She was wary of irritating him with so many requests. "He ultimately arrived at my cellar, though, for the All Hallows' Eve party—"

"Your annual crypt soirée," Vaudeline interrupted. "I attended a few, long ago."

"Right. As always, many of us from the Society were in attendance. Constable Beck and myself included."

"Given that you discovered his body in the cellar, that is where we'll have the séance." She made a quick note. "Did he come here, to Society headquarters, on the day he died?"

"Yes. He always took breakfast here on weekdays. Then he would look over the logs, respond to queries, and so on."

"The *logs*?"

Mr. Morley nodded. "We keep a visitors' log in the front foyer, where members sign in each day. Mr. Volckman reviewed it regularly to monitor whether any members were failing to meet their attendance quotas."

"And you feel fairly confident he might have thumbed through this log on the day he died?" At his nod, Vaudeline continued. "I should like to see it tomorrow, then. And did he have a study of some kind here at the Society? Where he might have left a pen or a pipe? Anything he would have touched that day."

Mr. Morley shook his head. "Some of the men prefer to do their work in the library, just above us on the second floor. Myself included—my study is at the back. But Mr. Volckman was a social man, more likely to do his work at any open chair in the dining room, the gaming room, even the smoking tower. I haven't any idea where in the building he spent his time on All Hallows' Eve."

While Vaudeline took a few more notes, Lenna felt herself grow brave. "Anything else?" she asked. She hadn't addressed Mr. Morley since the docks. "Any other journals, books, or papers he might have touched?" She wanted to be useful in some way; she was still playing the role of understudy, after all.

Mr. Morley narrowed his eyes. "I cannot agree to share any documentation of that sort. I can let you look through the public sign-in log, but Society records are, generally speaking, classified."

Vaudeline put on a thin smile. "Your sense of duty is admirable, Mr. Morley."

"Also, I won't be able to take the log out of the foyer tomorrow," he said. "We'll have members going in and out all day. But I can retrieve it for you now, as everyone has left for the night, and sign-outs will be complete. I'll get the second cot, as well. Give me a few minutes, please."

Out he went, his footsteps echoing down the corridor.

"All Hallows' Eve," Lenna said the moment he was gone. "I can hardly believe Mr. Volckman and Evie were killed on the same evening."

Vaudeline nodded, a thoughtful look on her face. "On the surface, it seems a great coincidence. But last All Hallows' Eve was a new moon. When this happens—as it does every nineteen years, in accordance with the ancient Metonic cycle—it portends death in shocking numbers. Many mediums refuse to leave their houses when a new moon falls on All Hallows' Eve. The barrier betwixt the living and the dead is so terribly delicate that night."

The ancient Metonic cycle. Vaguely, Lenna remembered Evie mentioning something about this last fall, but she'd written it off as nothing more than another of her sister's preposterous theories.

A moment later, the door opened, and Mr. Morley stepped in. He first handed Vaudeline a thick leather-bound book. "The sign-in log," he said. Then he busied himself with maneuvering the second cot into place. Beads of sweat formed at his hairline, despite the cot looking relatively light. He was not the fittest of men, Lenna mused.

Vaudeline sat down in the chair beneath the window, letting the logbook fall open in her lap. She ran her hands delicately over the pages, closing her eyes as she did so. Lenna wanted to ask what, exactly, she aimed to do or feel or sense, but she also did not want to interfere with Vaudeline's technique.

With her eyes closed, Vaudeline turned a few more pages at random. Then she stopped, a curious look on her face. She opened her eyes, and suddenly there came a loud thumping noise, somewhere in the corridor outside the room. All three of them jumped.

The noise came again. It sounded like a knock on the servants' door they'd used to access the building. Lenna began to feel sick. Had someone seen them come in, someone who was not meant to know about Vaudeline's arrival in the city? It didn't make sense: they'd been covered in darkness when they walked into the building. "Let me see who it is," Mr. Morley said. He glanced warily at the log in Vaudeline's lap. "I'll be back in a moment."

When he'd gone, Lenna knelt next to Vaudeline, who had just turned to the sign-in log entries for All Hallows' Eve.

"There," Lenna said, pointing midway down the page. *M. Volckman,* it read. *In 10:14 a.m., out 3:30 p.m.* Vaudeline ran her fingers over the hand-scrawled text, smudging the ink slightly.

"What do you...feel?" Lenna asked.

"If I'm quite honest, something odd..." She turned a few more pages at random.

"Wait," Lenna said. "Go back." When Vaudeline did not do so quickly enough, Lenna turned the book toward her and thumbed swiftly through the pages herself.

At once, she let out a cry. Then she thrust forward a sweaty hand to point at the page they were on, a sign-in entry from last summer.

There it was, written in pencil.

E.R. W—.

Lenna knew this handwriting, the whimsical curl of the *R* and the distinct loops of the *W.* Even the dash to hide her surname was not unusual; she'd seen Evie sign things this way before, her way of toying with old traditions. *E.R. W—.*

Evie Rebecca Wickes.

There were no illusions about it: these pencil scratches were undeniable. Lenna could measure the letters if she liked, or weigh the piece of paper, or run her finger through the tiny graphite crystals sitting on the page in the shape of a name.

Evie had not just been associated with Mr. Morley in a yet-to-be-determined way.

She'd been here, *inside* of the London Séance Society headquarters.

In a place where women were not permitted, Evie had somehow maneuvered her way in.

12

LENNA

London, Saturday, 15 February 1873

In the small storage room on the ground floor of the London Séance Society, the air in the room grew thin. *Evie was here,* Lenna thought. *Here, in this very building.*

The door opened. Mr. Morley stepped in, having returned from interrogating whoever it was who had knocked on the door a few moments ago. In his hands was something Lenna recognized. It took her a moment to place it: her kerchief.

"You left this in the carriage," he said. "My driver kindly brought it back. Best not let it happen again. Imagine if another member went out for a morning ride in the omnibus and found a woman's kerchief in the seat." He raised his eyebrows. "You remember what I said about women partaking in Society affairs."

"Of course," Lenna said breathlessly.

Vaudeline snapped the book shut and handed the log over. "I have what I need, Mr. Morley." She ran her hand once more over the cover. "I think we would all benefit from a night's rest. What time should we expect you in the morning?"

They agreed on eight o'clock, and Mr. Morley made his way

out with the log. Vaudeline immediately unlaced her boots, but
Lenna remained standing, listening closely as Mr. Morley's footsteps echoed down the corridor. When she could no longer hear
him, she clasped her trembling hands together, knowing what
she soon intended to do.

Vaudeline removed her second boot, then tugged at one of
her stockings. "Tomorrow, I'm keen on talking with the widow,
Mrs. Gray, when we visit her residence. Far as I'm concerned,
she's our first order of business."

First order of business? For Vaudeline, maybe. But not for Lenna.
She'd just seen her dead sister's name in the sign-in log of the
very building in which they were to reside for the next thirty-
six hours. Lenna's first order of business was to get her hands
back on that log. She wanted to gather every possible clue to
Evie's activities in the months before her death.

She hadn't considered it until now, but maybe she was closer
to the truth here inside the Society than she was running free
about the city.

Lenna would read every page of that log if she must.

And she intended to do it tonight.

She would give it an hour, at least, long enough for Mr. Morley to return the logbook to the foyer and make his way out of
the building. In the interim, Lenna thought she might as well
make use of her time: something to eat and a change of clothes.

She dug through her bag, searching for clean stockings. As she
removed a pair, something fell onto the floor, very near Vaudeline's
feet. An envelope, already opened. Lenna recognized it as a letter
from Stephen that he'd sent to her in Paris last week.

When Lenna received it, she'd torn it open—had there been a
break in Evie's case, perhaps?—but the letter contained nothing
beyond a few expressions of sentiment and affection. As she'd
read on, she grew fearful Stephen might allude to a future en-

gagement, but she was relieved to reach the end of the letter without any such suggestion.

Now Vaudeline passed the envelope over to Lenna, their knuckles brushing against one another. "Isn't this the letter you received last week? I never asked: Is it anything important?" Vaudeline watched as Lenna stuffed it back into her bag.

Lenna shook her head. "Just a note from a gentleman named Stephen Heslop—the twin brother of my friend Eloise, who died a few years ago. Stephen is the one who works at the museum and has taught me all about fossils. He wrote to tell me that he was already looking forward to my return."

"He must be quite fond of you." The tone of Vaudeline's voice had gone up a few notes. "Was he a former beau? Or is he a current one?"

Other than the brief conversation about Léon on the train, the two women had never discussed their romances, former or current. A question about beaus might not have been appropriate a few days ago, but Lenna remembered the brush of Vaudeline's lips against her cheek after the château séance, and the way they'd held hands so tightly earlier that evening, sitting on the docks in silence.

"He is interested in me, but I find him rather forgettable. I am more intrigued by his fossils and books, to be honest." She looked up. It might have been her imagination, but Vaudeline's eyes seemed to have brightened a bit.

"How about you? Any beaus?" Lenna felt nervous all of a sudden and wished she could suspend the moment to gather her breath, cool her cheeks. She had never been this jittery around Eloise. But they'd never been covertly stashed away in a building together, either.

"I've had plenty of them," Vaudeline said, smiling. "Men and women both."

"*Women*," Lenna repeated, feeling heat rise to her neck. "Quite unconventional. In such an instance, who pursues who?"

"Oh, there are no rules about it. Besides, such arrangements are not unconventional in Paris. It is not London, all concerned with manners and appearances. In Paris, we do not stifle our longings."

A few minutes later, Lenna sifted through the clothes left by Mr. Morley. But her heart began to thud in her chest: across the room from her, Vaudeline had started to undress. Lenna turned, glancing quickly at her. She hadn't yet told Vaudeline she intended to break out of the room and go in search of the visitors' log, but she would momentarily.

Vaudeline's silhouette was illuminated by the low light of the lantern on the table. She had loosened her skirt from around her waist and now briefly lifted her eyes upward. She caught Lenna staring, but she went on without any sign of inhibition, slowly undoing a few of the buttons on her bodice. Lenna could not pull her gaze away, and she wondered vaguely how the room had grown so hot and airless in the last few moments.

Soon, only Vaudeline's cotton chemise remained. Lenna had never seen so much of her—had never seen so much of any female, other than Evie years ago, when they were still girls. This was the first time Lenna had really laid eyes on a woman, sans gown, all flesh and dips and shadows. She tried to swallow and found she could not.

"At the château in Paris," Vaudeline said, "you expressed frustration with me, saying I've shown you no proof of ghosts." She paused, tucking back a loose hair. "I can show you something now, if you'd like. It is the most real thing I have to offer as evidence, outside of a séance."

Lenna blinked. Why had it taken Vaudeline so long to reveal this? "Of course," she said. "What is it?" She waited, expecting Vaudeline to reach into her traveling case and withdraw a book of incantations or perhaps a picture. But instead, Vaudeline remained standing and lifted the bottom edge of her chemise, sliding the cotton fabric slowly up her legs and stopping only when it was impossibly high and taut against her thighs.

Vaudeline spun her right leg slightly outward, displaying the pale, tender skin of her upper thigh. Lenna gasped. Even in the low light, it was unmistakable: a double-arched scar. A bite mark long healed over. It marred the otherwise-smooth surface of Vaudeline's inner leg, but Lenna found the imperfection exquisite.

Still, it must have hurt. "My God," she said, covering her lips with her hand. "How did this happen?"

"As I've long said, spirits can be quite volatile."

Lenna frowned, inspecting the scar again. Did Vaudeline mean to imply—

Vaudeline dropped her nightgown, smoothing it down with her hands. "You remember why I became a spiritualist?"

Lenna grew dizzy, tangled up in confusion and desire. She'd just seen so much skin. A sinking feeling—disappointment?—settled in her chest. "Yes," she said. "Léon. He took a fall, hit his head."

"Right." Vaudeline paused. "I told you that after he died, I taught myself the art of mediumship. I learned to manifest Léon, and then I did so repeatedly. I would go to the outdoor staircase behind his town house—the same place where he fell—and sit out there many nights, entranced by him underneath the stars. This is how I practiced the art of séance. I experimented with the incantations and sequences, and I learned to recover quickly from the fatigue of entrancement so I could go back to him again." She put her hand to her inner thigh, where the bite mark now hid beneath the fabric. "You know that wounds often appear under entrancement. It is one way that we, as mediums, know the spirit has made its way inside of us. But spirits can also act *upon* us—they can do things to us, make us feel things that should otherwise require flesh or touch."

It seemed very much like Vaudeline was implying she'd made love to Léon even after his death. Instantly, Lenna's imagination spun together an unpleasant vision of Vaudeline's back arched against the sharp tread of a staircase and blood, cherry red, dripping from her thigh.

Vaudeline went on. "I loved Léon very much, and I always will. I've found it impossible to unlove someone—impossible to fully extinguish feelings for any of my lovers. There's always a smolder of something left."

"When was the last time you—" Lenna cleared her throat "—manifested him?"

Vaudeline reached out and gave Lenna's knee a squeeze. "It has been many, many years. Conjuring a spirit is akin to leading them into a half existence. The opposite of love. Spirits lust for embodiment; they will not leave of their own accord. And so, to repeatedly conjure them is a form of torment, like putting a sparrow in a lush forest, but plucking its feathers so it cannot fly." She sat down on her cot, tucking a leg underneath her. "Wounds should disappear once a séance is terminated and the spirit has been expelled. But I did not know how to expel spirits in the beginning—nor did I understand how selfish it was to repeatedly manifest a spirit, to tempt them with existence. The scar on my thigh is what I have to show for this ignorance." She pulled the thin blanket toward her. "So while a part of me will always love Léon, I am wiser now than I was, and I will never conjure him again, precisely because of that affection."

Vaudeline lay back on her cot, nuzzling her head into the flat excuse of a pillow, and closed her eyes. Lenna wasn't sure what to make of the story she'd just heard. There existed the possibility that Vaudeline had just told a magnificent lie—that the scar had, in fact, been given to her by someone living, some former beau in London or Paris.

Soon, Vaudeline was asleep. Lenna watched her for a moment,

the steady swell of her breath, the plunge of her low belly between her hip bones. The cotton chemise did not hide much.

Lenna removed her own gown and swiftly changed into the first pair of trousers she found in the pile. They were too large at the waist, but they stayed up with a bit of tugging. She didn't have the energy to search the bag for a better size.

She checked her watch, then knelt down in front of Vaudeline, ready to wake her and let her know what she intended to do tonight. But first—

"Vaudeline," she whispered in the dark.

"Mmm?" came the soft reply, her eyes still closed.

"I am sorry Léon hurt you." Lenna hovered her hand over Vaudeline's thigh. "The scar, I mean. I imagine it was quite painful."

"Painful?" Vaudeline fluttered her eyes open. "*Mais au contraire.* He knew exactly what I liked." Slowly, she placed her hand over Lenna's, threading their fingers together. They remained like this a few moments, Lenna kneeling next to Vaudeline's cot, neither of them saying anything. Lenna could hear only Vaudeline's breath and the thrum of her own heart.

Together, their interlocked hands began to move toward Vaudeline's thigh, and then upward along her skin, toward the scar. Who was pushing, who was pulling? It didn't matter; neither woman resisted, neither spoke. The tendon running vertically along Vaudeline's thigh was taut beneath Lenna's fingers, like the string of an instrument, until finally Lenna felt a tiny ridge of scar tissue at one edge of the bite mark.

Painful? Vaudeline had said moments ago. *Mais au contraire*— on the contrary. *He knew exactly what I liked.*

Remembering these words, Lenna traced the scar with her finger, pressing hard, harder than she would have otherwise. She watched Vaudeline's face carefully for any sign of discomfort. There was none. She'd closed her eyes again, parted her lips slightly, and now dug her thumbnail into Lenna's hand.

In Paris, we do not stifle our longings. Yet in London, years ago with Eloise, this was precisely what Lenna had done.

Well, she would no longer. She exerted more pressure on the scar, sinew, and muscle resisting beneath her fingers. This would result in a bruise, surely, but the deeper she pressed, the harder Vaudeline squeezed her hand.

It was undeniable: Vaudeline liked this pain. And though the situation might have been troubling—the idea of deriving satisfaction from someone else's discomfort—there was something gratifying in it, too. Lenna had been powerless these recent months, her efforts futile against the police, Evie's secrets, even her own beliefs. At last, she was exerting control over something—someone.

Further, she wondered if this reversal of roles contributed to the roused expression on Vaudeline's face now. In her line of work as both mentor and medium, Vaudeline always stood in a position of authority. Did she relish, perhaps, letting someone else take over? In casting aside her stoicism and letting herself *feel* things, even—especially—pain? Léon had known it, and Lenna wanted to give her this, too.

In the distance, the toll of church bells rang the hour. Swiftly, Lenna pulled her hand away, out from underneath Vaudeline's chemise, away from the scar, away from Vaudeline's grip.

Have I forgotten myself entirely? she asked herself, acutely aware now of the passage of time, of manners. *Have I forgotten my reason for being here at all?*

Vaudeline's eyes sprang open. "What is it?"

"I'm sorry," Lenna said, standing now. "I need to—" She blinked a few times, not entirely sure how much time had passed since the moment she'd first touched her finger to Vaudeline's scar. Had it been a minute, or an hour? She shook her head, cleared her throat. "I need to see the log again. I need to know more about what Evie wanted from this place."

She looked at the door, then at Vaudeline. What more might have happened between them tonight? She knew, instinctively, that Vaudeline had wanted her to move her hand farther up; their push and pull had been equal and even. A few inches had been all that separated them from whatever they were, and whatever they might have been.

Not tonight, Lenna thought. *Not here, shuttered away in the storage room of the London Séance Society.*

Always, Evie would come first.

13

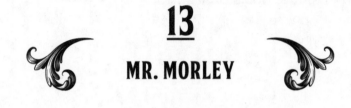

MR. MORLEY

London, Saturday, 15 February 1873

Head down, I hurried through the dark, making my way home from the Society. It was late, almost eleven. It had taken longer to get the women situated than I'd planned: the second cot, the forgotten kerchief, the bizarre request to see the visitors' log.

A bitter-cold drizzle had just begun to fall. The pavement was slick, and I pulled my coat up higher around my shoulders, thankful I did not have to travel far.

I stepped into the small parlor on the second story of my townhome, where I lived with my mother. I threw a log on the fire, then hung my hat and coat on the wooden pin next to the hearth. They'd need all night to fully dry.

I was feeling restless, ruminating on the women in the storage room at the Society. They'd likely be asleep by now.

I poured myself a brandy, took a seat in my armchair, and listened to the soft pops and crackles coming from the fireplace. The light was low, sensual. Shadows threaded themselves on the walls, reminding me of the lace Evie had once worn. Once, and never again.

She'd employed the garment wisely. I should have known what was coming, a request of such consequential nature.

That summer evening, in early August, she'd undressed more slowly than normal. I sensed some hesitation or nervousness on her part. Then, as the breeches and jumper came off, there she stood in the light of the lantern, wearing not only those god-forsaken stockings that sucked the air from my lungs but something else, some quasi corset thing that attached to her stockings and wrapped under and around. It was made of keyhole lace, and whatever alchemist designed the garment knew just where to place the little gaps and holes. The room was very cold, and yet still I thought I might ignite on the spot.

I began moving toward her, thinking this might, at last, be the rendezvous for which I'd waited.

"I need to ask you something," Evie suddenly said, putting her hand out to keep me from coming any closer.

I stopped short, tore my gaze off her waist to meet her eyes. "Yes?"

"I have attended one séance in my life. For my close friend Eloise Heslop. Her séance was performed by the London Séance Society."

"Yes," I said, wondering where she was going with this. "I didn't attend that one, but I was at her father's séance, a few days later."

She gave me a surprised look. "I wasn't aware of that."

I nodded. "It was a private affair."

"Right, of course," Evie said hastily. "In any event, I want to ask about attending another séance, but this time I want to be alongside you." Before I could reply, she went on. "It only makes sense, given how much you've shown me here at the Society. I have learned so much, and I want to see it all in practice. I will be there only to observe, and I'll dress in full disguise—a better disguise, even, than I wear here. No one will know, no one but you. I won't speak a word. You can say I'm a cousin or a friend or a prospective member."

I let out a little laugh, wanting to ask more, but it would complicate the conversation, perhaps lead this assignation astray.

"Let's talk it over in a short while, yes?" I asked in a hoarse voice, taking a step forward.

She took a step back.

She was against my desk now, her buttocks perched along the edge of it, my favorite pair of silver scissors just inches from her flesh. She leaned back on her hands and parted her legs a few inches. "Let's talk it over now," she said. "Make me a promise. You'll let me join a séance. Soon."

Cursed be the keyholes so artfully placed in that corset.

And so I said yes. *Yes.* And I knew I'd have to keep my end of the deal, else I might never have her on this desk again.

I moved toward her again, and she did not resist. At last, there on my desk, she permitted me to take all of her—

In my mother's parlor, the fire crackled, throwing sparks and disturbing my reverie.

No matter. I could draw in my mind every inch of Evie. That was the thing about memories. They were so lifelike, so full of texture and breath. Dimples on skin, tiny hairs on end. I could see it all, as if she were here in this moment, standing in front of the firelight.

After our lovemaking that night—my God, how long I'd hungered for it!—Evie remained very quiet. She didn't ask to see anything. No library volumes, no old meeting minutes. A sense of awkwardness hung in the air as we dressed.

"Evie," I'd ventured in the silence, my mouth suddenly dry.

She secured a button, looked up. "Mmm?"

"Might you—" My voice hitched, and I gave a little cough. "Well, there is a festival at Cremorne Gardens next week. Might you like to accompany me?"

"What sort of festival?" she asked.

"A festival of flowers. Extravagant displays," I said. "And several rare orchid species, or so I hear." I had no interest in this myself, but surely she would.

Her face did not light up as I'd hoped, and she returned her attention to her remaining buttons. "In fact, flowers do not inspire me in the least."

"Perhaps a riverboat tour, then, or I can chaperone you when—"

"Are you trying, yet again, to steer me into a traditional courtship?"

I blinked a few times, amazed as I often was by her brazenness. My invitation hadn't been any such maneuver. I merely wanted to spend more time in her company.

"I'm afraid I do not understand you at all," I finally said.

She gave me a rueful smile. "I'm very sorry, but I've no interest in flowers or festivals or riverboat tours."

A sinking feeling settled in my chest, heavy and cool. "Very well, then," I said, finding myself hardly able to look her in the eye.

She left soon after, not in the mood for any further conversation. In spite of everything, I missed her at once.

I realized only later that she'd slipped out with my hat and left her own. She must have confused the two. In her defense, they were similar in color, and I always kept the lantern low.

Though the conversation had not gone as I wanted and she'd left in such haste, I willed myself to move past the affront, and I resolved to honor our existing arrangement from that moment forward.

After all, she'd made it abundantly clear: permission to attend a séance was all she'd wanted of me that night.

14

LENNA

London, Saturday, 15 February 1873

Stepping away from Vaudeline, Lenna paced the small room, feeling recklessly determined. "The sign-in log," she said. "I'm going to find it. I'm going to look through it again."

"Lenna." Vaudeline sat up on her cot. Her tone was stern, cautionary. "To leave this room would be a grave mistake."

Lenna expected this. "Risky, yes. A mistake, no." She folded her gown, set it aside for now.

Vaudeline stood from her cot and crossed the room, grabbing Lenna's hand. "Stop," she said. When she had Lenna's attention, she shook her head. "You cannot do this. You don't know who may be stationed throughout the building. And what is it you hope to find, anyway?"

Lenna gently pulled back her arm, considering Vaudeline's question. What *did* she hope to find? It was unreasonable to think that the answer to Evie's death was buried somewhere in the pages of the log. Still, her sister had successfully breached a preeminent West End men's society and had cavorted, it seemed, with at least one of its members. Who knew how many others she'd involved herself with?

"Evie died on the same night as Mr. Volckman. What if...?" Lenna paused, trying to make sense of this possibility. "I know you believe the coincidence is due to the new moon, but what if the men who killed Mr. Volckman also killed her? What if she and Mr. Volckman had some kind of relationship or arrangement, and someone wanted them both dead?"

Vaudeline splayed out her hands, an exasperated look on her face. "All of this will become clear when I do her séance. We must only wait it out a few days."

"That's assuming you succeed at Mr. Volckman's séance."

"True, yes. But as dangerous as that affair will be, it still is not as dangerous—or reckless—as sneaking out of this room tonight." Her voice had risen in volume. "This building is enormous, and as Mr. Morley said, sometimes members stay the night. It's very possible you'll be—"

"Shhh," Lenna cautioned her. "Seeing as how loudly you're talking, I think that's more likely to get us caught."

Lenna stepped to the door, reaching for the handle. She couldn't blame Vaudeline for disputing the idea, but her mind was made up. She was going, no matter Vaudeline's opinion on the matter.

She placed her hand on the doorknob. "Perhaps I'll look again through the log and find nothing more," she said. "But if you mean to talk me out of it, you won't. I'm going to the foyer."

Vaudeline frowned in the low light, peering at her. "This is absurd, Lenna. Think of what you're risking. You were so worried for my safety earlier, and the possibility of the séance failing. What if we cannot even do it on account of your recklessness? If someone discovers that we're in here, Mr. Morley's plan will be entirely ruined..."

Lenna opened the door, and a cold draft flooded the room. She turned to Vaudeline, feeling suddenly—what?

Distrustful. Just as she'd felt after the château séance.

"I've told you what I'm doing, with or without your help," Lenna said coolly. "Yet you remain terribly opposed. It's almost as though you don't want me to look at the log again. Like there's something there you think I shouldn't see."

Vaudeline winced. "That couldn't be further from the truth."

"Good." Lenna glanced down the dark corridor. "I'll be cautious," she said, and she meant it in earnest. She agreed with the risks that Vaudeline had just outlined. But she could not pass this night without trying to find her way to the foyer. "I'll just have a look around," she said, not an entirely honest statement. She stepped over the threshold.

Before she could take another step, Vaudeline's hand tightened around her wrist. "You're a fool, Lenna," she whispered. She was trying to restrain her, to pull her back into the room, and Lenna briefly indulged in the fantasy of turning around, picking back up where they'd left off a few minutes ago.

No. Lenna tore out of her grip. Not a moment later, she was walking down the soft, carpeted corridor. Behind her, inside the room, Vaudeline made a final, unintelligible protest, something about *sentries.* Then she quietly pulled the door closed.

Lenna took a deep breath. Even if men were posted around the building, she felt well hidden in the dark hallways, skirting along the inky-black, wainscoted walls. She listened closely for any noise: voices, footsteps, the jangle of keys. But the night was mercifully quiet, and she spent several minutes wandering the maze of hallways, disappointed when a few of them ended in closed doors. She opened one of them, but when she stepped into the room, she bumped hard into a small, hexagonal piece of furniture—a card table. She spent a moment rubbing the tender place on her hip where she'd knocked it, spotting a nearby rack of billiards sticks. She was in the game room, then. Quickly, she closed the door and padded away from it, glad for the carpet that hushed her steps.

She kept on, turning down a passageway that appeared wider than the rest. Given the light emanating from a single gas lamp outside one of the windows, her eyes made out a wall of mounted paintings, a few leather-upholstered chairs, and ahead what appeared to be an atrium. The foyer.

A mahogany table sat in the central part of the room. On top was an inkwell and beside it a leather-bound book she recognized: the visitors' log, with proof of Evie's presence in this very place.

She rushed forward, realizing now that without a candle, she wouldn't be able to see what was within the pages. She'd have to snag the log, take it back to the room, return it safely somehow…

It would be a night of no sleep—that much was clear.

A thump echoed down the hallway, behind her. Lenna froze, sidestepping her way to the wall, but there was no place to take cover. She looked around, panicked, and nearly retched as she realized footfalls were approaching from the darkness, toward the end of the corridor.

She trembled, cursing the lack of light. *It must be a guard*, she thought. *I am about to be discovered, and this will lead back to Vaudeline and Mr. Morley, and all of this will fail on account of me.*

She might have cried if she were not so bloody scared.

The footfalls grew closer, and Lenna braced herself for a confrontation. She needed to think of an excuse, any plausible explanation, and she needed to think of it quickly.

A candle began bobbing toward her. Lenna gasped as someone came into view, wearing dark breeches and a coat. A Society member, surely—but then Lenna spotted a few golden curls, catching the light of the candle's flame.

Vaudeline.

"Found you," she whispered, spotting her understudy. She hadn't bothered to put on a hat.

Lenna's heart still thumped furiously in her chest. "You didn't need to come," she whispered back in the dark. "I made it perfectly well on my own."

"I didn't think you had the nerve to do it. Quite frightened me, seeing you turn down that corridor and out of my sight."

Lenna motioned to the table in the foyer, aware of the passing minutes. "The log is over here," she said. "Let's be quick about it."

The women stepped up to the table, and Lenna gave another glance around the empty entryway before opening the front cover of the log. Vaudeline hovered the candle over the paper, and Lenna quickly located the page where, earlier, she'd seen Evie's initials. She pointed again to the name, *E.R. W—*.

It had not been her imagination, then, her brain spinning mirages after a long day of travel. "It will take quite a long time to go through each day," she muttered to herself, turning to the front of the book.

Next to her, Vaudeline had just opened one of the table's drawers. She withdrew a second leather-bound book, which had been pushed to the very back of the drawer. Without hesitating, she flipped it open.

"'DoS Lecture Assemblies—Invitation Only,'" Vaudeline read aloud.

"DoS?"

"*Department of Spiritualism*, probably. Morley's department." She kept reading. "'Lampadomancy and Flame Reading, 31 July 1872.'" She pursed her lips to one side. "It's like another sign-in log, I suppose, but for their lectures."

"What is *lampadomancy*, anyway?" Lenna stumbled over the word, sure she'd mispronounced it.

"A primeval divination technique. The theory goes that flames will move a certain way when a spirit is present and desires communication. A flame shifting left, for instance, might be interpreted as a *No* when the medium asks a question." Lenna glanced at the candle in Vaudeline's hand; the flame was very still. "Strange, though, because in my opinion, the technique is utter nonsense," Vaudeline went on. "A medium can exhale slightly, or even move their hand, to affect the flame in a certain way." She made a small movement, causing the flame to jerk wildly before going still again.

Suddenly, Vaudeline pointed back at the sign-in log. "Let's see if the dates she signed in align with any of these lectures."

Vaudeline held the candle steady while Lenna worked, running her finger down every lecture-attendance list, starting in early summer of last year, and comparing against the sign-in records. The gears of her brain worked efficiently now, very much like when she was hunched over a clay cast, studying fossil ridges and indentations. It was a strange reversal of roles, Lenna doing the work while her teacher looked on.

By the time they were done with their review, it was clear: Evie had signed in to the visitors' log on every day that a lecture had been held, meaning she'd somehow sneaked into every lecture held at the Society from June through October.

Lenna frowned. "Why would she have signed the log at all? If she wasn't meant to be here…"

Vaudeline shook her head. "She was hiding in plain sight. Imagine if someone caught her walking past the foyer without signing in. It would draw attention, surely. Recall, the Society has hundreds of members, many of whom may invite guests into the common areas. If her disguise were convincing enough— which it seems to have been—she would have been able to move around quite well."

Lenna pointed to one of the lectures, titled "Facial Transfigu-

ration Demonstration," and then to another one titled "Supernatural Substances and Ectoplasm."

"What's *ectoplasm?*" she asked.

Vaudeline sighed. "This doesn't make any sense to me." She
frowned, reading the headline again. "Ectoplasm is a substance
that some claim is discharged during a trance state," she explained. "All sorts of homemade recipes exist. Borax, glue, corn-
starch. Mediums pretend to vomit ectoplasm, or excrete it from
their ears, or evacuate it from their...well, from their genitalia.
When performed by women, such demonstrations often draw
enormous crowds."

Lenna kept flipping through the pages, shaking her head in
dismay. All those times Lenna had asked Evie of her whereabouts, and Evie refused to answer... Had she been coming
here, to the Society?

"Evie didn't miss a single lecture," Lenna said softly. "Quite
the devoted student."

"She always was," Vaudeline said. Then a look of consterna-
tion came over her face. "Flame reading. Transfiguration." Her
hands began to tremble. "These are the practices of fraudulent
mediums, not authentic ones. This is aligned with the sort of
rumors I'd heard about the Society before I left London—the
claims Mr. Volckman intended to investigate." She blinked several times, as though willing the records to rewrite themselves.
"The Society has more than two hundred members, but these
lectures were quite small." She pointed at a page. "Just nine attendees in this one, and the register says *Invitation only.* It seems
these lectures were private in nature. Attended only by a select few."

"I don't see Mr. Morley's name on any of the lists," Lenna said.

"I wonder if these lectures were happening right under his
nose."

Lenna scanned her eyes down one of the lecture-attendance

records, filled with shorthand names and initials. "Do you think the men involved in the Society's mischief are somewhere on these lists?"

"It would seem that way, yes." Vaudeline let out an exasperated sigh, then pointed to one of the lists. "Constable Beck is right here."

Lenna's mouth dropped open. "He has made me nervous from the moment we met him. I don't like him a bit."

"Nor do I. And while I would ask Mr. Morley if he's taken a close look at these, that would require my telling him that we left the storage room." She tapped the page. "This is very discouraging. Scientists and theologians are threat enough to those of us trying to make a living by way of mediumship. We do not need illusion in the mix, too."

This revelation unsettled Lenna. If this subset of Society members were frauds, and her sister had frolicked among them, then what did that make Evie?

They turned a few more pages. There was a lecture on dermography, or skin writing, attributed to ghosts, Vaudeline said, but easily done with cheap invisible ink, and another on the construction of spirit horns, which were merely wooden cones believed to amplify ghostly voices.

"Evie was too smart," Lenna said. "She would have seen through these ruses." She closed her eyes and ventured what she didn't want to admit aloud. "Evie wanted her mediumship business to flourish. She believed there was very good money to be had. I cannot help but wonder if she meant to learn from these men. To learn their tricks, if that is indeed what they were teaching some of their members."

"Yes," Vaudeline said grimly. "You remember when I told you my concerns about the phosphorous oil you found among her things."

Lenna nodded. She remembered too well. *A favorite tool of swindling spiritualists*, Vaudeline had said.

Lenna pushed the log aside, annoyed. Had Evie fallen victim to the claims of these men, believing their scams, or had she known they were liars and intended to learn a few profitable methods for herself?

If the latter were true, it raised another staggering question. Had Evie really believed in ghosts at all? Maybe this had always been about enterprise for her—opportunity and money. The more techniques she could learn, the more she could weave into her own mediumship business. It made Lenna reconsider those playful arguments the two sisters had had about the spirit world... Had it been an act, with Evie knowing that once she began her business, she'd need to appear the most fervent of believers, even to her own sister? It seemed unthinkable, but so did Evie's initials here in this log.

"I'm so angry with her," Lenna said. "I wonder now if she even believed in ghosts at all, or if it was just an act, knowing she could build a business on this." She crossed her arms, feeling suddenly very cold.

"I assure you, Evie believed in ghosts. I found her awake countless nights, long after my other students had gone to bed, practicing breath work and incantations. If she meant to fill her business with ploys, why would she have taken the time to learn the techniques and applications so thoroughly?"

This gave Lenna a small measure of comfort. Still, why had Evie been so secretive about everything? "She never let me look at her notebook," Lenna said, "and she often made excuses for her whereabouts. I just thought—" she grimaced "—well, I thought it had something to do with a man. A lover. I wish I'd asked more questions."

"Don't blame yourself for this," Vaudeline cautioned. "I know that road too well, blaming myself for the choices made by my family. As much as you loved Evie, she was a grown woman capable of making her own decisions."

It was strange, hearing someone call Evie *a grown woman*. To Lenna, Evie's memory would always evoke a sense of youthfulness. She spread out her hands in frustration, looking at the visitors' log. "Not a whit of this is authentic? You're sure?"

Vaudeline shook her head. "Much of what I believe—what I practice—cannot be observed. Entrancements during a séance, energy absorption via clairtangency…these are things that I experience internally—invisibly." She leaned her hip against the table. "But when you think about the lectures we've seen in this log, what do they all have in common?"

Lenna frowned. Flame reading, facial transfiguration, ectoplasm, spirit horns. According to Vaudeline's explanations, all of these techniques resulted in something that could be seen or heard or touched. "These techniques all result in something physical," Lenna said. "Something…observable."

"Precisely," Vaudeline concluded. "Recall what I said in Paris. The mission of this society is to foster tangible signs of the afterlife."

The irony was not lost on Lenna. These lectures were about feigning proof for people who refused to believe in spirits otherwise. People like her.

"But what's interesting," Vaudeline continued, "is the lecture in late August." She turned back a few pages and pointed at the heading, "Case Study: A Review of the Séance at the 22 Bow Street Bawdy House." Evie had signed in as a visitor on this day, as well. "This does not seem to be a demonstration," Vaudeline said, "so much as a discussion of a séance that had already taken place."

"At a brothel, no less." Lenna raised her eyebrows in surprise. "Evie always was enamored of the scandalous."

They closed the log, and Lenna recentered it neatly on the

table, just the way she'd found it. A knot had formed in her throat, the truth of Evie's activities weighing heavily on her now. She hadn't missed a single lecture over the course of five months. A dozen in all, and who knew what other visits she'd paid to the Society?

This wasn't just a clandestine adventure or two. Evie's very purpose was now thrown into obscurity—her obsession, her plans, her pursuits.

Who had Evie been, really?

15

MR. MORLEY

London, Sunday, 16 February 1873

The morning after the arrival of Miss D'Allaire and Miss Wickes, I returned to the Society just after sunrise. A young boy stood near the front steps with his tiny, dirt-stained palm extended. Wondering when he'd last eaten, I reached into my pocket and gave him all I had.

I stepped inside. Making my way through the sun-streaked foyer, I signed in to the visitors' log and went on my way. But suddenly I stopped, frowning at a filmy smudge on the floor.

I knelt down, using a fingernail to scratch at the surface of it. "Beeswax," I whispered, looking up above me. But it made no sense. There were no candelabras or chandeliers in this part of the foyer. How did a pale white orb of wax, resembling a tiny sand dollar, end up in the center of the entranceway? I picked a fragment of wax out from underneath my fingernail, thinking the situation curious but not worth further investigation. I had enough to worry about, what with the women locked away and tonight's planned séance.

Just then, junior Society member Mr. Armstrong called out

for me across the way, his eyes wide. "Morley. Were you by chance in the game room last night?"

I frowned, something in his tone leaving me...uneasy. "No," I said.

He gave a nod and beckoned me to the southeast corridor. *This*, I thought, *is indisputably worth further investigation.*

"I can't make sense of it," Armstrong said as we stepped into the game room. "A group of us played cards last night. We wrapped up late, after nine. When finished, I arranged the card decks in three neat piles as I always do." He pointed at the rosewood card table just in front of us. Where a tidy set of cards might have been, instead there was a mess of them: cards in disarray, some having slid all the way across the smooth surface. "It's almost as though someone pushed the table or tried to move it..." Armstrong said.

A peculiar riddle, the answer to which I knew immediately. But Armstrong was not privy to things—he had no knowledge that two women were, in fact, secreted away in the building.

I placed my palm on my forehead, feigning a look of forgetfulness. I had the sudden desire to throw a nearby vase against the wall. "In fact, I *was* in here, very briefly," I lied. "Last night, quite late, I misplaced my monocle and went in search of it. I'd nearly forgotten that when I checked the game room I bumped into the table." I leaned forward, immediately gathering up a few of the cards and setting them into their neat piles.

Armstrong let out a hearty laugh. "Perfectly sensible," he said, before helping me tidy the rest of the cards.

Afterward, I wasted no time. I made my way immediately to the library, heart thundering in my chest. What might I find there—or, God forbid, in my study?

Standing in front of the library door, teasing the handle, I let out a sigh of relief. All appeared well, locked and undisturbed. No fresh footprints were impressed into the carpet fibers. Far as I could tell, no one had been up here overnight.

I wondered, what was it the women were searching for? Something about Evie, or something about Mr. Volckman, or something about—

I shook my head. Women, and the gall they had. Wax drippings in the hall, a mess of cards in the game room.

Wiping my sweaty hands down my trousers, I unlocked the library and let myself in, then made for my study. In a short while, I'd have plenty to say to the ladies about this breach. Another romp through the building might jeopardize it all.

Hadn't they any idea the risk posed to them—posed to all of us—by running free about the building?

16

 LENNA

London, Sunday, 16 February 1873

Neither woman slept that night, both of them plagued by the disconcerting revelations they'd made overnight.

"I'm inclined to give Evie the benefit of the doubt," Lenna whispered. "Perhaps there is something more to learn here." Yet even as she said it, the statement felt disingenuous. To Lenna, her sister's trustworthiness had already begun to crack in two.

There was little way to pass the rest of the sleepless night, so Lenna held a candle over her notebook of incantations, practicing her breath control and the expulsive *Expelle* and *Transveni* injunctions, both of which were exceptionally challenging. Occasionally, Vaudeline would whisper a gentle word or two of correction, but generally she remarked on Lenna's easy grasp of what had always proved difficult for her other students.

At last, the early-morning light illuminated the room, and the women had a better look at the clothes Mr. Morley had left them. Last night, they'd put on whatever pieces they could grab, anything to swap out with their gowns. Now the women sorted through the meager offerings.

It was a bit like playing dress-up, Lenna thought, though this was more like dress-down. There were no tartan waistcoats or silk kerchiefs as might be seen on the gentlemen who frequented St. James's Square. These were laborers' clothes—soot-stained, commonplace, and mercifully inconspicuous.

Vaudeline lifted a pair of woolen drawers, then twisted her face into a look of disgust. "As if the rough-hewn waistband is not bad enough, think of where these have been." She dropped the drawers. "I'll keep on my cotton knickers. It's not as if Mr. Morley will know any better."

Lenna smiled. "I'll do the same, then. Our little secret."

Just like last night's little secret, she suddenly thought, thinking of the arched scar on Vaudeline's thigh. Across the room, Vaudeline gave a little cough, and Lenna swore she caught her smiling. Perhaps she was remembering the same.

In the end, Vaudeline donned a felted woolen smock and dark trousers, while Lenna found a knit jumper and canvas trousers that fit her better than what she'd worn last night. They experimented with a few hats, coats, and pairs of gloves. There was no mirror in the room, so Lenna relied entirely on Vaudeline's approval of her ensemble.

"Very convincing," she said, looking Lenna up and down, "if you keep a scarf pulled close around your face. Your chin and cheekbones will give you away, otherwise." She lifted a gray scarf from the pile and gently wrapped it around Lenna's neck, pulling it upward and around her ears. "There. Perfect." She glanced down at her watch, then lowered her voice to a whisper. "It's nearly eight o'clock. He'll be here any moment." She spread her hands out. "Now, how do I look? Can I pass for a man?"

Lenna couldn't help but smile. "Unfortunately, yes. Quite well."

A few minutes later, there came a knock on the door. Mr. Morley slipped in, an impeccably clean top hat wedged under his arm and a walking cane in tow.

"A pleasant night?" he asked.

"Quite," Vaudeline said.

He cleared his throat. "The game room," he said. He pursed his lips and waited, giving the impression of a disgruntled parent.

Vaudeline raised her eyebrows. "What about the game room?" Meanwhile, Lenna kept her gaze down; she had been the one to go in there, not Vaudeline.

"I saw the cards. The table in disarray, as though someone had bumped into it after stepping into the room." Mr. Morley's voice was low, calm. Kind, even. "I will not put you in the uncomfortable position of confirming or denying your activities last night. I will only say this: I implore you not to leave this room again without me." He stepped toward Vaudeline, put a gentle hand on her wrist. "If our intentions are discovered, Miss D'Allaire, by these men we aim to identify—" He looked away, shook his head. "Well, I shudder to even consider it."

Vaudeline gave a slight nod. "Yes. Yes, of course." She was protecting Lenna, even now.

With that, Mr. Morley opened the door an inch, peered out into the corridor, then waved the disguised women forward.

Outside, the Society omnibus was waiting. The same driver they'd had last night stood by one of the horses, running his hand along its muzzle. He silently gave the women a warm smile, a tilt of his hat.

The streets were slick, the sky a pale blue. Constable Beck waited by the coach, leaning against it with his ankles crossed casually and a slight scowl pasted to his face.

Settled in the omnibus, Mr. Morley took the slate and, with a short piece of chalk, jotted down *Albemarle Street*, and showed it to Bennett. The driver slapped the reins against his horses, and the coach was off.

Albemarle was but a few minutes away. As the driver made his final turn, ahead Lenna spotted a block of Georgian brick townhomes, nearly identical with their dark paneled doors and fanlights above. Along the street were countless piles of horse dung, softened by last night's rain. The sight of it made Lenna feel sick—odd, given that she'd seen such street waste her entire life.

"As a reminder," Mr. Morley said, "the name of the woman we'll be meeting is Mrs. Gray. The Society held a séance here the afternoon of Mr. Volckman's death. This would have been one of the last places he visited."

The horses came to a gradual stop in front of one of the town houses. Peering out the window, Lenna could see a thick, black crepe ribbon hanging from the door, a symbol of mourning within the household. The ribbon fluttered erratically in the cold wind.

"It always amazes me," Mr. Morley said, "that the horses know precisely where to stop. This pair has been with us long enough. When they see the ribbon on the door, they know we've arrived."

The group exited the carriage and walked toward the house. A small cat, his fur the color of ash, approached the party from behind a holly shrub. Mr. Morley smiled and bent down, giving him a tender rub under the chin.

The drapes inside the house were drawn closed. Mr. Morley knocked twice, and the door opened. On the other side of the threshold was a young woman, dressed in a black gown with a high neck. She looked not much older than Lenna herself. A lace veil covered her face and hair, while a brooch with an inky gemstone, onyx or jet, was situated at her throat. Her hair was pulled back into a severe, low bun. The overall appearance was unsettling, even ominous.

The widow looked worn, Lenna thought—more worn than melancholic. She could empathize with this, for grief was not only made up of sadness, but of so much more: yearning to hear a voice that was now forever vanished. Revering trivial items, like a worn pocket-purse or a comb tangled up with hair. Scrutinizing those final days, wondering if you gave enough hugs, showed enough love. All of this made for a terribly exhausting way to pass the days.

"Mrs. Gray," Mr. Morley said, looking down and giving a small bow.

"No more inquiries about my husband's death. I've met with too many officials already. I have nothing further to say." She scowled and began to shut the door, but Mr. Morley put his hand out.

"Please, listen to why we're here." He shuffled his feet, gave a tap of his cane, and went on quickly. "I'm a vice president with the London Séance Society. We intend to do a séance, and we need your help."

From underneath her veil, Mrs. Gray raised an eyebrow, dropped her hand from the door. "The Society's first séance was unsuccessful."

Lenna and Vaudeline shared a quick, knowing glance. Given all they'd discovered last night in the lecture log, this news about an unsuccessful séance was not entirely surprising.

The widow looked at Lenna, studying her closely. They were standing but a few inches apart. Could she see through Lenna's boyish disguise? "Who are these two?" she asked.

"I'll explain everything inside," Mr. Morley said. "I assure you, there is a very good reason for our visit."

The widow looked at Constable Beck, her gaze falling on the revolver at his hip. "This is the last time I let any of you inside. I'll call for tea."

A few minutes later, the group was situated in the parlor. Lenna settled into the sofa and glanced around the room. A number of framed photos were turned downward, and several lengths of black linen hung on the wall—mirror coverings, Lenna presumed. Her mother had taken these same measures at Aunt Irene's house before Evie's wake, covering photos and mirrors lest the curse of death chase after someone else.

Lenna had held vigil at Aunt Irene's for several hours during Evie's two-day wake, and the memories of it still haunted her: the sight of her sister's pale, limp body on the cooling board. The stab wound on the left side of her neck, ineffectually covered over with a beige, pasty rouge. The sickly-sweet fetor of the white lilies piled high throughout the room, meant to mask the odor of decay.

Lenna never wanted to lay eyes on a white lily again.

Vaudeline was across the parlor, having placed herself in a wingback chair near the window, apart from the group.

"Vaudeline D'Allaire is a medium from Paris," Mr. Morley said, motioning toward her. She'd just picked up a tiny figurine on the table beside her, one glass ornament of a dozen: miniature dogs, various breeds and colors.

Mrs. Gray raised her eyebrows. "I remember when you left town. Quite a lot of speculation went on. For months."

"It's really a complicated story," Vaudeline offered.

"Well, no more mediums," Mrs. Gray said. "I've lost all faith in the lot of you."

Mr. Morley threw out his hands. "Oh, you misunderstand, Mrs. Gray." He seemed remorseful, apologetic in his tone. "I did not mean to imply that Vaudeline has come to contact your late husband. On the contrary, I presume you have heard about the death of our Society's president, Mr. Volckman, who you—" he writhed his hands together, visibly uncomfortable "—well, who you met on All Hallows' Eve, during the séance."

"Of course I've heard of his death. The papers report on it near daily. And his killer, still running loose about the city. And the Met? Not a lead."

At this statement, Constable Beck let out a little cough, looking embarrassed. Mr. Morley moved on quickly. "In fact, Vaudeline is here to trace the steps of Mr. Volckman on the day of his death."

"For what purpose?" Mrs. Gray set down her tea.

Vaudeline looked up, put the figurine back on the table. "I'm—"

"We cannot get into details," Mr. Morley interjected. He gave Vaudeline a cool look.

Vaudeline frowned at him. "I was only about to say I'm not authorized to share particulars." She turned to Mrs. Gray. "I hope to absorb whatever energy Mr. Volckman left behind before he died—to visit the places he went, to touch the things he touched."

Mrs. Gray reached forward for her tea again, taking the porcelain cup delicately in her hands. "My experience several months ago has left me skeptical about mediums and spiritualism in general," she said. "That being said, Miss D'Allaire, I must admit that of the eight chairs here in this parlor, you went directly to the one in which Mr. Volckman was seated on the night of the séance. Further, he spent several minutes toying with the very ornament you just touched yourself. The little spaniel—the entire set is an heirloom, given to me by my grandmother."

Vaudeline nodded along, acting unsurprised, while Lenna's mouth fell open. Could Vaudeline's choice of chair and figurine have merely been coincidence? Or had she—sensed something?

"The séance was here, in this room?" Vaudeline asked.

"Yes. We arranged the chairs in a circle around a table. Mr. Volckman sat in that chair, and he remained there until…" Again, Mrs. Gray faltered. "Well, one of the other Society men said he had a magnetic detector that he wanted to use in the place where my husband had last slept. That's the bedchamber upstairs, of course, and against my better instincts, I offered to show him. I did not see Mr. Volckman again until about ten minutes later, when he came to check on us."

Vaudeline had her hands placed firmly on the armrests and gave them both a gentle squeeze. It reminded Lenna of last night, of flesh and bruises. Flushing, she averted her gaze.

Vaudeline stood, nodding to Mrs. Gray. "You'll show us this room?"

Mr. Morley pushed himself from his chair, but Vaudeline thrust out a hand. "By *us*, I meant myself and Miss Wickes." Then, before he could protest, "I won't reveal anything confidential, Mr. Morley. My aim is to gather information, not share it."

Chastised, he sat back down.

The women left the parlor. In the hall, Lenna's eyes fell on a wall clock, reading half three. She frowned, thinking it broken. Then she remembered that her mother and Aunt Irene had done this, too: the customary setting of clocks to the time of the deceased's death. Half ten for Evie. It had been the police officer's best guess at her time of death.

Vaudeline paused. "Mr. Volckman went upstairs, but he did not use the main staircase. He used the servant staircase, over there."

Mrs. Gray's eyes grew wide. "Yes, that is right. The main staircase had just been painted. We had roped it off that day." They made for the rear of the house and went up the steps.

As they went, Vaudeline touched a few things—a scuff on the handrail, the shelf of an alcove. "A magnetic detector," she said to Lenna under her breath. "What a sham."

On the second story, they walked down a narrow corridor, turning right into a moderately sized bedroom. The curtains were drawn in here, too. Vaudeline paused in the doorway, touching a small gash on the wooden frame.

Mrs. Gray shook her head in disbelief. "When Mr. Volckman came upstairs to look for us, he touched that same mark in the wood—remarked on it, even."

"I am following his energy," Vaudeline said somberly. "It is very strong here."

Lenna couldn't deny it, the scene unfolding before her. Indeed, since arriving at the house, it seemed as though Vaudeline knew things, or perceived things, that were invisible to the others. And it didn't appear to be an act or a performance at all. "Why would his energy be so strong?" she ventured, the first she'd spoken since their arrival.

"Energies are most powerful when someone is under duress or in the throes of passion or even very angry," Vaudeline answered.

This gave Lenna plenty to think on. What had Evie been feeling in the minutes before her death, and would her state of mind at the time hinder, or assist, her future séance?

"Thinking back on that night," Vaudeline said to Mrs. Gray, "was Mr. Volckman particularly temperamental or excitable?"

"Perturbed, I'd say." Mrs. Gray took a seat at the edge of the four-poster bed, slumping forward slightly. "You see, when it was clear the séance downstairs was nearing its end and we had not contacted my late husband, the Society member who'd led the affair—his name was Mr. Dankworth—told me that his magnetic monstrosity functioned best in the room where the deceased had slept."

Lenna's stomach dropped. *Mr. Dankworth?* That was the same man who'd led Eloise's séance.

"Downstairs, I could hear the other men exiting the house and making plans to meet later, for a party," Mrs. Gray said. "Meanwhile, Mr. Dankworth seemed enlivened, even frenzied, as he unboxed the instrument. He set it on this cabinet and fiddled with it for a time." She approached the rosewood dresser near the doorway. Here, decaying flowers, pansies and forget-me-nots, hung limply over the edge of a vase filled with putrid water. Next to the vase sat a stack of calling cards, black-bordered. "Eventually," Mrs. Gray said, "the needle began to move and point at certain letters, and he claimed to interpret its movements. He insisted my late husband's spirit was present, and though he was at peace, he feared greatly for my loneliness."

Lenna couldn't believe what she was hearing. Absurd, to think any metal device could communicate such a thing. And quite a convenient statement the device made, at least for Mr. Dank-worth.

Mrs. Gray remained on the edge of the bed, her face in her hands. "On and on he went, claiming these words were spelling themselves out on the instrument. Finally, the thing went still, and Mr. Dankworth sat here, next to me. 'You do not want him to worry about your solitude any longer, do you?' he asked. And I was in such a state, so burdened and terribly sad, and they had given me too much wine downstairs."

She looked up, face red and damp. "He bent in and kissed me, and though I tried to push him away, I was no match for him. I felt so disoriented, and he put his hands on me, my waist, and tried to push me back onto the bed. A few moments later, I heard someone on the servant stairs. Blessed be, it was Mr. Volckman, calling out to ask if everything was quite well. Mr. Dankworth immediately rolled himself off me. When Mr. Volckman stepped into the doorway, he and Mr. Dankworth shared a glance. I wonder now if Mr. Volckman suspected something awry. Anyhow, he snapped his fingers, said it was time to leave, and then he was gone."

As she spoke, Lenna twisted her face in disgust, but Vaudeline's face was inscrutable. She was well trained at this; whether in the séance room or conducting inquiries, she seemed able to withstand even the most harrowing of revelations.

"Before Mr. Dankworth left the room," Mrs. Gray said, "he asked for a 10 percent tip on what was already an exorbitant sum, given the failed séance. When I declined to tip, he threatened me, said a few Society men who worked as newspaper columnists might like to know about this, my stingy nature and my desire to take him upstairs…" She shook her head. "How easily he might have twisted this all against me. So I gave him what he asked and told him to never come near me again."

She was nicer than Lenna might have been. Mr. Dankworth had seized on a woman's susceptibility, fed her too much wine, forced her onto the bed. He could go to hell, for all Lenna cared. All of that nonsense about magnets and needles and loneliness... Damned be these men, these money-hungry predators.

"The man downstairs, Mr. Morley," Vaudeline said. "Do you recognize him? Was he at the séance?"

Mrs. Gray shook her head. "No, I'm certain he wasn't." Downstairs, a dog let out a few barks. "Ah, he'll be back from his walk." She gave a small smile, the first Lenna had seen. "That's Winkle. One moment—I'll settle him down." She left the room, and the sound of her footsteps reverberated on the servant staircase.

"Mr. Dankworth was the one who led my friend Eloise's séance years ago. Nothing came of it," Lenna whispered. "And given all Mrs. Gray has just revealed, I can't help but wonder if he is one of the Society's crooks."

"Undoubtedly." Vaudeline closed her eyes a moment. "I am horrified. Simply horrified. The rumors I heard last year were one thing. The lecture records, too, only indicated the men were learning fraudulent tactics. But Mrs. Gray's account? She's one of their victims—evidence of what they did with those ruses." She placed a hand on her stomach. "It is clear Mr. Volckman suspected this and was trying to catch the men in the act. And thank goodness Mr. Morley's story remains clean, too. He didn't attend this séance or the questionable lectures."

Mrs. Gray returned a few moments later, a small black pug tucked under her arm. She gave him a rub between the ears, then said, "Tell me why you do this, Miss D'Allaire. Why solve a murder for a man who oversees such a dreadful organization? Why do him any favors at all?"

Vaudeline gave a sad smile. "A fair question. Recently, I've learned the Society is not as upstanding as I previously believed them to be."

"I quite agree with you on that. Women are talking, you know."

Vaudeline looked up. "They have been for some time."

Mrs. Gray gave a stiff nod. "The Society has been such a reputable organization for many years—I would not have commissioned them, otherwise—but after the failed séance and Mr. Dankworth's behavior, I spoke with my cousin and a few of my friends. Though none of them have commissioned séances themselves, all have heard stories—rumors—about the London Séance Society. Nothing that can be proved, but it appears I'm not the only woman in London these men have preyed on, financially or otherwise. Which is why, Miss D'Allaire, I must admit, I am not at all saddened to learn about the death of their president. I hope you will not take my callousness as an indication that I was involved in his death. It is only evident of the hurt the Society has caused me."

"Of course not," Vaudeline said, shaking her head. "But you must understand, Mr. Volckman aimed to rid the organization of its wrongdoers."

"Do you believe one of the Society members might be to blame in his death, then?"

"Possibly," Vaudeline said, "but assumptions are dangerous. His séance is late this evening. We will know the truth of his death soon enough."

"Very well," Mrs. Gray said now, leading the women to the door. The dog was wriggling in her arms, trying to get free. "I wish you success at your séance, and I encourage you both to keep an eye out for each other. These men, they cannot be trusted. Who knows what they're willing to pull? My cousin says there are rumors they've enlisted a female accomplice, so who knows wh—"

"A female accomplice?" Lenna interrupted. Her blood went cold.

"That's what people are saying, yes. She's young, with astonishingly blue eyes. They say she's been spotted at a few wakes, a few funerals, and has even shown up in a boy's disguise at some séances." Mrs. Gray lifted her hands, let them fall again. "Even if it's true, I cannot attest to it myself. I'm sure she wasn't here on All Hallows' Eve. I remember everyone around the table. They were all men, mark my words."

Lenna steadied herself against the dresser. *Astonishingly blue eyes.*

Evie. It could only be Evie.

Evie's learning about Society schemes had been bad enough. But this news? This was appalling, the idea that she'd been acting as accomplice and involved in their manipulative, dishonest behavior. And if someone at the Society was granting her access into the organization, it seemed plausible that young, wanton Evie would be giving something in return. Lenna placed her fingers to her lips, feeling light-headed. She was learning more about Evie—in death—than she'd bargained for.

Perhaps worst of all, this news widened the net of people who might be to blame in Evie's death. If people knew about her—if talk was spreading through London about this accomplice—then anyone might have killed her. Anyone who wanted vengeance against the Society.

After all, Evie seemed quite the villain nowadays.

17

 LENNA

London, Sunday, 16 February 1873

The group settled in the omnibus after the visit to Mrs. Gray's. Solemnly, Lenna looked out the window at the bright blue sky, ruminating on the conversation they'd just had with the young widow. It had been alarming in more ways than one, and Lenna found herself desiring nothing more than a lie-down in a dark, cool room.

Constable Beck ran a finger along the scar on his chin. Then he muttered something about a late breakfast at the Society headquarters. Mr. Morley shook his head. "We've another quick errand. Miss D'Allaire would like to call on Mrs. Volckman," he said.

Constable Beck balked at this, his eyes wide. "I'm famished," he said. "And I'd be surprised if her footmen even come out to greet us."

Vaudeline frowned. "Why is that?"

Beck wavered for a moment. "Oh, the Met has inconvenienced her enough with their interrogations. She knows that the Society has been making its own efforts, too. We've hassled her quite a lot. She told me herself, just a few weeks ago: she's exhausted by our efforts and has nothing more to offer."

What is it with these men? Lenna wondered. Constable Beck and Mr. Morley both seemed oblivious to the idea that a visit with a grieving wife could entail anything beyond interrogation.

"I have nothing to *ask* of her," Vaudeline said. "I only want to pass along my condolences to a friend. You and Mr. Morley needn't even leave the coach. I'll be just a few minutes."

Beck gave her a cynical look, then reached for the slate. "Very well," he said, snagging a loose piece of chalk and scrawling out *14 Bruton Street.* He thrust the slate toward Bennett, making no effort to hide his irritation.

They arrived at the Volckman residence, a four-story Georgian townhome, its facade and front entry impeccably maintained. Vaudeline and Lenna exited the carriage, approaching the front portico, which was flanked by enormous white columns.

Standing in front of the door, Vaudeline removed her hat and fussed a moment with her hair. She knocked, and a moment later, the door opened.

A maid in a pale blue apron opened the door. At once, she gasped. "Miss D'Allaire."

Vaudeline gave her a warm smile. "Miss Bradley," she said, nodding.

"Please, come in." Miss Bradley swung the door open, looking Vaudeline up and down as though hardly able to believe the two were standing in the same space. "You're in London. I—" She shook her head, visibly disoriented and delighted. "Let me go fetch Mrs. Volckman. One moment."

Not a minute later, a woman came rushing around the corner, breathless. She wore an inky-black woolen dress, unadorned. Merino wool, Lenna guessed—far nicer than anything she owned.

Spotting Vaudeline, Mrs. Volckman burst into tears. She outstretched her arms, and the two embraced a long while, there in the entry hall. Vaudeline whispered a few things into her ear, but Lenna caught only a few words: *Terribly sorry… Maddening… I wish.*

Lenna stood awkwardly to one side while they hugged, studying the stained-glass transom window above the door and the yellow patterned paper along the walls. It was an airy, cheerful space, quite in contrast to the mournful reunion happening just in front of her.

After the two women pulled apart, Vaudeline introduced Lenna, then briefly summarized her reason for being in London. She explained that Mr. Morley and Constable Beck were outside, waiting in the coach, and that she'd be assisting them with a séance that would, hopefully, shed light on Mr. Volckman's death.

"I hadn't any idea you'd get involved," Mrs. Volckman said, her eyes welling with tears again. "How terribly hopeful this leaves me…" She withdrew a kerchief, dabbed at her eyes, and eventually composed herself. She then asked about Vaudeline's and Lenna's attire, obviously a disguise.

Vaudeline hesitated, but she said nothing about hiding from any dangerous or rogue men within the organization. Instead, she skimmed the surface of the truth. "As you well know, women aren't permitted to engage in Society affairs. Our assisting Mr. Morley—even riding about town in the omnibus—would not be well received."

"Understood," Mrs. Volckman said. "I'm moved, truly, that you would take such a risk in order to seek vengeance for my husband."

Vaudeline looked down, silent. Lenna thought again of what Vaudeline had said in Paris, after reading Mr. Morley's letter: *Not only have I learned about the death of a friend, but it seems the rumors I brought to him might have sent him to his grave.* She wondered if Vaudeline was suffering such remorse now—indeed, if this

might have explained her insistence in calling on Mrs. Volckman as soon as possible.

"Would you like to attend the séance?" Vaudeline asked.

Mrs. Volckman thought carefully for a moment. "Mr. Morley
and Constable Beck will be in attendance, I presume?"

"Of course, yes."

"And it's tonight?" Vaudeline nodded, and Mrs. Volckman
crossed her arms, silent a moment. At last, she replied. "No.
No, I will decline."

This surprised Lenna. Was she fearful of what might transpire
at the séance or what information might be gleaned? Or did she
dislike the men so much that she'd rather forgo her own husband's
séance than participate with them in attendance?

It wasn't worth dwelling on, Lenna knew, and it was unfair
to make assumptions about her reason for refusing. It was Mrs.
Volckman's decision to make, and hers alone.

"You're not fond of the men, I gather," Vaudeline said.

Mrs. Volckman gave a nod. "Mr. Morley is a nuisance more
than anything, especially when drunk. I once caught him uri-
nating in a planter outside. Another time, he pulled a callous
prank on one of the children." She gave a small smile. "Pardon-
able, I suppose. But Constable Beck? Even my husband found
him unnerving. And that's saying something, seeing as how he
oversaw an organization full of lively men."

"*Unnerving* in what way?" Vaudeline asked.

Mrs. Volckman lowered her voice, giving a quick glance over
either shoulder. "Well, I understand the Met has almost fired
Constable Beck several times. He's been caught taking bribes,
falsifying reports. They investigated him last year for assault on
a fellow constable."

Now Lenna wondered if the dark scar on his chin was related
to the altercation Mrs. Volckman had just mentioned.

She went on. "As if this isn't enough, Constable Beck runs
around with another Society member, a Mr. Dankworth—"

"Oh!" Lenna interjected, unable to hide her look of horror. Vaudeline shook her head. "The man that Mrs. Gray—"

Lenna nodded.

"Bad eggs, Beck and Dankworth both," Mrs. Volckman said.

"So we gather," Vaudeline said, a troubled look on her face. "I'm surprised that your maid so much as let us in. I worried that the Society omnibus in which we arrived would not work in our favor. From what I hear, you're quite exhausted by the endless questioning."

Mrs. Volckman cocked her head, frowning. "Pardon?"

"Constable Beck said that between the Met and the Society, you've answered quite a few questions about your husband's death," Vaudeline explained.

"That couldn't be further from the truth." Mrs. Volckman splayed out her hands. "Immediately after his death, I answered a few questions, yes. But neither the Met nor the Society has been here since. To be honest, I'd have thought they'd show more concern than they have."

A look of dismay settled on Vaudeline's face. "Neither the Met nor the Society have come by in...months?"

"That's right."

Lenna and Vaudeline shared a glance; this news contradicted what Constable Beck had said on the drive here. He'd told them that he'd spoken with Mrs. Volckman just a few weeks ago.

Suddenly the three women jumped. Above the mahogany chiffonier next to them, a wall clock had struck the hour. The chime rang low and long, and by the time it ended, Vaudeline had taken a step toward the door. "They'll be impatient by now, I'm sure," she said. She turned to her friend, embracing her a final time. "I'll return soon. I promise."

Mrs. Volckman nodded. "It was so very good to see you. And to meet you, Miss Wickes." She gave Lenna a tender pat on the arm. But as they moved toward the door, Mrs. Volckman cleared her throat. "One more thing, if I may."

"Of course," Vaudeline said, pausing midstride.

"I only want to say that I am worried for you both." She spun her wedding band around on her finger, the marquise amethyst catching the light. "Promise me you'll remain wary and watch out for one another."

"We will," Vaudeline said. She tidied her hair, tucked it under her hat, and led Lenna out.

The door closed behind them. "Wary, indeed," Lenna said, keeping her face low. "We've already caught Beck in a lie. And his name in the lecture-attendance records..." she said, Vaudeline already nodding in agreement. He was looking worse and worse. He and Dankworth both.

"I can't make sense of it," Vaudeline replied. "The Society has maintained a spotless reputation for years." She exhaled hard. "But it seems there are even more blemishes than I feared."

18

LENNA

London, Sunday, 16 February 1873

Outside Mrs. Volckman's house, the group settled themselves inside the omnibus. Lenna fiddled with her coat buttons, thinking they would now return to the Society. The driver waited, reins in hand, for one of the men to pass over the slate.

On the bench between Mr. Morley and Constable Beck sat a small paper bag, the bottom soaked through with grease. Mr. Morley pointed out the window: a vendor with a cart strolled slowly down the street away from them, calling out to passersby.

"Meat pies," Mr. Morley explained. "While you were inside, we bought a half dozen, if you'd like one."

"Bit gristly," Constable Beck added, wiping a smudge of pale brown gravy from his lip. "But still quite good." He held out the bag, seeming much more cheerful than he had a while ago.

Both women declined, and Vaudeline cleared her throat. "Mr. Morley, a point of consideration. Volckman died at your private cellar near Grosvenor Square."

He went still. "Yes, that's right."

"Which means that, after leaving this part of town, we would expect him to have gone north or west. But I can assure you, with as much confidence as I had while tracing his steps through Mrs. Gray's house, he did not go north or west at all. *Croyez-moi*, he went south. Toward Piccadilly."

Earlier, toward the end of their visit, Mrs. Gray had made much of Vaudeline's clairvoyance, informing the men that the medium had indeed traced Volckman's path through the house step for step. Now Mr. Morley blinked dumbly, visibly surprised by Vaudeline's suggestion.

Constable Beck belched. Then he thrust his hand into the paper sack and removed another pie. "We ought to go that way, then, toward the Circus."

"We've risked quite enough already," Mr. Morley said, hovering his hand protectively near Vaudeline's shoulder. "I'm not about to brandish her through the busiest part of town in our omnibus."

"The Met has repeatedly questioned Volckman's whereabouts that evening. This could be helpful for the investigation." With greasy hands, Constable Beck reached for the slate, wrote *Piccadilly Circus*, and then handed it over to Bennett. "And she's in disguise, Morley. No need to be melodramatic about it."

Mr. Morley might have been a vice president of the Society, but Constable Beck was a member of the Met. The tension between the two men was palpable, and Lenna looked away, uncomfortable. Mr. Morley clenched his hands, looking as though he might dispute further, but finally the carriage began to move.

As they drove, Vaudeline leaned forward in her seat, a look of concentration on her face. A long, stray lash sat perched on one of her cheeks, and it took Lenna great effort to keep her hands in her lap, to not brush it away.

Going eastward, Mr. Morley took a few additional directions from Vaudeline and wrote them on the slate. They passed Haymarket, then Leicester Square, and soon approached the busy north end of Covent Garden.

"Inform the driver we'll turn up here," Vaudeline said suddenly.

At this, the two men exchanged a long glance.

The omnibus slowed and turned. At last, the horses came to a stop. Lenna peered out the window, her heart suddenly thudding. Last night, when looking through the visitors' log, she and Vaudeline had found Evie's name on the same day there had been the lecture on the bawdy-house case study.

And to Lenna's great surprise, 22 Bow Street was the exact address at which they'd just arrived.

Constable Beck threw his head back and laughed. "My God, he came to the brothel," he said. "How foolish of us to have not considered it."

"We all have our vices," Mr. Morley added, though even he looked surprised.

Lenna took her time exiting the carriage, wondering what information might be gleaned here. The Society had not only done a séance at a brothel, but the president had apparently paid a visit on the day of his death.

"We'll go inside," Vaudeline told the men, "for a quick walk-through, just as I performed at Mrs. Gray's."

Whatever mystery surrounded this place, Lenna knew this opportunity to investigate would be short-lived. It was imperative she play along, acting as though she'd never heard of this place. As they walked away from the coach, she feigned a look of curiosity, as a child might.

They approached the front of the brothel, and Lenna gazed up at the modest building. Blackened, soot-stained brick gave way to several arched single-paned windows, finished with uninteresting millwork. A bird perched on a windowsill above, watching.

A middle-aged man—the proprietor, Lenna guessed—opened the door when Mr. Morley knocked. "Morley," the man said.

His cheeks were pockmarked, his hair greasy and thin. "Back so soon?"

Mr. Morley flushed, motioning to the women behind him. "Peter, I've a small favor to ask," he said, before briefly explaining that this visit was related to Mr. Volckman's death and a few new communicative techniques the Society aimed to try.

Peter frowned. "I've no problem with them having a look around, but Mr. Volckman didn't—"

Vaudeline stepped forward. "Please, we'll be quick," she said, placing her hand lightly on Peter's arm.

He gazed down at her fingers as though a woman hadn't touched him in years. He nodded stiffly and let the group through, crossing his arms over his peacock-colored vest, which looked like something cast off by a livery servant. As Lenna passed him, he snaked his eyes over her. "Why are they in men's clothes?" he muttered.

"Leave it, Peter," Mr. Morley said. "It's of no importance."

Once inside, it took Lenna's eyes a moment to adjust. Despite the bright morning sun outside, the hall where they now stood was terribly dark. The hour could have been mistaken for dusk: a few lanterns were lit in the parlor and drawing room either side of them, while heavy, mismatched curtains were drawn closed in both rooms. The wood floors creaked underfoot as Lenna stepped forward.

In the parlor, a dusty oil painting hung unevenly on the wall. Dark stains marred the upholstered roll-top edge of a nearby chaise lounge, and an insect, flat and rust-colored, crawled its way into a seam. Lenna looked away, grimacing. To call this place unwelcoming would be a compliment; it was ramshackle, downright repulsive.

But not to Vaudeline, it seemed. She had begun to run her hands along one of the walls, ignoring the flaking plaster in places, and she eyed curiously the staircase going to the second story. Mr. Morley and Constable Beck watched her movements closely. It was very much how she'd acted at Mrs. Gray's house.

A movement in the drawing room caught Lenna's eye, startling her. Sitting on a two-person sofa, a young woman in a faded black gown held a cordial glass in her hand, swirling it in a circular motion. Her bodice fell low around her bosom, and she wore no shoes or stockings. The bottom edge of her gown draped high on her pale, thick ankles. She caught Lenna looking and smiled. "I'm Mel," she said, locking eyes with Lenna. "And you are?"

"L-Lenna." The word sputtered out, hesitant and full of distaste for this place.

Knowing Evie had attended a case study about the Society's séance at the brothel, Lenna wondered how she might possibly ask for more detail without attracting attention. She walked toward the sofa, taking a seat at the very edge of it, in spite of her disdain.

In the other room, Peter had called Mr. Morley and Constable Beck over to the sideboard, where he now offered his visitors something urine-colored from a decanter.

"I recognize the shorter one," Mel said. "Mr. Mott-something?"

"Mr. Morley," Lenna corrected her, assuming she recognized him because he was a regular customer. But what Mel said next caught her by surprise.

"He attended a séance here, last summer." Mel swirled her cordial again and took a sip. "Though the word *séance* is hardly fair. A farce, the whole thing was. Teeming with tricks."

Lenna's eyebrows shot upward. She seized the opportunity, brief as it would be. "Let me guess." She thought of the visit to the widow's house. "They didn't find any ghosts at all and tried instead to seduce the women here?"

"Precisely." Mel kept her voice low. In the other room, the men grew animated and began to laugh as they flipped through a catalog Peter had withdrawn from a drawer.

Mel bent over to set her glass down on the floor next to her bare feet. "Our old bawd, Betty, passed last summer—in July.

One of the girls found her dead in the back garden. She'd been separating lily bulbs. We think she tripped and hit her head on a rock. She loved flowers." Mel worried at a hem on her dress, running her fingernail along the fabric. "We hired the London Séance Society for a final goodbye. In the end, none of us got to say it. Still haven't." She composed herself, straightening in her seat. "Peter is Betty's son. He's unimaginably horrid."

"And you said Mr. Morley attended this séance?" Lenna thought of what Mel had said a moment ago: *A farce, the whole thing was. Teeming with tricks.* She wondered what role he'd played in the séance. Had he been an observer? Had he been at the séance table, or standing aside?

"Oh, yes," Mel said decisively. "But he was not only in attendance." She lowered her voice even further. "Mr. Morley led the whole affair."

19

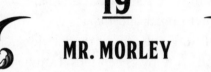

MR. MORLEY

London, Sunday, 16 February 1873

As I stood with Constable Beck and Peter near the sideboard, I glanced into the other room. Miss Wickes was in conversation with one of the brothel girls.

Suddenly, she looked in my direction.

Our gazes met. I took a sip of brandy, eyeing her over the glass. I'd been surveilling her and Miss D'Allaire all morning, even if they weren't aware of it.

At Mrs. Gray's house, for example. After they'd gone up the back stairs, I'd immediately gone up, too. I hadn't taken the wooden servant stairs but rather the carpeted steps off the foyer, which allowed me to tread discreetly. Constable Beck had looked on as I went up, an inscrutable expression on his face—amusement, maybe, or had it been exasperation? No matter. I hid in the corridor outside the bedchamber, where the women were, while the whole bloody thing unfolded. I'd overheard bits and pieces of what Mrs. Gray shared with the women: a few details about Dankworth, the magnetic instrument. *Who knows what they're willing to pull?* she'd said.

Now I wondered what the girl might be saying to Miss Wickes. What suspicions she, too, might be unveiling.

All of this talk about crooks and tricks. Had Miss Wickes and Miss D'Allaire put the puzzle together yet?

Had they any idea the illusionist at the Society was...me?

The Department of Spiritualism was mine to steer, after all, and the Society's mission stated *peace* and *satisfying curiosity*.

No one said anything about *truth*.

And illusion? It sufficed—it got the job done.

I was very good with my deceptions. I studied the playhouse mirages, the way light could fool an eye. I kept the right friends, too: chimney boys to take a penny and hide behind walls; ventriloquists to whisper from the far side of the séance table; vaudevillians to act as though they'd been bewitched.

The other men in the department were aware of the ruses, sure. But every last one of them had signed my oath, agreeing to never reveal aloud what they'd seen at the séances or what they might suspect. They weren't permitted to discuss anything—not among themselves, not in the presence of Mr. Volckman, and certainly not around anyone from the Department of Clairvoyance.

It was why I had hired Bennett to drive our omnibus. A driver was bound to overhear a few puzzling or peculiar things. I'd learned this the hard way and wouldn't make the mistake again.

Should my department members break their oath of discretion, they knew the power I wielded. I could fabricate an unpaid debt, slander them in the papers, write up their Society eviction notice. And should they be expelled, think of all they would lose. The exclusive parties, the theater boxes, the dividends.

All they had to do was *cooperate*. Not a terribly big ask.

Of the members in my department, there were a select few— like Mr. Dankworth—whom I considered deft and trustworthy enough to run the schemes themselves. I'd begun giving private lectures to these members, relaying my methods and techniques. More fraudsters meant more money, better dividends. And I didn't have the time to attend every séance, anyway. If a more desirable evening engagement arose, I was perfectly happy to let a member like Mr. Dankworth lead a séance.

But then those pesky rumors bubbled up, and there was the conversation with Volckman—the one in which he threatened to turn me out if I didn't get to the root of things in my department.

My techniques, I suppose, had gotten sloppy over the years. I'd let my men be too brazen with the post-séance flirtations. I'd been too quick to declare the meaning of a flickering flame during a séance. Too confident while reading the message on a sheet of trick paper.

The root of the problem—the blemish on the Society's otherwise-impeccable reputation—was *me*.

20

 LENNA

London, Sunday, 16 February 1873

*H**e'd led the whole affair.*

Sitting on the sofa at 22 Bow Street, Lenna balked at what Mel had just revealed to her. She sat up straighter, ready to ask more, including whether anyone of small stature and blue eyes had joined the fraudulent séance led by Mr. Morley. But the sound of footsteps interrupted them, and Lenna turned to find two people descending the staircase: a woman skipping lightly down the steps, and behind her, a flush-faced gentleman fiddling with the buckle of his trousers. Peter rushed over to them, and there was a flurry of fingers as money changed hands. Peter pocketed it all.

"As you can see, we're all in mourning." Mel nodded to the girl who'd just come down. She also wore a black gown, though it was not nearly as faded as Mel's. "Peter has begged us to pull our bright dresses back out. He insists mourning rules don't apply in a whorehouse. He wears that vest to *liven the place up,* as he says. Hideous, isn't it?"

The girl who'd come downstairs spotted Mel and smiled.

Then she walked over and sat cross-legged on the floor at their feet. She introduced herself as Bea. Across the hall in the parlor, Vaudeline was bent close to the hearth, studying the woodwork and inspecting the coal scuttle. How odd, her methods and techniques. And here at the brothel, she seemed to be moving especially slowly...

"Stingy, that one," Bea whispered, pointing to the man with whom she'd just been upstairs. He was gathering his coat, about to make his way out. "Slipped me only half the tip he promised."

Mel reached out, squeezed Bea's hand. "How much more do you need?"

Bea pursed her lips. "Three shillings." She turned to Lenna. "My mother recently fell ill, and she hasn't the funds to purchase the medicine she needs. I've been sending home what I can." She turned to look at the newcomers chatting with Peter.

"Have they found a girl yet?"

"Oh, that's not why we're here—" Lenna stammered. How embarrassing for Bea to think they'd accompanied these men on a brothel visit.

But Bea was already standing from the floor, eyeing the men.

"She's determined," Mel said sadly, as Bea approached the men. "She and her mother are very close."

Lenna admired Bea's resolve, but it would never work. No chance Constable Beck or Mr. Morley would let Vaudeline and Lenna out of their sight.

Bea approached the men at the sideboard and removed the faded black shawl covering her shoulders. They in turn stared at her, seemingly transfixed by the pale, bare flesh of her shoulders. Even Peter looked surprised: perhaps he hadn't expected this strange visit to make him any money.

Bea had other ideas, it seemed. She gave Constable Beck a long look. Then she reached for his glass—it appeared he'd declined the brandy and accepted only water—and took a slow, lingering sip. She put her lips softly to his. Lenna, recalling the way Beck had so gluttonously devoured the meat pies on the drive over, stifled a grimace.

Bea pulled out of the kiss. Then she turned to Mr. Morley as though about to repeat the action. He put out a hand. "No," he said. He turned, glancing sidelong at Lenna. "Not in front of them."

Peter's face twisted into a look of disgust. "I cannot believe you'd deny her." He shoved a hand in his pocket, toying with the coins inside.

Suddenly, the front door opened. A pair of disheveled men, unsteady on their feet, stepped in. Peter eyed them warily. "Christ," he muttered. "These two have a way of causing problems." He stepped toward them, pulling his shoulders back.

Constable Beck hardly noticed them. "I won't refuse the girl," he called out to Peter, before running his eyes up and down Bea's torso. In turn, she smiled at him. Then she took his hand and began to pull him away.

"Beck," Mr. Morley said, splaying his hands. "In front of the ladies, my God—" He waved a hand toward Vaudeline and Lenna.

"Miss D'Allaire and Miss Wickes aren't fools," Beck called back, frustration now in his voice. He'd stopped at the bottom of the stairs, his body turned toward the group. "They know what goes on here. Peter greeted you like an old friend, anyhow."

"What's the trouble?" one of the newcomers interrupted, his voice slurring. He was drunk—very drunk.

"Nothing that concerns you," Peter said, putting a hand on the man's shoulder. "Say, how about you come back later? In an hour or so?"

"How about we don't?" the man replied, pushing past Peter. He rubbed his hands together. "Have we a fight brewing? I put my money on him." He pointed at Beck. "Come on, gentlemen. Let's see it."

The room went silent, every man eyeing the others. At last,

Peter broke the tension. He nodded to Beck. "You go on. The rest of us gentlemen will step outside, get a breath of air, enjoy a drink."

This time, Mr. Morley didn't refuse. He followed Peter and the two newcomers through a corridor leading to the back of the building. Upstairs, Lenna heard a door open and shut.

With the men now gone, the air in the parlor instantly felt lighter, cooler.

Vaudeline stepped away from the hearth and joined Lenna in the drawing room. "Do you have what you need?" Lenna asked her.

"That depends. Have you?"

"No, I—" Lenna cut off, frowning. "What do you mean, *That depends?*" But Vaudeline only looked at her. Suddenly, Lenna's mouth dropped open.

"Right," Vaudeline said, giving a small grin. She lowered her voice to a whisper. "I made up the whole story about Mr. Volckman coming this way. Who says we can't pull a few tricks of our own?"

Vaudeline pulling a ruse: the grandest of ironies. Lenna felt the sudden urge to pull her forward by the scruff of her coat and kiss her hard.

Though impressed by her recklessness, Lenna now felt a greater sense of responsibility to use this time wisely. She turned to Mel, speaking quickly. "The séance. Can you tell us more about it?"

"Come here," Mel said, motioning the women forward. They went to where the men had been standing a few minutes ago, and Mel opened a middle drawer. She handed Lenna a tapered candle, partially burned down. "They left their candles. Have a look at this one."

Lenna turned the cream-colored candle over in her hands, frowning. "Is there something I should be looking for?" she asked.

"Let me see it," Vaudeline said. She took it, then ran her fingernail over a subtle line of discoloration in the wax, running down the length of one side. "A trick candle," she concluded.

"Right," Mel said. "We suspected the same when, halfway through the séance, the overwhelming scent of tulips surrounded us."

"I don't understand," Lenna said, looking again at the candle. "Tulips? A trick candle?"

"Odors can suggest a successful manifestation," Vaudeline said. "But they're so easily faked in a séance room. One must only make, or buy, the right sort of candle. There's typically a layer of beeswax, then a layer of perfumed wax. To those in the room, it appears nothing has changed—the candle is merely burning down—but the sudden change in the room's aroma is a convincing ploy. Adept fraudsters will match the perfume to whatever the deceased might have been known to use. A favorite fragrance, for instance. Imagine being in the séance room, and suddenly it fills with the scent of your dead husband's eau de cologne."

"Oh," Lenna said. "Yes, that would be quite convincing." She eyed Vaudeline carefully, marveling at how very much she knew about all of these schemes. She seemed to know every game in the book. Not to mention, she'd just pulled her own move against the men, and her acting had been good. A little too good, if Lenna was honest with herself. She ignored a flutter of unease that had begun to trouble her.

Vaudeline turned to Mel. "Is there anything else?"

Mel nodded. "There was a photographer here during the séance, and the men brought us the developed photograph the week after. They said it was proof they'd conjured Betty, but they asked for more money before showing it to us."

Vaudeline's eyes narrowed. "Do you have the photograph?"

Mel nodded again, putting the trick candle back in the sideboard. "Let me go find it. I'll just be a moment."

When she was gone, Vaudeline turned to Lenna. "A veritable league of illusionists," she concluded in a low voice. "How did Volckman not know what was happening just beneath his nose?"

Mel returned, holding something close to her chest. She thrust it out, and Vaudeline took the four-by-four-inch print. In it, several of the brothel girls stood around a table. Lenna recognized the paintings on the wall: the photo had been taken in the drawing room, where she'd been sitting earlier. In the image, the girls looked solemn—tearful yet anticipatory. It reminded Lenna very much of the expression on the mother's face at the château séance, grief awash with a shadow of hopefulness.

On one side of the image, hovering slightly above the ground, was the cloudy and diaphanous form of a woman. Her hair appeared a pale color, and she wore a thin, light-colored lace gown.

"You can't see the face very well," Mel said, "but Betty had black hair. Not to mention, she would never wear a frock so ugly. The photograph is a fake, without question."

Lenna asked to see the photograph herself. Then she turned it over. She read the photographer's stamp on the back: *Mr. Hudson's Studio, Holloway.* She tapped her finger against it, thinking the name vaguely familiar. Suddenly, she remembered. This was the studio Evie had mentioned while reading *The Spiritualist* magazine last year.

"This studio was shut down," Lenna stated, recalling her conversation with Evie. "The owner had been accused of superimposing images onto photographs." She handed the photo back, remembering how Evie spoke of this Mr. Hudson, almost in a defensive manner. Had she been in collusion with him, too? Or the trick candlemaker, or any of the other swindlers enlisted by the London Séance Society? She ran her hand over the back of her neck, suddenly exhausted.

Vaudeline nodded at the photograph. "You said they wanted more money for it?"

Mel nodded. "We had pooled our money already for the séance. Still, we came up short. On the night of the séance, the men said we could make up the shortage with another sort of...currency. It's what we do here, after all." A flash of shame crossed Mel's face. "The following week, the men returned with the photograph. But they wouldn't show it to us until a few of the girls agreed to yet another assignation."

Toward the back of the building, Lenna heard footsteps, movement. She needed to ask about Evie, and quickly. "Mel," she said, "I need your help with something, please. My sister, well, I believe she was involved with the Society in some way. Learning from them, or perhaps even assisting them. I don't suppose there was anyone at the séance that struck you as out of place. A young woman, disguised in men's clothing?"

Mel raised her eyebrows. "Evie, you mean."

An invisible tremor rippled through the air, and Lenna's knees went weak. Vaguely, she felt Vaudeline grip her elbow. "Y-yes," she stammered. "Evie. You know of her?"

"Of course. She was here during the séance, wearing men's clothes, like you are. Unmistakable eyes, though. One of the girls recognized her, having once met her at a fortune-telling shop on Jermyn Street."

"Yes," Lenna said. "Evie was often there."

Mel shook her head as though recalling a bad memory. "Quite scheming, that one."

Lenna steadied herself against the sideboard. Evie had been here, at the brothel, in disguise. At a séance full of tricks. It was all just as the widow, Mrs. Gray, had said.

"Evie is my sister," Lenna said. Her voice was more urgent now. "Did she return with the men when they brought the fake photograph?"

Mel cocked her head to one side, a perplexed expression in her eyes. "If she's your sister, can't you ask her this yourself?"

Lenna bit her bottom lip, shook her head. "Evie was killed on All Hallows' Eve."

The photograph in Mel's hand fluttered to the floor, and she clasped her hands over her mouth. "Oh, oh dear..." She blinked several times, a dazed expression on her face. "I am terribly sorry," she finally said. "Though, given her connection to the Society, I cannot say I am all that surprised."

21

MR. MORLEY

London, Sunday, 16 February 1873

Peter and I ushered the two drunken men out the back door, to the garden. It took us quite the effort to keep the men pacified; they were absurdly inebriated for this time of day, hankering for a fight between anyone—it didn't matter who.

Once tempers had calmed, Peter conversed with the men at a table underneath the ivy trellis, while I walked the short garden circuit, admiring none of it. There were too many memories hovering about this place.

Memories, and mistakes.

As my summer with Evie progressed, I noticed something peculiar. No matter how many documents or so-called ghost-hunting implements I put in front of her—and no matter how outlandish they were—she always inspected them carefully, without judgment or accusation. The ectoplasm lecture, for instance. It was obvious that the substance I'd left on the table was a blend of potato starch and egg white. One could smell the rotting eggs, for God's sake, and yet Evie hadn't so much as furrowed a brow.

The spirit horns that she'd asked to see, too: they did not have any more noise-transmission ability than the clay pipe often perched in my mouth, and any of the horns' sounds were due entirely to ambient noises coming through from the room, the street, and so on. Evie had to have known this. The girl was too smart.

Yet she kept coming back for more. The lectures, especially. I let her sit backstage, where she would not be seen by the other attendees. She marveled at these hour-long discussions, always hounding me with a slew of intelligent questions about the instruments and whether any of it might be corroborated. I reminded her once that although my techniques weren't provable, they were not *unprovable*. That was all that mattered, wasn't it?

She'd nodded along in agreement.

Her hunger for information became a sort of game for me. I unveiled technique after technique, some of them quite preposterous, and damn if she didn't play along magnificently.

I wondered, initially, what she was after. She'd made it clear that it had only a little to do with me. Then, midsummer, she told me about the mediumship business she intended to start in the new year. It all made sense to me then. She must have seen the advantage in fraud—not just the money in it, but the ease with which it could be carried out. Mourners *wanted* to believe in what unfolded in the séance room. Their desperation made my job so terribly easy.

And I never forgot about that time she said, *I do enjoy breaking a few rules, Mr. Morley.*

Eventually, an idea formed in my mind. With rumors swirling and commissions down and Mr. Volckman breathing down my neck, I thought Evie could be of great benefit. She could attract fresh clientele. She could dispel rumors at funerals and make up stories about satisfaction with our services. Most importantly,

she could challenge wake-room slander—convince the mourners that grief had blinded their senses, hindered their rationality.

Evie was what I needed to stifle the groundswell of gossip.
Rich widows would believe someone vulnerable, someone ap-
proachable. Someone like Evie. She could tamp down the rumors, certainly.

Think of the tricks to be turned in widows' parlors, with an
accomplice like Evie on my side!

Then came that all-important occasion, the night Evie and
I first made love. The night she begged me to let her attend a
séance.

After agreeing to her request, I spent considerable time looking through the forthcoming appointments for the Department
of Spiritualism. I decided upon the one at the bawdy house,
somewhat amused by the fact that my department worked in
venues far more interesting than anything Shaw pursued with
the Department of Clairvoyance. So wholesome, his side of
things. Those department members favored fêtes and fairs, not
whorehouses.

The affair at 22 Bow Street would be well attended. Plenty of
girls, plenty of Society members. This was important, so better
to keep attention off the boy in disguise.

I told Evie about the plan several days in advance, and I took
the opportunity to toy with the question on which I'd been ruminating for some weeks: Evie's thoughts on what really went
on with the Department of Spiritualism. Before proposing anything about being an accomplice, I needed her to admit that she
knew about, and accepted, our deviant techniques.

I began vaguely enough. "Evie, tell me what you envision
for your mediumship business." We were in our usual place,
my study. I was sifting through old receipts while she perused
her notebook, a pensive look on her face. She'd always been especially protective of that thing, keeping it turned askew so I

couldn't catch a glance at what was within. Not that I particularly cared for the inconsequential musings of women.

She looked up, cocked her head to one side. "Why, séance after séance. I'd like to model my business after Vaudeline D'Allaire's. Only, I will not limit my séances to murder victims."

"She's quite reputable," I said. "Doesn't even use a cabinet, I hear."

"Not a trick in her bag." Evie held my gaze as she said it, her face inscrutable.

"You don't think she's pulled one or two? In all these years?" The palms of my hands began to sweat. We were circling the beast.

"I suppose there's no way to be sure, but she has made plenty of money without resorting to ploys."

Money. There she was, my greedy little Evie. "What would you do," I asked then, "if your own skills didn't garner as much success? Would you resort to ploys?"

She paused, tapping her pen on her notebook. "Yes," she said. "Absolutely, yes."

I nearly slapped my knee in delight. "And how would you study and practice such ploys?"

She closed her notebook and leaned forward. "Probably, I'd find a way to learn from the best." One side of her mouth turned upward.

I could work with these insinuations. I knew this game as well as anyone. "And what if you had the opportunity to join the best? Not just to learn from them but to work alongside them?" I paused, watching her closely. "For quite a lot of money, even."

Her jaw opened slightly, the pink of her tongue visible. "What kind of work?"

A shrug. "Someone to spread the word about our expertise, to brag about all we've accomplished in séance rooms across London. Someone to visit funerals, dispute any slurs against us."

A thoughtful look came over her face. "You need an actress, then."

There it was.

"An actress, yes, but even more than that, an accomplice."

Her eyes glinted, all mischief and youth. "And you would continue to grant me access to the department's reference materials? To let me attend séances?"

How brave of her, to shift the conversation in the way she just had. This was no longer hypothetical. No more insinuations. She'd made this about us. About *her*. "Yes. That's right."

"And how will I know which funerals to attend? Would I ask around at my own discretion, or—"

"Oh, no, absolutely not." I waved my hand in the air, emphasizing this next point. "I will tell you exactly which affairs to attend."

"And you would *pay* me for this?"

"Indeed. Quite well."

She began to laugh, shaking her head as though she could not believe what she was hearing. I watched her, my arms crossed, feeling faintly that I'd missed something just now.

"Consider it done," she finally said. She thrust her notebook into her bag and declared it time to get home.

The brothel séance took place in late August. As the omnibus departed the headquarters, I informed the other members that a prospective member would be joining, a young foreigner I'd befriended at one of the gin palaces. I told the men he spoke almost no English, and thus there would be no use engaging him in conversation. The other members did not question it. My role as vice president, and the oath they'd signed, worked nicely in my favor that day.

Evie—in impeccable disguise—was waiting outside the brothel, as was the ventriloquist we'd hired for the evening. We all went inside. As séances tended to go, it began with a solemn discussion of the deceased's manner of death. In this case, the deceased was Betty, the former bawd. We were informed that she had died in the garden at the back of the house on the sixteenth of July, shortly after dusk. Her manner of death was an undetermined head injury: the girls said Betty had tripped and fallen onto a stone near her feet.

We then went to the garden and set up a table and a dozen chairs by the ivy trellis, but our candles would not stay lit in the evening breeze—and by God, I needed them to stay lit! So we moved to the drawing room, after which things proceeded nicely.

We did our humming, our hand-holding, our question-asking. We kept the room very dark, short of the candles, and a few of the girls got quite teary when faint whispers began to emanate from one corner of the room, not incidentally in the place where I'd situated my ventriloquist. The photographer, Mr. Hudson, stood alongside his tripod, taking pictures.

On it went like this for several minutes. We went round the table then, and anyone who wished to ask a question of the spirit was free to do so.

The girls were terribly emotional, worried only for Betty's peace and well-being. The gentlemen were more practical about things, posing inquiries regarding the brothel's fate. I asked Betty if she should like the brothel to remain open, and I was pleased at her reply in the affirmative. (It was in the ventriloquist's best interest to whisper *yes* to my question, for he pays quite a few visits to the brothel himself. His disguise was top-notch, though. The pasted-on facial hair nearly fooled me.)

When we ran out of questions, I asked the girls for a few moments of silence. In truth, I was waiting for the trick candles to burn down. I'd bought them from a candlemaker new to town, one I vowed to never use again, for they took far too long. At bloody last, the wax melted down. A floral aroma began to swirl about the room, and the reaction on the girls' faces—even a few of my men—was spectacular.

I could not resist a furtive glance at Evie then. She'd withdrawn her notebook and was making notes. She looked thoughtful, solemn. I was greatly encouraged by this; all night, she had played the part perfectly.

After a few more photographs and aimless mutterings, the séance reached its conclusion. We brought up the topic of money. We had not given the girls a fee prior to the affair, knowing that no matter how much they paid, we'd still ensure a deficit.

When the girls told us how much they'd pooled together, a few of the Society members convincingly lamented the shortage, then suggested another way to pay up. It was quite persuasive, I'll admit, and the women agreed to take a few of the men upstairs. (What choice did they have? Our services had been rendered; it was only fair.) But first, Peter brought out the brandy, and the mood lightened tremendously.

Evie crept toward the door. I followed. As she put on her coat, I pretended to rummage through my own, looking for something.

"Perfectly done," I muttered quietly to her.

She gave me a slight nod, as though we hardly knew each other, and then she slipped out the door and into the night.

22

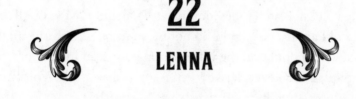

LENNA

London, Sunday, 16 February 1873

At the brothel, footfalls echoed at the back of the building, and the women turned toward the sound. The men were returning from their reprieve outside, and Lenna knew her conversation with Mel was over. She'd gotten all she would get today.

"Beck still occupied?" Mr. Morley asked as he came in. He walked to the staircase, propped a boot up against a balustrade. Meanwhile, Peter took a seat in the parlor with the two drunken men, who were visibly calmer now.

Lenna could hardly look in Mr. Morley's direction. Mel's comments a moment ago had confirmed her suspicions. Evie had been involved with the fraudulent side of the Society, by way of a séance that Mr. Morley himself had led.

"I'm going to wait in the coach," Mr. Morley finally said. "Miss D'Allaire, Miss Wickes, please join me. Our return to the Society is long overdue."

Lenna told Mel goodbye, quietly lamenting the fact that there was so much they hadn't been able to discuss about Evie. But how could they, now under the watch of Mr. Morley?

Besides, how much more did Lenna even want to know? She'd already learned more about her sister's true activities than she'd bargained for. It had been hard enough grieving the loss of what she considered her innocent, if not free-spirited, younger sister. But in death, Evie had taken on a new persona: a deceiver at best, a villain at worst. One who'd kept very bad company.

A few minutes later, situated in the omnibus, Mr. Morley spoke in a calculated tone, looking at Vaudeline. "Miss D'Allaire, you and I are friends, and I do not mean to question your methods or throw doubt on the information you glean by way of your techniques. However, I asked Peter—outside—if Mr. Volckman did indeed come here on the day of his death."

No. Oh, God, no. Lenna's stomach lurched.

"He said he did not. Not that day, not that week. He can't, in fact, recall seeing Volckman here at all, ever." Mr. Morley gave Vaudeline a suspicious look. "Is there something here we need to resolve between the two of us?"

Vaudeline's face reddened, but her voice remained steady. "His denial doesn't surprise me in the least. With so much mystery surrounding Mr. Volckman's death, do you really believe Peter is inclined to admit he was here mere hours before he was murdered? I suspect he wants to wash his hands of any knowledge about Mr. Volckman's activities that day." She paused, then said, "If I may say so, Peter doesn't exactly strike me as the most trustworthy sort, either."

Given the ensuing silence, this rejoinder caught Mr. Morley off guard. Still, Lenna knew that Peter had been telling the truth, and Vaudeline was the one now spinning tales. In spite of this, she glanced sidelong at Vaudeline, feeling defensive of her, terribly fond of her. It had been risky, directing the men here. And yet look what else they'd learned about the men and their methods.

"Very well, then," Mr. Morley said, his tone unconvincing. "Perhaps that does explain it." He turned in his seat and tapped the driver on the shoulder, passing over the slate. Constable Beck still had not come out of the brothel. A moment later, the carriage began to move. "Beck can manage his own way back," Mr. Morley said. He leaned his head back and closed his eyes.

As the horses trotted their way back to the Society headquarters, Lenna ruminated on all that had transpired in the last twenty-four hours. Sifting through the lecture records, which proved that Evie had infiltrated the Society. Hearing the widow's account, and subsequently learning that Evie had been an accomplice of the men. And then Vaudeline's cunning ruse to get them to the brothel, where Mel had confirmed the worst: Evie had attended the phony séance.

"Mr. Morley," Lenna said, disrupting the quiet inside the carriage. Was it nervousness making her voice tremble, or the way the carriage shook over the cobbled pavements?

"Mmm?" he mumbled, his eyes still closed.

"I have a sister named Evie Wickes." Mr. Morley's eyes sprang open, and Lenna went on. "Well, I had a sister. She was killed on All Hallows' Eve. The same night as Mr. Volckman."

Next to her, Vaudeline tensed. "Lenna," she said, her tone cautionary.

But Lenna ignored her. Evie was already dead, and she didn't need to protect her anymore. "My sister was enamored of ghosts. Spiritualism, séances. While you were outside a short while ago, Mel told me—" she cleared her throat "—she told me something quite alarming. She said that Evie attended a séance with the men of the London Séance Society last summer. I hadn't any knowledge of her involvement with the Society. Is it true?"

He gave a stiff shake of his head. "No. Heavens, no. That would be grossly against policy."

Lenna pursed her lips, undeterred. "Interesting, because Mrs. Gray said something similar. That there were rumors the Society had a female accomplice. Someone who went about town joining in on your séances."

Mr. Morley studied her carefully, then tilted his head slightly. She didn't necessarily believe he'd killed Evie—the two may have been coconspirators, even lovers, and she couldn't peg him with a motive. Still, she hoped that by confronting him so unabashedly now, he might slip up and reveal some crucial detail. "I'd only like to know if it's true," Lenna said, maintaining her cool. "It seems my sister might have kept some things from me. She never mentioned running around with a men's society."

"You don't mean to imply the Society had something to do with her death?" He placed his hand on his chest as though personally offended.

Lenna's hands grew clammy. "Not necessarily. I just want to know if what Mel and Mrs. Gray said is true. Did you know my sister? Did she ever join the Society's séances?"

Mr. Morley ran his hands along the wooden bench either side of him, a pensive look on his face. "No," he finally said. "No, I did not know your sister, and she certainly did not partake in any Society affairs. As you well know, women are not permitted any involvement with the organization."

Lenna maintained a look of indifference, though inside, she was reeling. His responses had been maddeningly unsatisfying. This was not good enough for her, not yet. "I saw Evie's initials," she persisted. "In the visitors' log when you let us look through it last night. Evie was at the Society. I saw it myself."

Mr. Morley narrowed his eyes. "A set of initials is hardly proof of anything. I'd wager I could match any set of initials if I looked through the log long enough."

Lenna gritted her teeth. This man was impossible. Still, he had a point. Evie hadn't written her full name in the log, so it wasn't as though she could point a finger at the page and prove her argument. It was almost as though Mr. Morley had instructed Evie, long ago, to keep her log entries abbreviated. Unverifiable.

"I admire your investigative nature, Miss Wickes, but worry not about what you've heard. These sound like mere women's rumors to me. A grieving widow, a brothel girl? You cannot trust them. They've fabricated these stories, far as I'm concerned. Parlor-room gossip."

Quite the statement, coming from him. Lenna crossed her arms, remembering one final piece of evidence against him— the hat he'd worn to the docks. But to mention this would only extract yet another excuse from him. *A thousand caps like it in the city,* he'd probably say.

It had begun to rain, and the traffic grew heavier as the omnibus neared St. James's Square. The carriage came to a complete stop for a few long minutes at an intersection. The driver flipped through a book to pass the time, annotating and doodling on a few pages. Meanwhile, Mr. Morley grew more and more agitated, checking his watch constantly.

"If I weren't so worried about you being spotted," he said to Vaudeline, "I'd propose we walk."

Lenna would have liked to walk. She hated this omnibus; every time they went somewhere, the movement of the carriage left her feeling unwell. But Vaudeline gave a shrug. "We're certainly in no hurry to return to our storage room."

"Yes, well, some of us have things to get done." He forced a tight smile, then: "Apologies for my tone. I'm quite tired today." He closed his eyes and did not speak for the remainder of the drive.

Several minutes later, the carriage came to a halt behind the Society building. Mr. Morley exited first and made his way quickly toward the back entrance. Vaudeline stepped out of the carriage, but as Lenna followed, she felt a slight brush against her shoulder. She turned to see the driver, pivoted slightly in his seat, with his arm stretched toward her.

Between his fingers, a tiny piece of paper.

Lenna took it, clasping it in her palm, and the driver retracted his arm, turning in his seat again. The movement had been so quick, Lenna might have believed she'd imagined it if the scrap of paper were not tucked snugly against her skin now.

Settled back in the storage room, she waited anxiously for the echo of Mr. Morley's footsteps as he disappeared down the hall. Instead, there came a low muffled sound, like a case or box was being dragged down the hallway. A few moments later, the noise ceased.

"Psst," Lenna said, getting Vaudeline's attention. She unfurled her palm, revealing the tiny scrap of paper.

Vaudeline frowned. "What is that?"

"The driver passed it to me as we alighted from the carriage."

"Well, what does it say?"

With trembling fingers, Lenna unfolded the little square. She read it once, twice, and then a third time.

"My God," she whispered. "I do not think—" she grew lightheaded "—I do not think the driver is deaf at all."

Vaudeline stepped close to her, and together they read the note again.

He lied.

You must get away from him.

23

 ## MR. MORLEY

London, Sunday, 16 February 1873

What a day it turned out to be, one interminable errand after another.

My patience was nearly gone as Bennett drove us from the brothel back to the Society. I wasn't in the mood to converse and wanted only to get on with my day, my plans. I'd leaned my head back, nearly about to doze off—

It was then that Miss Wickes decided to pepper me with questions about her sister.

I maneuvered my way out of her interrogation as best I could, though it was clear to me that the women had learned more than I'd have liked them to. As the coach drove on, I pondered the situation, determined to not let it worry me. *Let them muse on Evie's involvement with the Society,* I thought to myself, closing my eyes again. *Let them even believe we run rampant with fraudsters. If that's the worst they discover about us, then we've made out all right.*

We neared the headquarters just as the rain began falling in sheets. It reminded me of that stormy day, last October, when my feelings about Evie began to shift.

I'd been at my desk, fingers cold and numb. I'd just arrived at the Society, my trousers soaked through from the walk outside, all squalls and sideways rain. I gathered a stack of letters to be read and sorted, and I fought off a chill, feeling ill-tempered. Storms did that to me, the darkness and damp.

I began to open the envelopes. At long last, something I'd been waiting for. Two inquiries, both of them name-dropping the woman who'd praised the London Séance Society so highly at a recent funeral: Miss Evie Wickes.

This was business, *new* business—exactly the sort of update Volckman would be thrilled to hear. Each week, I'd been reviewing the death notices and Obituaries of Eminent Persons in the newspapers, skipping over the epitaphs and words of affection. Instead, I looked at the surnames, seeking out the wealthiest of them. With this information, I'd been providing Evie with a list—even a roughly drawn map—of funeral locations and dates.

Now here was the fruit of our efforts.

The chill in the room lifted, and I was terribly proud of her in that moment. I began to think it possible that she and I might single-handedly repair the Society's tarnished renown.

We might bring it back from the brink.

A resurrection.

Only, Evie had something very different in mind.

24

 LENNA

London, Sunday, 16 February 1873

With only a matter of hours until the séance, Lenna could not calm her thudding heart. Between her tingling fingers, the scrap of paper from Bennett was creased, damp with sweat.

The note had taken her by great surprise. If anything, Constable Beck was the one she hadn't trusted, and she'd gone so far as to assume he might be one of the Society's rogues, along with Dankworth. But Beck hadn't been in the carriage when Bennett passed her this note, so there was only one person he could have been referring to. Mr. Morley.

And this note was an outright condemnation of him.

He lied. This part of the note was accusatory, but not necessarily surprising. When Lenna asked Mr. Morley if he'd known Evie, or if she'd participated in Society séances, she'd been testing him. She already knew the truth. Bennett must have known about Evie from seeing her interact with the men. Perhaps she'd even ridden in the omnibus a time or two.

The more ominous message was what the driver had written next. *You must get away from him.*

What did he know? Was this indicative of something Mr. Morley had already done, or something he intended to do? It was maddeningly vague.

After all they'd learned that day, Lenna believed wholeheartedly that Evie's involvement with the Society had gotten her killed, and there existed the very real possibility that it was related to Mr. Volckman's death, also on All Hallows' Eve. But who might have wanted both the offender, Evie, *and* the virtue-seeker, Mr. Volckman, dead? Was it possible someone had been out for the Society—not realizing that Mr. Volckman wanted to purge his organization of fraud—and this had led them to Evie, too?

Given these questions, Lenna wasn't sure she even wanted to heed the note's warning. Did she want to escape if the answer— or part of the answer—to Evie's death might be gleaned during the Volckman séance, mere hours away?

"I suppose Bennett's note could also be a ploy," Lenna mused aloud. "He works for the Society, after all, and we've no idea who to trust within this organization."

Vaudeline raised her eyes at this. "I'm apt to trust Bennett over Mr. Morley, given what we learned at the brothel. His leading the séance, and all of those tricks..." She grimaced. "It makes me wonder what else he has hidden. About the Society. About Evie."

Lenna toyed with the note in her fingers again. "But if Mr. Morley and Evie were both crooks, working the same schemes, why would he hurt her? I'm convinced of a different scenario. I think someone killed Mr. Volckman—a woman seeking vengeance on the Society, perhaps—and maybe the same person killed Evie, knowing she was an accomplice to the Society. Or what if—" She gasped, surprised she hadn't considered it sooner. "Well, we suspect Mr. Morley and Evie were intimately involved. What if Evie was also involved with Mr. Volckman, and Mr. Morley learned about it? What if this is a crime of passion and has nothing to do with the Society's fraud at all?" As she said it, she cringed, repulsed by the idea that her sister might have taken yet another Society member to bed.

"In which case," Vaudeline said, "Mr. Morley looks quite guilty again. He might not have attended the séance at Mrs. Gray's house, but even still, I can't ignore what is right in front of me. I no longer trust the man a whit." Vaudeline sat up slowly, then crossed the room. She knelt in front of Lenna and gently pulled her hand away from her face. Lenna hadn't realized it, but she'd been biting away at her thumbnail; it was pink and raw, the nail bitten down almost to the quick, and damp with saliva.

Now Vaudeline kissed the very tip of her tender thumb. "Your nail-biting is driving me mad."

Lenna exhaled hard. "I'm going to find Bennett," she said decisively. "Forget Mr. Morley's admonitions about leaving the room. I want to know what Bennett means by this." She held up the note, and without waiting for Vaudeline's reply, she went to the door and gave it a push.

The door, however, didn't budge. It gave an inch or so, meaning it wasn't locked or latched, but instead blocked by something outside.

Lenna frowned, turning to Vaudeline. "What on earth?" She pushed the door again, leaning against it with her shoulder. Still, it wouldn't give. "Did he—" she splayed her hands, not believing what this could mean "—did he barricade us in?"

Vaudeline's comment a moment ago—*I no longer trust the man a whit*—suddenly seemed all too accurate.

Vaudeline stood, her face grim. She, too, tried to push against the door, to no avail. Even together, their efforts wouldn't budge the thing any farther.

"The bookcase," Lenna said, her underarms prickling now with effort and—fear. "It's been in the hallway this whole time. And a few minutes ago, we heard that noise, like something dragging outside."

"Given the bookcase's position in front of the door," Vaudeline said, "it must be taking up the entire width of the corridor."

Lenna nodded. Any force exerted outward on the door would merely push the bookcase up against the hallway's opposite wall. A perfect barricade, only able to be maneuvered out of place by someone in the hallway.

"Unbelievable," Vaudeline said.

"I wonder if he thought we would abandon the séance…"

"You give him far too much credit. I suspect worse."

Lenna paused. She understood Vaudeline's skepticism, but something still nagged at her. "Why, then, has he orchestrated this entire thing? Your arrival into London, your protection, your lodging, the séance as a whole. He's been helpful in many ways."

"Yes," Vaudeline said. "A little too helpful." She turned away from the door and crossed her arms. "I think we ought to abandon this entire endeavor," she said solemnly.

Lenna's breath caught. "Pardon?"

"When we arrived in London last night," she said, "I anticipated this séance being dangerous. Today, however, has brought to light horrifying truths about these men. Bennett's ominous note, now this blocked door. You're right in that Mr. Morley has arranged this séance, but we do not know what else he might have in mind for tonight."

Here it was, Vaudeline in her usual authoritative role, her tone decisive. Still, Lenna felt a wisp of disappointment, knowing the answer to Evie's death could very well be gleaned from the Volckman séance.

"How, exactly, do you think we'll manage to *abandon* the séance?" she asked. "It isn't as though he'll open the door for us and bid us *adieu*."

"No, he most certainly won't. We must use something else against him."

Lenna gave it a moment's consideration, but she didn't have

the energy for Vaudeline's games and intimations tonight. "And that is?"

"*Lust*. For all we know, Evie worked her way into the Society by wielding it herself. And earlier today, you saw how Bea so effortlessly got Beck upstairs. I'd think it unbelievable if I hadn't once been in Evie's and Bea's shoes."

"Please tell me you haven't seduced Mr. Morley in the past," Lenna said, forgetting the note crushed between her fingers for a moment.

Vaudeline shook her head. "No, of course not. But at the very beginning of my career, during my first few séances, I quickly realized the benefit of seduction. In order to protect myself, I had to ensure the others in the room were feebler than me. We have talked about the disadvantages of drunkenness, youth, emotion. Lust is but another one of them. Only, this weakness I would *evoke*, before and during a séance."

Lenna shook her head, trying not to guess how many times Vaudeline had needed to resort to this form of protection.

"How exactly did it work?" Lenna asked, her voice cool. "You paused the séance, removed a few articles of clothing, and danced around the men?" She'd seen pictures of this type of thing in some of Evie's pamphlets over the years, half-naked women circling the séance room in a sort of erotic trance.

"That is the thing about you science-minded people," Vaudeline whispered, a sliver of frustration in her voice. "Everything must be so terribly simple. A hypothesis, either proved or disproved. Black-and-white." She fiddled with the door once more. "Might you allow a few shades of gray in your life? Might there be some things you couldn't classify on a taxonomy chart of emotions, if one even existed?"

She had no idea what she was asking—no idea how badly Lenna wanted to say, *There are a thousand feelings I can't classify, all of them new since I met you. Every one of them a shade of gray.*

"Yes," she managed to choke out. She hated that the air between her and Vaudeline had shifted in the last few minutes. The warmth between them dwindling.

"So it is with men. They are not as simple as you seem to believe." Vaudeline turned away. "Men want to feel pursued, but still superior. They want to feel understood, but not exposed. They want control over you, but they want to believe you're a fool, unaware of it."

Lenna thought of Bea's seduction of Constable Beck earlier that day. She'd gotten exactly what she wanted, using her allure to her advantage. And though she'd never seen it firsthand, Lenna assumed Evie had done the same in order to get inside the Society.

"The goal of seduction," Vaudeline continued, "is to make a man surrender his resistance so he cannot act rationally. This is when he is susceptible to dangerous spirits in the séance room, or any enfeebling maneuver, for that matter. It will be our strategy tonight. Or, more correctly, *my* strategy."

Vaudeline straightened, a determined look on her face. "*Seducere.* In Latin, it means *to lead astray*. So that is what we will do. Mr. Morley said he will come for us at eleven, and when he does, you will be standing behind the door. I will be here, well within his view, and mostly undressed. He'll be distracted a few moments, at least. You will take one of the two candlesticks and—"

"A candlestick?" Lenna blurted out. Her throat grew tight, choked up with tears. She'd hoped Vaudeline would have a better idea, something less…violent. "I've never hurt anyone. I'm not strong enough, I don't think."

Vaudeline ran a finger through one of her waves, separating it into two. "I will pretend that I am changing clothes, and Mr. Morley has stumbled on me in a state of undress. I'll move closer to him, and then you'll come up behind him and… Well, you understand. It is meant to surprise him, not to kill him. Just enough time for us to rush out of the room and barricade him in as he has done to us." She closed her eyes, stretched her neck from side to side. "This is the plan, then. Unless..." She cleared her throat, looking uncomfortable.

"Unless what?"

"Well, unless your strike does not take him down as we hope. You will only get one chance, you understand. If you miss, or don't injure him severely enough, he'll be enraged. I will restrain him as long as I can, but you must go—get out as quickly as possible and escape to safety. Home, or wherever you deem the safest place."

"And lock you in here with him?"

Vaudeline didn't miss a beat. "Exactly." She nodded to the door. "Mr. Morley is no stronger than you. I suspect the bookcase isn't very heavy. It's the positioning of it that you'll need to be diligent about."

Lenna remembered too well the feeling yesterday on the docks, when she and Vaudeline were about to say goodbye. The same miserable melancholy now plagued her. She didn't want to be apart from Vaudeline. Not tonight, of all nights. She walked to the small table, lifted one of the candlesticks, and felt the heft of it. It was solid, made of brass. She ran her finger along the edge of the base, sharp as flint.

Lenna set the candlestick down and blinked a few times. *Home*, Vaudeline had just said. The idea of seeking out her father at the Hickway House should have been an appealing one. It meant normalcy, familiarity. And certainly, it was a safer place than here.

But going home also meant returning to the frustration and mystery surrounding Evie's death. She sensed that now she was closer than she'd ever been. So much had come to light today about Evie's involvement with the Society. And the driver, Bennett—he seemed to know something, too.

Clearly, Vaudeline's mind was made up. And though Lenna considered arguing it further, she realized that getting away from

Mr. Morley might, in fact, allow her to investigate something else. A different trail of clues.

With that in mind, perhaps Vaudeline's idea wasn't as absurd as she'd initially thought. Maybe she could raise the brass candlestick above her head and bring it down upon Mr. Morley. Maybe she could hurt this man to avenge her little sister.

Only, Vaudeline was very wrong about one thing.

If they safely managed a way out of the room, *home* was not the place Lenna would be going first.

25

 MR. MORLEY

London, Sunday, 16 February 1873

With a few hours until the séance, I sat in my study, a pipe dangling from my lips. There came a soft knock on the door, and I opened it to find Constable Beck on the other side. I was still irritated with him for taking Bea upstairs. It had been a rakish move and a waste of time, too.

"I see you made it back," I said, opening the door.

"Indeed." Beck motioned to the sofa. "May I have a seat?"

"As you wish." I ushered him in.

"Given the way Vaudeline's séances are known to go, I think we ought to ask the women what to expect tonight," he said. He sat at the edge of the sofa, tapping his foot nervously. He'd been so confident a few days ago when we'd discussed the risks of her séances, but now his expression—usually so cool and impassive— revealed his apprehension.

How convenient it would be if Beck pulled out of the séance; his decamp would be a stroke of unexpected good fortune. "If you're having second thoughts about attending, I can handle things perfectly well on my own," I said.

"Not at all. I only think it would be wise to know of any special preparations we might take in order to reduce the chance of—" he grimaced, shook his head as though he couldn't believe what he was saying "—well, the chance of something chaotic unfolding."

I blinked a few times, absentmindedly rubbing my fingers together. A bit of black powder—residue—made them feel slick. I caught Beck looking, and I quickly pushed my hands into my pockets.

"I suppose it can't hurt," I replied. I needed to be agreeable from this point forward. Anything to suppress suspicion.

We went downstairs. As we padded through the hallways, I kept a close eye on the rooms we passed, ensuring we didn't draw any unnecessary attention from other Society members.

As we made for the storage room, I leaned in close to Beck. "As you'll see, I moved a bookcase in front of the door," I said. "I discovered that they took a gander through the building overnight. Couldn't risk them going on yet another adventure."

I gave the bookcase an easy push, maneuvering it away from the door. Then I knocked on the storage-room door and slipped inside with Beck.

The women were sitting together on Vaudeline's cot, both still in the clothes they'd worn that morning. They looked up at us with eyes wide in surprise and—alarm? I wondered, briefly, if we'd walked in on them conspiring about something.

"You locked us in," Vaudeline said immediately. Her voice, like ice.

It took me a moment to recover from the surprise of such a bold statement. "I felt compelled to do so," I finally said, "given the situation with the game room last night."

"You don't trust us."

I scratched the back of my neck, considering my reply. I didn't trust her, no. I didn't trust her understudy, either. "Tell me, Miss

D'Allaire, how is it possible to know a door is locked or obstructed, unless one attempts to *open* it?" Then I raised my eyebrows at her. I'd caught her, and she knew it.

Her response was little more than an incensed glare, and I nodded at Beck to go ahead.

"The séance," Beck began. "We'd like to discuss a few things in advance."

"Certainly," Vaudeline muttered. She motioned to the lone chair in the room, and Beck took it without missing a beat. I glowered at him, suddenly imagining what it might be like to wrap my fingers around his prickly neck.

"Let's begin with the order of things," Beck said, leaning forward. "The *sequence*, I believe you call it."

"Right. My séances typically follow a seven-stage sequence." Vaudeline held up a single finger. "Phase one is the *Ancient Devil's Incantation*, arguably the most important phase of them all. It protects those of us in the séance room from rogue spirits—demons and the like. I will not begin a séance without it."

Beck withdrew a small notebook from his pocket and jotted down a few notes.

"Phase two is the *Invocation*," Vaudeline went on. "This is the summoning of all spirits. Here, I solicit any spirits in the area and welcome them to the séance room. This is often when strange things begin to happen in the room, falterings and flickerings."

Beck cocked his head to one side. "Should we be concerned about this?"

"Aware of it, certainly. During this phase, participants may suffer brief, albeit volatile, entrancements, a phenomenon known as *absorptus*. There may be arguing, physical outbursts, manifestation of injuries. Even violent or erratic movement of items in the room." She cleared her throat. "Once the *Invocation* incantation has been recited, spirits will be present. Quite simply, the séance is underway, and it must be brought to completion."

"Or what?" I asked.

"If we do not proceed through the rest of the sequence?" She crossed her legs. "Why, then we've a roomful of lively spirits free to do as they please."

I was struck by her casual manner about this whole thing. "What's phase three?" I asked, moving us along.

"The *Isolation* phase." Vaudeline watched Beck as he continued making notes. "At this stage, I ask all spirits to depart, excepting the target spirit—the one I aim to conjure, which is Mr. Volckman in this instance. This phase often comes as a great relief to the sitters. It clears the room, quite literally. Though at any point in the séance, if stubborn or dangerous spirits try to entrance the sitters, I have at my disposal two expulsive—purgative—injunctions. The *Expelle* injunction, which expels a spirit out of a sitter, and the *Transveni* injunction, which transfers a spirit from a sitter to the medium."

Beck's eyes grew wide, and he hovered his pen over his notebook. "How interesting, all of these incantations…"

"No need to write the injunctions down," Vaudeline explained. "Very unlikely we would need to resort to them." She gave him a smile and continued. "Stage four is the *Invitation*. Once I have determined that all but the target spirit have left the room, I recite the *Invitation* incantation, which is a summons for the target spirit to entrance me. This step takes less time if I can gather latent energy the deceased left behind just prior to their death. Which is why we went to the widow's house and then to the brothel. As I've said, these latent energies are strongest in the places the deceased occupied in the hours before their death."

Beck and I shared a glance. We in the Department of Spiritualism conducted our séances much differently. We read a few passages, yes, but all of this about *summoning* and *manifestation* and *expulsion*—why, constructing illusions was easy in comparison. I wondered if Beck was thinking the same, or if, on the contrary, he was impressed by Vaudeline's techniques.

Beck went on. "I apologize, Miss D'Allaire, for my elementary questions, but the manner in which you go about your séances is not like anything I've heard before. Having said that, can the spirit refuse the invitation?"

"A curious question, but no. The incantation is quite powerful. By reciting it, I am compelling the spirit to entrance me."

"So it is not really an *invitation* at all," I said. "It's a demand."

She cocked her head to the side. "I don't think of it in such forceful terms. These are murder victims, Mr. Morley. They anxiously await embodiment—and justice. Which brings us to stage five, *Entrancement*. For a medium, entrancement is akin to a dual existence, or a split psyche. It allows us to penetrate the memories and thoughts of the deceased, because, indeed, in that moment they are within us—part of our own experience and existence. The trance state is unspeakably fatiguing. It's hard enough existing as one person, what with all of those unfulfilled desires and walled-up secrets. Still, it is the most effective way to ascertain what we need to know."

"The identity of the killer." Beck excitedly rubbed his hands together.

"Precisely. Accessing the victim's memory provides not only this information, but it often reveals the deceased's last moments, as well. These memories can be helpful in guiding police or families to evidence which might not have been obtained. Hidden weapons, and so on."

I crossed my arms. "How long does all of this take?"

"Could be thirty minutes. Could be two hours."

"No less than thirty, though."

Vaudeline frowned at me. "No."

"I'm bloody excited about it myself," Beck said, face flushed now. All pink except the dark, sinewy scar on his chin.

"And once you have determined the killer?" I asked.

"Things wrap up quickly then. Stage six is *Dénouement*, the moment in which I ascertain the killer and declare it to the room. Stage seven, the final one, is the *Termination*, an incantation to expel all spirits from the room. Which, in this case, would be the target spirit that has entranced me. Without the *Termination* incantation, a spirit may be—we might say—*stuck* in this realm and unable to find their way back."

"Wouldn't that be a nightmare."

"Indeed." Vaudeline spread her hands out. "What else would you like to know?"

"Why must we wait until midnight?" Beck asked. "We ought to go now. We could have this solved for the commissioner in an hour or two."

"Midnight is what we agreed upon," I said decisively. I turned to Vaudeline. "Anything else we should know? Or preparations we should take?"

She proceeded to list a few items. I pretended not to hear the rule about refraining from wine beforehand, for I had no intention of adhering to it. I'd have a few fortifying nips before the séance.

Maybe more than a few.

God knew I'd need the nerve.

Late that night, after my final errand, I returned to the Society feeling more at ease than I had in many days. I had a very good feeling about the evening, now that I'd gotten a few things in order.

I went to my study and sat down at my desk. First, I withdrew my address book from a drawer. *Confidential Contacts*, it read. The pages inside were well-worn, for I accessed this book at least weekly. It contained the names and addresses of vaudevillian actors and stagehands, trick candlemakers and papermakers, photographers and chemists, ventriloquists, set designers, firemasters, lawyers. There were asterisks next to the best of the best, my most preferred associates.

I set the address book aside, sifting now through some other drawer contents: a few sheets of blank paper, which were not, in fact, blank at all. It was expensive, specially designed paper, three-ply. The middle layer had the faintest of ink within, spelling out certain words or names. The text became visible only once the paper had been dampened with water.

I situated the pages next to the address book, a smirk on my face. This trick paper had long been a profitable prop.

I continued looking through my items. I spotted a notebook— Evie's notebook, the one she'd always kept turned away from me. I tossed it aside; I knew the contents of it now, and it wasn't this I was interested in.

What I wanted was the folio.

I lifted the vellum-bound book out of the drawer. No gilt lettering on the front, no sprayed edges. I set the portfolio on my desk and opened it, skipping past the old newspaper clippings and going straight to the sheets of parchment at the back, with handwritten memorandums for future reference. I located the page I'd written on last week, hovering my pen over the entry I'd made.

Quickly, I plunged my split-nib dip pen into the inkwell.

I pressed the pen to paper.

I made a short note.

Once I'd finished, I blotted the excess ink from the page and closed the portfolio. Then I tucked it back into place in the drawer.

No sooner had I stood than I heard it again: outside, the warbler had struck up yet another bleak tune. I listened but a moment, and then the melody was drowned out by the discordant symphony of steeple bells ringing out all over the city, marking the eleven o'clock hour.

It was time.

I meandered out of the study, closed the door behind me, and made my way downstairs. I realized, as I went, that my step was lighter than it had been in months.

By God, I even felt a smile coming on.

26

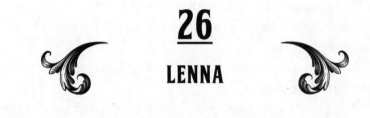

LENNA

London, Sunday, 16 February 1873

As the women waited for the time to pass, Lenna paced the room, unable to keep her restlessness at bay. Outside, a bird warbled hysterically, further grating on Lenna's nerves. "How much time left?" she muttered.

"Twenty-five minutes," Vaudeline replied, looking at the clock. Even she nibbled at her bottom lip, visibly agitated. "Let's play the word game. Anything to distract ourselves." She retrieved her novel, opened it up, and took a seat next to Lenna. She flipped through a few pages, then pointed at one. "I'm ready. It's two words. Your clue is…" She thought a moment. "…*sky fire.*"

Lenna pondered on this a moment, already glad for the diversion. Anything was better than thinking about Bennett's note, or Evie's involvement with the organization's rogues, or the candlestick sitting on the table across the room. Instead, she thought of the way that some stars blinked red or orange, like fire, in the night sky. But the answer could not be *stars* or *planets*. "The answer is two words, you said?"

"Yes."

"May I have another clue?"

Vaudeline leaned close, bumping her shoulder against Lenna's. For a brief moment, their faces were but an inch apart. "It is something many have experienced," she said, "but no one can explain."

Lenna blinked, her mouth dry. *"Love,"* she said. "Or—*in love?"*

"That has nothing to do with *sky fire.*"

"You're right." Lenna groaned, rubbing her temples. "I can't think straight at all."

"Nor can I. The answer is *aurora borealis.*" She closed the book, patted the front cover.

"Ah," Lenna said, feeling slightly embarrassed now at her guess. "I've seen the aurora borealis."

"Have you?"

"Yes. Evie and I went to see it together." And Eloise, too, but Lenna left this detail out.

Evie had suggested the trip for Lenna's birthday two years ago. The three girls had traveled north by train to Sheffield in the dead of winter. Huddled together under a blanket, they'd lain awake on their backs and watched the celestial display for hours. The dancing light of the aurora borealis resembled a dream: sky-wide arcs of viridian, luminescent bands of vermilion. It had been one of the happiest moments of Lenna's life. She'd been nestled between Evie and Eloise, the warmth of them on either side of her. The two people she most adored, safe with her in that moment.

Lenna had studied the way the bands of light moved, observing the motion like a scientist might. The undulations didn't resemble a vapor or gas but instead reminded her of bright ink dropped into a vessel of water. Whatever the case, there must have been a logical explanation for the way the colors diffused and re-formed. There must have been tiny particles of something in the air.

"What do you think it's made of?" Lenna had asked, directing the question at neither girl in particular. Next to her, hidden underneath the blanket, Eloise moved her thumb in slow circles against Lenna's palm.

"I think it's a type of cloud," Eloise said thoughtfully. "A night cloud. Made of steam or fog."

"How interesting. A night cloud." She squeezed Eloise's hand. "And, Evie? What do you think?"

Evie paused, then: "Spirits, of course." Above them, a cylinder of bright green light billowed and rippled. "It is almost as though they're dancing."

"I quite like that possibility," Eloise said. Lenna glanced over at her, watching as a flash of green light, the color of limes, twirled in her eyes. Eloise looked back at her. "What do you think it is, Lenna?"

"Particles of something," she said. The light dimmed slightly just above them, revealing a cluster of stars. Then it came back to life. "Maybe dust."

"Dust?" Evie said. "How terribly dull." Yet as she said it, she tucked her head into the crevice between Lenna's neck and shoulder, nuzzling against her. "No matter. I still love you, sister." Above them, a falling star dropped vertically across the sky. "Happy birthday," she said.

"Yes, happy birthday," Eloise echoed.

If there were a single moment of her life that Lenna could relive, it would have been that one—a time when she'd passed her days in blissful ignorance, believing in her sister's goodness and the many years that lay ahead for the three of them to adventure, to explore, to love.

It was nearly eleven o'clock. Mr. Morley would be arriving in just a few minutes. Vaudeline had just finished undressing and now stood near the corner of the room, shivering in her cotton chemise.

Lenna kept her eyes down, the reality of their looming objective weighing heavily on her. If Lenna did not succeed in hitting Mr. Morley hard enough, and if the women were somehow separated, when would they see each other again? And under what circumstances?

She remembered her resolution to be braver, to not make the same mistakes she'd made in the past, like waiting to make apologies. Or waiting to state, loud and clear, what she wanted. *Who* she wanted.

She cleared her throat, lifted her eyes. "Vaudeline, I must tell you something."

Vaudeline raised her eyebrows. "Yes?"

"On the docks, when we arrived in London, you said that your affection for me is not a tangible thing. You feared I would not believe in its existence."

"Yes." She gave a nod. "I feel that way even now. The affection, and the fear."

They stood across the room from one another, nothing but chilled air and possibility between them. How easy it would be to end the conversation now, to let the reminder of Vaudeline's feelings be enough.

But there was nothing brave in that.

Lenna took a deep breath, then ventured the truth. "After this—" she waved her hand around the room "—after *all* of this, I want to explore what else might exist between us. Something more than our relationship now as teacher and student, and as friends. Even if our beliefs aren't entirely aligned. Even if I can't see or touch the proof of your work." She looked Vaudeline hard in the eye. "I can see *you*. I can touch you. And it is you I want anyway. Not your work, or what you believe." She held her breath, wondering how that would land.

In spite of the circumstances—the cold room, the darkness, Mr. Morley's imminent arrival—Vaudeline dropped her head and let out a little laugh. "Although I suspected you felt this way, I wondered if you would ever permit yourself to say it aloud.

I'm quite in awe of you, Lenna Wickes. And yes, we do indeed have much to explore between us."

Lenna's tummy lurched, a brief moment of glee amid such distress.

"As you said, though, first we must deal with—" Vaudeline might have finished her statement, if not for the sound of something being moved just outside the door. *The bookcase.*

The women eyed each other and quickly moved into place. Vaudeline tugged downward on her chemise an inch, and Lenna gripped her hands tightly around the brass candlestick. In an instant, the metal warmed beneath her fingers.

The door slowly swung open. Lenna took a silent step back, tucking herself into the V-shaped crevice quickly forming between the door and the wall.

Mr. Morley stepped in, oil lamp in hand. He was formally dressed, wearing a heavy coat and a tall hat bordered with a ribbon of black bombazine. His back was to Lenna as he stepped in—he didn't see her, not yet. Then he came to a sudden halt. Just in front of him, Vaudeline stood in her thin chemise. She trembled harder now, and even from here, Lenna could see the gooseflesh on her arms, the swell of her nipples under the fabric.

Vaudeline pretended to gasp in frustration. "I cannot undo the button here at the bottom," she said, holding up a gentleman's vest that she'd chosen earlier from the clothing pile. "We meant to be dressed long ago, but..." she said, fiddling with the fabric.

Mr. Morley stood motionless. Surely any moment he would turn, having realized Lenna was not in his line of sight in the small room. She had but seconds to raise the candlestick and bring it down. Her arms began to violently shake.

"You'll help me?" Vaudeline said to him now, her voice impossibly thick and throaty. She bent forward, allowing the top of the chemise to fall partially open. *Seducere,* Lenna remembered Vaudeline saying. *To lead astray.*

Mr. Morley's breath hitched. Lenna's might have, too, if she hadn't been holding it. In this moment, she and Mr. Morley were no better than each other. Both of them hungered for Vaudeline.

"I'd be glad to h-help," Mr. Morley managed, stepping toward Vaudeline. Lenna could not see his face, but she could imagine the flush in it now, the thrumming of his heart. Vaudeline handed him the vest, letting her hand trail over his. Did he think it an accidental caress?

"How about Miss Wickes?" he said. "Is she—"

He stopped, cut himself short, as though his senses had finally returned.

He knows, Lenna thought. *He knows I am behind him.*

When she'd imagined this moment, it had unfolded slowly. A step or two, a slow turn. But it was nothing of the sort. At once, Mr. Morley spun on his heel like an animal, like prey catching a predator's scent on the wind. As he turned, Lenna's skin prickled, the sensation of a thousand pins inside of her clawing their way out.

He glanced down at her hands. "Miss Wickes," he said, gazing at the candlestick. She'd not yet raised it. He might have thought she merely intended to light it, or he might have sensed her more sinister aim. "I see you're ready for the séance, at least," he said, looking her up and down.

Over his shoulder, Vaudeline stood very still, the prop vest hanging limply in her hands. She gave Lenna a single, slow nod—a silent go-ahead, communicated with only her blazing eyes.

"I won't be joining the séance, actually," Lenna replied, her voice cracking.

Mr. Morley cocked his head to the side. "Pardon?" He turned slightly, looking to Vaudeline for an explanation.

Lenna seized the moment. With every ounce of fury she could muster, she lifted her arm. She let out a forceful exhalation—how long had she been holding her breath, anyway?—and swung the candlestick down and around, battering it against Mr. Morley's cheek and the bridge of his nose. As she swung, Vaudeline's words echoed in her ears: *You will only get one chance, you understand.*

A crack sounded—bone, or brass?—and then came his savage wail of outrage and pain, the most horrifying sound she'd ever heard. He squeezed his eyes shut, tears instantly seeping from them. He crumbled to the floor with a yowl.

Lenna eyed the door while Vaudeline—still shivering in her chemise—reached for a coat. Yet this single moment proved a delay too long. From his prone position on the floor, Mr. Morley reached out a hand and gripped Vaudeline's ankle. Even in the dim light, Lenna could make out the whites of his knuckles, the fury on his face.

He would not be letting go of Vaudeline—that much was clear.

Lenna let out a cry, covering her mouth with her fingers. She'd failed. She had not hit him hard enough.

As Vaudeline tried to kick her way out of Mr. Morley's grip, she mouthed two silent words to Lenna. *Go. Now.*

There wasn't time to think, not now. They'd talked about exactly this situation. Lenna ran from the room, not bothering to look back a final time at Vaudeline. She couldn't bear the inevitable expression on her face, whether pride or tenderness or dread. Nor could she bear to look another moment upon Mr. Morley's bloody glower.

She must only get out, get out. She rushed from the room and moved the bookcase easily into position, knowing that within she'd locked the woman she most wanted with a man she couldn't trust.

All of this, for Evie.

Still, she'd done it. She'd bought herself time, and she'd paid a heavy price for it, not the least of which was Vaudeline's safety. Lenna needed to use this opportunity wisely.

She hurried toward the servants' door, the one she and Vaudeline had used since their arrival at the Society, always accompanied by

Mr. Morley. She pushed it open a few inches, glancing outside into the dark alleyway. It was empty, save a pair of carts stowed to one side. She slipped out the door and sauntered along the back wall of the building, moving as stealthy and silent as a cat.

After a moment, she reached the heavy wooden gate, the entrance to the stables. The mews.

Above this, the window of the second-story living quarters shone with the light of a low lamp. *Bennett's awake*, she thought. He'd be waiting, after all, to take them to the séance in a short while. Lenna hurried into the mews, which smelled of fresh hay and oiled leather. At once, she let out a sneeze.

She spotted a narrow, wooden staircase leading up, the wall on one side lined with bridles and bits hanging on pegs. At the top of the staircase, she knocked on the door. She waited, blowing hot hair into her hands, wondering about Mr. Morley's condition—and Vaudeline's.

The door opened. If the handwritten note wasn't proof enough, this certainly was. Bennett could not be deaf, not if he'd heard the knock on his door. "You're not deaf at all," Lenna said, her breath low.

Bennett shook his head. "No," he said, glancing at the empty steps behind her.

She followed his gaze, then frowned. "Why did you open the door? It could have been Mr. Morley standing here."

"I heard you sneeze."

Perfectly sensible. Lenna gave a nod, then: "Tell me what you know."

"Where is—"

"Please," she said again, more insistent this time. "I only have a minute or two. Mr. Morley—what was he lying about?"

Bennett let out a long exhalation, leaning his weight against the door frame. "She and I were friends," he said, his mouth set hard.

"She?"

He nodded. "Evie." His voice was raspy and thick, like he hadn't used it in many days.

Lenna blinked. "You knew my sister?"

"Yes. Though, I didn't realize she was your sister until earlier today, when you spoke so directly to Mr. Morley about it." He shifted his weight from one foot to the other. "We met a couple of years ago. I sometimes drove my father's coach to make extra money, and Evie was once one of my passengers. We became friends. Then, early last year, she told me the London Séance Society had posted a vacancy for a driver. Why she watched the Society's vacancies, I haven't the slightest idea. The pay was— is—very good. The vacancy said that they'd recently become involved with a newly formed charity supporting the deaf, and thus they would give preferential consideration to applicants who fell within that category." He splayed his hands, then let them fall. "It's really not a hard act to put on."

She shook her head, incredulous. "You're in good company. Much about the Society is an act."

"Yes, well, after a few weeks of working here, Evie began asking me questions. What members took the omnibus, where they went, what they talked about. She always wanted to know what I'd overheard. She occasionally paid me a few coins for the information."

This was a surprise. Lenna understood Evie's motives for wanting to know about the Society's techniques, but it sounded as though her curiosity into the Society's inner workings—the who and the what—went even deeper. "Did she say why she wanted to know?"

Bennett shook his head. "Never. Though, I didn't push the matter. I'd always liked Evie and saw no reason to meddle in her business."

Lenna glanced back down at the staircase, glad to find it empty. But still, Bennett hadn't answered her question. "Your note said Mr. Morley was lying. What is he lying about?"

"Evie's involvement with the Society. He said she did not partake in any séances, which is downright false. I spotted her—
though she was disguised—in front of 22 Bow Street before
their séance last summer. And one or two other times. Mr.
Morley and Evie would always walk into the affairs together.
I'm sure I caught her sneaking into the Society's back door once
or twice, too."

This was not new information, and Lenna fought off a growing sense of impatience. She forged on. "Why did your note say
You must get away from him?"

Bennett pursed his lips. "I have always wondered if something happened between Mr. Morley and Evie on the night of
All Hallows' Eve. Evie told me she'd intended to sneak into
his crypt soirée, which I knew many of the Society members
planned to attend. She asked if I had any idea when Mr. Morley would be arriving at the party. I wasn't sure when he would
call for me, but she seemed quite concerned that she might run
into him while there. I didn't understand why on earth she
would want to avoid him at the soirée, given how much time
they spent together.

"Mr. Morley acted odd that evening, too. I asked him when
I should return to pick him up from the party. To my dismay,
he instructed me to leave the coach, telling me I would need to
make my way home some other way. He said the soirée would
go late, and he'd drive the carriage home himself. It made me
very nervous—the horses do not like him one bit—but it is
the Society's coach, the Society's horses. What could I do but
agree?" Bennett gave a small shrug, a defeated look on his face.
"All of these strange occurrences that night, and now your sister, my friend, is dead.

"I'm sure Mr. Morley knows something," he went on. "After
that night, he spent days in his study. I heard the other members talking about how he would not leave, how he took his
meals there, slept there." Suddenly, he frowned. "Where is Mr.

Morley, anyway? And the séance, is it still...?" He checked his watch. "We should be leaving in only a few minutes."

She'd heard enough. "Thank you for this," Lenna breathed. "I wish you—" she paused, looking Bennett hard in the eye "—I wish you the very best."

"Where are you—"

Lenna didn't hear the rest of his question. In a few moments' time, she was down the staircase and back out in the alleyway, rushing toward the Society's servant entrance again.

Stepping inside, she froze. At her left, down the corridor where Vaudeline and Mr. Morley were locked in the room, came a thunderous battering against the door, then a string of expletives. It was Mr. Morley's voice. He was awake, alive, trying to beat his way out. Lenna paused a moment, fearing she might retch, hoping desperately to hear Vaudeline's voice within, even a cry.

She didn't. Not so much as a breath.

Lenna didn't waste another moment. She turned right, headed for the staircase. She took the steps two by two, far easier in breeches than it would have been in a gown. Still, she slipped once, landing hard on her knee. She forced herself upright, her hands damp with tears she hadn't realized were falling from her cheeks.

Furious and determined, she made her way to the library. Given Bennett's comments about Mr. Morley spending days locked in his study after All Hallows' Eve, she had to have a look around.

She didn't have a candle, so at the top of the staircase, she felt her way along the passageway. Ahead, a wall of glass revealed the library. Just yesterday, Mr. Morley had said his study was at the back of it. It was a detail he'd been unwise to share.

Time, she thought, willing the word through the floorboards and down into the room where Vaudeline and Mr. Morley were locked inside. *Buy me time, Vaudeline, to look around.* If she could, that was. She hadn't heard Vaudeline a moment ago, and it wasn't lost on Lenna that in his crazed state, Mr. Morley might have already gravely harmed her. But if Vaudeline couldn't buy Lenna time, the bookcase in front of the door would. The barricade Mr. Morley had put up himself. Had he any idea it would ultimately be used against him?

The library door was locked. She paused for a moment. Then she turned her body, drew back her arm, and thrust her elbow toward the door's glass pane. With an ear-piercing crack, it shattered. She reached her hand through the jagged opening and turned the lock.

Inside the library, the far wall consisted of windows. Lenna rushed forward to one of them and pulled back the drapes; enough light came in from the street to see her way around. Book stacks rose around her. There must have been a thousand volumes in this room, if not more. As she walked through the center aisle, she bumped into a wooden footstool, cursing at the sudden sharp pain in her shin. She could feel a welt forming instantly, but she pressed on, making her way to the back of the library—to Mr. Morley's study.

Might there be a sign of Evie somewhere inside? Her notebook, or an article of clothing?

She reached a closed door—the only door, from what she could tell. This must be it. She pushed it open.

Stepping inside, Lenna frowned. The meager space could hardly be called a study. It was more so a cupboard: windowless, with a small desk, a few framed items, and a sofa pushed against one wall. It wouldn't take long to search, at least.

She began first with the desk. It was an old mahogany thing, heavy-looking and scratched all over. An oil lamp sat on top, matches close by, and Lenna didn't waste a moment lighting it. The desk, newly illuminated, was scratched and scuffed. It had not been well taken care of, but nothing in this room seemed to be. Pitiful for a vice president, really.

She began with the papers on top of his desk. Receipts, logs, memorandums, letters. She recklessly sifted through them, not bothering to pick up the ones that fell to the floor.

She then went to the first drawer. A half-dozen dip pens rattled and rolled when she yanked it open. Several bottles of ink, black and blue, were pushed to one side. A small tray held tarnished and stained nibs, and beside this was a blotting pad covered in fat, black ink rings. She pulled the drawer from its brace and set it aside, onto the carpet. She searched the opening in the desk, feeling around for anything loose. Nothing.

Next, she searched the second drawer, but the contents were just as menial and uninteresting: thick stacks of blank parchment, spare candles and matches, a handkerchief, a pewter hip flask. Underneath the flask were a few pamphlets of smut. She sifted through them quickly, not bothered by the vulgar images. She set this drawer on the ground, too, beads of sweat now forming at her hairline.

The third and final drawer revealed nothing other than a folder annotated *Morley Estate Papers*—family accounting records of some kind?—and a thin book, the frontispiece of which read, *Woman Disrobed: A Curious and Amusing Love Tale*. She removed the contents, setting them aside.

She began to cry. There was no sign of Evie here, and it seemed foolish now, the notion that Mr. Morley would keep any sign of her around. Either way, Lenna couldn't stomach the idea that everything they'd uncovered about the Society had led to this—a place of no answers, no resolution.

She pulled the third drawer out of its casing, ready to search behind it. But as she removed it from its brace, she frowned. This drawer, despite being empty now of its contents, was heavy. Much heavier than the other two drawers had been.

She pressed down on the bottom of the drawer, and one edge of it tilted downward slightly. Frowning, she pressed harder on that side of the panel.

The opposite side popped upward, enough to slide her finger beneath. Carefully, she maneuvered the panel up and out of the drawer.

She gasped. The drawer's bottom panel was not the bottom at all. It was a false panel; there was a hidden compartment beneath.

A trick. Like so much else Lenna had discovered here.

Two books were visible inside the hidden compartment: a burgundy, vellum-bound portfolio, along with the corner of a notebook—one she recognized. Her heart began to thud. Months ago, after Evie's death, this was precisely the sort of discovery she'd hoped to make when rifling through her sister's things.

She lifted the notebook out, running her hands over the shiny black cover as though it were a relic. She'd been in search of this since Evie's death—it had been conspicuously missing from her desk and her satchel—and here it was now, in Lenna's hands.

She handled the notebook delicately, her eyes welling with fresh tears as she pried it open. Evie had never let her peek inside, and Lenna couldn't ignore now the feeling that she was invading her dead sister's privacy. Still, she flipped through a few pages, looking through Evie's copious notes and lists. It was clear, very soon, that the notebook contained detailed notes about the ruses and procedures carried out by the men of the London Séance Society, indicating exactly how and when she'd identified each technique.

In some places, Evie's handwriting was blocky and thick, made with a forceful hand. This was how she wrote when she was angry—she'd written more than a few letters to Lenna in similar print over the years, sisters' squabbles.

Lenna held the notebook at arm's length for a moment, knowing she'd located the most damning evidence yet against Mr. Morley. Here was one of Evie's most personal possessions, hidden in a trick drawer of his desk. This all but proved he'd been involved, somehow, in her death. A crime of passion seemed more and more likely.

Lenna turned a page of the notebook, surprised to see an envelope tucked within. But her surprise turned to alarm when she spotted the return address on the envelope and the postmark.

The letter was from Paris, sent to Evie in the second week of October, two weeks before her death.

And the letter was sent by none other than Vaudeline D'Allaire.

This was unsettling. Vaudeline had never once said a word about having written to Evie a mere fortnight before her death.

Lenna flipped the envelope over and yanked out the letter, not caring when one of the creases tore between her fingers. She held the letter to the lantern light, racing her eyes across the faint ink strokes. The scrawl was recognizable, for she'd seen it countless times in recent days, studying alongside Vaudeline.

On the matter of the exposé and the Society secrets to be shared with The Standard Post *in the new year...*

Lenna frowned. The *exposé*? This didn't make any sense. She pulled at the collar of her jumper, which had begun to rub uncomfortably at her skin. She was so bloody dizzy all of a sudden. Dizzy and misreading things, obviously.

She glanced at the bottom of the letter, verifying the sender of the letter—Vaudeline—and then she reread the first sentence. *On the matter of the exposé...*

"I don't understand," Lenna muttered to herself. Her hands went numb. Her vision grew dim, blurry. In the low light, distorted and swirling with tears, she scanned the letter, making out only fragments.

...impressive work, your months of information-gathering from the outside and the inside, and your skillful seduction of Mr. Morley...

...you simply must find a way to filch the burgundy portfolio—it could be the coup de grâce—and submit it along with the exposé...

...I cannot do so, being in Paris as I am...

...vengeance for Eloise and to set all of this right...

Lenna began to tremble so hard, the letter fell from her fingers and floated to the ground.

Exposé. Vengeance. Evie had not been working with the Society at all. She'd been working *against* them.

Lenna thought of Evie's strange comings and goings before her death, the diligent research and note-taking about questionable spiritualism tactics, and Evie's attendance at every Society lecture.

It hadn't been fanaticism, as Lenna had originally believed.

It hadn't been collusion with criminals, as Lenna believed mere hours ago.

It had been sleuthing, reporting.

But although this revelation redeemed Evie's motives in an instant, it shifted the blame elsewhere: Vaudeline. According to this letter, she'd encouraged—even begged—Evie to take her place in investigating the Society after she departed London and went to Paris. This letter was a plea for action. *You simply must find a way,* it read.

Lenna fell to her knees and kept reading.

> *...very close associates with Mr. Volckman, which meant I went to many of the cellar parties hosted by his friend Mr. Morley. The most lavish and legendary of these are his All Hallows' Eve parties—crypt soirées, they're called. Why not disguise yourself as you have been and slip into the party?*
>
> *...the parties always begin at seven. By nine, the room will be rollicking with drunkards. Sneak in then, and make your way to the vermouth vault. Mr. Volckman once revealed that this is where Mr. Morley keeps his most private documents. I can guarantee nothing, but I wonder if perchance the portfolio is there...*

The message here was clear: *get your hands on the portfolio.* In this letter, Vaudeline had called it the coup de grâce. Lenna looked at the second item that had been hidden in the drawer. It was, indeed, a burgundy portfolio. She lifted it now, turned it over in her hands. Perhaps it contained information about the strategies wielded by the rogue men within the organization, written in Morley's own hand? Damning evidence, surely.

Whatever the case, it was obvious that Vaudeline had used her friendship with Volckman, and knowledge of Morley's parties, to send Evie into a dangerous predicament. She'd encouraged Evie to do the dirty work. The infiltration. The digging. The writing of the exposé, the snitching of the portfolio, the delivery of both to *The Standard Post*.

And this dirty work had gotten Evie killed.

"No, no," Lenna said, still on her knees on the floor. She bent forward, thinking she might heave, and retraced the last few weeks, beginning with the moment she'd arrived on Vaudeline's doorstep. She had told Vaudeline that her sister, Evie Wickes, had been killed. Vaudeline had invited her in immediately, independent of her normal cohort schedule. She'd then gone on to expedite her training, anything to seek vengeance for Evie as quickly as possible. Lenna had chalked it up to sympathy for a former student—perhaps tinged with something more, an affinity for Lenna—but now she wasn't so sure.

Intentional or not, Vaudeline had sent Evie into the snake pit with these men. Lenna recalled how Vaudeline had begun crying after receiving Mr. Morley's letter, announcing Volckman's death. In that moment, it must have dawned on Vaudeline that, in her hunt to identify the Society rogues, she'd sent *two* people to their deaths.

Everything was distorted through this new lens of truth. Every interaction Lenna and Vaudeline had had in the weeks past—their closeness, their vulnerability, the affection between them—what of it had been real? She considered, again, Vaudeline's adept acting on the drive to the brothel earlier today. A sense of unease had taken root in Lenna even then, knowing how well Vaudeline had tricked the men. Lenna should have listened to that feeling.

How very much Vaudeline had kept hidden. Lenna would

have preferred the truth about Evie to a lingering kiss on the cheek. She would have exchanged every hand-hold, every expectant glance, for even a mote of honesty from Vaudeline.

Lenna didn't know Vaudeline at all, not in light of this news. She seemed as much a liar as the men of the London Séance Society themselves. Who was the woman downstairs, really?

For a moment, Lenna forgot where she was—in this suffocating room, this Society of lies, this city where her sister was killed—and her vision began to swirl and twist. She felt terribly alone, knowing her only ally—Vaudeline—was no longer an ally at all. She was, instead, a stranger. A liar, a withholder, a master of deceit.

Worse, she was a liar for whom Lenna had just confessed her feelings. *It is you I want*, she'd said to Vaudeline a short while ago.

But not anymore, not after this. Lenna didn't want any part of Vaudeline.

She set the letter and Evie's notebook aside. Unable to resist a moment longer, she lifted the vellum-bound portfolio, pried open its cover, and began to read the book Evie and Vaudeline had so desperately wanted to get their hands on.

27

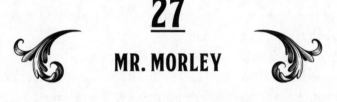

MR. MORLEY

London, Sunday, 16 February 1873

I should have noticed Lenna's absence the moment I stepped into the storage room, but when I saw Vaudeline in a state of undress, lust obscured my senses.

The pain and shock of what happened next prevented the formation of any memory of it. I sensed something behind me, turned quickly, and asked a question—which I cannot recall—of Miss Wickes.

When I came to my senses a moment later, blood seeped hot from my nose and onto my hands. I reached for the thing nearest me, Vaudeline's ankle.

As soon as I could stand, I threw myself toward the door, tried to push it outward—and then I dropped my hands at my sides, dumbfounded. She'd barricaded us in, the same way I'd done.

I threw my body at the door, dizzy and sputtering expletives. Looking down at my breeches, I made the horrifying realization that I'd urinated myself after I'd been struck. Vaudeline remained against the far wall, her back pressed against it, a timid look on her face. She looked to be weeping, maybe.

I thought I heard the click of a door—the one leading outside, to the back alleyway. If it was Miss Wickes, I hoped she meant to run home, to get out of here. Yet I wondered if she was smarter than this, and it terrified me, the idea of what she might be after: the library, my study.

I kicked harder at the door, and a crack formed slowly around the knob. On and on I went for minutes. If I could only break part of the door away, then reach through and try to maneuver the bookcase out of position...

How long would the door hold? I glanced around, wishing for something sturdy to slam against it. Suddenly, a cracking of glass came from somewhere above me. *The library*, I realized, almost crying out.

I rushed for the chair at the side of the room and slammed it against the door. I did this for a few minutes, but it was less effective than my own shoulder, and one leg of the chair broke in two. I threw myself against the door once again, aware that every passing moment was one in which Miss Wickes might uncover the hidden compartment beneath the third drawer of the desk.

On that rainy afternoon in October, as I finished with the post—excited about the two new inquiries praising Evie's work—I frowned. Something had caught my eye a few yards away, underneath the sofa where Evie and I had been just last night. It looked very much like *another* envelope. Had one fallen from my pile? Impossible, unless it had scampered its way across the room. I set down my letter opener and crossed the room to retrieve it.

I read the front—the sender and addressee were neatly printed by hand, in block letters—and at once, the palms of my hands grew clammy. The letter was addressed to Vaudeline D'Allaire, and the sender was none other than Evie Wickes. It was stamped, ready for the post. And the envelope was quite thick. Around the edge of it were little illustrations, sparrows and birds' eggs.

I furrowed my brow, looking again at the sofa. Last night,

Evie had set her leather satchel very near where I'd found the letter. It must have slipped out.

I blinked a few times, considering my options. I could return the unopened letter to Evie next time she visited. Or I could drop the letter in the pillar box myself; I needed to send off some Society post today, anyhow.

But there was a third option.

I walked to the door of my study and latched it. Then I thrust the blade of my letter opener into the envelope and tore it open.

I withdrew the missive inside, six pages in all, and began to read.

I'd known, upon reading the first paragraph, that the contents would be grim.

As your former student, I feel as though I must share this information with you. I have found myself in possession of information relating to the London Séance Society, and I have determined that some of the mediumship activities performed by the organization are in no way legitimate, licit, or moral. At least one of the men within the Society is little but a nefarious actor and swindler, and I have spent the better part of the year compiling notes for a lengthy, anonymous exposé which will reveal these behaviors in detail, including names, dates, and locations where possible.

My doubts about the Society originated more than a year ago, after the death of my very best friend, Eloise Heslop. The Society performed her séance, and I thought it suspiciously lacking in validity. I had a few other hunches about them, too. I intended to sneak into the Society headquarters once or twice and perhaps glean some information about their real activities.

What I did not anticipate was being swept up into these activities myself. But the closer I got to the inside workings of the place, the more I realized how deep the schemes went. What began as

*frustration and resentment following Eloise's séance soon evolved
into more. I am, to put it simply, horrified at what I've discovered.*

*I am in a unique position to author such an exposé, having
attended (in disguise) multiple lectures and séances put on by
the Society. Further, I was sent on assignment to several wakes
and funerals, at which I was tasked with seeking out wealthy
mourners and praising the reputation of the organization. In
fact, I didn't praise much of anything at all, but rather remained
mostly in silence, paying my respects. I then forged a pair of letters to the Society vice president who'd sent me to these affairs,
making him believe the mourners did, indeed, want to commis-
sion the Society's services.*

*I can only feign my way through this for so long. I intend to
send my exposé to* The Standard Post *in the new year. The
Society has marred the art of spiritualism and turned it rotten,
but this is not even the worst of it. They abuse the vulnerable,
particularly women.*

She went on to list more than twenty of the Society's tactics
and techniques; this alone took up more than half of the letter.
The schemes were detailed, terribly precise. I knew them all—
by God, I had been the one to share them with her.

As I read, the words on the page in front of me blurred, so
consumed was I by disbelief, by fear. I'd thought Evie greedy,
like me—thought she yearned for success and fortune, just as
the Society did, and would scam and feint her way there.

But *this*? This meant she'd been playing an act the entire time.
I recalled her enthusiasm about the paid accomplice idea, and
how she'd begun to laugh when she realized what I was offering her. How shamed I was now. I should have been able to spot
my own kind. The only difference between me and Evie was
that, as a woman, she could work her blade into my Achilles'
heel: my lustfulness.

My stomach lurched as I remembered something else. *I find it exquisite,* she'd said to me, very early, *the ways in which you are different.* How encouraged I'd been by this, the idea that not every woman in London was repulsed by my birthmark. Yet now I believed it a lie. A lure. This blow to my self-respect—I'd actually begun to believe myself desirable—was as bad as the letter itself.

I am in a unique position to author such an exposé, she'd written. *A unique position,* indeed—a double entendre if there ever was one. I eyed the corner of my desk where Evie had been perched many times, garments twisted and pulled to the side.

I kept reading the letter, and while I hadn't believed it possible, the contents grew worse.

I have been discreetly following one of the members since the beginning of this year, a departmental vice president, Mr. Morley.

"My God," I uttered, recalling our first encounter, when Evie had dressed as a boy and attended the lecture on ectoplasm. I'd had a vague sense of recognition that day, like maybe I'd seen her once or twice around the city. I should have trusted that instinct.

I've noticed that Mr. Morley sometimes carries with him a small burgundy portfolio. I've come to suspect that this portfolio might hold damaging evidence against the Society—evidence of their most severe deeds, written in their own hand.

As I read these words, my stomach curdled.
The portfolio. She'd spotted it.

I intend to continue pursuing Mr. Morley and hope to safely pilfer the portfolio. Once I have done so, I will submit it with my exposé. Though I will submit it anonymously, I am confident he will know that I am the author. Once the exposé has come to light, I will need to seek asylum for some time—possibly months.

Perhaps you could permit me to join a second cohort, this one in Paris. Might this be something you'd entertain?

As a final note: I have always wondered about your swift, discreet departure from London. I wonder if you were onto a similar trail? Nevertheless, I hope that this letter comes as welcome news to you. A form of vengeance against men who manipulate and take advantage of mourners. Vengeance, after all, is the principle on which you've built the whole of your career.

I look forward to your response.

Sincerely, your devoted friend and student,
Evie R. Wickes

I set the letter down, chilled. Then I looked at the pair of inquiries I'd read moments ago with such delight. She'd forged them. And now that I looked closer, I could see it: the penmanship of each letter bore similarities to the other. The same slant of hand, for one. I'd been a fool to not spot it at once.

What else might Evie try? I would put nothing past her now.

My clothes, still damp from the October rain, felt cold as ice against my skin. "I let her frolic among our secrets," I muttered to myself, mortified. For as many times as I'd stripped down with the woman, I suddenly felt as naked—as exposed—as I'd ever been.

I stepped to my desk, lifted my fist into the air, and brought it down hard. The force of it reverberated around the room, shaking the thin walls. The Society's printed mission statement, affixed to the wall in its wooden frame, dislodged and plummeted to the floor.

28

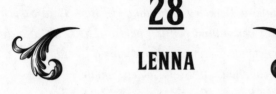

LENNA

London, Sunday, 16 February 1873

Portfolio in hand, Lenna took a few cautious steps toward the lantern, sidestepping the heap of papers and the drawers she'd set aside. She angled the portfolio toward the light, studying it more closely.

It had no lettering or markings on the outside; it was conspicuous in its subtlety. On the inside cover was a small annotation: *TLSS Special Arrangements.*

It wasn't a printed volume but rather a collection of newspaper clippings and assorted ephemera toward the front, followed by brief handwritten notes at the back. Lenna began with the clippings: obituaries and death notices and, strangely, a number of reports about marriages, inheritances, and property deeds relating to wealthy London families. In the obituaries, someone had underlined the names of surviving wives and children. Odd, but it aligned with what she'd come to suspect about the Society. They preyed on the rich.

She turned to the sheets of parchment at the back of the portfolio, noting that the pages contained names, each with a short paragraph below.

Lenna turned to a page at random, an entry made more than a year ago, and quickly read.

Mr. J. Flanders, Berkeley Square, thirty-one years old. Newly married to Henrietta, twenty-nine, only child and heiress of Lord Stevens. Estate at Berkeley a wedding gift from Lord Stevens, plus significant per annum pension paid to Henrietta. No children. Flanders tends to leave the bank late on Tuesdays, dines 8 o'clock at the chophouse west of Golden Square.

Member candidate oathman to secure: Mr. Steele.

Estimated payment to Society per annum: £550.

Case reviewed & agreements signed 4 September 1871.

Lenna frowned at the strange entry, the focus of which was clearly on the wife, Henrietta, and her wealth. Who had made this note? And why the specific details about Mr. Flanders's comings and goings?

She turned a few pages to read another.

Sir Christopher Blackwell of Lincolnshire, now resident of Westminster.

At this first line of the entry, Lenna's breath caught. Everyone in London knew of Sir Christopher Blackwell's death late last February. The newspapers had reported heavily on it, given his renown. Police had determined that he was bludgeoned in his study. The culprit was never caught.

Lenna turned back to the handwritten entry.

Blackwell recently broke hip; homebound for foreseeable future. Spends most time in his study; direct entrance on north end of house.

Member candidate oathman to secure: Mr. DeVille.
Estimated payment to Society per annum: £830.
Case reviewed & agreements signed 18 February 1872.

Lenna's skin began to tingle. Something was very wrong about this. An entry about Blackwell—including mention of his study, and a way into it—mere days before he was found dead in that very room? Too coincidental. A deep chill overtook her. Steeling herself, Lenna flipped through a few more pages.

Mr. Richard Clarence, department omnibus driver. Has made repeated threats to reveal inside knowledge he's acquired about the Society.
Member candidate oathman to secure: ——
Estimated payment to Society per annum: ——
Case reviewed & agreements signed: reviewed 8 March 1871, no agreements.

"My God," Lenna whispered to herself. These entries, all of them, were pointing to one terrible truth. No wonder this folio was hidden under a false bottom of Mr. Morley's desk drawer. It was a *kill book.*

Lenna didn't waste a moment turning the pages again, making her way to the very back of the portfolio—the entries from October.

There was another name she sought. Not an earl, not an heir, but someone far more important. Someone who'd infiltrated the Society, uncovered a few of its secrets, and was hot on the trail of the biggest one yet.

Flipping through the portfolio, at last Lenna spotted the entries made in October. She'd spot Evie's name, surely, at any moment...

But then she frowned. September, October, even into November. Evie's name wasn't in the book at all. It didn't make

SARAH PENNER

sense. Knowing that Evie had in fact been working against the Society, Mr. Morley would have had a perfect motive to kill her. Not to mention, her notebook was hidden in his desk. Why, then, hadn't he recorded her name in his folio?

She didn't have time to consider the possible reasons. Drawing herself upright, Lenna took a steadying breath. She'd discovered the Society's real secret. This portfolio was potent evidence against Mr. Morley; no wonder Evie wanted to get her hands on its contents. *The police and the papers would enjoy a look through this,* Lenna thought to herself. *Evie would have known it, too.*

At once, Lenna resolved to snag the portfolio and Evie's notebook, exit via the servants' door, and make her way straight home. There existed the possibility she would encounter Mr. Morley on her way out—if he'd broken his way through the door, that was—so she grabbed a letter opener sitting in plain view on the desk. She was so overcome with fury and grief, she believed she could thrust the letter opener right through his eye, if needed.

And what of Vaudeline—was she safe? Alive? Indisposed? *It doesn't matter,* Lenna thought to herself. *She betrayed me—and Evie, too.* Her throat tightened, and she decided she didn't care what became of Vaudeline tonight. Let her die. She should have gone after the Society herself, not asked a student to do the dirty work for her.

Lenna glanced down once more at the letter Vaudeline had written to Evie. It mentioned *Eloise.* How odd. What had Evie written to Vaudeline about her? Perhaps she'd mentioned that the men of the Society had performed a ridiculous séance after Eloise's death, or perhaps this had been about—

Lenna gasped. The kill book. What if Evie had suspected *this?*

She turned, quickly, to the entries from January 1870, the month Eloise had died. There, at the bottom of the page, was the entry:

Mr. L. Heslop, significant financial interest in the rail and steel industries. Walks every evening approx. 7:30 along southwest edge of the Regent's Park; enters via York Gate and walks counterclockwise along boating lake.
    Member candidate oathman to secure: Mr. Cleland.
    Estimated payment to Society per annum: £1,000.
    Case reviewed & agreements signed 12 January 1870.

Lenna could not believe it. She hiccuped through tears, tempted to throw the book against the wall. Mr. Morley had killed Mr. Heslop. And because Eloise had accompanied her father unexpectedly on his walk, she'd been murdered, too.

For years, Lenna—and Eloise's family and friends—believed Mr. Heslop had died trying to rescue his daughter from an icy slip into the lake. How very wrong they'd all been.

But there was another puzzle to solve. This entry mentioned Mr. Cleland, the man whom the widowed Mrs. Heslop had gone on to marry. He was known to have accrued significant gambling debts, and he was listed in this entry as the *Member candidate oathman*, owing an enormous fee to the Society each year.

This could only mean one thing. Mr. Cleland was a pawn in a costly arrangement. Marrying a wealthy widow meant not only the repayment of his debts, but the ability to pay the Society such an extravagant annual fee. The Society had coordinated the whole thing, it seemed. And they'd probably begun the process at Mr. Heslop's séance. No one had been permitted to attend, other than Mrs. Heslop.

This news was so appalling, Lenna found herself glad that Eloise wasn't here to learn the sordid truth.

Mr. Morley was not only a fraudster and manipulator. He was not only a wielder of illusion, a master of pretense. He was doing much more than conducting fraudulent séances across the city while letting his men take the women to bed.

He had a second scheme, this one much worse: he'd murder rich men, marry off their widows to one of his Society members—*oathmen*, he called them—and siphon a nice annual fee off of the arrangement.

A wicked business model if there ever was one.

But how could Morley use a séance to convince these widows to remarry one of the oathmen? This, Lenna didn't understand.

She pitied Mr. Richard Clarence, too, the omnibus driver who'd threatened to reveal Society secrets. Mr. Morley obviously wasn't above killing his own—anyone who threatened the exposure of their inside knowledge. Bennett had said he was hired early last year, so it must have been soon after Mr. Clarence was killed. Mr. Morley had posted a vacancy for a deaf driver, supposedly because the Society was involved with a related charity, but this was a claim Lenna no longer believed. Mr. Morley needed a driver who posed no threat to his secrets.

Evie, Eloise. Mr. Morley had taken from Lenna all that she'd once held dear. She gripped the letter opener harder.

It was time to go, but she'd just heard something. A thump.

She froze, mouth gone dry. Another *thump*, then a shout. The abrupt break in silence startled her, and the portfolio slipped from her hand and onto the floor.

Someone had just come in through the library door, the one she'd broken into. Someone was making their way in, toward her, at this very moment.

She looked quickly around—no window in here, no exit except into the library—and then her eyes fell on the portfolio at her feet. It had fallen open to the most recent page.

She hadn't seen it until now, but there was a name she recognized, hastily jotted on the most recent page. Two names, actually:

Vaudeline D'Allaire and Constable Beck.

And beneath this:

Loc: Volckman séance.

Lenna gasped.

Was this why Mr. Morley had called Vaudeline back to London? Not because he needed her help solving Volckman's murder but because he intended to kill her? She was a loose end, after all. She'd known about the rumors and clearly corresponded with Evie in ways that Mr. Morley had discovered.

And Constable Beck—now, he seemed little more than one of Mr. Morley's pawns. Vaudeline's agreement to return to London had been due, in large part, to the protection he could offer her. He'd been an instrument for Mr. Morley to coerce Vaudeline back to the city.

The air left Lenna's lungs as she took a moment to absorb all she'd just discovered.

Then she spotted what was written next to this entry. In the right-hand margin, written in fresh ink, were three words: *and Lenna Wickes.*

Mr. Morley must have made this note only within the last day or two. She'd been an unexpected companion, after all. He hadn't known he would need to deal with her, not until she'd arrived on the docks with Vaudeline. Lenna had unknowingly put her own life on the line. She should have parted ways with Vaudeline the moment they'd arrived in London.

But she hadn't. She'd become embroiled in this mess, in Mr. Morley's schemes.

And now he intended to kill her—all three of them—at tonight's séance.

29

LENNA

London, Sunday, 16 February 1873

It took Lenna a moment to realize that the sudden musty, salty odor in Mr. Morley's study was the smell of her own sweat.

If Mr. Morley wanted her and Vaudeline dead, it could only be because they'd come too close to the truth about Mr. Volckman. Or Evie. Or both. He meant to squash all they'd learned thus far or all they might learn at the séance.

Lenna might have spent more time reviewing the pages, if not for the approach of footsteps in the library. It could only be Mr. Morley or Vaudeline.

Vaudeline. The woman for whom Lenna had fallen in recent days. Yet all the while, Vaudeline had been withholding vital information about Evie and the Society. She was no longer a friend. And though her name was also mentioned in the portfolio, Lenna didn't care. *Let her suffer at the hands of these men,* she thought. *But not me. I will get out of this, somehow.*

Quickly, she bent down to close the folio. If Mr. Morley found out what she'd discovered, he wouldn't let her leave this building alive. She kicked it aside, back toward the desk, as though she hadn't read it all. She held the letter opener steady, waiting.

The door to the study flew open, revealing the wounded face of Mr. Morley. He was alone, his body hunched forward as though he might collapse. Lenna let out a scream. He looked half-dead, his face an inflamed mess. Dried blood clung to the collar of his shirt. A stench hung on him, sweet and pungent, like urine. His left cheek had swollen to twice its normal size, leaving his eye partially closed and seeping tears. Still, there was no mistaking his expression. The eye that remained open was wide and fearful, full of hate.

Had Evie known this gaze? Had she seen it, too, in her last few moments?

Mr. Morley lunged for her, taking a long step, but just as Lenna raised the letter opener in defense, he came to a sudden stop. His gaze was on the floor, the chaotic mess of papers and books all around. "What in the bloody hell...?" he said, a dumbfounded look on his face. He scanned the pile of disarray—was he searching for the folio?—and then his eyes fell on it, adjacent to the far wall. Immediately, he crossed the room to retrieve the kill book.

He held it up. "Did you look at this?"

Lenna clung to the letter opener with such force, the muscles in her hand began to cramp. "No," she lied. "I didn't look at much of anything after finding this." She pointed at Evie's notebook on the desk. "You lied to me in the omnibus earlier today. Why do you have my sister's notebook?"

He couldn't answer because, behind him, there came a flurry of movement as Vaudeline rushed into the room, half limping and still in her chemise, which was now bloodied and torn. She stopped next to Mr. Morley, her face tear-streaked, bands of dried blood smeared across her pale arms. Was it her blood or his? It shouldn't have mattered now to Lenna, but still, she gave Vaudeline a quick look-over. Nothing looked broken, no serious wounds.

"Why are you here?" Vaudeline cried aloud, looking at Lenna. Only then did it occur to Lenna how unexpected this discovery must have been for Vaudeline. Earlier, Lenna had told her that after escaping from the storage room, she intended to make her way to safety. Instead, she'd gone to Bennett's residence above the stables, and then she'd returned to the building, breaking her way into the study.

"I'd like to know the same," Mr. Morley said, coming closer now, his step unsteady. He looked as though he might faint, and a few beads of perspiration dripped from his cheek.

"I found it," Lenna said again. "Evie's notebook, full of details on the Society's schemes. I know about the exposé she planned to submit." Her chest heaved as she took in small gasps of air. "Vaudeline's letter, I saw that, too." Lenna turned slightly, facing Vaudeline head-on. "You're as much a liar as any of them."

The look of dismay and confusion on Vaudeline's face was so whole, so complete, Lenna might have applauded her for it. *A perfect actress*, she thought.

"A *liar*?" Vaudeline choked out.

Before she could reply, Mr. Morley yanked the letter opener from Lenna's hand in a swift movement. The pain was instantaneous. She let out a cry and looked at her hand, only to find that the textured handle had torn open the delicate skin of her palm.

Mr. Morley threw the letter opener across the room. It fell to the ground, out of reach. "Your sister was a rat," he hissed, eyeing a rubbish bin nearby, like he might vomit. "Surely you already knew of the exposé. She would have told you. She told you everything."

He was wrong about this, but Lenna kept it to herself.

Vaudeline stepped toward Lenna and grabbed her hand, putting pressure directly on the fresh wound. Lenna winced, feeling the sting of salty skin on the gash.

"We need to wrap this," Vaudeline said. "It's bleeding badly." She looked to Mr. Morley, eyeing the handkerchief protruding from his pocket. Without asking, she pulled it out and secured it around Lenna's hand. She didn't concern herself with gentleness or delicacy; she drew the fabric taut, not bothering to ease up even when Lenna grimaced.

Lenna hated how she liked it, how something in the pit of her stomach kindled at the rough affection. She dared to watch Vaudeline as she worked, studying the dip of her collarbone and the edges of her lips, all the little details she wished to know better and now never would. How conflicted she felt in that moment. She abhorred this woman as much as she wanted to drink her in, the sweetest of poisons.

"There," Vaudeline finally said, tying the knot. Through her lashes, she pulled her gaze upward to Lenna, as though trying to silently communicate something.

Lenna looked away. She couldn't trust this woman anymore, couldn't look long into her eyes, that deep place where so much warmth had begun to bloom between them in weeks past.

Or so Lenna had believed.

Suddenly, she wanted to scream. She wanted to shake Vaudeline by her pale, tender shoulders, to tear her hands through those decadent curls. What a charlatan she was! A seductress, a tease, one without bounds or morals.

Lenna turned to the desk, locating Evie's notebook. Within it, she retrieved the letter, the one Vaudeline had written to Evie. She unfolded the letter, ready to hurl accusations, when Mr. Morley stepped forward and snatched it from her. He thrust it into a pocket.

The abrupt movement took Lenna by surprise. She froze, frowning at him. It was incriminating, she realized. The letter and Evie's notebook shouldn't have been in his possession at all. "Did you take her things before or after you killed her?"

He chuckled. The bleeding from his nose had ceased. "You think you have it all figured out, don't you?" He checked his watch, motioned to the door. "We're late," he said. "Beck will be waiting."

He was referring to the séance, of course. Lenna's blood ran cold.

Mr. Morley walked across the room, toward the sofa. He bent down, feeling along the base of it, then withdrew a small revolver hidden underneath. He gave it a quick wave, displaying it to the women, then tucked it into his inner coat pocket.

That's how he intends to kill us, Lenna thought to herself.

He made his way to the door. As he went, he retrieved a canvas bag hanging on a wall, and then he stuffed the folio inside. He approached the desk and grabbed Evie's notebook and Vaudeline's letter, too. Putting them inside his bag, he slung it over his shoulder and beckoned the women forward.

Still, Vaudeline had no idea what was in store—that Mr. Morley intended to strike both of them from the record, to get them out of the way before they could do any more damage. Lenna couldn't tell her this, not with Mr. Morley in the room.

But even if she could tell her, would she?

Would she try to save this woman who'd betrayed her?

30

MR. MORLEY

London, Sunday, 16 February 1873

I grabbed a spare pair of breeches from my study and followed the women downstairs. We made for the washroom first, where I changed my clothes and splashed cold water on my face, wiping away as much dried blood as I could. Vaudeline did the same, but she still wore her bloodied chemise, so we returned to the storage room, where I waited outside—revolver in hand—with Miss Wickes while Vaudeline changed into something decent.

As I stood there, I studied the splintered door, which only minutes ago I had forced my way out of. It had taken more effort than I'd anticipated, to be sure. I'd kicked against the wood until, finally, a piece splintered outward. Using my hands, I broke off as much of it as I could, providing a gap wide enough for me to push the bookcase to one side.

Out I'd gone, not giving Vaudeline so much as a glance. I knew, instinctively, that she would follow me. She'd want to protect Miss Wickes, help her in whatever way she could. All those looks they'd exchanged—the unquenched longing between them was evident. I knew that wherever Miss Wickes went, Vaudeline would not be far behind.

On the second floor, the library door stood open, its glass pane shattered. Beyond the stacks, I could see a faint light glowing from the back of the library. *My study.* I cursed, rushing in, vaguely aware of Vaudeline's footsteps close behind me. I wiped a hand across my eye, a viscous secretion smearing its way across my palm. Too early to be pus, too thick to be tears.

I stepped into my study, glowing golden on account of the lantern I kept on my desk, which Miss Wickes must have lit. Immediately, my worst fear materialized, for a pile of papers and broken drawer pieces lay in disarray on the floor.

Protectively holding a letter opener in front of her, Lenna began the accusations immediately: the ruses, the notebook. But then, to my great surprise, she turned on Vaudeline and said something about the letter, the one with Vaudeline's signature at the bottom. *You're as much a liar as any of them,* Lenna accused her.

At once, I ripped the letter opener from Lenna's hands.

Anything to sever the moment, to divert this line of discussion.

In October, after discovering Evie's damning letter to Vaudeline, I left my study, astonished by what I'd found.

With long, slow strides, I made my way through the corridors and down to the foyer. I passed a few meeting rooms, aware of my name being called out once or twice. I ignored them, not interested in conversation. I had an errand to run—an urgent one, well suited for a vice president who tended to take a few liberties.

I signed out of the log in the foyer, taking a moment to study the tiny scribbles and slanted numbers on the page in front of me. I thought I ought to study the pages for a few minutes, pick apart the handwriting. Perhaps even practice a few rows of text.

I went out the front entrance, intending to go around back,

in search of Bennett. But as I made my way down the paved sidewalk, I paused, turning at the sound of hurried steps.

"Mr. Morley," Evie whispered breathlessly, pulling up alongside me.

Was I surprised? Not a whit. I'd expected something like this. How many hours had she watched and waited for me out here?

We stood on the street in plain view, she in her usual disguise. Still, much was changed about her today. Her blue eyes were fearful, her porcelain forehead wrinkled with concern. I knew precisely what this was about.

"Evie," I said, giving her a wide smile. "What is it? You look terribly worried."

"There's s-something—" She stammered over her words and shoved her hands into her pockets. "I dropped something inside. I'm not sure where it fell out." She gave the building an uneasy glance.

I tilted my head to one side, as I might if speaking to a woeful child. "The letter?"

She went rigid. "Yes. A letter, ready to be posted. You found it?"

"Indeed. I posted it a short while ago, along with a stack of Society business." I arched backward, soft pops traveling down my spine as I stretched.

At once, the creases in her forehead diminished. "Oh," she said, giving a small nod. "Very well, then. Thank you."

I wasn't finished with her, not yet. "I couldn't help but notice the letter was addressed to Miss D'Allaire. Forgive me, but curiosity has gotten the best of me. Do you and Vaudeline correspond regularly? I know you've long idolized her, but perhaps I did not realize to what extent..."

Evie gave a nervous laugh and looked at her feet. "Not really, no, but having trained under her some time ago, I considered it time to give her an update on my progress."

"Quite an update, then, judging by the heft of the letter."

She tugged at the edge of her sleeve. "Yes, I suppose."

We locked gazes on each other, and it was not lost on me: this was the first time I had truly laid eyes on Evie Rebecca Wickes. The first time I'd seen her for who she really was. *A rat.*

What of the last few months had been real, and what of it had been illusion? Briefly, I considered inviting her inside, but as I surveyed her small, boyish frame, I found I could hardly muster the desire. Nothing stirred within me.

Curious, how quickly the truth could extinguish affection.

"Well, I wish you a good day," I said at last. Evie paused— was she surprised I had not invited her in?—and then she wished me the same before walking off in the direction from whence she'd come.

After she'd gone, I placed my hand over my chest. I pressed lightly on the padded letter within my coat, smiling at the rustle of paper within.

Evie's damning missive would never go to the post.

It would never cross the Channel.

She'd learn this, soon enough.

31

LENNA

London, Sunday, 16 February 1873

What a sight they must have been, loading into the Society's omnibus! Mr. Morley with a bruised and swollen face. Lenna with a white handkerchief wrapped tightly around her right hand. Vaudeline lugging her case of séance books and *outils*, a tiny smear of dried blood along her hairline. She must have missed it when they'd cleaned up in the washroom.

Bennett sat at the front, reins in hand. There was no need for the slate tonight, as they all knew the destination. As Lenna settled herself in the carriage, her small bag of personal items at her side, Bennett turned to give her a wary, fearful glance. He let his gaze linger on her bandaged hand; his lips parted, like he desperately wanted to say something.

They drove north and then west, toward Grosvenor Square, coming upon a narrow street lined with brick residences. Several times, Lenna side-eyed Mr. Morley, scheming how she might lunge for him, pull the gun from his pocket. But he kept his arms crossed close over his chest, and besides, what could she do with the gun once she had it in her hand? She didn't know how to fire a gun—had never so much as touched one—and throwing it aside would only buy her a few moments of time. Even if she managed to put several yards between herself and Mr. Morley, he'd reach for it, and a bullet could cross such distance in a second's time.

Eventually Bennett pulled the horses to a stop, and out the omnibus window, Lenna spotted a man standing on the cobbled walkway nearby. Constable Beck.

Vaudeline leaned in. "You're not supposed to be here at all," she said stiffly. "But seeing as how you disregarded our agreed-upon plan, you might like to know that the cellar where we're going is beyond that walkway, down a set of stairs."

Lenna didn't give her the courtesy of a nod, though privately, she appreciated the explanation. She'd all but forgotten that Vaudeline had attended a few parties here.

Mr. Morley retrieved a lantern and a box of matches from underneath one of the carriage seats. With the lantern lit, the group began walking toward Constable Beck, their heads down against the cold. They went down the pathway, eventually coming upon the set of steps Vaudeline had mentioned. Next to the stairs was a ramp, which must have been for the purpose of wheeling casks in and out of the cellar.

"My God," Constable Beck said, eyes alighting on the three of them. He studied Mr. Morley's injured forehead, his swollen eye. "Your face. What on earth happened?"

"I could ask the same of you," Mr. Morley spit back, pointing at the pronounced scar on Beck's chin.

Constable Beck let out a laugh. "I wish I had a better story to tell. Fell off a pony when I was sixteen."

Lenna had always assumed a more sinister reason behind the constable's scar. Mr. Morley must have, too, for he moved on quickly. "I dealt with a—situation," Mr. Morley said. "Involving these two, as if it's not obvious enough."

"Does that explain why you brought your gun?" Beck asked, nodding to the weapon protruding from Mr. Morley's coat.

"Certainly a more valid reason than you have."

"You know my reservations about tonight."

The hostility between the men was palpable, but the gun on Constable Beck's hip did give Lenna a measure of relief. Despite being a member of the unprincipled Society, he was more of an ally than Mr. Morley. His name was in the kill book along with hers, and this situated them on the same side of things.

Mr. Morley unlocked an exterior wooden door and led them inside. He proceeded to walk the perimeter of the cellar, lighting the candle sconces affixed to the stone walls every few yards. He went to the hearth next, but Vaudeline advised him not to light it; she'd cover it with black linen shortly, anyhow.

With the room newly illuminated, Lenna widened her eyes in surprise. It was as much a crypt as any room she'd ever been in. The arched stone ceiling above them lent a feeling of encapsulation, coffin-like. The far end of the room lay in shadow, and Lenna could imagine passages leading deeper into the cellar. Still, despite the ominous impression of the room, there was something sensual about it. The candles softened the space with a flaxen glow, and the air felt damp—breath-like, as though someone panted close by.

Lenna estimated there were fifty casks, maybe more, lined up in the cellar. On a few shelves sat dark glass bottles—gin, whiskey, wine. A few of the labels indicated these hailed from exotic, far-off places like Spanish Town and Siam. No small expense, surely.

As Lenna stepped deeper into the room, her breath constricted. A vibrant, cobalt blue aura flashed in her left eye. It had become almost familiar to her now, these strange mirages in her vision, paired with tingling fingertips and a queasy stomach. Standing near one of the walls, she placed a hand against the cold stone. *It is knowing what Mr. Morley intends to do*, she thought. *It is knowing that I am on my own. I am the only one re-sponsible for saving myself.*

She let this notion sink in, then shook her head.

No, there is something else. Something more...peculiar.

The blue aura flashed and whirled in her vision. She thought back on the other times she'd experienced this: the morning of Evie's death; during the séance at the château; and, most recently, after reading Bennett's note about Mr. Morley. She'd always chalked it up to nervousness, but now she wasn't so sure. She remembered Vaudeline's comments about her natural skill in mediumship, even her question on the night of the château séance: *Did you feel anything strange tonight when performing the incantations?*

Lenna had lied and said *no.*

Now she wondered if there was something else to this. Perhaps this feeling was less about nerves and more about intuition. An inherent—if unfounded—awareness that something significant would soon be unfolding.

"This way," Mr. Morley said, motioning for the group to follow him. They walked a few yards, passing underneath a low archway. Here, the air smelled of must and dirt. Behind a row of barrels was a circular wooden table with several candles on it. "Shall I light these, Miss D'Allaire?"

"No," she whispered. "I will use my own candles." She approached the séance table, placing her bag on the stone floor. But when she set it down, the *thump* was hollow, as though it had been set upon wood, not stone. Frowning, Vaudeline tapped her foot against the floor. "Is there another room beneath us, Mr. Morley?" she asked.

He eyed her warily. "Indeed. There's a subcellar where I keep the vermouth. It's a few degrees cooler; the spirits age better down there. It is also where I found...well, it is where I found Mr. Volckman's body."

Vaudeline frowned. "Why, then, are we not doing his séance down there?"

"There is hardly room for four of us to stand, much less arrange a table and chairs. But as you've just noticed, the subcellar is indeed directly below us."

Vaudeline nodded, satisfied with this. Then she removed a few items from her bag. At the same time, she leaned close, placing her lips close to Lenna's earlobe. "Why did you call me a liar?" she hissed.

Lenna had never heard such chill in her voice. Perhaps Vaudeline was angry that she'd been found out, or maybe it had something to do with Lenna's change of plans. After hitting Mr. Morley with the candlestick, she was supposed to have escaped. Vaudeline knew this séance would be dangerous and had wanted to protect her. Yet Lenna hadn't escaped. Instead, she'd gone deeper into the Society's belly of secrets. Maybe Vaudeline feared she'd be responsible for the death of a third person, too.

"The exposé was your idea, wasn't it?" Lenna whispered back, full of loathing. "I saw the letter. You told Evie to come here. You got her killed." She let out a shaky breath, knowing that she could never take back what she was about to say. "I hate you for it, and I will never forgive you." She blinked back tears, regretting nothing.

"I never wrote your sister," Vaudeline said, mouth set hard.

Lenna narrowed her eyes. She was a liar. Vaudeline would never admit to it; this woman thrived on lies and fraud, no better than the men.

Mr. Morley stepped close to them, and the women ceased their conversation. He approached the row of casks and hovered a few moments, inspecting things. All the while, Lenna kept her eyes close on him, wondering if—and when—he would reach into his pocket. Constable Beck seemed to be keeping a close

eye on him, too, though Lenna couldn't understand why he was
so suspicious of his fellow Society member.

Vaudeline began to lay out several of the things she'd packed
before they left the Society: her book of incantations, the cedar
box of basic *outils*—candles, gemstones, feathers, black ribbons—
plus a pair of pens, a journal, and a small inkwell. Lenna wondered, briefly, if one of the pens inside the bag was the same
pen Vaudeline had used to craft her letter to Evie.

"Where shall we sit?" Lenna asked Vaudeline, unable to look
her in the eye.

Vaudeline glanced at the table, but Mr. Morley interrupted
before she could reply. "I think the two of you ought to be
over here," he said, motioning to the chairs closest to the row
of casks where he stood.

"Whatever you'd like," Vaudeline replied.

Lenna took her seat, then withdrew her notebook from her
bag and flipped to a blank page. She fought the urge to write
a scathing note to Vaudeline and slide it to her. *You knew what
Evie was up to from day one. You're as much of a swindler as they are.
What other lies have you kept from me?*

As Lenna's heart burned with these questions, so too did her
lower belly, the place in her body that fueled want and desire.

*Has the memory of my fingers on your scar tormented you, like it
has me? Has your every glance, your every touch, been a lie? Have you
enjoyed making me your fool?*

But she wrote none of this. Instead, she shook her head and
blinked away the heat in her eyes.

Vaudeline went to the hearth and draped a length of black
linen over it. Then she laid another length of fabric over the
table. She smoothed it with her hands, and then she lit three
candles and placed them equidistant between the sitters.

Everyone took their places around the table.

The candle in front of Lenna flickered. From her nervous
exhalations, probably. She clasped her hands tightly together,

thinking vaguely of the last time she'd been in this scenario—the château in Paris.

That night had been disappointing in more ways than one, but at least no one had wanted her dead. She looked across to Mr. Morley, holding his gaze, wondering when he would reach for the revolver in his coat—wondering if she would be fast enough to knock it from his grasp.

Vaudeline took a long breath.

The séance had begun.

32

MR. MORLEY

London, Monday, 17 February 1873

My placement was perfect: the cask, the slow-match fuse, the table, the chairs in which the women now sat. The gun nestled against my chest was just there for show, to keep the women in line.

The retired firemaster on Fleet Street had sold me the length of slow-match—a fuse cord of cypress bark and flax, soaked in a saltpeter solution—which burned at the rate of one yard every three hours. Carefully, he'd measured and cut the precise length I needed. I trusted his counsel. He might have gone rogue and rheumy in his old age, but he'd worked with the Society before and had proved himself proficient and reliable.

"Thirty-five minutes, not a minute more," he'd warned, handing over the cord. Then, "What will be at the end of the fuse?"

"A barrel of black powder," I said.

He gave a low whistle. "Anyone within the immediate vicinity will be gravely injured."

"Yes," I replied. This was precisely my aim.

I'd quickly and discreetly set the fuse when the group walked into the cellar, noting the time as a minute past midnight. This meant that by the time we were seated, the cask—less than a yard away from the women—had twenty-eight minutes until explosion. Less than.

I would make an excuse to step outside in twenty minutes or so, cellar key in hand.

Stone walls, wrapped tight around wooden casks of whiskey, gin, and wine: the blaze would be extraordinary. I almost wished I'd be there to see it, to delight in the single-swoop resolution of every last nuisance. Let the secrets burn, and the meddlers, too, Vaudeline being the worst of them.

She'd always been a loose end.

I was fortunate that her séances often went awry. The papers had long reported on the chaotic nature of Vaudeline's affairs, and this would be but another séance gone wrong. A spontaneous fire, one lucky survivor—*me*.

Yet how much easier it all would have been if Beck did not have a revolver at his hip and a shrewd eye on me. Did he suspect me of something? I wasn't sure. As tempting as it might have been to shoot them all the moment we stepped into the cellar—I could make my way out and wait for the explosion to rid the room of evidence—Beck was a better marksman than me. If I dared to pull my gun, I feared he'd be on me like a dog.

Thus, I'd put on the act until the last possible moment.

Now, as Vaudeline opened her book—presumably to begin her first incantation—I studied Miss Wickes from across the table. She was as much a varmint as her sister.

I could not let any of them learn what had happened down here on All Hallows' Eve, how it had all transpired. Certainly, I couldn't let them take such information up the stairs and out of the cellar. Which was why I'd make sure that none of them left this place alive.

Vaudeline pulled her book close, drew a long breath.

I checked my watch again, heart thundering.

Twenty-four minutes.

33

LENNA

London, Monday, 17 February 1873

"*C ircum hanc mensam colligimus…*"

    Vaudeline recited the first verse of the *Ancient Devil's Incantation* in perfect Latin as Lenna looked down at her notebook on the table in front of her, following along with the English translation of each verse.

The *Ancient Devil's Incantation* was seven quatrains—twenty-eight lines in total. Lenna had heard Vaudeline recite it several times during their practice sessions together, always impressed with her impeccable breath control. Now the words came out of her in a steady, rhythmic melody.

We gather around this table in a spirit of mourning and mystery.
Seeking truth and light, fortify us against malice and malevolence.
Defend us against rogue spirits and evil intentions…

Lenna squeezed her eyes shut, treating the incantation like a prayer. And yet it wasn't demons she was scared of tonight. It was the man across the table.

Vaudeline went on for nearly a minute. Just as she'd done in the parlor-turned-séance room at the château, she'd established a quiet control in the space. This was power, subtle and unlike anything Lenna had witnessed a woman exert over a man. In London, there were so few ways for a woman to wield this sort of influence.

Once finished, Vaudeline took a long breath and turned her palms upright. Dampness glinted off them like tiny salt crystals: she was sweating, flushed. "We will now hold hands and join the circle," she said softly, "and I will perform the *Invocation*— the summoning of all spirits."

Across the table, Constable Beck swallowed hard. "This is when strange things may begin to happen, is that right?"

Vaudeline nodded, and the party exchanged wary glances. Reluctantly, Mr. Morley reached his hand across the table. Lenna eyed it like a snake, then let him place his fingers against hers. It was good if they were all holding hands, she reasoned—it would keep his hands off his gun.

Lenna then placed her left palm in Vaudeline's, feeling the dampness of their skin intermingle.

"Our departed friends," Vaudeline began, "*transite limen*. I invite you now to cross the barrier that separates us. Commune with us, *intrate*…"

The *Invocation* went on, easy and controlled, but suddenly Lenna felt unwell. Vertigo seized her, followed soon after by a ringing in her ears—a humming like summer insects, low and constant. She squeezed her eyes shut, flashes of white blinking behind her eyelids, aware of a strange tightening sensation around her throat. Tendrils of confusion wrapped around her. Instinctively, she yanked her hands away, shoving them into her lap, and blinked her eyes open just as the cellar went completely dark.

Every candle in the room, sconces included, had just extinguished simultaneously, as though in a synchronized theater act. There was not a flicker to be found as the odor of sulfur began to swirl. Lenna had never been in a room so dark.

Across the table, expletives and muttered words from one of the men. Next to Lenna, the clatter of a box, then the strike of a match as Vaudeline relit one of the candles. In the faint glow, Lenna looked down at the table. Innumerable handprints, waxy and wet-looking, were visible on the black linen tablecloth— some large, the size of a man's hand, and some small, as though belonging to a child.

"Nearby spirits," Vaudeline whispered, lighting a second candle. "They are here. And quite a lot of them. I suspected this might happen, seeing as how we are so close to the old Tyburn gallows."

The gallows. They'd talked about this en route to the cellar: the risk of so many spirits, having been hung at nearby Tyburn, entering the room during the *Invocation*. How many were here now? How many martyrs and mothers and murderers and thieves?

"No one has been executed at the gallows for a century. More than," Mr. Morley said.

"*C'est sans importance.*" Vaudeline gave him a vexed look. "Irrelevant."

If Lenna needed something tangible, something to see, now she had it. This was no ploy, no illusion. She placed the tips of her fingers against the tablecloth where a handprint had just faded into oblivion. The linen felt warm, damp. She placed her fingers to her nose, sure she smelled something fetid.

"Christ," Mr. Morley said, voice trembling. "It is one thing to hear the rumors. It is quite another to experience it." A candle in the center of the table began to rise. Lenna gasped, only to realize that he had lifted it, brought it closer to him. He withdrew his pocket watch and checked the time.

Next to him, Constable Beck sat motionless, a petrified look on his face. His burly frame didn't much serve him tonight, Lenna thought.

"Very common to lose our light," Vaudeline said, striking another match to light the third and final candle. Still, the cellar was very dark without the sconces lit. "Let's proceed."

The party linked hands again, and Vaudeline resumed her recitation, her words slow and thick. Lenna gripped Mr. Morley's hand again.

A few moments passed. Through a haze of candlelight, Lenna looked upon Mr. Morley, studying his jawline. *How well I know it*, she thought. *How well I remember it! I can nearly taste his skin, the salt and musk.*

Lenna jolted upright in her chair, appalled by what very much felt like a...memory. Yet she had never tasted Mr. Morley's skin before. It could only mean she'd briefly experienced *absorptus*, the temporary entrancement sometimes suffered by séance participants. During their training, Vaudeline had said entrancement was marked by the intrusive inflow of thoughts that didn't belong to the medium, like memories, recollections, or knowledge of technical matters that the medium could not possibly possess.

The realization jarred Lenna. And how strange, that memory of Mr. Morley's skin! If the *absorptus* she'd just experienced was due to Mr. Volckman's spirit, then it left her wondering if his relationship with Mr. Morley had, perhaps, been intimate in nature...

Suddenly, the vertigo began again. Lenna grimaced, and within moments, her entire body began to tingle. From some detached place within, she was aware that something was attempting to penetrate its way into her chest, her skull. She was anxious for Vaudeline to move on with the séance. The *Isolation* phase would take care of this.

Lenna looked across at Mr. Morley again. *He trimmed his mustache recently*, she thought. *I quite like it this way; it accentuates the natural sharpness of his jawline. I'd be inclined to reach across the table and touch it like I used to—if I didn't hate him so much.*

Lenna bit her lip hard, the pain superseding the memory and bringing her back to her senses. She writhed in her chair, begin-

ning to feel stiff and sore in her bones. When would Vaudeline
move on to the next phase?

Faintly, the aroma of bergamot seeped into Lenna's nose. She
blinked, confused. *Bergamot?*

Then she gasped. The stiffness in her bones had gone as
quickly as it came on. She suddenly felt gloriously warm, nim-
ble. *Alive.*

She turned her head, glanced at the woman sitting next to her.
How entirely surprising—the woman was Vaudeline D'Allaire.
Her former teacher. Her idol.

At once, Vaudeline turned to look at her. "Lenna?" she asked
warily, looking her hard in the eye.

Lenna felt her head shake back and forth. *No.* She bit her lip
again, tasting blood, and tried to force herself up and out of this
absorptus entrancement, but found she could not do so.

The scent of bergamot continued to fill her nose.

"Evie," she heard herself say. "I am Evie, not Lenna."

Lenna had no control of herself; she was a mere witness now.

Something like joy—utter glee—sparked inside of her as
she reveled in embodiment once again. How terribly fun, this
strange affair!

In those brief few moments, Evie marveled at the sensations
she hadn't known for three months. Saliva damp and salty on
her tongue. The pressure of her toes against her shoes. A welcome ache in the muscle along the left side of her neck. How
beautiful the pain was now, its easy way of reminding her how
very splendid it was to be alive.

Still, Evie was not sure why they were all gathered in this
place or what exactly was unfolding at this table. She knew
only that she'd been called forth, invited to return by a powerful summons. Around her in the room, she sensed the presence
of benevolent others in the same realm as her. Dozens of them,
hovering and waiting.

"Suum corpus relinque," Vaudeline suddenly commanded, looking her directly in the eye. *Leave her body.*

No longer was Evie exhilarated. She suddenly felt scorned, unwanted.

She looked down at her hands. But where she'd once had long, strong nails, now she saw only bitten-down nail beds and pink, irritated cuticles. They looked just like Lenna's fingernails, always chewed down. A terrible habit, one for which she'd always chided her big sister...

She placed her hand to her hair, pulling a lock of it away from her face. It was long, honey-colored. Lenna's hair.

"Suum corpus relinque," Vaudeline commanded again, and this time she grabbed her hand, intertwining their fingers, and Evie could not resist the invisible force of expulsion that Vaudeline issued through their touching skin. She felt a great impact, like a slam against a wall, and then she was above the table, looking down at the flickering candles and the bowl of feathers and the young woman with tawny hair—her big sister, Lenna, eyes wide in shock and surprise, like a newborn baby seeing light for the very first time.

34

MR. MORLEY

London, Monday, 17 February 1873

How bizarre, the way things unfolded once the séance had commenced. First the requirement to hold hands with Miss Wickes and Constable Beck; then the extinguishment of every last candle; and lastly, the odd look Lenna gave me—one of familiarity, almost *intimate* familiarity.

All the while, my pocket watch ticking away, and my canvas bag nestled close by my feet. Within the bag: the folio. Evie's black notebook. And that letter to Evie, the one with Vaudeline's name on the signature line.

That October day, after Evie had inquired about her lost missive to Paris, Bennett dropped me off at the stationer's boutique, Le Papetier. The shop was in Chelsea, between a point-lace maker and a confectioner. The afternoon was bright, clear... promising.

I'd not been to this particular boutique before. I preferred to shop at the Hughes emporium for Society stationery, where I typically bought plain white paper and inexpensive bound tablets. Sometimes, I ventured to the specialty papermaker on the Strand for the three-ply trick paper. But this afternoon, I needed something especially fashionable. Something especially French.

Stepping into the shop, I might have mistaken the place for a perfumery. Unfamiliar scents swirled around me, all floral and nauseating.

A demure young woman approached, greeting me warmly. "May I help you?" she asked. Her hands were splattered with ink stains, quite in contrast with the shop front's bow windows, which were shined to perfection.

I cleared my throat. "Paper," I said, glancing around. Ceramic ink vessels and boxes of India rubber were neatly arranged on various tables.

"Of course." She brought me over to a wall made up of compartments, each with a stack of loose-leaf paper inside. White and dyed, of various sizes. Gilt-edged stationery and mourning notes were specially marked.

I thanked her, then started with the stationery at the very middle of the wall: midsize sheets with a light dye, no gaudy embellishments. I sorted through a few, finally settling on a pink-bordered octavo. I counted out ten sheets. In the event of a blunder.

I brought my selection to the front desk. "Quite feminine," the woman said, smiling. "Will you be needing envelopes?" At my nod, she led me to a nearby cabinet and pulled out a few drawers. "Gummed envelopes are in this drawer, and over here we have sealing wax and wafers." She withdrew an envelope with a small pink flower bud printed at one corner. "This would match nicely," she said.

I agreed. "Ten of them, too," I said.

She took them to the counter, then gave me an expectant look. "Will this be all?"

I paused a moment, then shook my head. "In fact, there is something else."

The woman tilted her head quizzically, her lips slightly parted.
"Yes?"

"French stamps. Might you have any on hand?"

"Stamps? Why, the post office can—"

"Not English-issued stamps," I interrupted. I glanced around,
glad there were no other patrons. I was nervous all of a sudden,
wanted only to be on my way. For all of the illusions I'd con-
strued, the frauds I'd fashioned, I'd never asked for this. "As I
said, French-issued. I thought, given the nature of your shop,
you are probably from France yourself, and—"

"I am, yes." She paused a moment, glancing at a leather bag
on the floor next to her. "But I don't understand. If you are to
post the letter from here in London, why do you need a French
stamp?"

I ignored her question and pulled a bill from my pocket, sliding it across the desk. She blinked a few times at it. I wagered
it was more than a month's pay for her.

Shortly thereafter, I walked out of Le Papetier. The tiny bell
on the door jingled when I left, terribly delicate and frail. Tucked
under my arm was a brown paper sleeve smelling of daffodils.
Inside the sleeve were ten sheets of pink-bordered paper, ten
gummed envelopes, and a single stamp. French-issued, bloodred.

I couldn't help then what I muttered under my breath.

A ruse for a ruse, Evie.

35

LENNA

London, Monday, 17 February 1873

L enna pushed her chair back from the séance table, dry-heaving.
She placed her head in her hands, letting the waves of nausea
roll through her.

Something extraordinary had just happened. The *absorptus*
phenomenon.

Vaudeline had read the *Invocation* incantation, and then everything had gone so dark, so astonishingly dark. Lenna had not
disappeared, not entirely, but she had been rendered powerless.
She'd not been in control of her own body, her own thoughts. At
least until Vaudeline had recited that strange *Expelle* injunction...

What surprised her wasn't that she'd experienced *absorptus*. It
was that the brief entrancement had been...Evie.

If Evie hadn't died anywhere near here, how had Lenna just
manifested any part of her? It was grossly against the tenets of
mediumship. Evie was killed in the garden of the Hickway
House, and thus she could not be conjured here. As Vaudeline
had said many times, spirits never traveled far.

She jerked her head upright. Upon finding Evie's body in the garden, her hair had been in disarray, and her skin bruised and blanched, which police—and therefore Lenna—believed was a result of a struggle in the garden.

But what if the struggle had happened elsewhere? What if the trauma to her body was due, in part, to being *moved* after her death? Lenna had never considered it, not until this very moment.

How badly she wanted to discuss this possibility with Vaudeline—but Vaudeline's face looked pained, and across the table, Constable Beck had begun to writhe in his seat, looking as though he, too, were fighting something off.

"Your throat," Constable Beck suddenly cried out. He reached his hand across the table toward Lenna, then pulled it back. Gone was his typically gruff expression. Now he looked so struck with fear, Lenna wondered if he might hurl himself from the room.

Lenna frowned: she did indeed feel something strange on the left side of her neck, damp and tender, and she moved her fingers toward the spot, only to pull them away and find them smeared with a trace of bright red sticky blood. She palpated the wound. It wasn't painful, nor did it go very deep, but it had formed spontaneously on Lenna's body. In the exact spot where Evie had been stabbed.

"Did s–someone hurt me?" she whispered. She looked up at Mr. Morley. Whatever strange thing had happened a moment ago, perhaps he had seized on her disorientation. But there was nothing suspicious about him. No gun lay on the table, no blood soiled his hands. He hadn't moved. None of them had.

She grimaced, trying hard to remember what she could about the experience she'd just had. She couldn't grasp a complete picture of it, but she could feel the lingering impressions it left behind: a sense of familiarity with this cellar, with Mr. Morley. A brief sensation of glee and freedom. Then the feeling that she'd intruded on something and was no longer wanted...

"I am going to be sick, I think." Lenna looked toward the

stairs leading out of the cellar. "I need to step outside, straight-away—"

A deafening clamor interrupted her. On a shelf some yards away, several wine bottles plunged to the ground. Amid the shattered glass, puddles of dark red wine dispersed, saturating the porous stone floor. Lenna eyed the puddle seeping toward her. Then she flinched as a tiny chip of stone fell onto her lap.

She looked up. A thin crack, several feet long, slithered its way across the stone ceiling.

"You cannot," Vaudeline said, her voice haggard. She nod-ded weakly to the broken wine bottles, the ceiling. "If any one of us dares to leave, this will get worse."

Lenna remembered what Vaudeline had said earlier that day, when the group had discussed the stages of a séance. Once the *Invocation* had been read, the séance was underway and must be brought to completion.

Now Vaudeline coughed hard, releasing her grip on the table. "The *Isolation* incantation," she said, voice weak. "I need your help with it, please. There is too much energy here, probably on account of the gallows, and I cannot—" She coughed again, then slid her notebook in front of Lenna and turned to a page. "Read this," she said, "but specify the name of Mr. Volckman. Quickly, Lenna. We need to clear the room of all but him. I do not want to have to resort to the *Expelle* injunction again."

Dutifully, Lenna took the notebook, all the while keeping an eye on Mr. Morley. He had still not made any moves toward her or Vaudeline, and she began to wonder when, exactly, he planned to pull his gun. He seemed overly concerned about the timing of things—that much was clear.

It was then that Lenna wondered whether his plan might not involve a gun at all. Might he have some other idea in mind? It disoriented her, the possibility that she'd misinterpreted his scheme.

Lenna pulled the notebook toward her, absentmindedly

touching her wound once again. The blood had begun to dry around the edges. *"'Omnes sunt cogniti,'"* she read aloud, glancing quickly at the translation written in the margin of the page. *We acknowledge all of you.* She read on, saying the Latin incantation aloud, surely mispronouncing certain words. *We acknowledge your pain. We acknowledge your desire to return. In a spirit of justice, we are here to commune with only—*

Lenna paused. Here, the incantation read *unum*—one. Lenna read this aloud, but silently in her mind, she replaced it with something else: *duos*—two.

The spirit of Mr. Volckman, she continued, while simultaneously thinking to herself *and Evie Rebecca Wickes.* It was less an incantation now, more so a plea. As illogical—and against doctrine—as it seemed, Lenna knew something very unusual had happened a short while ago. She had accessed Evie in some strange, inexplicable way, and she was not done with her yet.

Lenna finished reading the *Isolation* passage. In an instant, several of the sconces around the room spontaneously revived, flooding the room with a soft golden glow. Lenna felt the wound on her neck begin to itch, as though healing.

"Thank God," Constable Beck muttered, relief writ on his face. He slumped forward slightly, no longer fighting off whatever had plagued him a moment ago. He looked as though he might cry.

With the incantation behind them, Vaudeline, too, was visibly calmer. The sweat had disappeared from her brow, like a fever had lifted. "Thank you," she said, reaching for Lenna's hand, not minding the smear of blood on it. She gave it a squeeze, letting her fingers linger, and Lenna found herself suspended again between distrust of Vaudeline and absolute want of her.

"Now," Vaudeline said, "the *Invitation.*" It was the fourth stage of the sequence. "If you'll give me a few moments, please." She closed her eyes, lifted her face up to the low ceiling of the cellar, and began her slow recitation.

Lenna had not memorized this incantation, either, but as Vaudeline said the words, she silently repeated them to herself. She made just one change to the recitation: instead of *Mr. Volckman*, she said *Evie Rebecca Wickes*.

When Vaudeline finished, Lenna caught a movement across the table. Mr. Morley had just reached into his coat. It happened so fast, Lenna could hardly react. He withdrew his hand, something metal between his fingers. Lenna stood, ready to lunge for him—

But it wasn't his gun. It was a flask, tucked inside his coat. He put it to his lips and sucked hungrily from it. Lenna lowered herself back into her chair, pretending that she'd been shifting in her seat. As Mr. Morley twisted the cap of the flask back on, his fingers trembled. Lenna might have chided him for breaking Vaudeline's rule against drink, but it seemed a minor concern as things stood.

Vaudeline cleared her throat. "I'll proceed now with the *Entrancement* incantation, if we're all ready?" she asked the group.

Lenna gave a weak nod. She was as ready as anyone else at the table, which was to say not at all. The answer to Mr. Volckman's death was but moments away. In truth, she wished for a flask of her own.

"This is all going quite a bit faster than anticipated," Mr. Morley said suddenly. "Might we take a few minutes, have a stretch?"

Vaudeline ignored him and uttered the next incantation. *Introitus, concessio, veritas.* And just like last time, Lenna silently repeated the words, specifying the name *Evie Rebecca Wickes*.

Two séances were being performed tonight, but Lenna was the only one in the room who knew it. It was reckless, she knew, and dangerous and desperate.

After she finished silently repeating the incantation, she touched her fingers to her neck. Where the blood had dried a moment ago, now the wound had begun to weep again, sticky and trickling and warm.

A moment later, a jolt went through her, feeling very much like a wedge hammered between boards.

Lenna's hand moved toward Mr. Morley. She could not stop it, could not retract her arm even though she commanded it to do so.

"Hello," she whispered to him, her voice equal parts tease and hate. She ran a delicate finger along the top of his hand.

"Miss Wickes," he muttered. "What is this? What are you—"

Another jolt, and finally the signals coursing through Lenna's body—brain to wrist to fingers—caught fire, like a wick steeped in oil and put to flame. She pulled her arm back, horrified. *Evie,* she said silently. *Evie, you must ease up.*

Vaudeline had long said that entrancement was a form of dual existence, a split psyche. To Lenna, the sensation was more like a battle of wills waged inside flesh. She and Evie had always been equally strong-willed, equally stubborn. It was why they'd quarreled often, and it certainly didn't make for a pleasant interaction now.

At her left, where Vaudeline sat, Lenna sensed cold air and the acrid odor of something rotten. It gave her the impression of hostility and ugly, unresolved memories. She looked at Vaudeline; gone were her soft, nuanced gray eyes. Now her eyes were but featureless spheres of black. "Are you quite w—" she began to ask.

The woman in front of her interrupted, cutting her off, a glower in her eyes. "Evie. Hello again." Her voice had deepened, and her left wrist had suddenly taken on a grotesque appearance, jutting out at an unsightly angle.

Helplessly, Lenna heard the next words leaving her own lips. "Mr. Volckman, good evening."

At once, Lenna—or the part of her that existed now, somewhere in the far reaches of consciousness, surmounted by her dead sister—understood what this meant. Even if she didn't know how it had all happened.

Mr. Volckman had entranced Vaudeline.

Evie had entranced Lenna.

There were four of them now, in the bodies of two. And Mr. Volckman and Evie seemed to have a recent history.

Stage six, *Dénouement*, was next. Vaudeline, sitting next to her, would already be working away on Mr. Volckman's memory, trying to ascertain how he had died and who had killed him. She could be finished any moment, skilled as she was.

Which meant that Lenna needed to get to work. She didn't understand how she'd managed to conjure Evie here in this cellar, but she remembered what Vaudeline had said about repeat conjurings and teasing a spirit with embodiment. *The opposite of love*, Vaudeline had said. *Like putting a sparrow in a lush forest, but plucking its feathers so it cannot fly.* Lenna would never do that to her little sister. She'd use this single chance best as she could.

All Hallows' Eve, Lenna thought, knitting her brow together. *This room. You must have been here, Evie…*

Her heart thundered in her chest as she waited to apprehend a memory that she, Lenna, could not claim as her own. This was how Vaudeline solved murder crimes, after all—by accessing the memory of the deceased during entrancement and seeing it all for herself.

As Lenna surveyed the situation—the dual entrancement, the blood weeping from her neck, the acrid odor of death—it dawned on her that this was precisely the reason Vaudeline's séances were known worldwide for being so dangerous, so unpredictable.

She did not have much time. Once Vaudeline had ascertained the truth of Mr. Volckman's death, she would announce her *Dénouement* and recite the *Termination*. It would banish Mr. Volckman's spirit from the room, and Evie's, too. It seemed impossible that Lenna might glean the information she needed before Vaudeline did, but she had to try. She squeezed her eyes shut.

All Hallows' Eve, she thought again, the night she had walked along the Thames in search of shells and mollusks. The night she had stumbled upon the dead body of her sister. The night she had helplessly stood by while the police declared her sister yet another unfortunate victim of London's sordid underbelly.

And yet no sooner had Lenna dwelled on these memories than they dimmed and altered themselves. She couldn't recall if she'd found any mollusks along the river that night, but she remembered rushing down High Street toward Grosvenor Square with an important letter in her pocket...

Her eyes sprang open, and she let out a little laugh, feeling a flip in her belly like she'd just done a somersault. She looked down at her hands again—the same raw, bitten nails.

Yes, I am quite sure of it, Evie thought to herself. *On All Hallows' Eve, I was here. Not along the Thames at all. I'd been dressed in dark men's clothes so better to skirt any attention, Vaudeline's letter tucked into my coat. I'd sent her a letter mid-October, revealing the truths I'd learned about the Society. It was very nearly intercepted by Mr. Morley, but he said he'd posted it on my behalf. I was glad to receive Vaudeline's reply, postmarked at Paris on the nineteenth of October.* The parties always begin at seven, *the letter read.* By nine, the room will be rollicking with drunkards. Sneak in then, and make your way to the vermouth vault. Mr. Volckman once revealed that this is where Mr. Morley keeps his most private documents. I can guarantee nothing, but I wonder if perchance the portfolio is there...

The reference to a separate vault had taken me by surprise. I'd gone immediately to Bennett, asking if he had any knowledge of such a thing. Perhaps he'd heard Mr. Morley refer to it during one of his rides.

Indeed, said Bennett, there was a subcellar where Morley aged the vermouth. He gathered it was accessible via a door toward the back of the main cellar...

A strange odor—sulfur, wood—pierced the memory. Lenna

hadn't realized entrancement could be so delicate, so easily interrupted. Frustrated, she opened her eyes, expecting to see that one of the candles on the table had extinguished again. But to her surprise, all three remained lit.

She looked over at Vaudeline; her eyes flickered open. The odor had disturbed her entrancement, too. "Your letter sent her straight to her death," Lenna said now. "You told Evie precisely where to go, and at what time."

Vaudeline pinched the bridge of her nose. "What *letter*?" she replied, impatience in her voice. Had she been close to her *Dénouement*? "I haven't the slightest idea what you're talking about."

"Don't try to lie your way out of this," Lenna snapped back. She recalled Evie's memory, the one she'd just accessed. "Postmarked at Paris on the nineteenth of October. You told her to go to the vermouth vault at nine o'clock. Sound familiar?"

Across the table, Mr. Morley pushed himself out of his seat. "Uh…" he interjected.

Weakly, Vaudeline lifted her arm. Her inner wrist had turned a dull, mottled blue. She snapped a finger, glaring at him. "Sit," she demanded, pointing to the crack in the ceiling, "lest the entire room cave in. It would not be the first time it's happened."

Mr. Morley obeyed, and Vaudeline turned in her chair to face Lenna. "I did not, until minutes ago, even know this cellar had a vermouth vault." Then she furrowed her brow. "And the nineteenth of October? I spent most of the month in the medieval village of Lisieux, performing séances. I was not even in Paris on that date. How could I have sent a letter from the city?" Suddenly she bent forward, coughing, her eyes darkening again.

Lenna blinked, considering what this meant. *It was very nearly intercepted by Mr. Morley*, Evie had revealed in her memory. *But he said he'd posted it on my behalf.*

Very slowly, Lenna looked across the table at Mr. Morley. "You didn't post Evie's letter, did you?" She put her hands on either side of her forehead. "You forged the reply," she sputtered. "You lured her here." Just as he'd lured Vaudeline to London.

"How w-would—" he stammered, then shook his head. "What an absurd accusation."

Lenna turned to Vaudeline, remorseful, but she couldn't apologize. Vaudeline's eyes were closed as though she'd sunk back into her entrancement, willingly or not.

Lenna had called her a liar, let herself boil over with loathing. But how perfectly obvious it seemed now! For all the tricks Mr. Morley pulled, she should have questioned the authenticity of the letter the moment she found it in his study. She should have trusted the woman she'd come to know. She found herself retreating, trying to purge the animosity toward Vaudeline that she'd indulged in earlier that night while reading the letter in Mr. Morley's study. The letter wasn't real, she was now convinced. It was as good as a theater prop.

Following suit, Lenna closed her eyes, trying to sink back into Evie's memory. How far along was Vaudeline in Mr. Volckman's memory of that night? Did she know yet what had happened to him? But as Lenna tried to concentrate, the sulfuric stench in the room grew in intensity. "Do you smell that?" she asked, opening her eyes again, glancing either side of her.

Constable Beck nodded. "I do, yes." He lifted his hands in disbelief. "But what on earth is happening here? Who the bloody hell is *Evie*?"

Lenna could only imagine how confused he must be. Evie's name had come up several times now.

Before anyone could reply, Mr. Morley pointed to a candle sconce on the wall behind them. "The odor," he said, "is coming from that candle, licking against the wooden beam. God forbid, it catches the place on fire…" He stood from the table, taking a candlestick to guide his way. In her trance, Vaudeline couldn't stop him this time. He made his way around the casks to the wall behind Lenna and Vaudeline. As he went, he knit his brows together in concern.

He would have shot us already, Lenna thought to herself. She turned slightly in her chair, following him with her eyes. *I'm sure of it now: he has another plan in mind.*

36

MR. MORLEY

London, Monday, 17 February 1873

The bloody fuse had extinguished. I knew it the moment I smelled the sulfur swirling about the room.

I might have smashed my fist through the stone wall. This séance did not oblige malfunction.

The firemaster had promised thirty-five minutes. Not a minute more, not a minute less. I had, quite literally, set my watch by it. With the wretched fuse now smothered, I'd have to relight it and estimate how much time was left on the cord. The notion of approximations made me feel ill. This was a barrel brimming with explosive black powder, for God's sake.

Nevertheless, the act I maintained. I approached the candle sconce—which was not a threat to any wooden beam at all—and as I went, I eyed the slow-match fuse, irate. The middle of the cord had indeed inexplicably fizzled out.

I blew out the sconce. As I began to make my way back, I pretended to knock my shin against one of the barrels. Reaching down with a feigned cry of pain, I very carefully hovered my candlestick near the expired fuse and relit it.

The slow, low hiss began again.

The countdown had resumed. I needed to get out, and soon.

37

 LENNA

London, Monday, 17 February 1873

As Mr. Morley leaned over in pain, Lenna noticed something odd.

Whereas the other casks in the row had a bright blue stamp with the barreling date printed on one side, the cask near which Mr. Morley now stood had no date at all. It was, in fact, entirely unmarked.

Strange, she thought to herself. But before she could draw any conclusions about the matter, she begged Evie to bring the memory back, to start again.

No sooner had she shut her eyes than it recommenced, vibrant and intrusive.

Before the crypt soirée, I'd dressed in a new disguise, wearing some of Father's looser clothing items to make me look heavier than I was. In the event Mr. Morley and I crossed paths at the party, I hoped my new disguise would keep me inconspicuous. I couldn't risk him spotting me in my usual garb.

At about half eight, I made my way on foot to the cellar near Gros-

venor Square. I hid behind a few holly shrubs, watching the door. It was terribly dark, a new-moon night. I knew it was dangerous being out that night—on All Hallows' Eve, a new moon promised an increase in death rates—but I also knew the danger of letting these men go on with their havoc-wreaking across the city.

The number of partygoers exceeded my expectations. In a span of ten minutes, I watched as two dozen guests, maybe more, arrived and filed down the staircase, making their way into the cellar. A few wore simple costumes—bat wings affixed to bodices, faux tails clipped to trousers— but most were dressed in gowns and tailcoats, standard evening attire. There was a ramp to the side of the stairs—for the ease of moving casks, I guessed—and one man, obviously inebriated, forwent the stairs and opted to use the ramp as a sort of slide into the party.

When the church bells tolled nine o'clock, I made my move. A coach dropped off a group of five partygoers, and as they descended the steps, I filed in behind them, pretending to be part of their group. The noise and commotion were such that no one paid me any mind as I stepped over the threshold and into the cellar. A trio of musicians stood in one corner, playing violas and a cello. As I stepped inside, a liveried boy handed me a cup of mulled wine, which I was glad to accept. Another offered candied nuts. I scanned the room quickly—I did not see Mr. Morley. Then I turned my face downward, resolving to keep a low profile.

The letter had told me to make my way to the vermouth vault at the back. As I skirted the edge of the room, a pair of women eyed me strangely. Worried that my false mustache was not as convincing as I'd hoped, I moved on quickly, trying to keep my cup of mulled wine close to my face.

I pressed on through the throng of guests. A gentleman dealt a game of euchre to his mates. Next to them, an unruly group played snapdragon, plucking raisins from a bowl of burning brandy. Everywhere, fortune-telling cards lay discarded on the floor. I marveled at the merriment, thinking that on any other night, this was precisely the sort of party I'd have liked.

The crowd thinned the deeper into the cellar I went. I passed a couple kissing against the wall, and then ahead, I spotted a wooden door, inconspicuous behind a few wooden crates. With a quick glance behind me to ensure no one was watching, I opened the door and slipped through, now in the subcellar. The vault.

There wasn't much of a landing, and I gasped, nearly stumbling. Several candles were lit, placed every few steps. As I descended, my heart thundered in my chest. This adventure was far more dangerous than anything I'd yet done at the London Séance Society. I believed the Society's greatest secret was somewhere here in this unassuming subcellar. And I suspected that Mr. Morley was more than a liar.

I had a hunch he might be a murderer.

It had all begun with the drowning death of my dear friend Eloise Heslop and her father. The séance the Society performed for Eloise was laughable, yes, but what concerned me more than this was the hasty remarriage of Eloise's widowed mother to the insolvent Mr. Cleland, a new member of the organization. The way it all transpired seemed too...coincidental.

Still, I needed to get closer to the inner workings of the Society to determine if my suspicions might be true.

As I spent more and more time with Mr. Morley, I noticed that he occasionally carried with him a burgundy folio. He hid it in an inner pocket of his coat, but he removed his coat around me plenty of times, and I could see the folio sticking out, so near and yet so unattainable. Still, he seemed to take great care of it, and I couldn't help but wonder if it held notes about a more sinister side of the Society. If it were true, I badly wanted to get my hands on it.

He didn't always have the folio on him. I suspected he stored it somewhere for safekeeping when he didn't have need for it, but I hadn't any idea where this might be. Vaudeline's letter helped greatly with this. She stated that he kept his most private documents in his subcellar. It was the missing piece I needed.

I couldn't wait to have a look around.

While the soirée carried on above me, I spun in a circle in the subcellar, frowning. Where might he hide his things? There were no cupboards, no cabinets, no drawers of any sort. Just open shelves and glass bottles.

I reminded myself that this man was a master of disguise. If he had something to hide, why, he certainly wouldn't put it in a place as conspicuous as a cupboard or a desk. It might very well be hidden in plain sight, so I began to feel along the wall, my fingers searching for a loose stone.

"Pardon, sir, have you lost your way?"

I gasped, jerking my head upright. At the top of the stone steps was a man in shadow, silhouetted by the light behind him. "I've only just arrived, but surely we have not run out of vermouth, not yet," he added in a cheerful voice. He descended the first few steps, going on about another party, some family commitment he'd left early.

Then he came into view, illuminated by the candles placed on the steps. Mr. Volckman.

As he looked more closely at what I had been doing—searching the wall for something—his eyes narrowed.

He took the remaining few steps quickly. A moment later, he stood just in front of me. We were eye to eye. Just as I prepared to speak— I'd deepen my voice, futile as it might be—he reached out and grabbed the hat from my head, yanking it off. Strands of dark hair fell around my ears, and the false mustache wiggled loose.

"Who are you?" he asked.

I blinked up at him. A moment ago, I might have told him the truth about his organization, all I'd learned about his delinquent vice president. But now, given the heat in his eyes, I instinctively feared him.

I would drop Vaudeline's name, I decided. They were close colleagues; I'd seen illustrations of them standing side by side in The Spiritualist *magazine several times. If I told Mr. Volckman that I'd trained under her, perhaps he would show me some mercy for trespassing. "My name is Evie," I said. "I was one of Vaudeline's students, two years ago."*

At this, he frowned. "Vaudeline," he repeated.

"Yes. Your associate, your...friend."

He threw his head back and laughed. Then he stepped closer and tore the loose mustache from my skin.

I gasped, my upper lip suddenly on fire.

"She was a friend, once," he hissed. "Until she started meddling."

38

 ## MR. MORLEY

London, Monday, 17 February 1873

Lenna's accusation—*You forged the reply. You lured her here*—didn't bother me a whit. She would be dead in a matter of minutes. Soon, this old mess would be resolved.

As those last few minutes ticked down, I could hardly curb the relief sprouting inside of me, and I kept my head down, for fear someone at the séance table might catch me smirking. This night would be a fitting end to the department dilemma that had begun more than a year ago. January 1872, before Vaudeline left the city. Before Evie sneaked into the ectoplasm lecture. Before Volckman threatened to dismiss me.

It had been a time when the merrymaking was still terribly good.

But that all ended with a knock on my study door, that Tuesday so long ago.

I'd been sitting at my desk. At the sound of the knock, I checked the time. It would be Volckman, ready to discuss numbers. This was a recurring appointment, the first Tuesday of every month at eleven o'clock.

"Come in," I said, clearing off my desk. He'd have a stack of papers with him and would be looking to set them down.

But he stepped into the room with empty arms and a shaken, pale look on his face. He walked to the sofa, sighing as he sank into it. "I've just had a very uncomfortable conversation," he said, wringing his hands together.

I leaned forward, concerned. "With who? And about what?"

"Vaudeline D'Allaire," he said. "She's…hearing things. Around town. You know she has her ear to the ground."

I cleared my throat. "What sort of things is she hearing?"

He took a long breath, tilted his head to the side. "You've done good work with the department, Morley. I've let you do things Shaw could never get away with. I don't always understand your methods—your hoaxes and ploys—but you know my foremost concern is *reputation*, not truth. The two are entirely separate aims." He paused, let this sink in. "According to Vaudeline, people are catching on to the hoaxes. The instruments, the voices, the automatic writing. I believe you've gone too outlandish, which is exacerbated by the fact that your department members attending these séances have a tendency to, how should I say—" he snapped his fingers "—coerce the women into bed." He shook his head. "They're talking. These women are talking. I need you to clean it up."

I felt punched in the gut. Not at his reprimand, necessarily, but at the news that people were talking as much as they were. I hadn't any idea, not until now. Of course, forever beholden to Mr. Volckman, I would take his concerns very seriously. "What about Vaudeline, then? Do you think she's encouraging the rumors?"

"Encouraging them? No. But she's interfering—asking around,

trying to help me with matters. I can't have her involved. I can't have her learning about—" He stopped, shaking his head.

There was no need to finish the statement. He was referring to the most profitable—the most sinister—of our schemes.

There was the Department of Clairvoyance—the Society's reputable facade, run by Shaw. Then there was my unit, the Department of Spiritualism—subsisting on tricks and ploys.

But what Volckman alluded to just now? It was the most wicked of our endeavors.

"Vaudeline and my wife are close friends," Volckman said. "It makes me uneasy, the thought of what she might learn or share. I need her out of here."

"Out of London."

"Out of London, yes, and out of our business." He leaned his head against the wall. "Rumors about what you do is one thing. Rumors about what I do is another thing altogether. I've been impeccably cautious, covering my every track. But Vaudeline makes me nervous. She's wickedly sharp.

"I promised her I'd look into things at the Society, that I'll do some digging. Soon, I'll tell her that I've found areas of concern within the organization—a few rogue members causing problems. But I'm going to tell her that their scheme goes deeper than I feared, and that these miscreants know she's been meddling. I'll advise her to leave, for her safety."

"Lucky she trusts you."

"Lucky she does." He stood from the couch and approached my desk. With a quick glance at the door, he lowered his voice. "Any new arrangements for me to review?"

I nodded, removing the folio from its hidden place in the trick drawer. "A couple of ideas in the back. Sir Christopher Blackwell, for one."

He raised his eyebrows. "Ambitious."

I nodded. "Broke his hip. Homebound." He took the folio from my hand, tucked it under his arm.

As always, I was glad to be the purveyor of nothing but fraud. Leave the murders up to him.

39

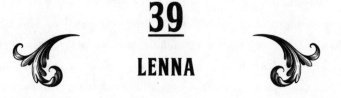

LENNA

London, Monday, 17 February 1873

In the cellar, Lenna bent forward in her chair, breathing hard. The deluge of Evie's memories continued, unyielding and brightly colored.

I felt sure I'd misheard Mr. Volckman a moment ago when he commented on Vaudeline. They were friends until she'd started meddling, he'd said.

And his eyes—now they were so very dark, and angry.

"What were you looking for?" he asked, coming closer. His teeth were yellowed and his breath foul.

"N-nothing," I stammered.

"Nonsense. You were just feeling along the wall for something."

It was Vaudeline's letter that had directed me here, but I could not say this. I saw the opportunity to direct Volckman's frustration away from her, and me, and toward someone else. "Mr. Morley, the documents he keeps down here, I know about them."

He sputtered a laugh. "There's nothing down here but vermouth."

I shook my head. "Do you even know what he's up to? What Society secrets he has told me?"

He wrapped his thick fingers around my wrist, squeezing too hard. "Impossible."

I gave a sly smile. If nothing else, I enjoyed the expression of distress on his face now. "Not impossible with a bit of a disguise and a few aptly timed exchanges." I glanced at the steps, considering a way out of his reach. "He's insatiable. He'll give up any secret if the price is right."

He narrowed his eyes. "Why are you after us?"

I paused, considering how best to answer his question. This was not about the art of spiritualism as a whole and the damage these men had caused in London parlor rooms. It was not about their exorbitant fees and what was given in return—salacious propositions, sprinkled with a few ill-timed wall rappings.

This was about Eloise.

"Eloise Heslop," I said. "He killed her and her father, didn't he?"

At this, he laughed. "Mr. Morley's a coward. He hasn't killed anyone. He prospects quite well, though."

"Then it's…you."

"No one would ever peg a family man as a murderer, would they? Especially not one so concerned with the reputation of his organization."

Above us, the music grew louder. I realized, given what he'd just revealed, that he had no intention of letting me out of this subcellar alive. I was at the mercy now of some miracle or twist of fate. It was sobering but made me reckless in my questioning. "Have you been killing people since the beginning? Since the Society's establishment?"

"More or less," he said. "The Department of Clairvoyance has always been our honorable facade. The men in that department are good at what they do, but it doesn't make much money, fortune-telling and card games.

"The money is better in the Department of Spiritualism. Rich mourners will pay anything. They'll sell their land, for God's sake, if it means a few words from the dead. And Morley mastered the maneuvers early." He paused, gripping my wrist harder. "But the real money is in—"

"Marrying off certain Society members to rich widows," I said.

He raised his eyebrows. If I hadn't known any better, I'd have thought him impressed.

"Mr. Cleland," I continued. "Everyone knew he was a gambler, heavily in debt. He joined the Society around the same time my friend Eloise's father drowned, and then not a few months later, Mr. Cleland and Eloise's mother were married." I tried to pull out of his grip again, to no avail. "I wasn't allowed to attend Mr. Heslop's séance. No one was, other than his widow. It was rigged, wasn't it? A ploy to convince Mrs. Heslop that she should remarry Mr. Cleland..."

He narrowed his eyes. "You're good."

"Tell me how you do it. How do you convince the widows to marry your men?"

"Trick paper. Three-ply. Text in the center layer, visible once dampened with water. Imagine, a grieving, aimless widow in the séance room. A blank sheet of paper sits in front of her, but then words from her deceased husband begin to take shape before her very eyes. A letter encouraging her to love again, and even providing the name of a suitor he desires for her..."

I wasn't sure such a letter would convince me, but this was because I didn't trust the Society. I knew—thanks to Mr. Morley—the extent of their ploys.

But most of London did trust the organization. Until very recently, that was.

"And then you charged Mr. Cleland a hefty fee?"

He tilted his head to one side. "A lifetime per annum fee, yes."

It was more profitable than I even imagined.

"All of this would have continued to work quite well," Mr. Volckman said, "if not for Miss D'Allaire's meddling."

"You knew she'd get to the truth," I said. "Which would expose your fraudulent séances and fracture your reputation. Neither could happen if you hoped to keep marrying your men to widows."

"Precisely," he said. "I sent Vaudeline away with no intention of inviting her back." He grimaced. "What a charade, the whole idea of truth. There's no money in truth."

Suddenly, he thrust himself toward me, wrapping his fingers around my neck. He pushed me up against the wall, fingers tight against my throat. I squirmed with all my might. Then I drove a knee straight into his groin. Lenna had once shown me how to do it in case I ever found myself in a situation such as this.

His grip released instantly. I seized the opportunity, shoving him hard toward the center of the subcellar. He lost his balance, tumbled to the floor. I heard a quick snap, then a pained cry. Mr. Volckman held up his left hand, eyes wide. He'd broken his wrist in the fall.

I lunged for the steps, determined to get out of his reach, but I did so a moment too late. He caught my ankle with his good hand and pulled me down next to him, then got on his knees and reached into his coat. Aware that he'd withdrawn something—I could not see what it was—I reached for the only thing close by: a bottle of vermouth at the bottom of the stairs, ready for consumption by the oblivious partygoers in the cellar above.

I swung the amber-hued bottle toward him. With a horrible crack, the glass heel of the bottle shattered against his head. I managed to get myself upright again, while Mr. Volckman collapsed backward, a blank look on his face. I paused, the broken neck of the bottle still in my hand. Wine pooled around my feet, but it was intermingled with a thicker, darker substance. Blood.

Strange, as Mr. Volckman did not appear to be bleeding. Only then did I see the knife flung to one side and feel the dampness at my throat, the dizziness behind my eyes. I raised my fingers to touch the skin above my collarbone. When I pulled them back, they were crimson. Mr. Volckman had struck me with the knife, and I was now bleeding profusely.

He lay dazed on the floor, making futile motions to slide himself toward me. Several grunts, like a laboring animal, left his lips. The broken neck of the bottle remained in my hand. I had but a single strike left in me. I brought the fractured amber bottle down, piercing the side of Volckman's face. His cheekbone collapsed underneath it and his irises drifted backward, leaving orbs of white in their place.

I fell onto my knees, very warm, very at ease. As my heart slack-

ened, so too did the despair about leaving my family and any distress about the unknown. In its place, curiosity. Death had always been the known thing, the understood thing: eyes fluttering closed, a cessation of pain. But what lay behind it? What lay after it?

I knew there was something. I knew I was not disappearing, not really. I was merely going somewhere else. And Eloise would be waiting.

The secrets of the afterlife were what I'd always lusted after. So eager was I to see the truths hidden across this veil between life and death, I might have held my next breath in anticipation.

Only, there was not a next breath to be had. There was just this one, this final pull of air into my lungs.

Before I closed my eyes, a shadow. I looked up toward the door to the subcellar.

Mr. Morley stood there, looking down upon us two bloodied bodies, both of us near dead. He stepped down the stairs, and as he grew closer, I spotted a letter protruding from his pocket: my letter to Vaudeline. I recognized the sparrows and birds' eggs that I'd doodled on the exterior of the envelope.

He had not, in fact, posted it at all.

Which could only mean one thing. The letter that sent me here tonight— it had not been Vaudeline's doing. It had been a forgery. Morley's forgery.

He'd lured me here. The subcellar story was nothing but bait. Nothing was hidden down here at all.

I gave Mr. Morley a weak smile—I wanted him to see it, to realize that his lure had led to this, the takedown of the Society's president. Then I surrendered it all and lifted the veil.

The memory loosened and gave up its grip. At the séance table, Lenna's eyes sprang open.

Mr. Volckman was the mastermind. The worst of the villains all along. And he and Evie had killed each other. Here, in the subcellar. She'd just seen it—relived it—via Evie's memory.

She'd been looking at the situation all wrong, wondering who might have killed them both. Now she knew. They'd made victims of each other.

And the reason he'd killed Evie, the reason he'd stumbled upon her at all? It was due to Evie's suspicions about the Society following Eloise's death. She'd sought vengeance and exposure, both rooted in her devotion to mediumship—the *real*, illusionless version of the craft. She'd been faithful to her friend, to the art. Willing, even, to risk her life for it. A martyr.

This also meant that the folio Lenna had found earlier that night wasn't solely Mr. Morley's. He left notes on prospects and targets, but the actual murders? Mr. Volckman was responsible.

After Mr. Volckman's death, Mr. Morley must have snagged the folio for safekeeping and then added a few targets himself: the three of them sitting now at the table.

Indeed, Mr. Volckman appeared to be the source—the fountainhead—of the Society's rogue behavior. It was a complete shift in what she and Vaudeline had believed about him. They'd thought him honorable. Lenna remembered her and Vaudeline's visit to Mrs. Gray's house, when the widow had recounted the magnetic instrument used by Mr. Dankworth before he tried to take advantage of her. According to Mrs. Gray, Mr. Volckman had come up to check on them. *Mr. Dankworth immediately rolled himself off me*, Mrs. Gray had said. *When Mr. Volckman stepped into the doorway, he and Mr. Dankworth shared a glance. I wonder now if Mr. Volckman suspected something awry.*

With the truth now exposed, Lenna suspected Mr. Volckman had not meant to check on Mrs. Gray's welfare at all. Perhaps his intentions were worse—perhaps he wanted to see how Mr. Dankworth's pursuits, financial or otherwise, were progressing.

Lenna could still sense Evie's thoughts intermingled with her own. They were not as potent as the memories she had just accessed, but it was still a source of noise, a distraction. It would remain this way, with Evie suspended in Lenna's consciousness, until someone recited the *Termination* incantation.

"You killed Evie," Lenna said to Vaudeline, but she was speaking to Mr. Volckman, the man within. She wanted to strangle him. If only a man could die twice.

Vaudeline leaned in, a new and strange scent on her breath, like tobacco and whiskey. *She is still entranced*, Lenna realized. Any words leaving the medium's lips were not her own.

"And Evie killed *me*," Vaudeline said. Her *Dénouement*.

"You can blame Evie all you like, but—" Lenna pointed her finger across the table "—he's the reason for it all. Morley lured Evie here."

"No," Mr. Morley said, shaking his head like a child. He looked in Vaudeline's direction. "Volckman was supposed to be with his family that night, not here at the soirée at all." He looked at Vaudeline, eyes pleading. "I was going to fix this, all of this—" He suddenly stopped, looked at his watch, gasped. "I need to step outside for a breath of air." He pushed his chair back, but Beck gripped his arm, kept him in place.

"Wait," Lenna said. She remembered what Bennett had told her earlier that night, at the mews. He'd said that on the night of All Hallows' Eve, Mr. Morley had asked Bennett to leave the omnibus after dropping him off at the party. He'd told Bennett to make his own way home.

"You moved her body," Lenna said, still pointing a finger at Mr. Morley. Every piece of this puzzle was falling into place, including the mystery behind where Evie actually died. "When you realized your lover killed the president of the Society, you hid the evidence, didn't you?"

"What a ridiculous notion," Mr. Morley said.

"She's right. I saw it," Vaudeline—Volckman—said, breath still reeking of liquor. "I saw you haul her up the stairs, shove her into an empty barrel."

Lenna twisted in her chair. "What?"

Vaudeline gave a slow nod, rubbing her—Volckman's—disfigured and broken wrist. "Evie probably believed me dead. Little did the harlot know I was alive another few minutes after she hit me with the bottle, slowly choking on my own blood."

"Then you carted her body to the Hickway House," Lenna added, gaze directed at Mr. Morley. She clasped her hand over her mouth, thinking of the omnibus, how ill every trip had made her feel. She'd attributed it to the motion of the carriage, but now she knew it was something else: her intuition, that invisible awareness that came alive at the strangest of times, including when she'd been in the coach, near where Evie's dead body had been.

Mr. Morley remained silent, the truth unfolding quickly now.

Lenna went on. "After you carted her body over there, you dumped her in the side garden for me to find."

He'd made Evie's death look casual, incidental. Ever the illusionist.

"You meant to kill her yourself that night, didn't you?" Lenna asked. "Little did you know Mr. Volckman would do it for you."

"This Evie was your lover?" Constable Beck asked, gawking at Mr. Morley.

Lenna could only imagine how confused he was about the details quickly coming to light. "His lover, and my younger sister," she said.

Constable Beck kept his eyes on Mr. Morley. "The Society president, brought down by a woman with whom you cavorted... If you meant to avoid shame, Morley, you've done a terrible job of it. The Met will ruin you when they discover you've known the truth all along."

They were all turned against Mr. Morley now, it seemed. Everyone in the room, living or dead, had a score to settle with this man. He flushed. "The London Séance Society is facing enough slander. You must understand, Beck, I moved her body out of here to protect the Society's honor. She was after our secrets—"

Constable Beck frowned. "You thought it worth killing someone because they discovered our séances were rigged?"

"No, no. It is much worse than that. There are other secrets you don't even know about, and—" Mr. Morley halted, breathless.

He meant the killings, of course. Lenna nearly opened her mouth to spill the truth, but to do so would be risky. Both men had revolvers on them. To escalate the tension now might leave them all dead.

"It is my greatest duty, my greatest promise, to protect the Society," Mr. Morley sputtered. He tried to yank his arm free of Constable Beck's grip, but he was unable. A look of exasperation and something else—fear?—flickered in his eyes. "Better than you've done for the Met. Taking bribes, assaulting colleagues."

Beck flinched. "Old mistakes, Morley. Gave up the gin and bad friends. Not an infraction since." He tightened his grip. "I don't have a perfect past. Not a one of us does. We all do things we regret."

For the first time since meeting Constable Beck, Lenna wondered if she'd misjudged him. It had been easy to make assumptions, given his coarse manner, and she'd also placed too much importance on Mrs. Volckman's gossip about Beck's former misdeeds. Now she remembered how Beck had declined the brandy at the brothel, drinking water instead. He'd learned that liquor was his vice, then. Good for him for fixing his ways.

Besides, Beck was right when he said *We all do things we regret.* Lenna had her own regrets, including rashly tearing in two a certain drawing, which belonged to Evie.

From behind Lenna, near the unmarked cask, came yet another strange odor, something metallic. She looked at the others—did they smell it?—but to her horror, she saw that Vaudeline's lips were bloodstained. She seemed to be struggling to breathe.

Slowly choking on my own blood, Vaudeline—Mr. Volckman— had said moments ago. Which meant that what Vaudeline was experiencing now was but another séance-induced injury. Why had Vaudeline not begun to recite the *Termination* incantation, to put an end to all of this?

Behind Lenna, the metallic smell grew stronger. As Constable Beck and Mr. Morley continued to shout foul words at one another, she moved her arm toward the pen next to her. She pretended to make a quick, inadvertent motion, and then she nudged the pen off the table. It fell to the floor, rolling a few paces behind her, very near the unmarked barrel she'd noticed earlier.

Lenna stood from her chair. Reaching for the pen, she peered up at the barrel.

She clasped a hand over her mouth, lest she gasp out loud.

A thick fabric cord ran along the base of the barrel. Two-thirds of the way up the cord, something smoldered, a red-hot glow. Lenna recognized it as a fuse, remembering a festival at the Hickway House several years ago. She'd helped her father arrange several small illumination displays outside; the slow-burning fuses ignited periodically throughout the evening, surprising and delighting the festival attendees.

Now the fuse's ember inched its way slowly toward the barrel, the heat running parallel to the metal brace holding the cask together. This explained the odor.

And if it were a fuse, it could only mean something explosive lay within.

This was his plan, then.

It made perfect sense, given the sulfuric odor a short while ago, which Mr. Morley had insisted on inspecting. Not only this, but he'd been overly concerned with the timing of the séance, checking his watch and commenting on the progression of things. And he'd made several attempts to leave the cellar for a breath of fresh air...

Lenna glanced at the fuse again. If Mr. Morley had lit this upon their arrival at the cellar, the smolder had moved very slowly up the rope. She estimated another ten minutes, maybe more, until it reached the end. She snagged the pen and returned to her seat. She could not reveal aloud what she'd seen; if she did, Mr. Morley might resort to the gun after all.

Next to her, Vaudeline had grown pale, and a rivulet of blood dribbled from her bottom lip. Though her breaths were shallow, at least she was breathing and conscious. *She is too weak to recite the* Termination *incantation,* Lenna realized. *I am alone in this.*

But as soon as the thought crossed her mind, she blinked, shaking her head. She was not, in fact, alone. She remained entranced by Evie, even able to communicate with her. And spirits, she now knew, were capable of more than mischief.

They could cause utter devastation.

Even death.

40

 MR. MORLEY

I t is the truth: I have never killed anyone.

Yes, I accessed the portfolio on occasion, leaving notes or newspaper clippings within. But the folio belonged, foremost, to Volckman. A tidy collection of arrangements and plans: lineage charts, articles about landholdings, case notes for prospective targets. The who, the where, the when.

He'd always been the braver of us. There were no illusions about murder, no guise to hide behind. When the deed was done, it was done. And a family man makes the perfect killer. No one suspects a good husband, an attentive father.

Volckman had more grit than me, too. Trick candles and egg whites were my game, but Volckman thought nothing of raising a bludgeon and bringing it down upon a victim under the cover of dusk.

But the night of All Hallows' Eve? He was not meant to know at all—was not, even, supposed to be at my soirée. He was to attend a small household gathering with his wife and children. Puddings and parlor games. It was a perfect opportunity for me to take care of the problem in my department, the one I'd brought into the Society in the first place.

It would be my first murder, and Volckman would never know of it. Her name would never go into the folio.

Naturally, I planned a hoax. It was the subject I knew best, but make no mistake about it: the task was difficult. Imagination did me no favors here, for re-creating another's penmanship requires diligence and close examination. I studied a few old documents written by Miss D'Allaire herself—she'd corresponded plenty with Volckman in years past—and I analyzed her use of ink, how she must have angled her hand.

During the forgery, I made a few blunders, but I'd planned for this. Hence the spare sheets of pink parchment from Le Papetier.

My forged letter to Evie instructed her to arrive at the crypt soirée at nine o'clock. I considered that she might arrive earlier than this, but surely not too soon; she'd need a crowd, so better to go about unnoticed. There was nothing hiding in the subcellar, anyway. She could look for as long as she liked.

I arrived right at nine. Once at the party, I sent Bennett home. I needed the carriage, but no longer his services.

In the back of the omnibus was an empty barrel. Amid the partygoers, I rolled the barrel down the ramp and went around to the side where we move the casks in and out via a designated entrance. Once inside, I positioned the barrel very near the subcellar door.

The party, to my relief, was indeed rollicking. No one would be able to hear us in the subcellar, and any shouts or screams would be drowned out by the viola, the shrieks of debauchery above.

I stepped toward the door, ready to open it, knowing she would be down there, searching for something she wouldn't find.

Gently, I pulled the door open. In one of my pockets was the missive she'd written to Vaudeline. I couldn't wait to show it to her, to see the look in her eyes when I revealed all I knew about her. Perhaps I'd read a few of her passages aloud, just to watch her sweat.

With the door now open, I looked down the short flight of steps.

I was horrified at the sight that met my eyes.

There she was, lying prostrate on the floor, bleeding. Leather satchel flung aside, her notebook within view.

And she was not alone.

Upon spotting the pair of bodies—were they moribund, or already dead?—I let out a cry. I rushed down the stairs, closing the door behind me. I missed the last step, falling hard onto the floor, my hand brushing against a bloodied knife that I recognized as Volckman's.

"Volckman?" I cried aloud. I didn't understand. Why was he here at all?

Still, it was immediately clear what had happened. Relief and remorse waged war inside me. Evie was gone. And yet she'd taken him down with her.

I'd meant to keep them apart. I'd meant to deal with Evie that night, that very hour, and to rid the Society of the threat she posed.

Yet enemies have a way of sniffing each other out.

I went first to Volckman. He wasn't dead, not yet. The tips of his fingers quivered, and beneath the crushed bone protruding from one cheek, his eye fluttered in its socket. A faint gurgling sound came from his throat. I gave him a pathetic pat on the arm, feeling useless.

I recalled, so easily, the many admonitions he'd given me in the last year. *We need to figure out what's driving the rumors.* During the same conversation, he'd threatened to dismiss me. *Get it sorted, Morley,* he'd said. *The numbers, the talk, all of it.*

He wasn't talking about the men in my department or any rogues at all. The rogues were his own story, something to get

Vaudeline out of the city. When he said *Get it sorted*, he was talk-ing about *me*. About my methods. I needed to tighten things up.

Now, kneeling over his almost-dead body, I knew I should apologize to him. He had saved me, financially and socially, and look what I'd given him in return.

But in truth, an apology was not at the forefront of my thoughts. Instead, my mind was already hard at work on extri-cating myself from the situation.

At Volckman's side was Evie. Her face was not nearly as gro-tesque. She might have had a bleeding gash along her neck, but her countenance was...joyful. Her eyes were closed, her lips turned gently upward.

She'd always been enamored of the afterlife. Damn if I didn't think she was glad to greet it at last.

Getting rid of Evie's body—and her notebook, which I later found full of damning details—was paramount. She was very clearly Volckman's killer, which would result in a lengthy inves-tigation. Who was she? Why did she do it? What did she want? That would lead back to me, to Society secrets. It would reveal that I had been in blatant violation of Society rules. That I had played a role in the death of the president.

The Society's survival prevailed over the truth. Volckman would have wanted that, wouldn't he? My standing prevailed, too. Thus, I reasoned that the right choice was to proceed with removing her body to the cask and taking her away. Better to leave Volckman's killer in obscurity.

I snagged Evie's notebook and tucked it into my coat, next to the letter from Vaudeline that I'd forged only days ago. I'd take all of it back to the headquarters as soon as possible, then tuck it safely away in my hidden desk drawer. The folio was al-ready there; Volckman had consigned it to me last week, and I'd made a few good notes in it since, memorandums about fu-ture targets. Volckman's death was a stroke of good fortune for those potential victims, even if they'd never know it.

After I'd lugged Evie's body up the stairs and maneuvered it into the empty cask still smelling of oak and caramel, I went down to bid Mr. Volckman a final goodbye. The gurgling, the quivering, the fluttering had all ceased. He'd expired there on the stone floor, and I was glad his misery had not lasted long.

Eventually I made my way outside and rolled the barrel out to the waiting omnibus, glad for the new moon and the shroud of night. I heaved the barrel up the carriage-cask ramp. Then I mounted the box and snapped the reins.

Cursed be the horses, they would not move. Defiantly they stood there, the obstinate beasts. Were they toying with their new driver, or did they sense something odd about the cargo in back?

I reached underneath the seat, went after the driver's whip. The leather was hard, unblemished. I suspected Bennett had never needed to use the thing.

I came down with the whip, violent and quick. Their flanks seized up at the snap, and one of the horses whipped its head around, ears back and eyes wild.

Still, it was effective. Scourge in hand, I drove the horses toward the Hickway House, thinking all the while of Volckman's blood pooling and cooling on the stone floor around him.

Darkness is a steadfast friend, and activity around the hotel was quiet besides. It did not take me long to roll the cask out and toward the side garden. I rid the barrel of the body and then rolled the cask to an alleyway full of rubbish and discarded boxes. Though I had no lantern to confirm it, I suspected there might be blood at the bottom, so I dumped some discarded food scraps into it, putrid things I blindly found among the rubbish. A mélange of waste.

I then made my way back to the crypt soirée. As I drove the horses westward, I tried to forget all that had transpired. I tried to swipe clean the slate of memory, to reenvision the night en-

tirely, so better to play ignorant when the police inevitably in-
terrogated me. I would be the one to find the body, after all.
They would have plenty of questions.

Judging by the conviviality that greeted me upon my return, it
was clear no one had even noticed my absence. I walked through
the throng of partygoers feigning a smile, telling a few people
that I was headed down to get more vermouth.

To the subcellar I went.

I opened the door, let out a scream.

If I may say so, I think it was one of my better performances.

Alas, I can no longer get away with such ruses.

Not now.

Not here.

41

 LENNA

London, Monday, 17 February 1873

Slowly, almost imperceptibly, Lenna turned a few pages of her notebook. She went past the seven-stage séance incantations, not yet concerned with the *Termination*. It would not solve all of her problems, after all. It would expel Mr. Volckman's and Evie's spirits, yes, but that still left Mr. Morley alive and well. She needed to deal with him first. Then she, Vaudeline, and Constable Beck needed to get out—before the fuse expired.

Lenna turned to the page of expulsive injunctions, the ones used only in special circumstances. She might have forgotten about them if not for reviewing them yesterday while passing the sleepless night. Vaudeline had assisted her with a few corrections, and the enunciation rules were fresh in her mind. Among them, the *Transveni* injunction, meant to displace an entrancement and move a spirit from one séance participant to another, nearly always from a sitter to the medium. But in this instance, Lenna needed to accomplish the opposite. She needed Evie to leave her and entrance one of the sitters: Mr. Morley.

A short while ago, Lenna thought, *I did not even properly believe in an afterlife. Now I am hoping that the ghost of my sister will save my life.*

She knew this meant goodbye. Once Evie had gone from her, she would not conjure her again. She would never have her back. Not in life, not in death.

Lenna paused, hovering her fingers over the pages of her notebook. Then she remembered.

Quickly, she reached into her bag. She withdrew a tiny paper sack. Within, the warbler feather—the apportation she'd bought for Evie months ago.

Lenna laid the feather on the table in front of her, silently asking Evie to forgive her for so very much: years of disbelief in the spirit world. The countless stubborn, trivial arguments she'd initiated. Teasing her about boys and Evie's wanton behavior. Tearing Evie's drawing of the hexagon in half. Accusing her of rooting through her private things. She'd never apologized for any of it.

She felt something damp and warm on her cheeks. Lenna touched her fingers to her face; they came away wet with tears. She had not realized she'd begun to cry. Were these her tears, or Evie's? Both, perhaps.

Having made her apology, Lenna then began to read the short *Transveni* injunction. It consisted of two stanzas, eight lines in all. She read them silently, quickly, directing Evie to reverse course, to exit her body and enter Mr. Morley's.

Next to her, Vaudeline continued to breathe, slowly and shallowly. As Lenna approached the end of the incantation, she found her eyes blurring, unable to make out the last few lines.

And yet she wasn't crying anymore.

It was Evie, no doubt, stubbornly refusing the completion of this incantation.

My life is at stake, Evie, Lenna thought to herself. *You will not have died in vain. I will make sure of it.* Then, as a final goodbye: *I love you dearly, little sister.*

With her tearstained fingers, she touched the wound on her neck. The skin began to pull together at that very moment, healing beneath her fingers.

Evie was obeying. Evie was going.

Lenna finished the remaining lines quickly, coming to the end of the second stanza. A moment later, the *Transveni* injunction was complete.

Across the table, Constable Beck gasped, pointing a shaky finger at Mr. Morley's neck. In the low light, Lenna frowned. In the place where her own wound had begun to heal, a bloodied and raw slit had formed on Morley's neck.

Mr. Morley looked up, terror in his eyes. He touched his wound, inspected his fingers. But as he opened his mouth to speak, his voice was drowned out by a deafening noise. It sounded like a thousand fists knocking against the stone walls. Yet there was nothing and no one to cause the clamor. *Spirit rapping*, Lenna thought to herself. She put her hands over her ears, a smile pulling at her lips.

Next, the sconces extinguished, revived, extinguished, revived. As if by their own accord, spontaneous and synchronized.

Then the potent swirl of Evie's perfume. Bergamot, pungent and floral.

She was playing with their senses.

A horrified look crossed Mr. Morley's face. "Evie," he choked out. He turned to look behind him, finding nothing but a wall. He jerked his head left and right, but nowhere was Evie to be found. "Trick candles," he breathed then, talking to no one but himself.

Lenna shook her head, pointing at the table. "No trick candles here," she said.

Finally, the voices began.

From inside the walls and the ceiling and in the very air around them came the hollow, urgent voices of men and women and children. It would have taken a hundred ventriloquists to mimic the sound. All of them chanting the same word, over and over: *Evie. Evie. Evie.*

Mr. Morley stood from his chair, but he was quickly pushed back by some invisible force. He fell against the wall. He began to breathe heavily, his face red, and the wound on his neck bled harder. He stretched out his legs, pushed his head back against the wall, then cried out in what might have been pain or passion. His back arched as he fell victim to some pressure or sensitivity that Lenna could not see. She could only imagine how Evie was taunting him.

The rapping. The flames. The perfume. The voices. And now the lust. All of the fraudulent tactics he had used against grieving women throughout London, Evie was now using against Mr. Morley, filling him with fear and dread.

Lenna touched her hand a final time to her neck. The wound was healed, not so much as a tender spot. Evie was gone from her completely. It was time to read the *Termination* incantation.

She flipped quickly through her notebook. She read the passage as quickly as her eyes could flit over the page, knowing that once it was complete, Mr. Volckman and Evie would both be gone, set free of this half life. She didn't want it for Mr. Volckman—she'd have been perfectly fine dooming him to misery for eternity—but such was the nature of this séance. There were two spirits, one evil and one good, and any incantations applied to them both. Lenna would not doom her sister to this place forever.

Besides, even if it were malicious, spirits *could* be compelled to come forth time and time again. Perhaps she would—

Suddenly Mr. Morley cried out, now in the throes of something terrible. He looked half-dead, as though held down with invisible ropes.

The moment she finished the last line of the *Termination*, she stood from the table. She grabbed Mr. Morley's bag, which he'd brought from the Society. It contained the damning folio, the notebook. Then she grabbed Vaudeline's hand, the same one that had been bent at an awkward angle a moment ago. It had healed—straightened, no longer swollen. "Let's go," she said, knowing the fuse would ignite in a matter of minutes.

Lenna would let Mr. Morley die by his own devices.

Neither Constable Beck nor Vaudeline resisted. Both looked weak, pale—but free of influence, no longer invaded by something or someone sinister. Still, Lenna kept distance between herself and Constable Beck. Though he'd been ignorant of the murders carried out by Mr. Morley and Mr. Volckman, this didn't absolve him of everything. He had still taken part in a deceptive, manipulative organization. She might have changed her opinion of him tonight, but even so, she'd remain cautious around him.

As they moved toward the exit, Lenna turned back a final time. Where she'd left the feather on the table for Evie, there now remained something small and honey-colored.

Lenna frowned. She ran back to the table a final time, letting out a cry. The feather she'd left for Evie was gone, and in its place sat a tiny amber stone. The resin was void of inclusions, more beautiful than any in Lenna's existing collection. Almost as though the specimen were not from earth at all.

A feather for amber. Here to there. The exchange, Lenna knew, meant forgiveness. Love.

Lenna pocketed the stone. They exited the cellar, closed the heavy door, and made their way away from the building. When they were a safe distance from it, Lenna looked back. No shadows, no forms. Nothing and no one followed. Next to her, Vaudeline had turned to look, too. Her eyes had widened, vigilant and alert. Color returned to her face.

"We need to get away from the building," Lenna said. Vaudeline and Beck both turned to her, confused. "He set a fuse in the cellar—it was just behind the table. It will explode any moment. I don't know what's in the cask, but—"

"Black powder," Constable Beck said quickly, eyes wide. "I saw it on Morley's hands earlier today. That's why I kept a close eye on him tonight. I've never trusted the man. Not since the day I met him." He looked toward the street. "We'll go immediately to the Met to tell them the truth of Volckman's death."

"Yes," Lenna said, "and the rest of the story, too."

"Pardon?"

"The worst scheme of all. It's what Mr. Morley meant in the cellar, when he referred to the worst of the Society's secrets. He and Mr. Volckman kept a portfolio of names, rich men they murdered. After these murders, they would coerce the wealthy widows to marry certain Society members they called *oathmen*. These oathmen would then pay the Society a hefty annual fee."

"Impossible," Constable Beck breathed.

Lenna glanced into Mr. Morley's bag, the portfolio within. "The proof is right here," she said. "All of it."

Without another word, Constable Beck took off at a brisk walk, toward Bennett and the omnibus.

Lenna waved Vaudeline along for a few more yards, and then she stopped and turned. She reached for Vaudeline's hand, only to find it close. Vaudeline had been reaching for her, too, at the very same moment.

They faced one another, their bodies only inches apart.

"How did you do it?" Vaudeline asked. "How did you conjure her?"

Lenna swallowed. "I recited the incantations silently. I... changed a few of the words."

"*Téméraire*. How reckless of you. You might have compromised the entire séance." Vaudeline did not look pleased. And yet she took a small step forward. A wisp of her hair blew in the breeze, sticking to Lenna's cheek.

"You could not even perform the séance," Lenna reminded her. "I had to recite the *Isolation* incantation for you. The *Termination*, too."

"Any good understudy would have done the same. The gallows...
I did not expect such energy."

"Blame it on whatever you like. But you cannot say I compromised anything."

They were waltzing with words. Vaudeline stared at her as
though considering another rebuttal.

Enough of this, Lenna finally decided. Before Vaudeline could
say anything else, she loosened her grip and thrust her hand out,
wrapping it around the back of Vaudeline's neck. Then she tipped
forward and placed her lips firmly against hers.

Vaudeline might have gasped or pulled away, but instead she
put her hand on Lenna's lower back, pulling her in. It seemed
very much like she'd been waiting for this, perhaps even bait-
ing her with their quarrel a moment ago.

They stood that way a long moment, Lenna marveling at
how perfectly soft this woman's lips felt against her own. It was
nothing whatsoever like kissing Stephen, nor even Eloise. With
Eloise, there'd been a resistance between them—a sense of mod-
esty, even despite being behind closed doors.

Lenna wouldn't fall victim to that now. She took Vaudeline's
bottom lip and drew it between her teeth, having all but forgotten where they were and what had transpired tonight—

Suddenly, the cellar behind them exploded with enormous
force. Stone and dust mushroomed from the building. Lenna
pulled out of the kiss, clasped her hands to her ears. As dust
rained down around them, flames began to emerge from the
walls of the building.

No one could have survived such a blast.

Lenna blinked, remembering what she intended to do. She'd
made the decision while still in the cellar, toward the end of
the séance.

She turned, approaching the building once again. Constable
Beck was nowhere to be found; he must have already been in
the omnibus when the blast occurred.

"What are you doing?" Vaudeline cried, her hand frozen in place where Lenna's waist had been a moment ago.

Retrieving her notebook once more, Lenna got as close to the building as the heat and flames would allow. There, in the blinding light drawing sweat from her pores, she began again.

Tonight's second and final séance.

42

 MR. MORLEY

Before the explosion, as I lay writhing in agony on the stone floor, I believed there was no greater crime, no greater evil, than what Evie had done to me.

Then her sister did worse.

I could never have imagined how it would all transpire: that there would be a second séance, and that I would be one of two spirits conjured, and that Miss Wickes would not complete the seventh stage.

After reciting the first six stages of the sequence, she then performed the *Expelle* injunction to expel us from her, but she did not recite the *Termination* incantation—she did not release my spirit, nor Mr. Volckman's, from the smoldering pile of rubble.

Now we are here, suspended in this void of a realm, and I wish we were rotting away in prison. It would be better than this.

I hover over the place where the cellar used to be, and I can see them across the way: a legion of spirits. Something viscid and impenetrable separates us, a substance I cannot identify, for no such thing existed in the place from which I came. Among the spirits, there are women and men, children, infants, the unborn, and every conceivable beast. Flora, too, and colors I do not recognize.

Around all of them exists a sentiment of community and compassion. None of them are in pain. They do not long for anything. They do not seem to hear what I hear—the ceaseless, shrieking song of a warbler—nor do they appear haunted by memory and remorse. The ones we killed seem especially jubilant, as if they somehow sense that we are over here and will never be over there, with them.

I watch all of them enviously. It is clear they cannot see me.

I curse the illusions I spent a lifetime engineering. All of that feinting and feigning about the afterlife. How real it is to me now. It ravages me, an already-dead man.

Unless forgiveness strikes the heart of Miss Wickes or Miss D'Allaire—unless one of them opts to return to the place the cellar once stood and recite the final incantation—Mr. Volckman and I will be forever tormented.

May mercy be upon the man who finds himself the enemy of a vengeful medium.

EPILOGUE

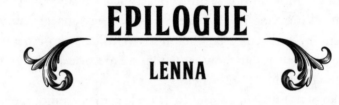

LENNA

Paris, March 1873

I n the parlor at Vaudeline's guesthouse in central Paris, Lenna sat at the small walnut desk by the window. It was early March. She peered outside, noticing the pink buds on the young apple tree outside. There must have been a thousand of them. A bumblebee hovered nearby; he wouldn't have to wait much longer, for the buds looked ready to blossom any moment.

She turned her attention to the volume on medieval mediumship in front of her. Toward the center of the book was a small scrap of paper—a page marker, affixed just above a list of otherworldly phenomena observed in the early fifteenth century. Lenna had placed the marker there several weeks ago, before the séance at the château. She'd expected to return to the book in a day or two, resuming her parlor-room studies.

Instead, she and Vaudeline had traveled to London.

They'd unmasked a criminal gentleman's Society.

They'd solved Evie's murder. Mr. Volckman's, too.

And then Lenna had single-handedly doomed Mr. Morley and Mr. Volckman to an existence of eternal misery.

Quite the accomplishment for an understudy, she thought now. Calling forth two spirits at once after the explosion had been not only dangerous but unspeakably fatiguing. Yet she'd forged her way through, harnessing as much willpower and focus as she could muster. She'd even successfully managed her breath control during the incantations.

Now, pencil in hand, she turned to the page marker and began again in the place where she'd left off.

After the Volckman séance, Vaudeline and Lenna had spent a long night, and part of the next morning, providing statements to the Met. Constable Beck proved a true and honest ally, vouching for all that the women said, even though it was clear that certain admissions—namely, the two killers sitting within the Society—would undoubtedly result in the disbanding of the organization.

It had been no easy task for Lenna to inform the police that Mr. Volckman's killer was, in fact, her sister. But she'd sought the truth, so truth was what she'd give.

Besides, the *why* was just as important as the *who*.

The policemen taking statements hadn't believed her at first, but Lenna had given them the contents of Mr. Morley's bag. Within was the portfolio listing everyone whom Mr. Morley and Mr. Volckman had killed, including Mr. Heslop; Evie's notebook of secrets, which detailed the Society's many schemes; Evie's letter to Vaudeline, which Mr. Morley had not posted at all; and even Mr. Morley's forged reply.

Evie was a heroine, Lenna told the police. Brave to a fault, yes, and not gone in vain.

With the answer to Evie's death uncovered, Lenna's mother returned from the countryside to London. Lenna was glad about it—for her father, especially. It would take time for their family to heal, but each day showed a glimmer of progress.

In time, the police returned a couple of the things Lenna had given to them—namely, Evie's notebook and the letter she'd written to Vaudeline. Lenna was glad to have the documents back, and she intended to make very good use of the information within.

News spread quickly that Vaudeline had returned to London, however temporarily. No longer under threat from the Society—all along, the most serious threat had been wielded by Mr. Volckman and Mr. Morley—she received enthusiastic attention from reporters and fans alike. It was discovered that, for now, Miss D'Allaire was residing at the Hickway House, and dozens of letters began arriving each day from grieving residents across London requesting séances.

She hadn't the time to address these requests, but she did make time for two séances in particular: one for the widowed Mrs. Gray, and another for Mel and Bea at 22 Bow Street. While at the brothel, Vaudeline slipped Bea more than enough money to cover her ill mother's medicine. Grateful, Bea had burst into tears.

Though Vaudeline no longer faced any threats in the city, it would take quite some time to clear the bad air, and she was not keen on returning to a place that had, only days prior, elicited in her so much distress. She didn't want to remain in London. Paris was home, and she made it known that in a matter of days, once the Met had gathered what they needed for their investigation, she would return to France.

There was no question in Lenna's mind. She would go with Vaudeline.

Foremost, she intended to continue pursuing her mediumship studies.

But there was that promise she'd made, too, just hours before the Volckman séance: *After all of this,* she'd told Vaudeline, *I want to explore what else might exist between us.*

"If you've any reservations, now is the time to change your mind," Vaudeline said on the morning of their return to Paris.

THE LONDON SÉANCE SOCIETY

Two weeks had passed since the Volckman séance. The women were seated next to each other on a bench at the railway station. Their train, which would take them from London to Dover, was scheduled to arrive in twenty minutes.

"I won't be changing my mind," Lenna said, scooting closer to her.

"Despite Stephen's pleading?" Vaudeline gave a little wink. She'd been there, last night, when Lenna had broken the news to Stephen. She'd told him that she'd be returning to Paris the following day, and the look of dejection on his face had been evident. Lenna hated to deliver this news, especially given all that had unfolded in recent days—namely, the fact that his father and twin sister had not drowned but had been murdered, and that his mother had been a pawn in an intricate scheme involving her second husband, Mr. Cleland.

Admittedly, Stephen had given Lenna a worthy reason to stay. The museum had just opened several entry-level vacancies in the geology lab. Stephen was well-liked by his superiors at the museum, and his recommendation could nearly guarantee a position for Lenna, which would make her one of only several women on staff.

Even if he hadn't outright said it, the meaning of his offer was clear: he wanted to keep her in London so he could continue courting her. But Lenna wasn't interested in him, nor would she ever be. On the surface, it should have been simple. They were of similar ages with similar interests. They would have had plenty in common if their relationship ever went further. These were the reasons Lenna had tried to conjure feelings for him in the past. How tidy it all would have been, if only Lenna's feelings for him were reciprocal.

But now Lenna understood: desire didn't require *trying* of any kind. Desire wasn't wrested out of someone. On the contrary, it tended to come to life on its own, bidden or not. Desire had certainly come to life in Lenna: the kiss she and Vaudeline had shared after the séance was proof of it. She knew, without a shadow of a doubt, that she wanted to kiss this woman again and again. She never wanted to stop kissing her.

The cellar explosion had pierced the moment. But the force of the blast, the heat of the fire, the destruction—all were representative, in many ways, of how Lenna felt about her life as of late. For one, her old views about science had shattered. She understood now that things did not need to be observed or touched to be real. Further, she'd learned that so-called proper courting behavior fancied by London society—a gentleman in pursuit of a wife—was, quite simply, not for her. Convention could burn, for all she cared.

But kissing Vaudeline? That *was* for her. And it was yet another reason she couldn't wait to board the train that would take her eastward, to Paris. She wanted away from London and back into the privacy of Vaudeline's guesthouse. Maybe, even, her bedroom.

With the train arriving in only a few minutes, the two women stood and gathered their things. Vaudeline put a novel back inside her bag while Lenna latched a small box of stones and amber specimens she intended to take to Paris. The box held her favorites, including the amber stone that Evie had left her after the séance—the apportation. Lenna continued to marvel at its clarity, the lack of inclusions. The amber was yet another reminder that the palpable could coexist with the invisible. Lenna could turn the honey-colored resin over in her hand, yet she could not explain from whence the stone had come or how Evie had gotten it to her. Nor could she explain how Evie had taken the blackcap warbler feather from the séance table.

Yet it had happened. The two objects had exchanged places, here to there—wherever *there* was.

Lenna couldn't make logical sense of it, but there was something freeing in this. She resolved, forevermore, to cease her stubborn efforts to assign logic to everything.

Vaudeline stepped into the parlor, sitting down next to Lenna at the walnut desk. She, too, looked out at the apple tree. "It will bloom any day," she said, rubbing her finger absentmindedly along the line of her jaw.

Lenna leaned forward, kissing the spot Vaudeline had just touched. How deliciously familiar it had all become: the coolness of Vaudeline's skin against her lips, the tiny freckles in the dip of her collarbone.

Last night, the women had taken a candle and a bottle of wine to bed. They'd hardly taken a sip before crawling under the white coverlet together. This had been their nightly routine since returning to Paris, but still Lenna relished every night together. Being tangled up with Vaudeline, the taste and smell of her, the way Vaudeline gasped and relinquished control over herself... It was intoxicating.

As was their ability to share, without hesitation, their affections for one another—no restraint in their intimacy, no ambiguous notes folded up as hexagons.

Lenna pushed aside the text she'd been studying and withdrew a folder of exposé notes. "Ready to finish this up?"

"Not a moment too soon, *ma chérie*," Vaudeline said.

Evie had not yet begun to draft her exposé—at least, Lenna could find no evidence of it back in London—but nevertheless, a slew of key information existed.

After their return to Paris, together with Evie's notebook close at hand, Lenna and Vaudeline had begun the work: hours and hours of summarizing schemes, unveiling ploys. Where possible, they included the names of victims, Society associates or coconspirators, and the dates of murders and manipulations. Anything that could be gleaned via Evie's notes or the women's own experience at the Society went into the exposé. This, in

conjunction with information the police promised to soon release about the Society's murder victims, would be the end of
the organization.

Now the exposé was nearly ready. The women worked carefully to transcribe several copies, writing it out word for word.
Should anything happen to the one they intended to send tomorrow to *The Standard Post*, they had several more copies at
the ready.

As Lenna gave the pages a final read, she couldn't help but
cringe a few times. Composition was not her strongest skill. In
some places, her words came across as dry and unsentimental,
a mere listing of facts. In other places, her penmanship was less
than ideal. But no matter these imperfections, she took comfort
in knowing that every word was true. And this was more than
Mr. Morley—once a Society vice president—could have said.

At the bottom of the report, Lenna left a personal note for
the reporters at *The Standard Post*.

*This exposé was compiled foremost by the late Miss Evie Rebecca
Wickes of London, with supplementary material and authorship provided by Miss Lenna Wickes, spiritualist understudy, and with counsel from internationally known medium Miss Vaudeline D'Allaire
of Paris.*

*After a forthcoming course of study, Miss Wickes and Miss
D'Allaire will commence an international tour. They will begin
in London in order to perform a series of séances, gratis, for anyone who unwittingly commissioned fraudulent séances from the
London Séance Society and still desires communication with their
deceased loved ones.*

*Without the contributions of the three authors listed herein,
it is very likely the Society's malfeasance would have continued
unhindered. For how long, we can only speculate.*

This exposé is approved for reproduction and dissemination with other outlets, and the contributors will endeavor to publish it in several leading spiritualist magazines throughout the world.

Miss Lenna Wickes has dedicated the international publication of this exposé to her late sister, Evie, who in her final known correspondence expressed a determination to take down the London Séance Society.

Gentlemen, your ruse has come to an end.

Signed,
The late Miss Evie Wickes
Miss Lenna Wickes
Miss Vaudeline D'Allaire

★ ★ ★ ★ ★

Author's Note

In the late Victorian era, the spiritualist movement—central to which was communication with the dead, especially through mediums—was in its heyday. Victorians were fascinated by anything supernatural, otherworldly, or occult. Parlor-room séances were a frequent occurrence, as were public theatrical displays of mediumship and physic power.

By and large, the most well-known mediums of this time were women. Spiritualism was one of the only professions in which women were more highly respected than men. This had to do with the belief that a woman's passivity, femininity, and intuition allowed her to access otherworldly realms more easily than a man, and because a man was considered less likely to submit to a spirit taking control of his psyche.

The Victorian era was a time of great prudence and sexual restraint, particularly for women. Yet mediumship events often unfolded in subtly erotic, suggestive ways. A séance was an opportunity for a woman to exert dominance in a way she otherwise could not. I sought to explore this dynamic when considered alongside the abundance of exclusive gentlemen's clubs in London in the nineteenth century, particularly in the affluent West End. Clubs existed for men interested in politics, travel, literature, and of course, ghosts. The Séance Society in my novel was based loosely on The Ghost Club, which was founded in London in 1862 and counted Charles Dickens and Arthur Conan Doyle among its members. The Club still exists today and continues to investigate hauntings and other spiritual phenomena.

In Victorian "clubland," dues were expensive, bylaws were strict, and membership waiting lists were long. A wait of fifteen to twenty years to join an especially prestigious club was not unusual. Given that these clubs often favored anonymity and discretion, oaths of secrecy among members were common. Women were not eligible for membership and, in many instances, were prohibited entirely from club premises.

At the time of this writing, one of the most prestigious clubs in the West End—the Garrick Club, founded in 1831—still does not permit women as members.

The seven-stage séance sequence discussed in *The London Séance Society* was entirely my invention, as were the incantations and injunctions.

The ancient Metonic cycle, or *enneadecaeteris*, is indeed real. Every nineteen years, a given lunar phase will recur at the same time of the year. This phenomenon was discovered by a Greek astronomer in 432 BC. I did, however, take a few liberties with the Metonic cycle. Foremost, there is no evidence that a new moon on All Hallows' Eve results in a higher number of deaths than any other night. Further, in the fall of 1872, the new moon did not fall on All Hallows' Eve, but rather one day later—the first of November.

VICTORIAN MOURNING CUSTOMS

The Victorians were highly superstitious. Immediately upon death in a household, window coverings were drawn closed and remained this way until after the funeral. Mirrors were covered with black cloth so the deceased's soul would not be trapped inside. Clocks were stopped at the time of death, and photographs of the dead were turned facedown to prevent others from being possessed.

In winter, funerals generally took place within one week. In summer, even less than one week. Once funeral details were confirmed, it was customary for the family to send out memorial cards stating the name of the deceased, age, date of death, and where interred—with a grave number identifier so that those wishing to pay their respects could do so.

The deceased's body was monitored until burial. Many families held wakes (vigils) for several days in the event their loved one was not dead but merely in a coma. Flowers were brought in during this time to mask the odor of the body, and caskets were often placed on a cooling board to slow decay. Bodies were not embalmed. Eventually, the dead were carried out of the house feetfirst, lest they look back at the house interior and call forth another unlucky person.

Wreaths or black bows were hung on doors to notify passersby that a death had occurred. Horses accustomed to funeral processions were known to spot the black fabric fluttering from certain doorways and—without the command of the driver—automatically come to a halt in front of the correct house.

Deep mourning attire was worn by close relatives or widowed spouses for one year. After this, "half mourning" attire was worn for another six to twelve months. During deep mourning, widows did not typically leave the house except to attend church. During this period, it was customary to employ black-bordered stationery and envelopes.

As many families had minimal mourning attire, several emporiums (warehouses) existed in which dressmakers and milliners would travel to the household to fit custom pieces for the bereaved.

For women's deep mourning attire, black fabrics were standard, often trimmed with crepe. Black gloves and a veil were commonplace. Jewelry was minimal and often featured black stones such as jet or onyx. In half mourning, gray or lavender fabrics were acceptable. After the death of her husband, Prince Albert, Queen Victoria wore mourning attire until her own death forty years later.

For men's mourning attire, black suits, gloves, and hats were standard. The width of the hatband was commensurate with the man's relationship to the deceased. Widowers may have worn a hatband of seven inches wide, whereas extended family members may have opted for hatbands only a couple of inches wide.

Children were not expected to follow mourning orders.

Postmortem photography was common. For many Victorians, the only photograph taken of them was after death. Often, corpses in these photos were propped up by metal stands or family members. At the request of family members, photographers sometimes manipulated the photos to make the subject appear alive (e.g., painting eyes on the picture).

Some family members, concerned their loved ones may rouse after being buried, placed a rope inside the grave and attached it to a bell aboveground. In the event the deceased awoke, they could tug on the rope and ring the bell, signaling for help.

Victorian Funereal Feasting

At funerals in the Victorian era, it was common to serve wine or punch and to give funeral attendees a take-home favor: several sweet biscuits (cookies) wrapped in wax paper and sealed with a daub of black wax. The wax paper, or the biscuits themselves, was often stamped with images: a coffin, cross, heart, spade, skull, etc. The biscuits were similar in consistency to shortbread and often made with molasses and ginger.

Below are two recipes adapted from well-known Victorian recipe books.

VICTORIAN FUNERAL BISCUITS

Adapted from the third edition of
Miss Beecher's Domestic Receipt-Book,
published in 1862.

1/2 C SUGAR
1/2 C SALTED BUTTER, SOFTENED
1 C MOLASSES
1/2 C WARM WATER
2 TBS FRESH MINCED GINGER
2 1/4 C FLOUR
1/2 TSP BAKING SODA

In a large bowl, use an electric mixer to beat the sugar and butter together until light and fluffy, about 1 minute. Add the molasses, water, and ginger, and beat until combined.

In a separate bowl, whisk together the flour and baking soda. Add flour to molasses mixture and use electric mixer to combine well. Dough will be stiff.

Split dough into two balls. Knead each dough ball several times to remove any air bubbles. Form dough into two even logs, approximately 8 inches long. Wrap each log tightly in plastic wrap. Refrigerate for several hours until firm.

Preheat oven to 350°F. Line two baking sheets with parchment paper. Slice each log of dough into ¼-inch rounds and place one inch apart on baking sheets. Each dough log makes approximately 25 biscuits. If desired, use a knife or stamp to impress an image onto the biscuits.

Bake 20 minutes. Let cool completely (biscuits should be crunchy). Wrap several biscuits in wax paper and secure with a black wax stamp or black string.

VICTORIAN HOT PUNCH

Adapted from
Mrs. Beeton's Book of Household Management,
published in 1861.

1/2 C SUGAR
JUICE OF 1 LEMON
1 PT BOILING WATER
1/2 PT RUM
1/2 PT BRANDY
1/2 TSP NUTMEG

Mix sugar and lemon juice. Add boiling water and stir well. Add rum, brandy, and nutmeg. Mix well and serve hot or chilled over ice. *Serves 4.*

Do-It-Yourself
Three-Layer
Trick Candle

Please see this link for photos of each step below, as well as directions to a handmade hexagonal love note: www.sarahpenner.com/bookclubs.

MATERIALS:

1 CANDLEWICK
1 GLASS JAR (8 OZ CAPACITY)
2 CHOPSTICKS OR SKEWERS (FOR HOLDING THE WICK IN PLACE)
2 RUBBER BANDS (FOR SECURING THE CHOPSTICKS TOGETHER)
2 1/4 C SOY WAX FLAKES
FOOD THERMOMETER
3 FRAGRANCES (ESSENTIAL OILS OR PERFUMES)
CANDLE DYE OR COLORED WAX CHIPS (OPTIONAL)
TOOTHPICKS

Note: A true "trick candle" is one color throughout, and only the fragrance will change as the candle burns down. If you're not looking to pull any ruses, feel free to add a different color to each of your candle layers!

Place the candlewick in the center of the jar. Secure the wick in place by putting a chopstick or skewer on either side of the wick (skewers should lie horizontally on the top of the jar). Keep skewers close together by securing with rubber bands.

To make the first layer of your candle: Using a double boiler or microwave, melt ¾ c soy wax flakes in a small bowl. Melt until wax reaches 160°F (don't overheat!). Add 5–10 drops of your desired fragrance, then add desired color according to package instructions. If using multiple colors in your candle, I suggest starting with your darkest color first (which will be the bottom layer). Stir well with toothpick. Carefully pour the prepared wax into the glass jar, filling no more than one-third full.

Let cool completely, at least one hour in fridge. Repeat the process for the second and third layers of your candle.

Let finished candles sit overnight to harden. Trim wick. Enjoy!

FURTHER READING

Black, Barbara. 2012. *A Room of His Own: A Literary-Cultural Study of Victorian Clubland.*

Braude, Ann. 1989. *Radical Spirits: Spiritualism and Women's Rights in Nineteenth-Century America.*

Cassell's Household Guide, New and Revised Edition, 4 vols. ca.1880s.

Doyle, Arthur Conan. 1926. *The History of Spiritualism,* 2 vols.

Flanders, Judith. 2012. *The Victorian City: Everyday Life in Dickens' London.*

Goodman, Ruth. 2013. *How to Be a Victorian: A Dawn-to-Dusk Guide to Victorian Life.*

Harrison, William Henry, ed. 1869–1882. *The Spiritualist* newspaper. London, England: E.W. Allen. Archives available at http://iapsop.com/archive.

Owen, Alex. 1989. *The Darkened Room: Women, Power, and Spiritualism in Late Victorian England.*

Woodyard, Chris. 2014. *The Victorian Book of the Dead.*

ACKNOWLEDGMENTS

I often count my lucky stars, and three of them shine extra bright: Stefanie Lieberman, Molly Steinblatt, and Adam Hobbins. For years, this team at Janklow & Nesbit has stood alongside me, advocating for my best interests with candor and kindness. I can't imagine doing this with anyone else. Thank you forever and ever. This has been insanely fun.

To Erika Imranyi, my editor at Park Row. This industry is an intimidating one, yet you have remained a warm and encouraging ally from day one. Thank you for taking me by the hand and inviting me forward.

To Natalie Hallak, who first championed this book and helped me brainstorm the initial outline. I count you as a forever friend.

To Emer Flounders, Justine Sha, Kathleen Carter, and Heather Connor, my fabulous publicity team. Despite the number of after-hours (panicked) emails I've sent you, you still seem to like me. Thank you for your flexibility, patience, and attention to detail.

To Randy Chan: you might be the nicest person I've ever met. I'm so glad we get to keep working together! To Rachel Haller, Lindsey Reeder, and Eden Church: the work you do is vastly important. Thank you for shining a light on good books everywhere. To Reka Rubin, Christine Tsai, Nora Rawn, Emily Martin, and Daphne Portelli: thank you for working so hard to get my books into the hands (and ears!) of readers across the globe.

To Kathleen Oudit and Elita Sidiropoulou, who take words

and sculpt them into stunning book covers: your talent has stopped many a shopper in their tracks, and we are so lucky to have you.

Massive thanks to the entire team at Legend Press, my UK publisher. I cannot fathom a more devoted team: Tom Chalmers, Lauren Parsons, Cari Rosen, Liza Paderes, Olivia Le Maistre, and Sarah Nicholson. And special thanks to Lauren for reviewing the manuscript for Americanisms.

Thanks to copy editor Vanessa Wells, who, in addition to catching my typos and redundancies, also advised on the Latin and French. Your wicked-sharp eye for detail saved me many a blunder. Thank you to Patrick Callahan, doctoral candidate in classics at UCLA, who also assisted me with the Latin translations. And to Judy Callahan, on staff at my former high school, who made the connection. Those Latin classes weren't all for naught, after all!

To Laurie Albanese and Fiona Davis, I cherish our candid Zoom calls. Let's keep swapping stories, advice, title ideas, and the occasional curse word. To Heather Webb: girl, you're my from-day-one mentor and a kindred spirit. Thank you for being my friend. To Nancy Johnson and Julie Carrick-Dalton, whose publishing paths have run parallel to my own. You two mean so much to me, and I love our check-ins. Thank you for your support in recent years. And to Susan Stokes-Chapman, with whom I share a long-standing love of old London. Funny how the universe brought us together. Thank you for your friendship.

To Bookstagrammers, book bloggers, and superfan readers who spread the love with their creative posts and epic pictures: we authors adore you. Please never stop doing what you're doing. Thanks to Jaimie (@booksbrewsandbooze), Christine (@theuncorkedlibrarian), Jeremy (@darkthrillsandchills), Jess (@just_reading_jess), Lisa (@mrs._lauras_lit), Barbi (@dreamsofmanderley), and Amanda (@girl_loves_dogs_books_wine), just to name a few. And a special shout-out to Bookstagrammer

Melissa Teakell (who also happens to be my adoring sister-in-law!). Give her a follow on IG: @reading.while.procrastinating.

To Pamela Klinger-Horn and Robin Kall, thank you for all you do to support and connect authors, readers, publishers, and indie bookstores. You're absolute gems. And to Annissa Joy Armstrong, who not only supports every author everywhere, but was brave enough to tell me I'd been mispronouncing her name wrong for months (it's a-*KNEE*-sa, for those of you wondering).

To librarians across the globe who tirelessly connect readers to books, and authors to archival material: you are invaluable. Thank you.

Indie booksellers, you are our boots on the ground. Special thanks to Laura Taylor at Oxford Exchange in Tampa, Florida, as well as Litchfield Books, Tombolo Books, M.Judson Books, Watermark Books & Café, Portkey Books, Book + Bottle, and Monkey & Dog Books.

To my circle of strong women: Aimee, Rachel, Megan, Laurel, Lauren, Roxy, and Mallory. I feel consistently supported and loved by each of you. What a priceless gift, to have such honest, devoted, and inspirational friends in my orbit. Thank you.

To the women hidden in these pages, you know who you are. Thank you. Especially Taylor Ambrose, *ma chérie*.

To my big sister, Kellie: much of the tenderness between Evie and Lenna was inspired by my adoration of you. You are one of my greatest gifts. Thank you.

To my husband, Marc: this now marks two books that I have written, and neither was dedicated to you, despite you being my most treasured person on this planet. But book dedications are a strange, paradoxical thing. You understand this, and it's precisely why I love you.

To my mom: I tell everyone I meet how much I cherish you. Our closeness is precious to me, and I do not take it for granted.

(And I'll never forget our secret trip to Cassadaga Spiritualist Camp in rural Florida. What a strange séance that was…)

To my dad, who passed away in 2015. Sometimes I look at the journal you gave me twenty-three years ago, in which you wrote, "Sarah, you will succeed. Now, start writing!" If only you could see all that has unfolded in recent years—but then, maybe you can. Thank you for everything, Dad.